SAPPHIRE BLUE

PRAISE FOR RUBY RED

"Humorous, romantic and suspenseful, the plot is fast-paced and impossible to put down."—*Justine* magazine

"Gier succeeds on her own terms, keeping the reader moving along, forward and backward in time, and ending with a revelation and a cliffhanger. Both will leave readers anticipating the publication of the next installment, *Sapphire Blue*." —*The New York Times Book Review*

"What makes this such a standout is the intriguingly drawn cast, stars and supporting players both, beginning with Gwen, whose key feature is her utter normality. . . . Adventure, humor, and mystery all have satisfying roles here." —*Booklist*, starred review

"The characters in Kerstin Gier's stellar story come fully to life, and veteran translator Anthea Bell (who translated Cornelia Funke's Inkheart books) preserves the book's abundant humor. . . . There's something here for everyone." —*Shelf Awareness*

"*Ruby Red* is a wonderfully intriguing adventure filled with mysterious time travel, breath-catching action and heart-fluttering romance." —TeenReads.com

"A page-turner." —ChannelOne.com

KERSTIN GIER

SAPPHIRE BLUE

Translated from the German
by Anthea Bell

HENRY HOLT AND COMPANY
NEW YORK

Henry Holt and Company, LLC
Publishers since 1866
175 Fifth Avenue
New York, New York 10010
macteenbooks.com

First published in the United States in 2012 by Henry Holt and Company, LLC.
Original title: Kerstin Gier, *Saphirblau—Liebe geht durch alle Zeiten*
copyright © 2010 Arena Verlag GmbH, Wurzburg, Germany,
published by arrangement with Rights People.

Library of Congress Cataloging-in-Publication Data
Gier, Kerstin.
[Saphirblau. English]
Sapphire blue / Kerstin Gier ; translated from the German
by Anthea Bell.—1st American ed.
p.   cm.
"Originally published in Germany in 2010 by Arena Verlag GmbH under the title
Saphirblau: Liebe geht durch alle Zeiten."—Copyright p.
Sequel to: Ruby red.
Summary: Sixteen-year-old Gwen, the newest and final member of the secret
time-traveling Circle of Twelve, searches through history for the other
time-travelers, aided by friend Lesley, James the ghost, Xemerius the gargoyle
demon, and Gideon, the Diamond, whose fate seems bound with hers.
ISBN 978-0-8050-9266-0 (hc)
[1. Time travel—Fiction.   2. Family life—London (England)—Fiction.
3. Secret societies—Fiction.   4. London (England)—Fiction.
5. England—Fiction.   6. Great Britain—History—Fiction.]
I. Bell, Anthea.   II. Title.
PZ7.G3523Sap 2012   [Fic]—dc23   2011034011

First American Edition—2012 / Designed by April Ward
Printed in the United States of America by R. R. Donnelley & Sons Company,
Harrisonburg, Virginia

3 5 7 9 10 8 6 4

Frank,
I could never have
done it without you.

PROLOGUE

London,
14 May 1602

THE STREETS of Southwark were dark and deserted. The air smelled of waterweeds, sewage, and dead fish. He instinctively held her hand more tightly. "We ought to have gone straight along the riverside. Anyone could easily get lost in this tangle of alleyways," he whispered.

"Yes, and there's a thief or a murderer lurking around every corner." She sounded pleased. "Wonderful, right? Much, much better than sitting in that stuffy room in the Temple building, doing homework!" She picked up the heavy skirts of her dress and hurried on.

He couldn't suppress a grin. Lucy had a real gift for seeing the bright side of any situation in any historical period. Even Shakespeare's England, which was supposed to be a Golden Age but looked distinctly sinister just now, held no terrors for Lucy. The opposite, if anything.

"A pity we never get more than three hours," she said, as he caught up with her. "I'd have enjoyed *Hamlet* more if

I hadn't had to see it in installments." She neatly avoided a squelchy puddle of mud. At least, he fervently hoped it was only mud. Then she performed a few dance steps and twirled around. *"Thus conscience doth make cowards of us all . . .* wasn't that great?"

He nodded, and had to make a huge effort not to grin again. He grinned too often when he was with Lucy. If he didn't watch out, he'd end up looking like some kind of village idiot.

They were on the way to London Bridge. It was a shame that Southwark Bridge, which would have been a much more convenient place for them to cross the river, wasn't yet built. But they'd have to hurry if they didn't want anyone at home to notice that they'd taken this secret trip to the early seventeenth century.

How thankful he would be to take off this stiff white ruff again! It felt like the big plastic collars that dogs have to wear after an operation.

Lucy turned the corner, making for the river. She still seemed to be thinking about Shakespeare. "How much did you give that man to let us into the Globe Theatre, Paul?"

"Four of those heavy coins—don't ask me what they're worth." He laughed. "To him, they could well be a year's wages."

"Anyway, it worked. The seats were super."

Walking fast, they reached London Bridge. Lucy stopped, as she had on their way to the theater, to look at the houses built right over the bridge. But he led her on.

"You know what Mr. George said: if you stand under a window too long, someone's going to empty a chamber pot on your head," he reminded her. "And you'll draw attention to yourself."

"You'd never know you were standing on a bridge, would you? It looks like a perfectly normal street. Oh, look, a *traffic jam*! It's about time they built a few more bridges."

Unlike the side streets, the bridge was crowded with people, but the carts, carriages, and litters trying to get across to the opposite bank of the Thames could hardly inch their way forward. From up ahead, Lucy and Paul heard voices, curses, horses neighing, but they couldn't see exactly what was holding up the traffic. A man in a black hat leaned out of the window of a coach right beside them. His starched, white lace ruff came up to his ears.

"Isn't there some other way across this stinking river?" he called to his coachman in French.

The coachman shook his head. "Even if there was, we can't turn back—we're stuck! I'll walk on ahead and find out what's happened. I'm sure it will start moving again soon, monsieur."

Grunting something, the man put his head, complete with hat and ruff, back inside the coach, while the coachman climbed down and made his way through the crowd.

"Did you hear that, Paul? They're *Frenchmen*," whispered Lucy, delighted. "Tourists!"

"Yes, terrific, but we must go on. We don't have much time left." He vaguely remembered reading that, at some point, this bridge had been demolished and rebuilt later fifteen yards farther along the river. Not a great place for time travel, then.

They followed the French coachman, but after a while, the people and vehicles were crammed so close together that there was no way of getting through.

"I heard a cart carrying casks of oil caught fire," said the woman just ahead of them, to no one in particular. "If they don't watch out, the whole bridge will go up in flames."

"Though not today, as far as I know," murmured Paul, taking Lucy's arm. "Come on, let's retrace our footsteps and wait to travel back on that side of the river."

"Do you remember the password? Just in case we don't make it in time?"

"Something about gutting caves, wasn't it?"

"*Gutta cavat lapidem*, you idiot. Dripping water wears away stone." Laughing, she looked up at him, her blue eyes bright with pleasure, and suddenly he remembered what his brother Falk had said when he asked about the perfect moment for doing what he wanted to do. "I wouldn't make long speeches if I were you. I'd just do it," Falk advised him. "The girl can only slap your face, and then you'll know."

Of course Falk had wondered aloud exactly who the girl in question was, but Paul didn't want any of those discussions beginning, "You do know, of course, that any links between the de Villiers and Montrose families are purely a business relationship?" and ending, "What's more, all the

Montrose girls are silly cows, and later on they get to be dragons like Lady Arista."

Silly cows, indeed! That might apply to the other Montrose girls, but definitely not Lucy.

Lucy, whom he loved more every day, to whom he'd confided things he had never told another living soul. Lucy, someone you could literally—

He took a deep breath.

"Why have you stopped?" asked Lucy, but he was already leaning down to press his lips to hers. For three seconds, he was afraid she was going to push him away, but then she seemed to get over her surprise. She returned his kiss, at first cautiously, then putting her heart into it.

In fact this was anything but the perfect moment, and in fact they were also in a tearing hurry, because they might travel back in time any minute now, and in fact . . .

Paul forgot about the third "in fact." Nothing counted but Lucy.

But then he caught sight of a figure in a dark hood and took a step back in alarm.

Lucy looked at him for a moment, rather annoyed, before she blushed and lowered her eyes. "Sorry," she muttered, embarrassed. "Larry Coleman feels the same. He said I kiss like someone pushing a handful of unripe gooseberries into your face."

"Gooseberries?" He shook his head. "And who on earth is Larry Coleman?"

Now she seemed totally confused, and he couldn't even blame her. He had to straighten out the turmoil in his head somehow or other. He drew Lucy into the light of the torches, took her by the shoulders, and looked deep into her eyes. "Okay, Lucy: First, you kiss kind of like . . . like strawberries taste. Second, if I ever catch up with this Larry Coleman, I'll punch his nose. Third, don't forget just where we left off. But right at this moment we have a tiny little problem."

Wordlessly, he pointed out the tall man who was now emerging from the shadow of a cart and strolling casually up. The newcomer leaned down to the Frenchman's coach window.

Lucy's eyes widened with alarm.

"Good evening, Baron," said the man. He, too, was speaking French, and at the sound of his voice, Lucy's fingers dug into Paul's arm. "How delightful to see you. You're a long way from Flanders." And he pushed back his hood.

A cry of surprise came from inside the coach. "The bogus marquis! How do you come to be here? What does this mean?"

"I wish I knew, too," whispered Lucy.

"Is that any way to speak to your own descendant?" the tall man cheerfully replied. "I'm the grandson of your grandson's grandson, and although people like to call me the man with no name, I assure you that I have one. Several, in fact. May I join you in your coach? It's not very comfortable standing here, and this bridge is going to be jammed for a good while yet." And without waiting for an answer or looking around again, he opened the door and climbed into the coach.

Lucy had drawn Paul two steps aside, out of the circle of light cast by the torches. "It really is him! Only much younger. What are we going to do now?"

"Nothing," Paul whispered back. "We can't go up to him and say hello! We're not supposed to be here at all."

"But how come *he's* here?"

"Just a stupid coincidence. He mustn't see us, whatever happens. Come on, we have to reach the bank."

However, neither of them moved from the spot. They were staring, spellbound, at the dark window of the coach, even more fascinated than they had been by the stage of the Globe Theatre.

"At our last meeting I made my opinion of you very clear." That was the baron's voice coming through the coach window.

"Yes, indeed you did!" The other man's soft laughter brought Paul's arms out in goose bumps, although he couldn't have said why.

"My decision is still the same!" The baron's voice shook slightly. "I will not hand over that diabolical device to the Alliance, whatever evil means you may employ to make me change my mind. I know you're in league with the Devil."

"What's he talking about?" whispered Lucy.

Paul just shook his head.

Once again, they heard a soft laugh. "My blind, narrow-minded ancestor! How much easier your life—and mine as well!—could have been if you'd listened to me, not your bishop or those unfortunate fanatics of the Alliance. If only you had heard the voice of reason, instead of telling your rosary. If only you had realized that you are a part of something greater than all your priest says in his sermons."

The baron's answer seemed to consist of the Lord's Prayer. Lucy and Paul heard him gabbling it under his breath.

"Amen!" said his visitor, with a sigh. "So that's your last word?"

"You are the Devil incarnate!" said the baron. "Get out of my coach, and never let me set eyes on you again!"

"Just as you wish. There's only one more little thing I should mention. I didn't tell you before, so as not to agitate you unnecessarily, but on your tombstone, which I have seen with my own eyes, the date of your death is given as 14 May 1602."

"But that," said the baron, "that's . . ."

"Today. Exactly. And it's nearly midnight already."

All that could be heard from the baron was a gasp.

"What's he doing?" whispered Lucy.

"Breaking his own rules." Paul's goose bumps had spread right up to the back of his neck. "He's talking about—" He interrupted himself, because a familiar queasy sensation was spreading through him.

"My coachman will be back at any moment," said the baron, and now his voice was distinctly alarmed.

"Yes, I'm sure he will," replied his visitor, sounding almost bored. "That's why I'm going to cut this short."

Lucy had moved her hand down to the region of her stomach. *"Paul!"*

"I know, I can feel it myself. Bloody hell. . . . We must run if we don't want to fall into the middle of the river." He seized her arm and pulled her on, taking care not to turn his face toward the coach window.

"You're really supposed to have died in your native land from the effects of a severe attack of influenza," they heard the other man saying as they slunk past the coach. "But since my earlier visits to you ultimately led to your presence here in London today, and it so happens that you are enjoying the best of health, the equilibrium of a rather sensitive state of affairs is now unbalanced. Correct as I am, I therefore feel it my duty to lend Death a helping hand."

Paul was concentrating on the queasy feeling inside him and working out how far it still was to the bank, but all the same, the significance of those words seeped into his mind, and he stopped again.

Lucy nudged him in the ribs. "Quick!" she whispered, breaking into a run herself. "We have only a few seconds left!"

Feeling weak at the knees, Paul started off again, and as he ran and the nearby bank began to blur before his eyes, he heard a terrible if muffled scream from inside the coach, followed by a gasp of "you devil!" And then all was deathly quiet.

Today, at 1500 hours, Lucy and Paul were sent to elapse to the year 1948. When they returned at 1900 hours, they landed in the rose bed outside the window of the Dragon Hall, wearing early seventeenth-century costume and drenched to the skin.

They seemed to be very upset; they were talking wildly, and therefore, much against their will, I informed Lord Montrose and Falk de Villiers. However, there turned out to be a simple explanation for the whole affair. Lord Montrose said he still had a vivid recollection of the fancy-dress party held in the garden here in 1948, during which several guests, evidently including Lucy and Paul, had unfortunately landed in the goldfish pool after the excessive consumption of alcohol.

Lord Montrose had taken responsibility for this incident and promised to replace the two rosebushes they had ruined, "Ferdinand Pichard" and "Mrs. John Laing." Lucy and Paul were strictly instructed to abstain from alcoholic beverages in future, no matter what the period.

FROM *THE ANNALS OF THE GUARDIANS*
18 DECEMBER 1992
REPORT: J. MOUNTJOY, ADEPT 2ND DEGREE

ONE

"YOUNG PEOPLE, this is a church! No kissing allowed here!"

Startled, I opened my eyes and hastily sat up straight, expecting to see some old-fashioned priest hurrying indignantly toward me with his cassock billowing, all set to deliver a stern lecture. But it wasn't the priest of this parish church who had disturbed our kiss. It wasn't a human being at all. The speaker was a small gargoyle crouching in the pew right next to the confessional, as surprised to see me as I was to see him.

Although that was hardly possible. Because basically my state of mind couldn't be called mere surprise. To be honest, my powers of thought had switched off entirely.

It had all begun with that kiss.

Gideon de Villiers had kissed me—me, Gwyneth Shepherd.

Of course I should have wondered why the idea came

into his head so suddenly—in a confessional in a church somewhere in Belgravia in the year 1912—just after we'd been running full tilt in headlong flight, and my close-fitting, ankle-length dress with its silly sailor collar kept getting in the way.

I could have made analytical comparisons with kisses I'd had from other boys, trying to work out just why Gideon did it so much better. I might also have stopped to remember that there was a wall between us, and a confessional window through which Gideon had squeezed his head and arms, and these were not the ideal conditions for kissing. Quite apart from the fact that I could do without any more chaos in my life, after discovering only two days ago that I'd inherited my family's time-traveling gene.

The fact was, however, that I hadn't been thinking anything at all, except maybe *oh* and *hmm* and *more!*

That's why I hadn't noticed the flip-flop sensation inside me, and only now, when the little gargoyle folded his arms and flashed his eyes at me from his pew, only when I saw the confessional curtain—brown, although it had been green velvet a moment ago—did I work it out that meanwhile we'd traveled back to the present.

"Hell!" Gideon moved back to his side of the confessional and rubbed the back of his head.

Hell? I came down from cloud nine with a bump and forgot the gargoyle.

"Oh, I didn't think it was that bad," I said, trying to sound as casual as possible. Unfortunately, I was rather breathless, which tended to spoil the effect. I couldn't look Gideon in the eye, so instead I kept staring at the brown polyester curtain in the confessional.

Good heavens! I'd traveled nearly a hundred years through time without noticing because that kiss had so totally and absolutely . . . well, surprised me. I mean, one minute here's this guy grousing away at you, the next you're in the middle of a wild chase to get away from men armed with pistols, and suddenly—like, out of nowhere—he's telling you you're something special and kissing you. And, wow, could Gideon kiss! I instantly felt green with jealousy of all the girls he'd learnt to do it with.

"No one in sight." Gideon took a cautious look out of the confessional and then emerged into the church. "Good. We'll catch the bus back to the Temple. Come on, they'll be expecting us."

I stared blankly past the curtain at him. Did that mean that now he was carrying on as if nothing had happened? After a kiss (or before a kiss would really be better, but it was too late for that), you'd think a few basic questions might be cleared up, wouldn't you? Was the kiss some kind of declaration of love? Or had we just been snogging a little because we had nothing better to do?

"I'm not going on a bus in this dress," I said firmly, getting to my feet with as much dignity as possible. I'd sooner have bitten off my tongue than ask any of the questions that had just been going through my head.

The dress was white, with sky-blue satin bows at the waist and the collar, probably the latest fashion in the year

1912, but not quite right for wearing on public transport in the twenty-first century. "Let's take a taxi," I added.

Gideon turned to me, but he didn't object. In that early twentieth-century coat, and with those neat trouser creases, he seemed to feel he wasn't necessarily dressed for a bus ride either. Although he did look really good in the costume of the time, particularly now that his hair wasn't combed right back behind his ears like two hours ago. Locks of it were falling untidily over his forehead.

I stepped out into the nave of the church to join him and shivered. It was icy cold in here. Was that because I'd had almost no sleep over the last three days? Or because of what had just happened?

I guessed my body had manufactured more adrenaline in those three days than in all my sixteen years of life before. So much had happened, and I'd had so little time to think about it. My head felt like it was bursting with new information and emotions. If I'd been a character in a strip cartoon, I'd have had a thought bubble with a huge question mark in it hovering over me. And maybe a couple of death's-heads as well.

I gave myself a little shake. So if Gideon was carrying on as if nothing had happened—well, thanks a lot, I could do the same. "Okay, let's get out of here," I said brightly. "I'm cold."

I tried to push past him, but he took hold of my arm and stopped me. "Listen, about all that just now . . ." He stopped, probably hoping I was going to interrupt him.

Which of course I wasn't. I was only too keen to hear

what he had to say. I also found breathing difficult when he was standing so close to me.

"That kiss . . . I didn't mean . . ." Once again it was only half a sentence. But I immediately finished it in my mind.

I didn't mean it that way.

Well, obviously, but then he shouldn't have done it, should he? It was like setting fire to a curtain and then wondering why the whole house burned down. (Okay, silly comparison.) I wasn't going to make it any easier for him. I looked at him coolly and expectantly. That is, I *tried* to look at him coolly and expectantly, but I probably really had an expression on my face saying, *Oh, I'm cute little Bambi, please don't shoot me!* There was nothing I could do about that. All I needed was for my lower lip to start trembling.

I didn't mean it that way! Go on, say it!

But Gideon didn't say anything. He took a hairpin out of my untidy hair (by now my complicated arrangement of strands must have looked as if a couple of birds had been nesting in it), took one strand, and wound it around his finger. With his other hand, he began stroking my face, and then he bent down and kissed me again, this time very cautiously. I closed my eyes—and the same thing happened as before: my brain suffered that delicious break in transmission. (Well, all it was transmitting was *oh, hmm,* and *more!*)

But that lasted only about ten seconds, because then a voice right beside us said, irritated, "Not starting that stuff up again, are you?"

Startled, I pushed Gideon slightly away and stared right into the face of the little gargoyle, who was now hanging upside down from the gallery under which we were standing. To be precise, he was the ghost of a gargoyle.

Gideon had let go of my hair and had a neutral expression on his face. Oh, God! What must he think of me now? I could read nothing in his green eyes, or at the most I saw slight surprise there—and annoyance?

"I . . . I thought I heard something," I murmured.

"Okay," he said, slowly but in a perfectly friendly tone.

"You heard *me*," said the gargoyle. "You *heard* me, you did!" He was about the size of a cat, and he had a catlike face, except that as well as his big, pointed, lynxlike ears, he had two round horns, little wings on his back, and a long, scaly, lizard tail ending in a triangular point. He was lashing the tail back and forth in excitement. "You can see me too!"

I didn't reply.

"We'd better go," said Gideon.

"You can see me and hear me!" cried the little gargoyle, delighted. He dropped from the gallery to one of the pews and hopped up and down on it. He had a husky voice, like a child with a cold. "I spotted that right away!"

Come to think of it, I *had* seen him before. In that church back in 1912. If I put a foot wrong now, I'd never be rid of him. I deliberately let my eyes wander over the pews with total indifference as I walked to the church door. Gideon held it open for me.

"Thanks, very kind of you!" said the gargoyle, slipping through onto the church porch with us.

Out on the pavement, I looked up at the sky. It was cloudy, so the sun wasn't in sight, but at a guess, I thought it must be early evening.

"Wait for me, wait for me!" cried the gargoyle, plucking at the skirt of my dress. "We have to talk! It's urgent! Hey, you're treading on my toes. . . . Don't pretend you can't see me. I know you can." A little water shot out of his mouth and formed a tiny puddle around my buttoned boots. "Oops, 'scuse me. Only happens when I get overexcited."

I looked up at the church façade. I gucssed it was Victorian architecture, with stained-glass windows and two elaborate, pretty towers. Brickwork alternated with cream-colored plaster, making a pattern of stripes. But however high I looked, I couldn't see a single statue on the entire building, let alone another gargoyle. Odd that the ghost was haunting it all the same.

"Here I am!" called the gargoyle, clinging to the masonry right in front of my nose. He could climb like a lizard, of course—they all can. I stared at the brick next to his head for a second and turned away.

The gargoyle wasn't so sure that I really could see him now. "Oh, *please*," he said. "It would be so nice to talk to someone else for once, not just the ghost of Sir Arthur Conan Doyle."

Quite ingenious of him, but I wasn't falling for that

one. I did feel sorry for him, but I knew what a nuisance those little pests could be. What's more, he'd disturbed me in mid-kiss, and all because of him, Gideon now probably thought I was a silly girl who didn't know her own mind.

"Please, please, pleeeeease!" begged the gargoyle.

I went on ignoring him as hard as I could. As if I didn't have enough problems already!

Gideon had gone to the edge of the pavement and was looking out for a taxi to hail. Of course a free one came along at once. Some people have all the luck. Or call it something like natural authority. My grandmother Lady Arista, for instance. She only had to stand at the roadside looking stern, and taxi drivers squealed to a halt right away.

"Coming, Gwyneth?"

"You can't just walk away like that!" The hoarse, childlike voice sounded tearful, heartrending. "When we've only just this minute found each other."

Very likely if we'd been on our own, I'd have let him persuade me to talk to him. In spite of his pointed fangs and clawlike feet, he was kind of cute, and he probably didn't get much company. (I'd bet the ghost of Sir Arthur Conan Doyle had more interesting things to do than talk to gargoyles. What was Sir Arthur's ghost up to in London anyway?) But if you start talking to ghosts and so on in front of other people, they think you're a liar or just showing off. That's if you're lucky. If you aren't, which is most of the time, they think you're totally crazy. Besides, the last gargoyle I talked to had been so affectionate and clinging that I could hardly even go to the toilet alone.

So I got into the taxi with a stony expression and stared straight ahead as we set off, with Gideon sitting next to me and looking out of the window. The taxi driver raised his eyebrows as he examined our costumes in the rearview mirror, but much to his credit, he made no comment.

"It's nearly six thirty," said Gideon, obviously trying to strike up a normal conversation. "No wonder I'm dying of starvation."

Once he'd said it, I realized that I felt the same. I'd hardly managed to get half my breakfast down because of the edgy atmosphere around the family breakfast table, and as usual school lunch had been inedible. I thought rather wistfully of the appetizing sandwiches and scones on Lady Tilney's tea table. We'd missed out on them as well.

Lady Tilney! Only now did it strike me that Gideon and I had better discuss our adventures in the year 1912. After all, our visit to her had gone wildly off course, and I had no idea what the Guardians, who considered time travel no joking matter, were going to think of that. Gideon and I had traveled back to 1912 on a mission to read Lady Tilney into the chronograph. (To be honest, I still didn't entirely understand the reasons for that, but the whole thing seemed to be enormously important. As far as I could make it out, the safety of the world itself was at stake, at the very least.) But before we could do anything about that my cousin Lucy and Paul de Villiers came barging in. They were the villains of the piece, or anyway that's how Gideon's family and Gideon himself saw it. Apparently Lucy and Paul had stolen the other chronograph and hidden in the past with it. No one had heard of them for years—until they turned up at Lady Tilney's house and wrecked our little tea party.

When exactly pistols were drawn was something I'd suppressed out of sheer fright, but at some point, Gideon had held a gun to Lucy's head, a pistol that, strictly speaking, he ought not to have brought with him at all. (Like me when I took my mobile phone into the past, but at least you can't shoot anyone dead with a mobile!) Then we ran for it and took shelter in the church. But all the time I'd been unable to shake off a feeling that the Lucy and Paul situation wasn't quite as black and white as the de Villiers family liked to paint it.

"What are we going to say about Lady Tilney?" I asked.

"Hm." Gideon rubbed his forehead wearily. "I'm not suggesting we should actually lie, but maybe, just this once, it would be a good idea to edit a few things out. You'd better leave the talking to me."

There it was again, that familiar tone of command. "Oh, sure," I said. "I'll just nod and keep my mouth shut, the way a nice girl should."

I instinctively, defiantly, crossed my arms. Why couldn't Gideon act normal? First he kissed me (more than once, at that!), then he was back talking like a lordly Grand Master of the Guardians' Lodge again. What was the idea?

We concentrated on looking out of our respective windows.

It was Gideon who finally broke the silence, which gave me a certain satisfaction. "What's the matter? Cat got your tongue?" The way he asked, he sounded almost embarrassed.

"What?"

"It's what my mother always used to say when I was little. If I was looking straight ahead and saying nothing, like you right at this moment."

"You have a *mother*?" Only when I'd said it did I realize what a silly question it was! Oh, for heaven's sake!

Gideon raised one eyebrow. "What did you expect?" he asked, amused. "You thought I was an android put together by Uncle Falk and Mr. George?"

"Well, it's not such an outlandish idea. Do you have photos of yourself as a baby?" Trying to imagine a baby Gideon with a round, soft, plump-cheeked face and a bald head made me grin. "Where are your mum and dad, then? Do they live in London too?"

Gideon shook his head. "My father's dead, and my mother lives in Antibes in the south of France." For a brief moment, he pressed his lips together, and I was just thinking he'd retreat into silence when he went on. "With my little brother and her new husband, Monsieur *Do-Call-Me-Papa* Bertelin. He owns a company making platinum and copper microparts for electronic devices, and obviously the cash is rolling in. At least, he called his showy yacht the *Croesus*."

I was really surprised. So much personal information all at once—it wasn't a bit like Gideon. "Oh, but it must be cool going on holiday there, right?"

"Of course," he said with derision. "They have a pool the size of three tennis courts, and the stupid yacht has gold-plated faucets."

"Sounds better than a cottage without any heating in Peebles, anyway." My family usually spent the summer up in Scotland. "If I were you, and I had a family in the south of France, I'd be off there like a shot every weekend. Even if they didn't have any pool or any yacht."

Gideon looked at me, shaking his head. "Oh, yes? And how would you manage that if you had to travel back to the past every few hours? Not so thrilling if you happen to be driving along the motorway at seventy miles an hour when it happens."

"Oh." Somehow this time-travel business was still too new for me to have thought out all the consequences. There were only twelve carriers of the gene—scattered over several centuries—and I couldn't yet fully grasp that I was one of them. My cousin Charlotte was supposed to have been the time traveler, and she'd prepared herself for the part with gusto. But for reasons that no one could understand, my mother had faked the date of my birth, and now we were in a real mess. Just like Gideon, I had the choice between controlled time travel with the aid of the chronograph or traveling back to the past unexpectedly at any time and from anywhere. And from my own recent experience, I knew that was not much fun.

"Of course you'd have to take the chronograph with you, so that you could always elapse to a safe year now and then," I said, thinking aloud.

Gideon uttered a joyless snort. "Yes, that would make nice relaxed travel possible, and I could get to know all sorts of historic places at the same time. But apart from the fact that I'd never be allowed to go around the country with the chronograph in my backpack, what would *you* do without it while I was away?" He was looking past me and out of the window. "Thanks to Lucy and Paul, there's only that one chronograph, remember?" His voice was heated again, as always when Lucy and Paul were mentioned.

I shrugged my shoulders and looked out of my own window. The taxi was making for Piccadilly at a snail's pace. Rush hour in the city, great. It would probably have been quicker for us to walk.

"You obviously don't quite realize that you won't have many chances to leave these islands in the future, Gwyneth." There was a touch of bitterness in Gideon's voice. "Or even this city. Your family ought to have shown you the whole wide world, not just Scotland. It's too late now. You'll have to accept the fact that the only way you can see all the places you dream of is on Google Earth."

The taxi driver reached for a well-worn paperback, leaned back in his seat and began to read, unmoved.

"But . . . but you've been to Belgium and Paris," I said. "To travel back to the past from there and get some of what's-his-name's blood, and put it into the—"

"Yes, sure," he interrupted me. "Along with my uncle, three Guardians, and a *costume designer*. What a fun trip! Apart from the fact that Belgium is such a wildly exotic country. Don't we all just dream of spending three days in *Belgium* sometime?"

Intimidated by his sudden bitterness, I asked quietly, "Where would you like to go, then, if you could choose?"

"You mean if I wasn't cursed with this time-travel gene? Oh, my God—I wouldn't know where to begin. Chile, Brazil, Peru. Costa Rica, Nicaragua, Canada, Alaska, Vietnam, Nepal, Australia, New Zealand . . ." He grinned faintly. "Well, just about everywhere except the moon. But it's no use thinking about the things you can never do. We just have to reconcile ourselves to our rather boring lives without the chance to travel."

"Except for time travel." I went red, because he had said "our lives," and somehow that sounded so . . . so intimate.

"At least that's something like fair compensation for all this control and being shut up here," said Gideon. "If it wasn't for the time travel, I'd have died of boredom long ago. Paradoxical but true."

"Watching an exciting film now and then would be enough of a kick for me. Honest."

Wistfully, I watched a cyclist weaving his way through the traffic jam. I wanted to get home! The cars ahead of us weren't moving an inch, which seemed to be fine by our cabby, who was deep in his book.

"If your family lives in the south of France, then where do *you* live?" I asked Gideon.

"In an apartment in Chelsea now, but I'm hardly there at all except to shower and sleep. If that." He sighed. Over the last three days, he'd obviously had as little sleep as me. Maybe even less. "Before I got my own place, I lived with Uncle Falk in Greenwich since I was eleven. When my mother met Monsieur Po-Face and wanted to leave this country, of course the Guardians objected. After all, there were only a few years to go until my initiation journey, and I still had a lot to learn."

"And your mother left you alone?" My mum could never have brought herself to do such a thing, I was sure of that.

Gideon shrugged his shoulders. "I like my uncle. He's okay when he's not putting on airs as Grand Master of the Lodge. Anyway, I'd a thousand times sooner be with him than my so-called stepfather."

"But . . ." I hardly dared to ask, so I just whispered it. "But don't you miss her?"

Another shrug of the shoulders. "Until I was fifteen, when I could still go away safely, I always spent the holidays in France with her. And my mother comes to London at least twice a year, officially to see me, but to spend Monsieur Bertelin's money is more like it. She has a weakness for clothes and shoes and antique jewelry. And four-star macrobiotic restaurants."

The woman sounded like a real cozy, picture-book mum. "What about your brother?"

"Raphael? He's a real little Frenchman now. Calls Po-Face *Papa* and is going to inherit the platinum-parts empire someday. Although right now it looks as if he won't even pass his final school exams, lazy kid. He'd rather hang out with girls than study." Gideon put an arm on the back of the seat behind me, and my breathing frequency instantly stepped up. "Why are you looking so shocked? Not feeling sorry for me or anything, are you?"

"A bit," I said honestly, thinking of an eleven-year-old boy left behind on his own in England. With mystery mongers who made him take fencing lessons and learn to play the violin. And *polo*! "Falk isn't even your real uncle, just a distant relation."

There was an angry hoot behind us. The taxi driver looked up only briefly to move the car on a yard or so, without taking much of his attention away from his book. I just hoped he wasn't in the middle of a really exciting chapter.

Gideon seemed to take no notice of him. "Falk's always been like a father to me," he said. He looked sideways at me with a wry smile. "Really, you don't have to look at me as if I were David Copperfield."

What was that all about? Why would I think he was David Copperfield?

Gideon groaned. "I mean the character out of the Dickens novel, not the magician. Don't you ever read a book?"

There he went again, the old supercilious Gideon. My head had been reeling with all those friendly confidences. Oddly enough, I was almost relieved to have my obnoxious traveling companion back. I looked as haughty as possible and moved slightly away from him. "To be honest, I prefer modern literature."

"You do?" Gideon's eyes were bright with amusement. "Like what, for example?"

He wasn't to know that my cousin Charlotte had been regularly asking me the same question for years, and just as arrogantly. In fact I read quite a lot of books, and I'm always ready to talk about them, but as Charlotte always dismissed with contempt whatever I was reading as "undemanding" or "stupid girly stuff," the time came when I'd had enough, and once and for all, I spoilt her fun. Sometimes you have to turn people's own weapons against them. The trick of it is not to show any hesitation at all as you speak, and to weave in the name of at least one genuine, well-known, bestselling author, preferably if you've really read that author's book. Oh, and in addition, the more exotic and outlandish the names, the better.

I raised my chin and looked Gideon right in the eye. "Well, for instance I like George Matussek, Wally Lamb, Pyotr Selvyeniki, Liisa Tikaanen—in fact, I think Finnish writers are great, they have their own special brand of humor—and then I read everything by Jack August Merrywether, although I was a little disappointed by his last book. I like Helen Marundi, of course, Tahuro Yashamoto, Lawrence Delaney, and then there's Grimphood, Tcherkovsky, Maland, Pitt. . . ."

Gideon was looking totally taken aback.

I rolled my eyes. "*Rudolf* Pitt, of course, not Brad."

The corners of his mouth were twitching slightly.

"Although I have to say I really didn't much care for

Amethyst Snow," I quickly went on. "Too many high-flown metaphors, don't you agree? All the time I was reading it, I kept thinking someone must have ghosted it for him."

"*Amethyst Snow*?" repeated Gideon, and now he was definitely smiling. "Yes, right, I thought it was terribly pompous too. Although I considered *The Amber Avalanche* remarkably good."

I couldn't help it—I had to smile back. "Yes, he definitely deserved the Austrian State Prize for Literature for *The Amber Avalanche*. What do you think of Takoshi Mahuro?"

"His early work is okay, but I get rather tired of the way he keeps going back to his childhood traumas," said Gideon. "When it comes to Japanese writers, I prefer Yamamoto Kawasaki or Haruki Murakami."

I was giggling helplessly now. "But Murakami is real!"

"I know," said Gideon. "Charlotte gave me one of his books. Next time we're discussing literature, I'll recommend her to read *Amethyst Snow*, by . . . what was his name again?"

"Rudolf Pitt." So Charlotte had given him a book? How—er, how nice of her. Fancy thinking of that. And what else did they do together, besides discuss literature? My fit of the giggles had evaporated, just like that. How could I simply sit here talking away to Gideon as if nothing had happened between us? There were a few basic points we ought to have cleared up first. I stared at him and took a deep breath, without knowing exactly what I wanted to ask him.

Why did you kiss me?

"Here we are," said Gideon.

Put off my stroke, I looked out of the window. Sure enough, at some point during our verbal fencing match, the taxi driver had obviously put his book down and gone on with the journey, and now he was about to turn into Crown Office Row in the Temple district, where the secret society of the Guardians had its headquarters. A little later, he was parking the car in one of the reserved slots next to a gleaming Bentley.

"Sure we're allowed to stop here, are you?"

"It'll be okay," Gideon assured him, and got out. "No, Gwyneth, you stay in the taxi while I get the money," he said as I started climbing out after him. "And don't forget, whatever they ask us, leave me to do the talking. I'll be right back."

"The meter's still running," said the taxi driver morosely.

He and I watched Gideon disappear among the venerable buildings of the Temple, and only now did I realize that I'd been left behind as a pledge that the driver would get his fare.

"Are you from the theater?" he asked.

"What?" What was that shadow fluttering overhead?

"I only mean because of the funny costumes."

"No. The museum." There were strange scratching noises on the roof of the car. As if a bird had come down on it. A large bird. "What's that?"

"What's what?" asked the taxi driver.

"I thought I heard a crow or something land on the car," I said hopefully. But of course it wasn't a crow dangling head down from the car roof and looking in at the window. It was the little gargoyle from Belgravia. When he saw my horrified expression, his catlike face twisted into a triumphant smile, and he spewed a torrent of water over the windshield.

True love knows no constraints, no locks or bars.
Past every obstacle it makes its way.
It spreads its wings to soar toward the stars,
No earthly power will make it stop or stay.

MATTHIAS CLAUDIUS

TWO

"SURPRISE, SURPRISE!" cried the little gargoyle. He'd been talking nonstop ever since I got out of the taxi. "You don't get to shake me off so easily!"

"Yes, okay, I know. Listen . . ." I looked nervously back at the taxi. I'd told the driver I urgently needed fresh air because I didn't feel well, and now he was glaring suspiciously our way, wondering why I was talking to a blank wall. There was still no sign of Gideon.

"And I can fly too!" To prove it, the gargoyle spread his wings. "I can fly like a bat. Faster than any taxi."

"Do please listen. Just because I can see you doesn't mean that—"

"See me *and* hear me!" the gargoyle interrupted. "Do you know how rare that is? The last person who could see *and* hear me was Madame Tussaud, and I'm sorry to say she didn't appreciate my company. She usually just sprinkled me with holy water and started praying. Poor dear, she was rather sensitive." He rolled his eyes. "Well, you can understand why, after seeing all those heads sliced off by the guillotine. . . ." He spouted another jet of water. It landed right in front of my feet.

"Stop that!"

"Sorry, just excitement! Harking back to when I was a gutter carrying rainwater away."

My chances of shaking him off again were slim, but at least it was worth a try. I'd adopt a friendly tone. So I bent down to him until our eyes were level. "I'm sure you're a really nice guy, but you can't possibly stick around here with me! My life is complicated enough already, and to tell you the truth, the ghosts I already know are as much as I can take. So would you please go away again?"

"I am not a ghost," said the gargoyle, offended. "I'm a demon. Or what's left of a demon."

"What's the difference?" I asked desperately. "I can't do with any more ghosts or demons right now, understand? You'll just have to go back to your church."

"What's the difference? Oh, really! Ghosts are only reflections of dead people who for some reason or other don't want to leave this world. But I was a demon when I was alive. You can't just lump me in with ordinary ghosts. Anyway, it's not *my church*. I simply like to hang out there."

The taxi driver was staring at me with his mouth wide open. Presumably he could hear every word through the car window—every word that *I* said.

I rubbed my forehead. "I couldn't care less about that. You can't stay here with me, anyway."

"What are you afraid of?" The gargoyle came closer, putting his head on one side in a confidential way. "These days no one gets burnt as a witch just for seeing and knowing a bit more than ordinary people."

"But these days people who talk to ghosts—er, and demons—get sent to mental hospitals," I said. "Can't you understand that—" I broke off. There was no point in this. Taking a friendly line with him wasn't going to get me anywhere. So I frowned and said as brusquely as possible, "I may be able to see you, that's just my bad luck, but it doesn't mean you have any claim on my company."

The gargoyle didn't seem in the least impressed. "But you have a claim on mine, you lucky—"

"Let me make this perfectly clear: you're a nuisance! So please go away!" I hissed.

"Won't! And you'd be sorry later. Here comes your boyfriend, by the way. Kissy kissy!" And he pursed his lips and made loud kissing noises.

"Oh, shut up." I saw Gideon striding around the corner. "And *go away*." I said that last bit without moving my lips, like a ventriloquist. But of course the gargoyle still wasn't impressed.

"No need to take that tone, young lady!" he said, sounding satisfied. "Don't forget that when you shout the echo comes back the same."

Gideon wasn't alone. I saw the stout figure of Mr. George puffing along after him. He had to run to keep up. But even from a distance, I could see him beaming at me.

I straightened up and smoothed down my dress.

"Gwyneth, thank God!" said Mr. George as he mopped the sweat from his brow with a handkerchief. "Everything all right, my dear?"

"Fatso there is right out of breath," said the gargoyle.

"Fine, thanks, Mr. George. We just had a few . . . er, problems . . ."

Gideon, who was giving the taxi driver several banknotes, cast me a warning glance across the car roof.

". . . with timing," I murmured, watching the taxi driver turn out into the street, shaking his head, and drive away.

"Yes, Gideon's told me there were complications. That's extraordinary. There's a loophole in the system somewhere. We'll have to analyze it thoroughly, and maybe do some rethinking. But what really matters is that nothing happened to you two." Mr. George offered me his arm, which looked a little odd because I was a few inches taller than him. "Come along, my dear. There are things we have to do."

"I'd really like to get home as soon as possible," I said. The gargoyle shinned up a drainpipe and made his way along the gutter toward us, hand over hand, singing "Friends Will Be Friends" at the top of his voice.

"Yes, of course you would," said Mr. George. "But you've only spent three hours in the past today. To be on the safe side until tomorrow afternoon, you'll have to elapse for another couple of hours now. Don't worry, it won't be any trouble. A nice comfortable room in the cellars where you can do your homework."

"But—my mum is sure to be waiting for me and worrying!" What was more, this was Wednesday, and Wednesday was our day for roast chicken and french fries. Not to mention the fact that a bathtub and my bed were waiting for me at home!

And pestering me with homework too, in a situation like this, was really too much! Someone ought just to write the school a note. *Since Gwyneth is away on important time-travel missions these days, she must be excused homework in future.*

The gargoyle was still warbling away on top of the roof, and I had to make a great effort not to put him right. Thanks to SingStar and karaoke afternoons at my friend Lesley's place, I knew the lyrics to all of Queen's greatest hits, and I knew for a fact that there were no gherkins in that song.

"Two hours will be enough," said Gideon, once again taking such long strides that Mr. George and I could hardly keep up. "Then she can go home and have a good sleep."

I hated it when he talked about me in the third person in front of me. "Yes, and she'll be glad of that," I said, "because she really is very tired."

"We'll call your mother and explain that you'll be brought home by ten at the latest," said Mr. George.

By ten? So long, roast chicken, it's been good to know you. I'd bet anything my greedy little brother would have guzzled up mine by then.

"*When you're through with life and all hope is lost,*" sang the gargoyle, coming down the brick wall half-flying, half-climbing, to land neatly on the pavement beside me.

"We'll say you still have lessons," said Mr. George, more to himself than to me. "Maybe you'd better not mention your trip to the year 1912. She thought you'd been sent to elapse in 1956."

We'd reached the headquarters of the Guardians. Time travel had been controlled from here for centuries. The de Villiers family was apparently directly descended from Count Saint-Germain, one of the most famous time travelers. We Montroses were the female line, which as the de Villiers men saw it, meant that we didn't really matter.

It was Count Saint-Germain who had discovered how to control time travel by using the chronograph, and he had also given the crazy order for all twelve time travelers to be read into the wretched thing.

By now the only travelers missing were Lucy, Paul, Lady Tilney, and some other female, a court lady whose name I could never remember. We still had to fix it for those four to give a few drops of their blood.

And the ultimate question was, What exactly was going to happen when all twelve time travelers really had been read into the chronograph, and the Circle of Twelve was closed? No one seemed to know for certain. As for the Guardians, they were like a lot of lemmings where the count was concerned. Blind devotion was a mild description of their attitude.

My own throat tightened up at the mere thought of Saint-Germain, because my only meeting with him in the past had been anything but pleasant.

Mr. George was puffing and blowing as he went up the steps to the house ahead of me. His small, round form always had something comforting about it. At least, he was just about the only one of the whole bunch I trusted an inch. Apart from Gideon—although, no, you couldn't actually say I trusted Gideon.

Outside, the Lodge building looked just like the other buildings in the narrow streets around Temple Church, most of them lawyers' chambers or offices occupied by professors of law. But I knew that the place was much bigger and a great deal grander than it seemed from the street, and there was a huge amount of space in it, particularly below ground level.

Gideon held me back just as we reached the door and hissed into my ear, "I said you were terribly scared, so look a bit upset if you want to get home early this evening."

"I thought I was looking upset already," I murmured.

"They're waiting for you in the Dragon Hall," panted Mr. George at the top of the steps. "You'd better go straight in, and I'll find Mrs. Jenkins and get her to bring you something to eat. You must be hungry by now. Anything special you'd like?"

Before I could tell him, Gideon had taken my arm and was leading me on. "Lots of everything, please!" I called back to Mr. George over my shoulder, before Gideon hauled me through a doorway and into a wide corridor. I was having difficulty not stumbling over the hem of my ankle-length skirt.

The gargoyle skipped nimbly along beside us. "I don't think your boyfriend has very good manners," he remarked. "This is more the way you'd drag a goat to market."

"Slow down a bit, can't you?" I asked Gideon.

"Look, the sooner we get this over with, the sooner you can go home." Was there a touch of concern in his voice, or did he simply want to get rid of me?

"Yes, but . . . maybe I'd like to be in on this whole meeting too—did you ever think of that? I have a lot of questions, and I'm sick and tired of no one ever giving me any answers."

Gideon slackened his pace slightly. "No one would give you answers today anyway. All they'll want to know is how Lucy and Paul came to be lying in wait for us there. And I'm afraid you're still our prime suspect."

That *our* cut me to the heart. I resented it.

"But I'm the only one who doesn't know anything about all this!"

Gideon sighed. "I've already tried to explain. *Now* you may be totally ignorant and . . . and innocent, but no one knows what you may do in the future. Don't forget, you can travel to the past yourself, and that way you could tell them about our visit." He stopped short. "Well—you *would* be able to tell them."

I rolled my eyes. "So would you! Anyway, why does it have to be one of us? Couldn't Margaret Tilney herself have left a message behind in the past? Or the Guardians?

They could give one of the time travelers a letter to take from any time to any other time—"

"Eh?" asked the gargoyle. "Can you explain what you're talking about? I can't make head or tail of it."

"Of course there are various possible explanations," said Gideon, definitely slowing his pace now. "But I had a feeling today that Lucy and Paul somehow or other . . . let's say *impressed* you." He stopped, let go of my arm, and looked at me seriously. "You could have talked to them, you could have listened to their lies, maybe you'd even have given them your blood for the stolen chronograph voluntarily if I hadn't been there."

"No, I wouldn't," I said. "But I really would have liked to hear what they wanted to say to us. They didn't seem all that evil to me."

Gideon nodded. "You see, that's exactly what I mean. Gwyneth, those two are out to destroy a secret that's been safely guarded for hundreds of years. They want something that isn't theirs. And for that they need our blood. I don't think they'd shrink from anything to lay hands on it." He pushed a curly strand of brown hair back from his forehead, and I instinctively held my breath.

Oh, God, he looked terrific! Those green eyes, the curve of his lips, the pale skin—everything about him was just perfect. And he smelled so good that for a split second I toyed with the idea of simply leaning my head against his chest. Of course I didn't.

"Maybe you've forgotten that we wanted their blood

as well. And it was you who put a pistol to Lucy's head, not the other way around," I said. "She didn't have a gun."

An angry line showed between Gideon's eyebrows. "Gwyneth, please don't be so naive. We'd been lured into a trap—as usual. Lucy and Paul had armed reinforcements. It was at least four to one!"

"Two!" I snapped. "I was there too!"

"Five if we count Lady Tilney. But for my pistol, we could be dead by now. Or at least they could have taken blood from us by force, because that's exactly what they were there for. And you wanted to *talk* to them?"

I bit my lip.

"Hello?" said the gargoyle. "Anyone got a thought to spare for me? Because I don't understand this one little bit!"

"I can see why you're confused," said Gideon, much more gently now, but you couldn't miss the patronizing note in his voice. "You've had too many new experiences over these last few days. And you were totally unprepared. How could you understand what it's all about? You ought to be at home in bed. So let's get this over and done with, fast." He reached for my arm again and made me go on. "I'll do the talking, and you confirm my story, right?"

"Yes, so you've said at least twenty times already!" I replied, annoyed, stopping when I saw a brass plate outside the door saying LADIES and bracing my legs. "You can all start without me. I've been needing to go to the loo since June 1912."

Gideon let go of me. "Can you find the way up by yourself?"

"Of course," I said, although I wasn't absolutely sure whether I could rely on my sense of direction. This house had too many passages, flights of stairs, doors, and nooks and crannies.

"Great! We're rid of that pest at last," said the gargoyle. "Now you can tell me what's going on."

I waited until Gideon had disappeared around the next corner, then I opened the door of the ladies' room and snapped at the gargoyle, "Okay, come on in here!"

"What?" The gargoyle was looking offended. "Into the ladies' toilet? I kind of don't think that would—"

"I don't care what you think it would be. There aren't many places where a girl can talk to demons in peace, and I don't want to risk being overheard. So come on."

Holding his nose, the gargoyle reluctantly followed me into the ladies', where the only smell was a faint one of lemony disinfectant. I glanced quickly at the cubicles. All vacant. "Right. Now listen to me. I know I'm probably not about to shake you off in a hurry, but if you want to stick around, you have to keep a few rules, understand?"

"No picking my nose, no rude words, no scaring dogs," chanted the gargoyle.

"What? No, what I want is for you to agree to leaving me alone in private. I want to be on my own at night, and in the bathroom, and if anyone happens to kiss me"—here I had to swallow—"I don't want any audience then either. Is that clear?"

"Tut, tut!" The gargoyle clicked his tongue. "And that from someone who's dragged me into a *ladies' toilet!*"

"Well, is it a deal? You respect my privacy?"

"No way do I want to watch you showering or—yuck, heaven preserve me!—kissing anyone," said the gargoyle emphatically. "You really don't have to worry about that. And as a rule, I think it's a dead bore watching people asleep. All that snoring and slobbering, not to mention the other stuff—"

"What's more, I don't want you gabbling away when I'm at school or talking to someone—and please, if you have to sing, keep it for when I'm not around."

"I can do a really good trumpet imitation too," said the gargoyle. "And a tuba imitation. Do you have a dog?"

"No!" I took a deep breath. I was going to need nerves of iron to cope with this little guy.

"Couldn't you get one? Or a cat would be better than nothing, but they always look down their noses at you, and it's not so easy to wind a cat up. A good many birds can see me, too. Do you have a bird?"

"My grandmother can't stand pets," I said. I was about to say she probably wouldn't have much time for invisible pets either, but I swallowed the words again. "Okay, now let's start over again from the beginning: My name is Gwyneth Shepherd. Nice to meet you."

"Xemerius," said the gargoyle, beaming all over his face. "Pleased to meet you too." He climbed up on the washbasin and looked deep into my eyes. "Really! Very, very pleased! Will you buy me a cat?"

"No. And now get out of here. I have to go to the loo."

"Urggh!" Xemerius stumbled hastily through the door without opening it first, and I heard him strike up "Friends Will Be Friends" again out in the corridor.

I spent much longer in the ladies' than really necessary. I washed my hands thoroughly and splashed plenty of cold water on my face, hoping it would clear my head. But that didn't stop my confused ideas from going round and round like a carousel. My reflection in the mirror looked as if crows had been nesting in my hair, and I ran my fingers through it to smooth it out, meanwhile trying to encourage myself. The way my friend Lesley would have done if she'd been here.

"Only a couple of hours and then you'll be through with it, Gwyneth. And, hey, considering you're so tired and hungry, you don't look too bad."

My reflection peered reproachfully at me out of large eyes rimmed by dark shadows.

"Okay, that was a lie," I admitted. "You look terrible. But you've been known to look worse. For instance when you had chicken pox. So chin up! You can do it."

I found Xemerius dangling from a chandelier in the corridor like a bat. "It's a bit creepy in here," he said. "A one-armed Knight Templar just walked by. Friend of yours?"

"No," I said. "Thank God, he isn't. Come on, we have to go this way."

"Will you explain time travel to me?"

"I don't understand it myself."

"Will you buy me a cat?"

"No."

"Come to think of it, I know where you can get cats for free. Hey, there's a *person* inside that suit of armor."

I cast a surreptitious glance at it. Sure enough, I had the feeling that I saw a pair of eyes glittering behind the closed visor. It was the same suit of armor I'd tapped cheerfully on the shoulder yesterday, naturally thinking it was just there for decoration.

Somehow yesterday seemed years ago.

I met Mrs. Jenkins, the secretary, outside the door of the Dragon Hall. She was carrying a tray and was glad that I could hold the door open for her.

"Just tea and biscuits for now, dear," she said with an apologetic smile. "Mrs. Mallory went home long ago, and I'll have to look around the kitchen to see what I can make for you children."

I nodded politely, but I was sure that with a little effort anyone could have heard my stomach begging, "Oh, do just send out for Chinese!"

They were already waiting for us in the Dragon Hall: Gideon's uncle Falk, who always reminded me of a wolf, with his amber eyes and mane of gray hair; Dr. White in his eternal black suit; and, to my surprise, my English and history teacher, Mr. Whitman, also known as Mr. Squirrel. I immediately felt twice as uncomfortable and tugged nervously at the pale blue bow on my dress. Only this morning Mr. Whitman had caught my friend Lesley and me skipping a class and read us a lecture. And he'd confiscated all Lesley's research work. So far we'd only had a strong suspicion that he belonged to the Inner Circle of the Guardians, but it was officially confirmed now.

"Ah, there you are, Gwyneth," said Falk de Villiers, in a friendly tone but without smiling. He looked as if he could do with a shave, but maybe he was one of those men who shave in the morning and already look as if they have a three-day growth of beard by evening. Possibly it was just the dark shadow around his mouth, but he looked a lot tenser and more serious than yesterday, or even at midday. A *nervous* leader of the wolf pack.

However, Mr. Whitman gave me a wink. Dr. White muttered something incomprehensible in which all I could make out were the words *women* and *punctuality*.

The little fair-haired ghost boy Robert was standing beside Dr. White as usual. He was the only one who seemed glad to see me, because he gave me a beaming smile. Robert was Dr. White's son, who had drowned at the age of seven in a swimming pool, and now, as a ghost, he stuck close to his father all the time. Of course, no one except for me could see him, and because Dr. White was always there too, I still hadn't managed to have a proper conversation with Robert.

Gideon was leaning against one of the lavishly decorated walls. His gaze moved only briefly over me and then stopped at the biscuits on Mrs. Jenkins's tray. With luck, his stomach was growling as loudly as mine.

Xemerius had slipped into the room ahead of me and was looking around appreciatively. "Wow," he said. "This place is quite something!" He walked all around it once, admiring the elaborate carvings on the walls. I never tired of looking at them myself. I specially liked the mermaid swimming above the sofa. Every one of her scales was carved in detail, and her fins shimmered in all imaginable shades of blue and turquoise. But the hall owed its name to the gigantic dragon winding its way along the high ceiling between the chandeliers, looking as lifelike as if it might unfold its wings and fly away any moment.

At the sight of Xemerius, the little ghost boy widened his eyes in astonishment and hid behind Dr. White's legs.

I would have liked to say, "He won't hurt you. He only wants to play" (hoping that was true), but talking to a ghost about a demon when you're in a room full of people who can't see either of them is not to be recommended.

"I'll just go and see whether I can find anything else to eat in the kitchen," said Mrs. Jenkins.

"You ought to have gone home some time ago, Mrs. Jenkins," said Falk de Villiers. "You've been doing too much overtime recently."

"Yes, off you go home," Dr. White snapped at her abruptly. "No one here's going to starve to death."

Oh, yes, they were! I was. And I felt sure that Gideon was thinking exactly the same. When our eyes met, he smiled.

"Biscuits are not what I'd call a healthy, well-balanced supper for children," protested Mrs. Jenkins, but under her breath. Of course Gideon and I weren't children anymore, but we could have done with a good meal all the same. A pity Mrs. Jenkins was the only one who shared my opinion, because unfortunately she didn't have much say in the matter. At the door she almost collided with Mr. George, still out of breath and now also carrying two heavy leather-bound folio volumes.

"Ah, Mrs. Jenkins," he said. "Thank you so much for the tea. Do lock up the office and go home now."

Mrs. Jenkins made a disapproving face, but she only replied politely, "See you tomorrow morning."

Mr. George closed the door behind her, with a loud snort, and put the thick books on the table. "Well, here I am. Now we can start. With only four members of the Inner Circle present, we don't have the necessary quorum to make decisions, but we'll be almost at full strength tomorrow. As we expected, Sinclair and Hawkins are not available, and they've both transferred their voting rights to me. Today we're just concerned with establishing a rough plan of action."

"We'd better sit down." Falk pointed to the chairs standing around the table under the carved dragon, and we each took one of them.

Gideon hung his Edwardian coat over the back of his chair, opposite the place where I was sitting, and rolled up his shirtsleeves. "I'll say it again: Gwyneth doesn't have to be at this meeting. She's tired and terrified. She should elapse, and then someone must take her home."

And first someone should give her a pizza. With extra cheese.

"Don't worry. Gwyneth will only be asked to give us a brief account of her impressions," said Mr. George. "Then I'll take her down to the chronograph myself."

"I can't say she appears to me particularly terrified," muttered black-clad Dr. White. Robert, the little ghost boy, was standing behind the back of his chair and casting curious glances at the sofa, on which Xemerius was now lounging.

"What's that *thingy*?" Robert asked me.

Of course I didn't answer.

"I am not a thingy. I'm a good friend of Gwyneth's," replied Xemerius for me, putting out his tongue. "You might even say her best friend. She's going to buy me a dog."

I cast the sofa a stern glance.

"The impossible has happened," Falk began. "When Gideon and Gwyneth visited Lady Tilney, they were expected. All of us here can confirm that we chose the date and time of their visit entirely at random. Yet Lucy and Paul were waiting for them. It can't conceivably be coincidence."

"Which means someone must have told them about that visit," said Mr. George, who was leafing through one of the folio volumes. "The only question is who."

"Or when, more like it," said Dr. White, looking at me.

"And why," I said.

Gideon frowned. "*Why* is obvious. They need our blood to read it into the chronograph they stole. That's why they brought reinforcements."

"But there's not a word about your visit in the *Annals*," said Mr. George. "And yet the two of you were in contact with at least three of the Guardians of the time, not to mention the guards posted at the doors. Can you remember their names?"

"The First Secretary met us himself." Gideon pushed a lock of hair back. "Burgess, or some such name. He said the brothers Jonathan and Timothy de Villiers were expected to elapse there early in the evening and Lady Tilney had already elapsed early that morning. And then a man called Winsley took us to Belgravia in a cab. He was supposed to wait at the door for us there, but when we came out of the house, the cab had disappeared. We had to get away on foot, find a place to lie low, and wait to travel back."

I felt myself blushing when I remembered the place where we'd been lying low. I quickly helped myself to a biscuit and let my hair fall over my face.

"The report that day was written by a Guardian in the Inner Circle, a man called Frank Mine. It's only a few lines long, says a little about the weather, then he mentions a suffragettes' protest march in the city, says Lady Tilney turned up punctually to elapse, and that's it. No unusual incidents, he adds. There's no mention of the de Villiers twins, but they too were members of the Inner Circle at the time." Mr. George sighed, and closed the folio volume. "Very strange. It all points to a conspiracy in our own ranks."

"And the main question," said Mr. Whitman, "remains how Lucy and Paul could know that you two would visit Lady Tilney's house at that time and on that day."

"Wow," said Xemerius from the sofa. "All these names. Enough to make your head spin."

"The answer to that is obvious," said Dr. White, his eyes resting on me again.

We were all staring thoughtfully and gloomily into

space, me included. I hadn't done anything, but obviously all the others were assuming that at some future date I'd feel that I had to tell Lucy and Paul when we were going to visit Lady Tilney, for a reason so far unknown. It was all terribly confusing, and the longer I thought about it, the more illogical it seemed to me. Suddenly I felt very much alone.

"What sort of freaks are you all?" said Xemerius, jumping up from the sofa to hang head down from one of the gigantic chandeliers. "Time travel—I ask you! I've seen a lot of things in my time, but this is new even to me."

"There's one thing I don't understand," I said. "Why were you expecting to find something about our visit in those *Annals,* Mr. George? I mean, if there had been, then you'd have seen it already, and you'd have known that we were going there that day *and* what would happen to us. Or is it like that film with Ashton Kutcher, *The Butterfly Effect*? And every time one of us comes back from the past, the whole future has changed?"

"That's an interesting and very philosophical question, Gwyneth," said Mr. Whitman, as if we were in one of his classes. "I don't know the film you're talking about, but it's true, according to the laws of logic, that the tiniest change in the past can have a great influence on the future. There's a short story by Ray Bradbury in which—"

"Perhaps we can put off philosophical discussion to some other time," Falk interrupted him. "At the moment I'd like to hear the details of the ambush in Lady Tilney's house and how you managed to get away."

I looked at Gideon. Right, it was up to him to give his pistol-free version of the story. I helped myself to another biscuit.

"We were lucky," said Gideon, his voice just as calm as before. "I realized that there was something wrong at once. Lady Tilney didn't seem at all surprised to see us. The table was laid for afternoon tea, and when Paul and Lucy turned up and the butler stationed himself in the doorway, Gwyneth and I escaped into the next room and down the servants' stairs. The cab had disappeared, so we got away on foot." He didn't seem to find lying difficult. No giveaway red face, no batting of his eyelids, no artificial looking up, not a trace of uncertainty in his voice. All the same, I still thought his version of the story lacked a certain something to make it credible.

"Strange," said Dr. White. "If the ambush had been properly planned, they'd have been armed and would have made sure that you two couldn't get away."

"My head's still spinning," said Xemerius, back on the sofa. "I hate all these crazy verbs, using a subjunctive to get what's happened in the future and the past mixed up."

I looked expectantly at Gideon. If he was going to stick to the pistol-free version, he'd have to come up with a bright idea now.

"I think we simply took them by surprise," said Gideon.

"Hm," said Falk. The others didn't look entirely convinced either. No wonder! Gideon had botched the job! If you were lying, you had to come up with confusing details that wouldn't interest anyone.

"We really did move fast," I said hastily. "The servants' stairs had obviously just been polished, and I nearly slipped, in fact I more or less slid down the stairs instead of running down them. If I hadn't held on to the banister rail, right now I'd be lying in the year 1912 with a broken neck. Come to think of it, what happens if you die while you're away time traveling? Does your dead body travel back of its own accord? Well, anyway, we were lucky that the door at the bottom of the stairs was open, because a maid was just coming in with a shopping basket. A fat blonde. I thought Gideon was going to knock her over, and there were eggs in that basket, which would have made a terrible mess, but we managed to run past her and down the street as fast as we could go. I have a blister on my toe."

Gideon was leaning back in his chair with his arms folded. I couldn't interpret the look on his face, but it didn't seem to be either appreciative or grateful.

"Next time I'm going to wear sneakers," I said into the general silence. Then I took another biscuit. No one else wanted to eat them.

"I have a theory," said Mr. Whitman slowly, toying with the signet ring on his right hand. "And the longer I think about it, the more certain I feel that I'm on the right track. If—"

"I'm beginning to feel rather foolish because I've said it so often already. But *she* ought not to be present at this discussion," said Gideon.

I felt the pang in my heart turn to something worse. I wasn't just offended anymore, I was downright cross.

"He's right," agreed Dr. White. "It's sheer stupidity to let her take part in our deliberations."

"But we also need to know what Gwyneth remembers," said Mr. George. "Any impressions, however small—what they wore, what they said, what they looked like—could give us a good idea of Paul and Lucy's present time base."

"She'll still remember all that tomorrow and the day after tomorrow," said Falk de Villiers. "I think it really would be best for you to take her down to elapse now, Thomas."

Mr. George crossed his arms over his fat little paunch and said nothing.

"I'll go down to the chronograph and supervise her journey," said Mr. Whitman, pushing his chair back.

"Right." Falk nodded. "Two hours will be plenty. One of the adepts can wait for her to travel back. We need you up here with us."

I looked inquiringly at Mr. George. He only shrugged his shoulders, resigned.

"Come along, Gwyneth." Mr. Whitman was on his feet. "The sooner you get it behind you, the sooner you'll be in bed, and then at least you'll be fit for classes at school tomorrow. I'm looking forward to reading your essay on Shakespeare."

Good heavens. What a nerve the man had! Starting on about Shakespeare now . . . it really was the end!

For a moment I wondered whether to protest, but then I decided not to. I didn't really want to listen to any more idiotic babble. I wanted to go home and forget this whole time-travel business, Gideon included. Let them go on mulling over mysteries in their stupid Dragon Hall until they dropped with sheer exhaustion. I wished that on Gideon most of all, plus a nightmare after he'd showered and gone to bed!

Xemerius was right, they were freaks, the whole lot of them.

The silly thing was that, all the same, I couldn't help glancing at Gideon, and thinking something crazy along the lines of *if he'd only smile just once now, I'd forgive him everything.*

Of course he didn't. Instead he just looked at me expressionlessly. It was impossible to tell what was going on inside his head. For a moment, the idea that we'd kissed was miles away, and for some reason, I suddenly thought of the silly rhyme that Cynthia Dale, our authority at school on everything to do with love, always liked to chant. "Green eyes, cold as ice, no idea that love is nice."

"Good night," I said with dignity.

"Good night," all the others murmured. All of them except Gideon, that is. He said, "Don't forget to blindfold her, Mr. Whitman."

Mr. George snorted crossly through his nose. As Mr. Whitman opened the door and propelled me out into the corridor, I heard Mr. George saying, "Have you stopped to think that this policy of excluding her could be the very reason why the things that are going to happen do happen?"

Whether anyone had an answer to that I didn't hear. The heavy door latched shut, cutting off the sound of their voices.

Xemerius was scratching his head with the tip of his tail. "That's the weirdest secret society I ever came across!"

"Don't take it to heart, Gwyneth," said Mr. Whitman. He took a black scarf out of his jacket pocket and held it under my nose. "It's just that you're the new factor in the game. The great unknown in the equation."

What was I supposed to say to that? Three days ago, I didn't even have an inkling about the existence of the Guardians. Three days ago, my life had still been perfectly normal. Well, reasonably normal. "Mr. Whitman, before you blindfold me . . . could we stop in Madame Rossini's sewing room and fetch my things? I've left two sets of my school uniform here now, and I'll need something to wear tomorrow. My school bag is there too."

"Of course." Mr. Whitman waved the scarf cheerfully in the air as he walked along. "In fact, you can change your clothes there. You won't be meeting anyone in the past. What year shall we send you to?"

"Makes no difference if I'm shut up in a cellar, does it?" I said.

"Let's see, it has to be a year when you can land in . . . er, in the aforesaid cellar without any problems. That's all right after 1945—for a few years before that, the cellars were used as air raid shelters. How about 1974? The year when I was born, a good year." He laughed. "Or shall we try 30 July 1966? That's when England beat Germany in the World

Cup final. But I don't suppose you're very interested in football, are you?"

"Particularly not when I'm holed up in a cellar without any windows, a long way below ground level," I said wearily.

"It's all done for your own safety." Mr. Whitman sighed.

"Hold on a moment," said Xemerius, who was flying along beside me. "I can't quite keep up with all this. Does it mean you're going to get into a time machine now and disappear into the past?"

"Yes, exactly," I told him.

"Then let's go for the year 1948," said Mr. Whitman happily. "The year of the London Olympic Games."

He was walking ahead, so he couldn't see me roll my eyes.

"Time travel! Wow! Interesting girlfriend I've found myself!" said Xemerius, and for the first time I thought I detected a note of respect in his voice.

THE ROOM where the chronograph was kept was deep underground, and although I'd always been brought down here and led up again blindfolded, by now I had some idea where it was. If only because in both 1912 and 1782 I'd been allowed to leave the room without a blindfold. When Mr. Whitman led me, blindfolded now, away from Madame Rossini's sewing room and along the corridors and staircases, the way began to seem quite familiar, and it was only at the end of it that I felt Mr. Whitman was taking an extra detour to confuse me.

"He really piles on the suspense, doesn't he?" said Xemerius. "Why did they hide this time machine down in a deep, dark cellar?"

I heard Mr. Whitman talking to someone, then a heavy door opened and latched again behind us, and Mr. Whitman took off my blindfold.

I blinked at the light. A red-haired young man in a black suit was standing beside Mr. Whitman. He looked slightly nervous and was sweating with excitement. I glanced around for Xemerius. He was putting his head back through the closed door, just for fun, while the rest of him was here in the room with us.

"Thickest walls I ever saw," he said when he reappeared. "So thick they could have walled up a bull elephant here sideways, if you see what I mean."

"Gwyneth, this is Mr. Marley, Adept First Degree," said Mr. Whitman. "He'll wait here for you to come back and then take you up again. Mr. Marley, this is Gwyneth Shepherd, the Ruby."

"It's an honor to meet you, Miss Shepherd." The redhead made me a little bow.

I smiled at him, feeling a bit embarrassed. "Er . . . pleased to meet you, too."

Mr. Whitman was doing something to an ultramodern safe with a display of flashing lights. I hadn't noticed it on my last two visits to this room. It was hidden behind a tapestry on the wall embroidered with what looked like scenes out of medieval fairy tales—knights on horseback with plumed helmets, ladies with pointy hats and veils obviously admiring a half-naked young man who had killed a dragon. As Mr. Whitman tapped a sequence of numbers into the keypad of the safe, Mr. Marley discreetly looked down at the floor, but you couldn't make anything out anyway, because Mr. Whitman's broad back hid the display from our eyes. The safe door swung open gently, and Mr. Whitman took out the chronograph in its red velvet wrapping and put it on the table.

Mr. Marley held his breath in surprise.

"This is Mr. Marley's first sight of the chronograph in action," said Mr. Whitman, eyes twinkling at me. With his chin, he indicated a flashlight lying on the table. "Take that just in case there's any problem with the electric light. So you needn't be afraid of the dark."

"Thanks." I wondered whether to ask for an insecticide spray as well. An old cellar was bound to be full of creepy-crawlies—and what about rats? It wasn't fair, sending me off all on my own. "Please could I have a stout stick too?"

"A stick? Gwyneth, you're not going to meet anyone there."

"But there could be rats—"

"Rats are more scared of people than vice versa, believe me." Mr. Whitman had taken the chronograph out of its velvet cloth. "Impressive, don't you think, Mr. Marley?"

"Yes, sir, very impressive, sir." Mr. Marley stared at the device in awe.

"Sucking up!" said Xemerius. "Redheads always suck up, don't you agree?"

"I'd have expected it to be larger, I must say," I said. "And I wouldn't have expected a time machine to look so like a mantelpiece clock."

Xemerius whistled through his teeth. "And look at those clunking great rocks! If they're real, I'm not surprised this thing is kept in a safe." The chronograph did have gemstones of an impressive size set in it, glowing like the crown jewels in among the painting and writing on the surface of the strange device.

"Gwyneth has opted for the year 1948," said Mr. Whitman, as he opened flaps and set tiny little wheels turning and whirring. "What was going on in London at the time, Mr. Marley, do you know?"

"The Olympic Games, sir," said Mr. Marley.

"Show-off!" said Xemerius. "Redheads are always showing off."

"Very good." Mr. Whitman straightened up. "Gwyneth will arrive at twelve noon on the twelfth of August and spend exactly a hundred and twenty minutes there. Are you ready, Gwyneth?"

I swallowed. "I really do wish I knew . . . are you sure I won't meet anyone there?" Not to mention rats and spiders. "When I was on my own before, Mr. George gave me his ring to take with me so I wouldn't come to any harm. . . ."

"That was when you traveled back to the documents room, which has always been much used. But this room will be empty. If you keep quiet and don't leave it—it will be locked, anyway—you definitely won't meet anyone. Hardly anyone ever came into this part of the vaults in the

postwar years. They were busy with reconstructing buildings aboveground all over London then." Mr. Whitman
sighed. "An exciting period."

"But suppose, just by chance, someone *does* happen to
come into this room at that time and sees me? I ought at
least to know the password for the day."

Looking slightly annoyed, Mr. Whitman raised his
eyebrows. "No one will come in, Gwyneth. Once again:
you'll land in a locked room, stay there for a hundred and
twenty minutes, and then travel back again, and no one in
the year 1948 will know anything at all about it. If they
did, there'd be something about your visit in the *Annals*.
And we don't have time now to find out the password for
that day."

"Not to Win but to Take Part," said Mr. Marley shyly.

"What?"

"The password for the duration of the Olympic Games.
It's from the Creed of the Games: 'The most important
thing in the Olympic Games is not to win but to take
part.'" Mr. Marley looked awkwardly down at the floor.
"I noticed because they're usually in Latin."

Xemerius rolled his eyes, and Mr. Whitman looked as
if he'd like to do the same. "Really? Well, there you are,
then, Gwyneth. Not that you'll need to know, but if it makes
you feel any better . . . come here, will you?"

I went over to the chronograph and gave Mr. Whitman
my hand. Xemerius flew down to the floor and landed beside me.

"Now what?" he asked excitedly.

Now came the uncomfortable bit. Mr. Whitman had opened a flap on the chronograph and put my forefinger through the opening.

"I think I'll just hang on to you," said Xemerius, clinging to my neck from behind like a monkey. I ought not to have felt anything at all, but in fact there was a general impression of someone putting a wet scarf around me.

Mr. Marley's eyes were wide with tense interest.

"Thanks for the password," I told him, and made a face as a sharp needle pricked my finger and the room was filled with red light. I clutched the flashlight, colors and the figures of people swirled around before my eyes, and a jolt passed through my body.

23 June 1542, Florence. I am asked by the leader of the Congrega-tion to inquire into a case that calls for the utmost discretion and delicacy. It is also extremely curious. Elisabetta, the youngest daughter of M.,[1] who has lived for the last ten years in strict seclusion behind convent walls, is allegedly with child by the Devil and will give birth to a succubus.[2] On visiting the convent, I was indeed able to convince myself of the girl's possible preg-nancy and of her somewhat confused state of mind. While the Abbess, who enjoys my full confidence and who appears to be a woman of sound mind and good understanding, does not exclude a natural explanation of the phenomenon, the girl's father ex-presses suspicions of witchcraft. He claims to have seen, with his own eyes, the Devil in the shape of a young man embracing the girl in the garden, and then dematerializing in a cloud of smoke, leaving behind a slight smell of sulphur.[3] Two other girls at school in the convent apparently bear witness that they have seen the Devil several times in the company of Elisabetta and that he has given her gifts in the form of valuable jewels. Improbable as the

---

[1] We may assume, with probability verging on certainty, that the initial denotes Giovanni Alessandro, Conte di Madrone, 1502–1572, cf. also Lamory, *Noble Italian Families of the Sixteenth Century*, Bologna 1997, p. 112 ff.

[2] Here, child of demonic origin.

[3] The conte may have invented the cloud of smoke and the smell of sul-phur to lend greater credibility to this story.

story may sound, in view of the close connection of M. with R.M.[4] and various friends in the Vatican, it is difficult for me to cast doubt publicly on his sanity and accuse his daughter merely of unchastity. Beginning tomorrow, I am therefore about to conduct interrogations of all involved.

FROM THE RECORDS OF THE INQUISITION
AS DRAWN UP BY FATHER GIAN PETRO BARIBI
OF THE DOMINICAN ORDER
ARCHIVES OF THE UNIVERSITY LIBRARY, PADUA
(DECIPHERED, TRANSLATED, AND EDITED
BY DR. M. GIORDANO)

---

[4] R.M.: probably Rudolfo, a member of the Medici family, who created a great stir with his spectacular suicide in the year 1559, see Pavani, *Legends of the Forgotten Medici*, Florence 1988, p. 212 ff.

THREE

"XEMERIUS?" The wet-scarf feeling around my neck had gone away. I switched the flashlight on. But the room where I'd landed was already lit by a dim electric bulb hanging from the ceiling.

"Hello," someone said.

I spun around. The room was full of a jumble of crates and pieces of furniture, and a pale young man was leaning against the wall by the door.

"Not to Win but to T-take Part," I stammered.

"Gwyneth Shepherd?" he stammered back.

I nodded. "How do you know?"

The young man took a crumpled piece of paper out of his pocket and held it out to me. He looked just as excited as I felt. He was wearing suspenders and a small pair of round-rimmed glasses; his fair hair had a side parting and was combed back with a lot of hair cream. He could have been in one of those old gangster films as the precociously clever but harmless assistant to the hard-boiled chain-smoking detective who falls for the gangster's moll, the girl with all those feather boas who always gets shot in the end.

I calmed down slightly and looked around. There was no one else in the room, and no sign of Xemerius. He might be able to walk through walls, but he obviously couldn't travel in time.

Hesitating briefly, I picked up the piece of paper. It was yellowed, a sheet out of a notebook torn hastily out of the perforations. The message scrawled on it, in surprisingly familiar handwriting, said

For Lord Lucas Montrose—important!!!
12 August 1948, 12 noon, the alchemical laboratory.
Please come alone.
Gwyneth Shepherd

My heart began beating faster. Lord Lucas Montrose was my grandfather! He'd died when I was ten. I looked at the curving lines of the two capital *L*s. No doubt about it, unfortunately; the scrawly writing was exactly like mine. But how could it be?

I looked up at the young man. "Where did you get this? And who are you?"

"Did you write that?"

"Maybe," I said, and my thoughts began frantically going around in circles. If I'd written it, how come I couldn't remember writing it? "Where did you get it?"

"I've had it for five years. Someone put it in my coat pocket along with a letter. On the day of the ceremony for admission to the Second Degree. The letter said, *He who keeps secrets ought also to know the secret behind the secret. Show not only that you can keep quiet, but that you can also think.* No signature. It was in different handwriting from the note, it was—er—rather elegant old-fashioned handwriting."

I bit my lower lip. "I don't understand."

"Nor do I. All these years, I've thought it was some kind of test," said the young man. "Another exam, so to speak. I never talked to anyone about it. I was always waiting for someone to mention it to me or drop more hints. But nothing of that kind happened. And today I stole down here and waited. I wasn't really expecting anything at all. But then you materialized out of nowhere right in front of me, just like that. At twelve noon on the dot. Why did you write me that note? Why are we meeting down in this remote cellar? And what year do you come from?"

"Two thousand eleven," I said. "Sorry, but I'm afraid I don't know the answers to those other questions myself." I cleared my throat. "So who are you, then?"

"Oh, sorry. My name is Lucas Montrose. No *Lord*. Adept Second Degree."

My mouth was suddenly dry. "Lucas Montrose of 81 Bourdon Place."

The young man nodded. "That's where my parents live, yes."

"In that case . . ." I stared at him and took a deep breath. "In that case, you're my grandfather."

"Oh, not *again*," said the young man, sighing heavily. Then he pulled himself together, moved away from the wall, dusted down one of the chairs stacked on top of each other in a corner of the room, and offered it to me. "Why don't we sit down? My legs feel like rubber."

"Mine too," I admitted, sinking onto the upholstered seat. Lucas took another chair and sat down opposite me.

"So you're my granddaughter?" He grinned faintly. "You know, that's a funny idea for me. I'm not even married. Strictly speaking, I'm not even engaged."

"How old are you, then? Oh, sorry, I ought to know that. Born 1924—that makes you twenty-four in 1948."

"Yes," he said. "I'll be twenty-four in three months' time. And how old are you?"

"Sixteen."

"Just like Lucy."

Lucy. I thought of what she'd called after me when we were on the run from Lady Tilney's house.

I still couldn't believe that I was sitting in front of my own grandfather. I looked for any likeness to the man who used to tell me exciting stories while I sat on his lap. Who had protected me from Charlotte when she said I was trying to show off by telling ghost stories. But young Lucas Montrose's smooth face didn't seem at all like the wrinkled, lined face of the old man I'd known. I did see a likeness to my mum, though—the blue eyes, the firm curve of his chin, the way he was smiling now. I closed my eyes, feeling that all this was simply . . . well, too much for me.

"So there we are, then," said Lucas quietly. "Am I . . . er . . . a nice grandpa?"

I felt a prickling in my nose as I fought back tears. So I just nodded.

"All the other time travelers arrive by chronograph officially and in comfort up in the Dragon Hall or in the documents room," said Lucas. "Why did you pick this gloomy old laboratory?"

"I didn't pick it." I wiped my nose with the back of my hand. "I didn't even know it *was* a laboratory. In my time it's just a normal cellar, with a safe where they keep the chronograph."

"Really? Well, it's not been a laboratory for a long time," said Lucas. "But originally this room was used as a secret alchemy lab. It's one of the oldest rooms in the whole building. Famous London alchemists and magicians worked here searching for the philosopher's stone hundreds of years before the Lodge of Count Saint-Germain was even founded. You can still see eerie drawings and mysterious formulas on the walls here and there, and it's said that the walls are so thick because bones and skulls are built into them." He stopped, biting his own lower lip. "So you're my granddaughter. May I ask which of my . . . er, my children is your mother or father?"

"My mum is called Grace," I said. "She looks like you."

Lucas nodded. "Lucy told me about Grace. She says she was the nicest of my children, the others were boring." His mouth twisted. "I can't imagine having boring children— or any children at all, come to that."

"Maybe they inherited it from your wife, not you," I murmured.

Lucas sighed. "Since Lucy first turned up here a couple of months ago, everyone's been winding me up because she has red hair, just like a girl I'm . . . er, interested in. But Lucy wouldn't tell me who I'm going to marry, because she thinks I might change my mind. And then none of you would be born."

"I expect the time-travel gene that your future wife must be going to pass on matters more than her hair color," I said. "You ought to have been able to identify her that way."

"That's the funny thing about it." Lucas sat a little further forward on his chair. "There are *two* girls from the Jade Line who seem to me really . . . well, attractive. The Guardians have classified them as observation numbers Four and Eight."

"Oh," I said.

"You see, the fact is that at this moment I can't really decide. Maybe a little hint from you might help me."

I shrugged my shoulders. "If you say so. My grandmother, that's your wife, is La—"

"No!" cried Lucas. He had raised both arms to stop me saying more. "I've changed my mind." He scratched his head, looking awkward. "That's the St. Lennox school uniform, isn't it? I recognize the crest on the buttons."

"Yes, that's right," I said, looking down at my dark blue blazer. Madame Rossini had obviously washed and ironed my things. At least, they looked like new and smelled slightly of lavender. She must also have done something clever with the blazer, because it was a much more elegant fit now.

"My sister, Madeleine, goes to St. Lennox, too. She won't be leaving until the end of this year because the war got in the way."

"Aunt Maddy? I didn't know that."

"All the Montrose girls go to St. Lennox. Lucy too. She had the same school uniform as you. Maddy's is dark green and white, and the skirt is checked. . . ." Lucas cleared his throat. "In case you're interested . . . but we'd better concentrate on working out why we're meeting here. So assuming you wrote that note—"

"Will be writing it!"

"—and you'll be leaving it for me on one of your future time-travel trips, why do you think you did it?"

"You mean why *will* I be doing it?" I sighed. "It must make some kind of sense. You can probably tell me a lot. But then again, I don't know. . . ." Baffled, I looked at my young grandfather. "Do you know Lucy and Paul well?"

"Paul de Villiers has been coming here to elapse since January. He's grown two years older in that time, which is rather creepy. And Lucy came for the first time in June. I usually look after them both when they visit. As a rule, it's very amusing. I can help them with their homework. I must say, Paul is the only de Villiers I've ever liked." He cleared his throat again. "But if you come from the year

2011, you must know them both. Funny to think they're nearly forty by now. . . . You must give them my regards."

"I can't do that." Oh, dear, this whole thing was so complicated. And I probably ought to be careful what I said, when I myself didn't really understand what was going on. My mother's words were still ringing in my ears. *Trust no one! Not even your own feelings!* But I simply had to trust someone, and who better than my grandfather? I decided to stake everything on a single card. "I can't give Lucy and Paul your regards. They stole the chronograph and traveled back into the past with it."

"What?" Lucas's eyes were wide behind his glasses. "Why would they have done that? I can't believe it. They'd never . . . When is this supposed to have happened?"

"Nineteen ninety-four," I said. "The same year I was born."

"In 1994 Paul will be twenty, and Lucy eighteen," said Lucas, more to himself than to me. "In two years' time, then. Because now she's sixteen and he's eighteen." He smiled apologetically. "Well, of course I don't mean *now*, I only mean their now when they come to this year to elapse."

"I haven't had much sleep the last couple of nights, so I get the feeling my brain is nothing but candy floss," I said. "And I'm useless at arithmetic anyway."

"Lucy and Paul are . . . Oh, what you're telling me makes no sense. They'd never do anything so . . . so *outrageous*."

"But they did. I thought you might be able to tell me

why. In my own time, everyone keeps telling me that they're wicked. Or crazy. Or both. Anyway, dangerous. When I met Lucy, she said I ought to ask you about the Green Rider. Okay. So who or what's the Green Rider?"

Lucas stared at me, baffled. "You met Lucy? But you just said she and Paul had disappeared the year you were born." Then something seemed to occur to him. "If they took the chronograph with them, how can you travel in time at all?"

"I met them in the year 1912. At Lady Tilney's house. And there's another chronograph that the Guardians use for us."

"Lady Tilney? But she died four years ago. And the second chronograph isn't capable of working."

I sighed. "It is now. Listen, Grandpa"—that word made Lucas jump—"this is all much more confusing for me than you, because until a few days ago, I hadn't the faintest idea about it. I can't explain anything to you. I've been sent here to elapse, for heaven's sake, I don't even know how to spell the stupid word—I heard it for the first time yesterday. This is only the third time the chronograph has sent me back to the past. I traveled back uncontrolled three times before that. Which was not a lot of fun. But the fact is that everyone thought my cousin Charlotte was the gene carrier, because she was born on the right day, and my mum lied about my birthday. So Charlotte had dancing lessons instead of me, and she knows all about the plague and King George, and she can fence, and ride sidesaddle, and play the piano—and goodness only knows what she learned during her introduction to the mysteries." The more I talked, the faster the words came tumbling out of me. "Anyway, I don't know anything except what they've told me so far, and I can't say that was much, or very enlightening—and what's worse, I haven't even had time to make sense of the whole thing. Lesley—she's my best friend—Googled it all, but Mr. Whitman confiscated her folder, and I'd only copied half of the stuff she found out anyway. Everyone seems to have expected me to be somehow special, and now they're disappointed."

"Ruby red, with G major, the magic of the raven, brings the Circle of Twelve home into safe haven," murmured Lucas.

"Yes, well, there you are—magic of the raven, blah blah blah. But I'm the wrong person. Count Saint-Germain throttled me even though he was standing several yards away, and I could hear his voice in my head, and then there were those men with pistols and swords in Hyde Park, and I had to run a sword into one of them because otherwise he'd have killed Gideon, who is . . . who's such a . . ." I took a deep breath, only to go headlong on the next minute. "Gideon is a pain in the neck, he acts as if I were a millstone around his neck, and this morning he kissed Charlotte, well, only on the cheek, but maybe it meant something, I never ought to have kissed him without asking about that first, after all, I've only known him a day or so, but suddenly he was so nice and then . . . oh, it all happened so fast . . . and everyone thinks *I* told Lucy and Paul when we were visiting Lady Tilney because we need her blood, and we need some of Lucy and Paul's blood too, but they need Gideon's blood and mine because that's still missing from their chronograph. And no one tells me what's going to happen when everyone's blood has been read into the chronograph, and sometimes I think they don't know for certain themselves. And Lucy said I ought to ask you about the Green Rider."

Lucas had half closed his eyes behind his glasses and was obviously trying desperately to make sense of my torrent of words. "I have no idea what this Green Rider could mean," he said. "I'm sorry, but it's the first time I ever heard of him. Maybe it's the title of a film? Why don't you ask . . . I know, you could simply ask me in the year 2011."

I looked at him, horrified.

"Oh, dear, I see," said Lucas quickly. "You can't, because I'll be dead by then, or old and blind and deaf drowsing away in some senior citizens' home. . . . No, no, please, I really don't want to know."

This time I couldn't hold back my tears. I sobbed for at least half a minute because—strange as it sounds—I suddenly missed my grandfather dreadfully. "I loved you very much," I said at last.

Lucas gave me a handkerchief and looked at me sympathetically. "Are you sure? I don't even like children. Little pests, if you ask me. . . . But maybe you were a particularly nice child. In fact, I'm sure you were."

"Yes, I was. But you were nice to all us kids." I blew my nose noisily. "Even Charlotte."

We said nothing for a little while. Then Lucas took a watch out of his pocket and said, "How much time do we have?"

"They sent me here for exactly two hours."

"Not very long, then. We've wasted far too much time already." He got up. "I'll get pens and paper, and we'll try to find some kind of system in all this chaos. You'd better stay here. Don't move from the spot."

I just nodded. When Lucas had left, I stared into nothing with my face buried in my hands. He was right. It was important to keep a clear head now.

Who knew when I'd meet my grandfather again? Which things that hadn't happened yet ought I to tell him about, which should I hush up? And looking at it the other way around, I was desperately anxious for any information he could give me that might come in useful. Basically, he was my only ally. But living in the wrong time. And how could he cast light, from here, on any of the dark riddles facing me?

Lucas stayed away for some time, and as the minutes passed, I began to doubt my own feelings. Maybe he'd been lying, and any moment now he'd be back with Lucy and Paul and a big knife, to get blood out of me. Finally, feeling worried, I stood up and looked around for something I could use as a weapon. There was a board with a rusty nail in it lying in a corner, but when I picked it up, it crumbled apart in my fingers. At that very moment, the door opened again, and my young grandfather came back with a notepad under his arm and a banana in one hand.

I breathed a sigh of relief.

"Here, to stave off hunger pangs." Lucas tossed me the banana, took a third chair off the pile, placed it between us, and put the notepad on it. "Sorry I was so long. That idiot Kenneth de Villiers was upstairs getting in my way. I can't stand the de Villiers family. Always sticking their long noses into everything, wanting to be in control and make the decisions and always thinking they know best!"

"How right you are," I murmured.

Lucas shook his wrist to loosen it up. "Then here goes—granddaughter. You're the Ruby, the twelfth in the Circle. The Diamond, from the de Villiers family, was born two years before you. So he'd be around nineteen in your time. What's his name again?"

"Gideon," I said, and just saying it out loud made me feel warm. "Gideon de Villiers."

Lucas's pen was hurrying over the paper. "And he's a pain in the neck, like all of them, but you still kissed him, if I caught the drift of what you were saying just now. Aren't you rather young for that kind of thing?"

"Goodness me, no," I said. "Far from it—I'm a late developer. *All* the girls in our class are on the pill but me."

Well, all except Aishani, Maggie, and Cassie Clarke, but Aishani's parents were conservative Indians and would murder Aishani if she so much as looked at a boy, Maggie fancied girls, and as for Cassie—one day I was sure those spots would go away of their own accord, and then she'd be nicer to other people and stop snapping, "What do you think you're gawping at in that silly way?" when anyone even glanced in her direction.

"Oh, and of course Charlotte won't have anything to do with sex either. That's why Gordon Gelderman calls her the Ice Queen. But now I'm not so sure if that's really right for her. . . ." I ground my teeth, because I was thinking how Charlotte had looked at Gideon—and vice versa. If you stopped to think how quickly Gideon had thought up the idea of kissing me, on only the second day after we met, I couldn't even imagine what had been going on between him and Charlotte over all the years they'd known each other.

"What kind of pill?" asked Lucas.

"How do you mean?" Oh, my God, in the year 1948 they probably had nothing but cow-gut condoms, if that. I didn't really want to know. "Honestly, I'd rather not talk to you about sex, Grandpa."

Lucas looked at me, shaking his head. "And I'd rather not hear that word in your mouth. I don't mean *Grandpa*."

"Okay." I peeled the banana as Lucas went on making notes. "What do you say instead?"

"Instead of what?"

"Instead of sex."

"We don't talk about it," said Lucas, concentrating on his notepad. "Or anyway, not to girls of sixteen. So let's go on. The chronograph was stolen by Lucy and Paul before the blood of the last two time travelers could be read into it. Then the second chronograph came into use, but of course the blood of all the other time travelers is missing from that one."

"Not anymore. Gideon has found nearly all of them, and they gave him some of their blood. There's only Lady Tilney to go, and the Opal, Elise something-or-other."

"Elaine Burghley," said Lucas. "A lady-in-waiting at the court of Queen Elizabeth. She died in childbirth aged eighteen."

"Right. And Lucy and Paul's blood too, of course. So we're after their blood, and they're after ours. Or that's how I understand it, anyway."

"And now there are two chronographs which might complete the Circle? This is really incredible!"

"What will happen when the Circle is complete?"

"Then the secret will be revealed," said Lucas solemnly.

"Oh, no, not you too!" I shook my head angrily. "Isn't there *any* more concrete information available, just for once?"

"Well, the prophesies speak of the rise of the eagle, the victory of mankind over disease and death, and the dawn of a new age."

"Oh," I said, no wiser than before. "So it's a good thing, is it?"

"A very good thing. Something of benefit to the entire human race. That's why Count Saint-Germain founded the Society of the Guardians. That's why the most brilliant and powerful men in the world joined our ranks. We all want to keep the secret so that it can be revealed at the right time and save the world."

Okay. A clear statement for once. Or at least the clearest anyone had yet given me since I got mixed up in all this mysterious secret stuff. "But why don't Lucy and Paul want the Circle to be closed?"

Lucas sighed. "I've no idea. When did you say you met them?"

"In the year 1912," I said. "June. June the twenty-second, I think. Or the twenty-fourth. I didn't notice exactly." The more I tried to remember, the less certain I was. "Or maybe the twelfth? It was an even number, I do remember that. The eighteenth? Anyway, sometime in the afternoon. Lady Tilney had the table laid for tea." Then it dawned on me what I'd just said, and I clapped my hand over my mouth. "Oh, no!"

"What's the matter?"

"Now I've gone and told you, and you'll tell Lucy and Paul, and *that's* why they can lie in wait for us there. So really *you* are the one who gives us away, not me. Mind you, I suppose it all comes to the same thing in the end."

"What? No, no!" Lucas shook his head energetically. "I won't do that. I won't tell them anything at all about you—that would be crazy! If I tell them tomorrow that they're going to steal the chronograph someday and disappear into the past with it, they'll fall down dead of shock on the spot. You have to think very, very carefully what you're going to tell anyone about the future, understand?"

"Well, no, maybe you won't tell them tomorrow, but there are years and years ahead when you could do it." I thoughtfully munched my banana. "On the other hand, what time did they travel back to with the chronograph? Why not this period? They'd always have a friend here in you. Maybe you're lying to me and they've been waiting right outside that door for ages to get a few drops of my blood."

"I haven't the slightest idea where they could have gone." Lucas sighed. "I can't even imagine them ever doing anything so crazy. Or why they'd do it!" He added, sounding discouraged, "I've no idea of anything at all!"

"So neither of us has any idea at this moment," I said, just as discouraged.

Lucas wrote down *Green Rider, second chronograph,* and *Lady Tilney* on his notepad, and added large question marks to all of them. "What we need is to meet again later. By then I could find out a good deal. . . ."

I had a bright idea. "Originally I was supposed to be sent to the year 1956 to elapse. Maybe we could meet again tomorrow evening."

"Ha, ha!" said Lucas. "1956 may be tomorrow to you— for me it's— But yes, let's think. If you get sent to elapse to a time after this, will it be to this room?"

I nodded. "I think so. But you can't wait for me day and night down here. What's more, Gideon could turn up anytime. After all, he has to elapse as well."

"I know what to do," said Lucas, with growing enthusiasm. "If you land in this room next time, just come up to me! My office is on the second floor. You'll only have to pass two guards, but that's no problem if you say you've lost your way. You're my cousin. My cousin Hazel from the country. I'll start telling everyone about you this very day."

"But Mr. Whitman says this room is always kept locked, and anyway I don't know exactly where we are."

"You'll need a key, of course. And the password for the day." Lucas looked around him. "I'll get a key made for you and leave it somewhere here. Same with the password. I'll write it on a note and leave it in our hiding place. Somewhere in the brickwork would be best. The bricks are coming a bit loose just there, see? Maybe we can make a hollow space behind them." He got to his feet, made his way through the junk in the cellar, and knelt down in front of the wall. "Look, here. I'll come back with tools and make a perfect hiding place. When you come back next, you just have to pull out this brick, and then you'll find the key and the password."

"But there are a lot of bricks," I said.

"Just remember this one, fifth row from the bottom, roughly in the middle of the room. Damn, that was my fingernail! Never mind, that's my plan, and I think it's a good one."

"But then you'd have to come down here every day from now on to change the password," I said. "How are you going to fix that? Aren't you studying at Oxford?"

"The password isn't changed daily," replied Lucas. "Sometimes we use the same one for weeks on end. Anyway, this is our only chance to fix another meeting. Remember that brick. I'll draw a plan as well, so that you can find your way up. There are secret passages from here that go over half of London." He looked at his watch. "Now, let's sit down again and make notes. Systematically. You wait, we'll both know more in the end."

"Or alternatively we'll still be two people without the faintest idea down in a musty cellar."

Lucas put his head to one side and grinned at me. "Maybe, just in passing, you could tell me whether your grandmother's name begins with an *A* or a *C*?"

I had to smile. "Which would you rather?"

THE CIRCLE OF TWELVE

NAME	GEMSTONE	ALCHEMICAL QUALITY	ANIMAL	TREE
Lancelot de Villiers 1560–1607	Amber	*Calcinatio*	Frog	Beech
Elaine Burghley 1562–1580	Opal	*Putrefactio et mortificio*	Owl	Walnut
William de Villiers 1626–1689	Agate	*Sublimatio*	Bear	Pine
Cecilia Woodville 1628–1684	Aquamarine	*Solutio*	Horse	Maple
Robert Leopold, Count Saint-Germain 1703–1784	Emerald	*Distillatio*	Eagle	Oak
Jeanne de Pointcarré, Madame d'Urfée 1705–1775	Citrine	*Coagulatio*	Snake	Ginkgo
Jonathan and Timothy de Villiers 1875–1944 1875–1930	Carnelian	*Extractio*	Falcon	Apple
Margaret Tilney 1877–1944	Jade	*Digestio*	Fox	Linden
Paul de Villiers b. 1974	Black Tourmaline	*Ceratio*	Wolf	Mountain Ash
Lucy Montrose b. 1976	Sapphire	*Fermentatio*	Lynx	Willow
Gideon de Villiers b. 1992	Diamond	*Multiplicatio*	Lion	Yew
Gwyneth Shepherd b. 1994	Ruby	*Projectio*	Raven	Birch

FOUR

"GWENNY! GWENNY, wake up!"

With difficulty, I struggled up from the depths of my dream. In the dream I'd been an ancient, hunchbacked old woman sitting opposite Gideon, who was looking terrific, and claiming that my name was Gwyneth Shepherd and I came from the year 2080. Now I looked into the familiar, snub-nosed face of my little sister, Caroline.

"At last!" she said. "I thought I'd never get you to wake up. I was asleep when you came in yesterday evening, though I tried so hard to stay awake. Have you brought one of those gorgeous dresses back again?"

"Not this time." I sat up. "I was able to change when I got there."

"Is it always going to be like this? You not coming home until I'm asleep? Mum has been so odd since this happened to you. And Nick and I miss you. Suppers don't seem right when you're not there."

"They didn't seem right before," I reassured her, dropping back on the pillow.

A limousine had brought me back yesterday evening. I didn't know the chauffeur, but redheaded Mr. Marley had come all the way to the front door of our house with me.

I hadn't seen Gideon again, and just as well. It was quite enough to dream of him all night.

My grandmother's butler, Mr. Bernard, had let me in, polite and otherwise totally impassive, as ever. My mum had come downstairs to welcome me home, hugging me as tightly as if I'd just come back from an expedition to the South Pole. I was glad to see her, too, although I was still rather cross with her. It was so odd, finding out that your own mother had been lying to you. And she still wouldn't tell me why. Apart from a few cryptic remarks—*trust no one . . . dangerous . . . secret . . . blah blah blah*—she hadn't told me anything to explain her behavior. So what with that and the fact that I was just about dying of exhaustion, I'd simply eaten a small piece of roast chicken and then fallen into bed without telling Mum about the day's events. And what exactly was she going to do with the information? She worried far too much anyway. I thought she looked almost as exhausted as me.

Caroline shook my arm again. "Hey, don't go back to sleep!"

"Okay." I swung my feet over the edge of the bed and realized that, in spite of my long phone call to Lesley before I went to sleep, I did feel fairly well rested. But where was Xemerius? He'd disappeared when I went into the bathroom last night, and I hadn't seen him since.

Under the shower, I finally washed my hair, using Mum's expensive shampoo, which wasn't really allowed, and some of her conditioner as well, even at the risk of being given away by the wonderful scent of roses and grapefruit. As I rubbed my head dry, I instinctively wondered whether Gideon liked roses and grapefruit and then called myself sternly to order.

I'd hardly had a couple of hours' sleep, and here I was thinking of *him* again! And just what was so great about what had happened anyway? We'd done a bit of necking in the confessional, but right after that, he'd gone back to being his old insufferable self, and my fall from cloud nine was not something I wanted to remember, whether or not I'd had enough sleep. As I'd told Lesley when she wouldn't drop the subject last night.

I blow-dried my hair, got dressed, and went down all the flights of stairs to the dining room. Caroline, Nick, Mum, and I lived on the third floor of our house. Unlike the rest of the place, which had been in my family's hands since the beginning of time (or even longer), it was at least reasonably comfortable.

The rest of the house was stuffed with antique furniture and pictures of assorted ancestors, few of whom were exactly a sight for sore eyes. And we had a ballroom where I had helped Nick learn how to ride a bike—in secret, of course, but these days traffic in central London was terribly dangerous, as everyone knew.

As so often, I wished Mum and the three of us could eat up on the third floor, where we had our own rooms, but my grandmother, Lady Arista, insisted on all of us meeting at mealtimes in the gloomy dining room. Its paneling was the color of milk chocolate; at least, that was the only nice comparison I'd ever thought of. The others were less appetizing.

Today the atmosphere was distinctly better than the day before, as I noticed the moment I came into the room. Well, that was something, anyway.

Lady Arista, who always seemed rather like a ballet teacher about to rap you over the knuckles, said "good morning" in friendly tones, and Charlotte and her mother smiled at me as if they knew something and I hadn't the faintest idea of it.

Since Aunt Glenda never normally smiled at anyone (unless you count a sort of sour lift at the corners of her mouth), and Charlotte had said some horrible things to me only yesterday, I immediately felt suspicious.

"Has something happened?" I asked.

My twelve-year-old brother Nick grinned at me as I sat down beside Caroline, and Mum pushed a huge plateful of scrambled egg on toast over to me. I almost fainted away with hunger as the delicious smell rose to my nostrils.

"Oh, my goodness," said Aunt Glenda. "I suppose you want your daughter consuming a whole month's supply of fat and cholesterol in a single day, do you, Grace?"

"That's right," said Mum, unfazed.

"She'll hate you later for not taking better care of her figure," said Aunt Glenda, smiling again.

"Gwyneth's figure is faultless," said Mum.

"For now—maybe," said Aunt Glenda. She was still smiling.

"Did you two put something in Aunt Glenda's tea?" I asked Caroline in a whisper.

"Someone phoned a few minutes ago, and ever since then Aunt Glenda and Charlotte have been on top of the world," Caroline whispered back. "You'd think someone had cast a magic spell over them."

At that moment, Xemerius landed on the windowsill outside, folded his wings, and came in through the glass of the windowpane.

"Good morning," I said cheerfully.

"Good morning," replied Xemerius, hopping down from the windowsill and up on an empty chair.

While the others looked at me, rather surprised, Xemerius scratched his belly. "Yours is rather a large family. I haven't quite managed to get the hang of it yet, but I did notice there are a lot of women about the place. Too many, if you ask me. And most of the time, half of them look like they need a good tickling." He shook out his wings. "Where are the fathers of all these children? And where are the pets? A great big house like this, and not so much as a canary! I'm disappointed."

I grinned. "Where's Great-aunt Maddy?" I asked as I happily began to eat.

"I am afraid my dear sister-in-law's need for sleep is greater than her curiosity," said Lady Arista, with dignity. She was sitting ramrod straight at the breakfast table, eating half a slice of buttered toast with her fingers delicately spread. (I'd hardly ever seen her anything but ramrod straight.) "Getting up so early yesterday left her in a bad temper all day long. I don't think we'll see her before ten this morning."

"Glad to hear it," said Aunt Glenda. "All that talk of sapphire eggs and clocks on towers really gets on my nerves. Well, how are you feeling, Gwyneth? I imagine this must all be very confusing for you."

"Hm," I murmured.

"It must be so dreadful, finding out all of a sudden that you're born to higher things when you can't live up to expectations." Aunt Glenda forked up a small piece of tomato from her plate.

"Mr. George says Gwyneth has acquitted herself very well so far," said Lady Arista, although before I could feel cheered by this evidence of solidarity she added, "In the circumstances, anyway. Gwyneth, you'll be fetched from school again today and taken to the Temple. This time Charlotte will go with you." She sipped her tea.

I couldn't open my mouth without letting scrambled egg drop out, so I just gawped at her in alarm, while Nick and Caroline spoke for me. "Why?"

"Because," said Aunt Glenda, wagging her head in a peculiar way, "because Charlotte knows all the things that

Gwyneth ought to know if she's to do any kind of justice to her task. So on account of the chaotic events of the last few days—and as I'm sure we can all imagine only too vividly, they must indeed have been chaotic—the Guardians want Charlotte to help her cousin prepare for the rest of her time traveling." She looked as if her daughter had just won an Olympic gold medal. At the very least.

The rest of my time traveling? What was this all about?

"Who's that skinny, redheaded battle-ax with the sharp tongue?" inquired Xemerius. "I hope for your sake she's only a distant relation."

"Not that the request surprised us, but all the same we did wonder whether to go along with it. After all, Charlotte really has no kind of obligation to them now. However," and here the skinny, redheaded battle—er, Aunt Glenda—sighed theatrically, "Charlotte is also fully aware of the importance of this mission, so she is unselfishly ready to do what she can to contribute to its success."

My mother also sighed, and gave me a sympathetic glance. Charlotte tucked a strand of her glossy red hair back behind her ear and batted her eyelashes in my direction.

"What?" said Nick. "So what's Charlotte supposed to be teaching Gwenny to do?"

"Oh, my word!" said Aunt Glenda, her cheeks flushing red with emotion. "There's a very great deal she should be taught, but it would be absurd to think that in such a short time Gwyneth can catch up with all the skills Charlotte has acquired over many years, not to mention the . . . er, unequal distribution of natural talents in this case. In particular, Gwyneth's lack of general knowledge is positively disastrous, and she has no idea of the good manners appropriate to various historical periods—or so I have heard."

What a nerve! And who was she supposed to have heard it from?

"Yes, and a person really needs to mind her manners, sitting around for hours alone in a locked cellar," I said. "I mean, a woodlouse might see her picking her nose."

Caroline giggled.

"Oh, no, Gwenny, I'm sorry to have to tell you, but it's going to be just a *little* bit trickier for you in the near future." Charlotte gave me what was probably meant to be a sympathetic look, but it came across as nasty and gloating.

"Your cousin is right." I'd always been a bit afraid of Lady Arista's penetrating gaze, but this time it really made me jump. "On orders from the highest places, you will be spending a good deal of time in the eighteenth century," she said.

"And in company," added Charlotte, "with people who would think it very odd if you didn't even know the name of the king on the throne or what a reticule is."

A reti-what?

"What's a reticule?" asked Caroline.

Charlotte gave her a thin smile. "Get your sister to tell you."

I stared crossly at her. Why did she always get so much pleasure out of making me look stupid and ignorant? Aunt Glenda laughed quietly.

"Kind of a silly handbag, usually full of stuff that no one needs," said Xemerius. "Sewing things. And handkerchiefs. And little bottles of smelling salts."

Aha!

"A reticule is an old-fashioned word for a handbag, Caroline," I said, without taking my eyes off Charlotte. She blinked in surprise, but she kept the thin smile going.

"Orders from the highest places? What's that supposed to mean?" My mother had turned to Lady Arista. "I thought we agreed that Gwyneth would be kept out of the whole thing as far as possible. She was only going to be sent to safe years to elapse. How can they change their minds now and decide to expose her to such danger?"

"It's none of your business, Grace," said my grandmother coolly. "You have done enough damage as it is."

My mother bit her lower lip. Her angry glance went once from me to Lady Arista and back, and then she pushed back her chair and stood up. "I must start for work," she said. She dropped a kiss on Nick's head and looked over the table at Caroline and me. "Have fun at school. Caroline, don't forget to brush your hair before you go. See you later."

"Poor Mum," whispered Caroline as my mother left the room. "She was crying yesterday evening. I don't think she likes it one little bit that you've inherited this time-travel gene."

"No," I agreed. "I'd noticed."

"And she's not the only one," said Nick, with a meaningful look at Aunt Glenda and Charlotte, who was still smiling.

* * *

I'D NEVER ATTRACTED as much attention on walking into the classroom before. That was because half the kids there had seen me being fetched in a black limousine yesterday afternoon.

"The betting's still open," said Gordon Gelderman. "Top odds on possibility number one: that cool-looking guy yesterday, the gay one, is a TV producer, and he was auditioning Charlotte and Gwyneth for a show, but Gwyneth won the part. Possibility number two: the guy is your gay cousin, and he runs a limo service. Possibility number three—"

"Oh, shut up, Gordon!" spat Charlotte, tossing her hair back and sitting down.

"Charlotte, couldn't you explain how come you were necking with the guy but then Gwyneth got into the car with him?" asked Cynthia Dale in a wheedling tone of voice. "Lesley's been trying to make out he's a teacher giving Gwyneth private coaching after school."

"Yes, and a teacher giving coaching is likely to turn up in a limousine and hold hands with our Ice Queen, right?" said Gordon, giving Lesley a nasty look. "That's pathetic as a cover-up, if you ask me."

Lesley shrugged her shoulders and grinned at me. "Couldn't think of anything better in a hurry." She sat down in her usual place.

I looked around for Xemerius. Last time I'd seen him, he was perched on the school roof, waving cheerfully down at me. He did have instructions to keep away from me during classes, but I didn't think he was likely to follow them.

"The Green Rider looks like a dead end," said Lesley under her breath. Unlike me, she hadn't had much sleep last night. She'd spent hours on the Internet again. "A famous jade figurine from the Ming Dynasty goes by that name, but it's in a museum in Beijing, and there's a statue of a Green Rider in the marketplace of a German town called Cloppenburg, and it's the title of two books—one a novel published in 1926, and the other a children's book that wasn't written until after your grandfather's death. That's all so far."

"I thought it might be a painting," I said. Secrets always get hidden behind or in paintings in films.

"No such luck," said Lesley. "If it had been a Blue Rider, well, that would be different, but it isn't. Then I hunted THE GREEN RIDER through an anagram-making site. But . . . well, unless DITHER GREENER means anything, no luck there either. I printed out a few. Anything ring a bell with you?" She handed me a sheet of paper.

"DEER THREE GRIN," I read out. "ERRED HERE TING. Let me think for a moment. . . ."

Lesley giggled. "My favorite is REGRET HEN RIDE. Hang on, here comes Mr. Squirrel."

She meant Mr. Whitman, of course. At the time we nicknamed him that, we had no idea who he really was.

"I keep expecting us to be called to see the principal and told off because of yesterday," I said, but Lesley shook her head.

"Don't worry," she said. "Do you think he wants Mr. Gilles knowing his English and history teacher is an important member of a terribly secret secret society? Because that's what I'd say if he told on us. Oh, shit, here he comes. And looking so . . . so supercilious again!"

In fact, Mr. Whitman did come over to us. He put the fat folder that he'd confiscated in the girls' toilets yesterday down in front of Lesley. "I thought you might like to have this . . . very interesting collection of papers back," he said, with a touch of sarcasm.

"Oh, thank you!" replied Lesley, going a little red in the face. The *collection of papers* was her big file of research into time-travel phenomena. It contained absolutely everything that the two of us (but mainly Lesley, of course) had found out so far about the Guardians and Count Saint-Germain. On page thirty-four, just after all the entries on the subject of telekinesis, there was a note about Mr. Whitman himself. *Squirrel also member of the Lodge? Ring, meaning of?* We could only hope that Mr. Whitman hadn't jumped to the connection with him.

"Lesley, I don't like to say this, but I think your energy could be better invested in some of your school subjects." Mr. Whitman was smiling, but there was something other than just sarcasm in his voice. He lowered it. "Not everything that seems interesting is necessarily good for you."

Was that by any chance a threat? Lesley picked up the folder in silence and put it away in her school bag.

The others were looking at us curiously. Obviously they were wondering what Mr. Whitman was talking about.

Charlotte was sitting close enough to hear him, and she definitely had a gloating expression on her face. When Mr. Whitman said, "And, Gwyneth, by now you should be beginning to understand that discretion is not only desirable but essential," she nodded in agreement. "It is a pity that you are turning out to be so *unworthy*."

How unfair! I decided to follow Lesley's example, and Mr. Whitman and I stared at each other for a few seconds in silence. Then his smile grew wider, and he suddenly patted my cheek. "Chin up! I'm sure there's still a lot you'll be able to learn," he said as he moved on. "Now, then, Gordon, is your essay copied from the Internet again lock, stock, and barrel?"

"You're always telling us to use all the sources we can find," Gordon defended himself. His voice covered two octaves from bass to squeaky treble in the process.

"What was Whitman saying to you two?" Cynthia Dale leaned back and looked at us. "What was that folder? And why did he *stroke* you, Gwyneth?"

"No need to be jealous, Cyn," said Lesley. "He doesn't like us a bit better than he likes you."

"I'm not jealous," said Cynthia. "I mean, *hello* . . . why does everyone think I'm in love with the man?"

"Maybe because you're president of the William Whitman Fan Club?" I suggested.

"Or because you've been seen writing *Cynthia Whitman* twenty times on a piece of paper, saying you wanted to find out what it felt like?" said Lesley.

"Or because—"

"Okay, stop that," hissed Cynthia. "Anyway, it was only once, and it was ages ago."

"It was the day before yesterday," said Lesley.

"I'm more mature and adult now." Cynthia sighed and looked around the class. "It's all because of the boys—stupid, overgrown babies! If only we had reasonably sensible boys in this class, no one would need to fancy one of the teachers. By the way—tell us about the cool guy who picked you up in the limousine yesterday, will you, Gwenny? Is there something going on between you?"

Charlotte let out a snort of amusement, which instantly attracted Cynthia's attention. "Oh, don't keep us on tenterhooks, Charlotte. Do you have something going with him, or does Gwenny?"

By now Mr. Whitman was behind his desk, telling us to put our minds to Shakespeare and his sonnets.

For once I was truly grateful to him. Better Shakespeare than Gideon! The chatter died down around us, giving way to sighs and the rustling of paper. But I did hear Charlotte saying, "Well, certainly not Gwenny."

Lesley looked at me sympathetically. "She has no idea," she whispered to me. "Really, you can only feel sorry for her."

"Yes, right," I whispered back. But in fact I was sorry for no one but myself. I could see that an afternoon in Charlotte's company was going to be a whole load of fun.

THIS TIME the limousine wasn't waiting at the school gates, but parked discreetly a little way down the street.

Red-haired Mr. Marley was pacing nervously up and down beside it. He got even more nervous when he saw us coming.

"Oh, it's you," said Charlotte, very obviously displeased, and Mr. Marley blushed. Charlotte took a look through the open door at the interior of the limousine. It was empty except for the driver—and Xemerius. Charlotte looked disappointed. That gave me a real boost.

"Did you miss me?" Xemerius sprawled contentedly in his seat as the car purred away. Mr. Marley was sitting in the front, and Charlotte, beside me, was staring out of the window in silence.

"Glad to hear it," said Xemerius, without waiting for an answer. "But I'm sure you realize I have other duties too. I can't be looking after you the whole time."

I rolled my eyes, and Xemerius giggled.

In fact I really had missed him. Classes had dragged on slowly, and by the time Mrs. Counter was going on for-ever about the mineral resources of the Baltic states, if not sooner, I'd been longing for Xemerius and his comments. Also I'd have liked to introduce him to Lesley, so far as that was possible. Lesley loved listening to my descriptions, even though my attempts to draw the gargoyle demon for her hadn't turned out very flattering. "What are those clothes-pegs for?" she had asked, pointing to the horns on his head.

"At last!" she said enthusiastically. "An invisible friend who might come in useful! Think about it: unlike James, who just stands about in his niche doing nothing but complaining of your bad manners, this gargoyle can go around spying for you, *and* he can tell you what goes on behind closed doors."

That hadn't occurred to me before. But it was true—over that business this morning with the reti . . . reti-thingy . . . the old word for a handbag, Xemerius had definitely made himself useful.

"You could have an ace up your sleeve with Xemerius" was Lesley's opinion. "Not just a useless ghost always taking offense like James."

I'm afraid she was right there. James was—yes, what exactly was he? If he had rattled chains or made chandeliers swing, he could have been officially described as our school ghost. But the Honorable James Augustus Peregrine Pympoole-Bothame was a handsome young man aged about twenty who wore a powdered white wig and a flowered coat, and he had been dead for 229 years. The school had once been his parents' house, and like most ghosts, he couldn't understand that he had died. As he saw it, the centuries of his life as a ghost were just a strange dream, and he was still expecting to wake up. Lesley suspected he had simply slept through the part of dying where you see a bright light at the end of a tunnel and go toward it.

"James isn't totally useless," I had objected. After all, only yesterday I'd decided that as a child of the eighteenth century, he could be genuinely useful to me, for instance as a fencing teacher. For a few hours, I'd reveled in the fantasy of being as good with a sword as Gideon, thanks to James. Unfortunately I'd made a big mistake there.

Our first (and probably last) fencing lesson just now, in the empty classroom at lunchtime, had left Lesley rolling about the floor in fits of laughter. Of course she couldn't see James's movements, which looked to me very professional, or hear his instructions—"Parry, Miss Gwyneth, just parry! Tierce! Prime! Quint!" She'd only seen me waving Mrs. Counter's pointer desperately about in the air, fending off an invisible sword that could be sliced through like thin air. Useless. And ridiculous.

When Lesley had quite finished laughing, she said she thought James had better teach me something else, and for once James himself agreed with her. Fencing and all other kinds of fighting were a man's business, he said. In his opinion, embroidery needles were the most dangerous weapons a girl ought to pick up.

"I guess the world would be a better place if men stuck to the same rule," Lesley had said. "But as long as they don't, women ought to be prepared." And James had almost fainted away when she produced a knife with a seven-inch blade from her school bag. "So you can defend yourself better if another of those unpleasant lowlife characters in the past is out to get you."

"That looks like a—"

"Japanese kitchen knife, yes. Slices through vegetables and raw fish like butter."

I'd felt a shiver running down my spine.

"Only for emergencies," Lesley had added. "To help you feel a little safer. It was the best weapon I could get in a hurry without a license."

The knife was now in my school bag, in Lesley's mum's old spectacle case converted into a sheath, along with a roll of tape that, if Lesley was to be believed, would also come in useful.

The driver swung around a bend, and Xemerius, who hadn't been holding on tight, went slithering over the smooth leather upholstery to collide with Charlotte. He hastily scrambled up again.

"Rigid as a church column," he remarked, shaking his wings. He inspected her sideways. "Are we going to be lumbered with her all day now?"

"Yes, unfortunately."

"Yes unfortunately what?" asked Charlotte.

"Unfortunately I skipped lunch again," I said.

"Your own fault," replied Charlotte. "Although to be honest, it won't hurt you to lose a few pounds. After all, you'll have to fit into the clothes that Madame Rossini made for me." She tightened her lips for a moment, and I felt something like pity. She'd probably been genuinely pleased by the prospect of wearing Madame Rossini's costumes, and then I came along to spoil everything. Not on purpose, of course, but all the same. . . .

"The dress I had to put on for visiting Count Saint-Germain is in my wardrobe at home," I said. "I'll give it to you if you like. You could wear it to Cynthia's next fancy-dress party—I bet you'd bowl everyone over!"

"That dress isn't yours to give away," said Charlotte brusquely. "It's the property of the Guardians. And it has no business being in your wardrobe at home." She went back to looking out of the window.

"Grouse, grouse, grouse," said Xemerius.

Charlotte really didn't make it easy for you to like her. She never had. All the same, I hated this frosty atmosphere. I tried again. "Charlotte—"

"We're nearly there," she interrupted me. "I can't wait to see if we'll meet any of the Inner Circle." Her grumpy face suddenly brightened. "I mean apart from those we know already. It's so exciting! Over the next few days the Temple will be teeming with living legends. Famous politicians, Nobel Prize winners, highly decorated scientists will be in its hallowed halls, and the rest of the world will never know. Koppe Jötland will be here, oh, and Jonathan Reeves-Haviland . . . how I'd love to shake hands with him." For her, Charlotte sounded really enthusiastic.

I had no idea who she was talking about. I looked hopefully at Xemerius, but he simply shrugged his shoulders. "Never heard of any of those stuffed shirts, sorry," he said.

"No one can know everything," I said with an understanding smile.

Charlotte sighed. "No, but it doesn't hurt to read a serious newspaper now and then, or look at a news magazine to inform yourself about international political events. Of course, you have to switch your brain into gear for that . . . always supposing you have one."

Like I said, she really didn't make it easy.

The limousine had stopped, and Mr. Marley opened the car door. On Charlotte's side, I noticed.

"Mr. Giordano is expecting you in the Old Refectory," said Mr. Marley, and I had a feeling he'd almost added "ma'am." He continued, "I'm to take you there."

"There's something about you that makes everyone want to order you around," observed Xemerius. "Like me to come with you?"

"Yes, please," I said, as we made our way along the narrow alleyways of the Temple district. "I'd feel better with you there."

"Will you buy me a dog?"

"No!"

"But you do like me, don't you? I think I'll have to make myself scarce more often."

"Or make yourself useful," I said, remembering what Lesley had said. *You could have an ace up your sleeve with Xemerius.* She was right. Who else had a friend who could walk through walls?

"Don't dawdle like that," said Charlotte. She and Mr. Marley were a few feet in front of us, walking side by side, and only now did it strike me how like each other they were.

"Yes, Miss Manners," I said.

Let's withdraw; And meet the time as it seeks us.

WILLIAM SHAKESPEARE,
THE TRAGEDY OF CYMBELINE

FIVE

TO CUT A LONG story short, coaching by Charlotte and Mr. Giordano was even worse than I'd expected. That was mainly because they were trying to teach me everything at the same time. While I was struggling to learn the steps of the minuet (rigged out in a hooped skirt with cherry-red stripes, not very chic worn with my school uniform blouse, which was the color of mashed potato), I was also supposed to be learning how greatly the political opinions of the Whigs and the Tories differed, how to hold a fan, and the difference between "Your Highness," "Your Royal Highness," "Your Serene Highness," and even "Your Illustrious Highness." After only an hour plus seventeen different ways of opening a fan, I had a splitting headache, and I couldn't tell left from right. My attempt to lighten the atmosphere with a little joke—"Couldn't we stop for a rest? I'm totally, serenely, illustriously exhausted"—went down like a lead balloon.

"This is not funny," said Giordano in nasal tones. "Stupid girl."

The Old Refectory was a large room on the ground floor, with tall windows looking out on an inner courtyard. There was no furniture except for a grand piano and a few chairs pushed back against the wall. Xemerius was dangling head down from a chandelier, as so often, with his wings tidily folded on his back.

Mr. Giordano had introduced himself with the words, "Just Giordano, if you please. Qualified historian, famous fashion designer, Reiki master, creative jewelry designer, well-known choreographer, Adept Third Degree, expert on the eighteenth and nineteenth centuries."

"Oh, wow," said Xemerius. "Someone must have dropped him on his head when he was a baby."

I could only agree with him, if in silence. Mr. Giordano—sorry, *just* Giordano—bore a most unfortunate resemblance to one of those demented presenters on the TV shopping channels, always talking as if they had clothes-pegs on their noses and there was a miniature pinscher dog under the table snapping at their calves. I was just waiting for him to twist his plump lips (had they been Botoxed?) into a smile and say, "And now, viewers, take a look at our indoor water feature, the Bridget model, top quality, a little oasis of happiness, only twenty-seven pounds, a real snip at the price, you can't do without one of these, I have two at home myself. . . ."

Instead he said—without any smile at all—"My dear Charlotte, hello-hello-hellooo!" and kissed the air to the left and right of her ears. "I heard what's happened, it is simply in-cred-ible! All those years of training, so much talent gone to waste. Terrible, a crying shame, and so unfair. . . . Well, so this is the girl, is it? Your *understudy*." As he inspected me from head to foot, he pursed his fat lips. I couldn't help it—I stared back, fascinated. He had a peculiar windblown hairstyle which must have been cemented in place with huge amounts of gel and hairspray. Narrow black strips of beard crisscrossed the lower half of his face like rivers on a map. His eyebrows had been plucked to shape and then drawn in with some kind of black eyebrow pencil, and if I wasn't much mistaken, he had powdered his nose.

"And *that* is supposed to fit seamlessly into a soirée of the year 1782 in the very near future?" he asked. By *that* he obviously meant me. By *soirée* something else. The only question was what?

"Hey, looks like Puffylips has hurt your feelings," said Xemerius. "If you're looking for a nasty name to call him back, I'll happily prompt you."

Puffylips wasn't bad for a start.

"A soirée is a boring evening party," Xemerius went on. "Just in case you didn't know. People sit together after supper, play little pieces on the pianoforte, and try not to go to sleep."

"Oh, thanks," I said.

"I still can't believe they're really going to risk it," said Charlotte, draping her coat over a chair. "It's against all the rules of secrecy to let Gwyneth go into company. You only have to look at her to see there's something wrong."

"My own idea exactly," said Puffylips. "But the count is famous for his eccentric notions. Her cover story is over there. Hair-raising. Take a look at it."

Charlotte leafed through a folder lying on the grand piano. "She's to play the part of Viscount Batten's ward? And Gideon's going to pretend to be his son. Isn't that rather risky? There could be someone at the soirée who knows the viscount and his family. Why didn't they pick a French viscount in exile?"

Giordano sighed. "Because of her poor command of foreign languages. The count is probably just testing us. Well, we'll show him we can magically transform this girl into an eighteenth-century lady. We *must*!" He was wringing his hands.

"I guess if Keira Knightley could do it, I can do it too," I said confidently. I mean, Keira Knightley was about the most modern girl in the world, and still she was terrific in costume films, even wearing the craziest wigs.

"Keira Knightley?" The black eyebrows almost touched his hair extension. "That may pass muster in a film, but Keira Knightley wouldn't last ten minutes in the eighteenth century without being unmasked as a modern woman. Even the way she keeps showing her teeth when she smiles would do it, or the way she tosses her head back and opens her mouth wide when she laughs! No woman would have done that in the eighteenth century!"

"You can't know for certain," I said.

"What was that, may I ask?"

"I said, you can't know for—"

Puffylips flashed his eyes at me. "We had better get one thing settled right away: you don't question what the master says."

"And who's the master—oh, I see, *you* are," I said, going a bit red, while Xemerius cackled. "Okay, no showing my teeth when I laugh. I get that bit." I didn't expect any problem there. It wasn't likely I'd find anything to laugh about at this soirée thing.

Slightly mollified, Master Puffylips cranked his eyebrows down again, and as he couldn't hear Xemerius up under the ceiling shouting, "Silly old fool!" at the top of his voice, he began taking stock of the sad state of affairs. He wanted to find out what I knew about politics, literature, and habits and customs in the year 1782, and my answer ("I know what they *didn't* have then—flushing toilets, for example, and votes for women") made him bury his face in his hands for a couple of seconds.

"I'm falling about laughing up here," said Xemerius, and unfortunately he was beginning to infect me. It was only with a great effort that I managed to suppress the laughter bubbling up from deep inside me.

Charlotte said, gently, "I thought they'd explained to you that she really is *completely* unprepared, Giordano."

"But I . . . at least the basic principles, surely . . ." The master's face emerged from his hands. I dared not look, because if his makeup was smeared, it would finish me off.

"How about your musical skills? Can you play the piano? Can you sing? Perform on the harp? And then there are the dances usual in polite society. I suppose you will have mastered a simple *menuet à deux*, but what about the other dances?"

Harp? *Menuet à deux*? Oh, sure! I just couldn't control myself any longer. I began giggling helplessly.

"Glad to see that at least one of us is enjoying herself," said Puffylips, baffled, and that must have been the moment when he decided to torment me until I didn't want to laugh one little bit.

In fact it didn't take him long. Only fifteen minutes later, I was feeling like the greatest idiot and worst failure in the world. Even though Xemerius, up under the ceiling, was doing his best to encourage me. "Come on, Gwyneth, show those two sadists that you can do it!"

There was nothing I'd have liked better. But unfortunately I couldn't do it.

"*Tour de main*, left hand, you silly child, now turn to the right, Cornwallis surrendered and Lord North resigned in 1781, which led to— Turn to your right—no, I said right! Dear heaven! Charlotte, please show her how to do it again!"

Charlotte showed me how to do it again. She danced wonderfully well, you had to give her that. It looked like child's play when she did it.

And basically, that's what it was. You walked this way, you walked that way, you walked around in a circle and smiled nonstop without showing your teeth. The music came from loudspeakers hidden in the paneling on the walls, and I have to say it wasn't exactly the kind of music that made your legs itch to get moving.

Maybe I could have memorized the sequence of steps better if Puffylips hadn't also been going on at me about history the whole time. "Very well, then. At war with Spain from 1779 on . . . now the *mouline*, please, curtsey low, with rather more charm, if you don't mind. Now, step forward again, don't forget to smile, head straight, chin up. Great Britain has just lost her North American colonies, good heavens, no, right, turn right, arm at breast height and outstretched, it was a bitter blow, and no one has a good word for the French, that would be unpatriotic . . . don't look down at your feet. You can't see them in those clothes anyway."

Charlotte confined herself to sudden peculiar questions ("Who was king of Burundi in 1782?"), shaking her head all the time. That made me even more uncertain.

After an hour of this, Xemerius was getting bored. He flew down from the chandelier, waved to me, and disappeared through the wall. I'd have liked to tell him to go and look for Gideon, but there was no need for that, because after another fifteen minutes of torture by minuet, Gideon himself came into the Old Refectory, along with Mr. George. They arrived just as Charlotte, Puffylips, I, and a fourth imaginary dancer were performing a figure that Puffylips called *le chain*, in which I was supposed to give my invisible dancing partner my hand. Unfortunately I gave him the wrong hand.

"Right hand, right shoulder, left hand, left shoulder,"

cried Puffylips angrily "Is that so difficult to remember?
See how Charlotte does it. It's perfect that way."

Charlotte went on dancing in her perfect way long
after she'd noticed our visitors, while I stood there feeling
embarrassed and wishing the ground would open and
swallow me up.

"Oh," said Charlotte at last, pretending that she'd only
just seen Mr. George and Gideon. She sank into a charming curtsey, the sort that I now knew you performed at the
beginning and end of a minuet, and from time to time in
the middle as well. It ought to have looked silly, particularly as she was wearing her school uniform, but she somehow managed to make it sweetly pretty.

I immediately felt twice as bad, for one thing because
of the hooped skirt with its red and white stripes worn
over my own uniform (I looked like one of the traffic cones
they put around roadworks and building sites), for another
because Puffylips lost no time in complaining of me:
". . . doesn't know right from left . . . clumsiest creature I
ever saw . . . not very quick on the uptake . . . an impossible
task . . . stupid thing . . . can't turn a duck into a swan . . .
no way she can go to that soirée without attracting the
wrong sort of attention . . . I mean, look at her!"

Mr. George did just that. So did Gideon. I went bright
red. At the same time, I felt fury gathering inside me. I'd
had enough of this! I quickly unbuttoned the hooped skirt
and took off the padded frame that Puffylips had strapped
around my waist under it, and as I did so, I snapped, "I really don't know why I have to talk about politics in the

eighteenth century. I don't even talk about politics today—I haven't the faintest idea of them! So what? If someone asks me about the Marquis of Thingy, I'll just say that politics don't interest me. And if anyone is really hell-bent on dancing a minuet with me, which I think is more than unlikely because I don't know a soul in the eighteenth century, then I'll smile nicely and say no thank you, I've sprained my ankle. I expect I can get that much out without showing my teeth."

"See what I mean?" asked Puffylips, wringing his hands again. It seemed to be a habit of his. "Not even prepared to show willing! And shocking ignorance and lack of talent in all areas. Then she bursts out laughing like a five-year-old, just because the name of Lord Sandwich is mentioned."

Oh, yes, Lord Sandwich. Imagine, he really was called a sandwich! Poor man.

"She will certainly—" Mr. George began, but Puffylips cut him short.

"Unlike Charlotte, the girl has no . . . no *espièglerie* at all!"

Whatever that might be, if Charlotte had it, I was happy to do without.

Charlotte had put out the sheet music and was sitting at the grand piano, giving Gideon a conspiratorial smile. He smiled back.

As for me, he'd condescended to give me only a single glance, although it said a lot. And not in any very nice way. He was probably embarrassed to be in the same room as a failure like me, particularly when he seemed to know only too well how good he looked himself in his old jeans and a close-fitting black T-shirt. For some reason, that made me even angrier. I was almost grinding my teeth.

Mr. George looked from me to Puffylips in a worried way and back again. Then, frowning anxiously, he said, "I'm sure you can do it, Giordano. And you have an expert assistant in Charlotte. Anyway, we still have a couple of days to go."

"Even if we had weeks, it's never going to be long enough to prepare her for a grand ball," said Puffylips. "A soirée, maybe, with a lot of luck and if there are not many guests, but a ball, possibly even in the presence of the duke and duchess—out of the question. I can only assume that the count is allowing himself a little joke."

Mr. George's eyes were chilly. "He most certainly is not," he said. "And it is not for you to cast doubt on the count's decisions. Gwyneth will manage all right, won't you, Gwyneth?"

I didn't answer. My self-esteem had taken too much of a battering over the last two hours. If it was only a case of not making a disagreeable impression, I thought I could get by. I'd just stand in a corner and wave my fan about. Or rather, not wave my fan about, because who knew what that might mean? I'd stand there and smile without showing my teeth. So long as no one disturbed me or asked me about the Marquis of Stafford or wanted me to dance.

Charlotte began tinkling the piano keys. She was playing a pretty little tune in the style of the music we'd been dancing to earlier. Gideon went to stand beside her, and she looked up at him and said something I couldn't make out, because Puffylips was sighing so loudly.

"We have tried teaching her the basic steps of the minuet in the conventional way, but I fear we shall have to resort to other methods."

In spite of myself, I couldn't help admiring Charlotte's ability to talk, look Gideon in the eyes, show her delightful little dimples, and play the piano all at the same time.

Puffylips was still grousing away. "Diagrams might help, or chalk circles on the floor, we could try. . . ."

"You can go on with the lessons tomorrow," Mr. George interrupted him. "Gwyneth has to elapse now. Coming, Gwyneth?"

I nodded, relieved, and picked up my coat and my school bag. Let off the hook at last! My sense of frustration instantly gave way to a certain excitement. All being well, today I'd be sent to elapse to a date *after* my meeting with Grandpa, and then I ought to find the key and the password in the secret hiding place.

"Let me carry that." Mr. George took the school bag from me and gave me an encouraging smile. "Only four hours, and then you can go home. You don't look nearly as tired today as yesterday. We'll find you a nice quiet year— how about 1953? Gideon says it's very comfortable in the old alch—in the chronograph room. He tells me there's even a sofa there."

"Nineteen fifty-three is perfect," I said, trying not to sound quite so enthusiastic. Five years after my last meeting with Lucas! I could expect him to have found something out in all that time.

"Oh, and Charlotte, Mrs. Jenkins has ordered a car for you. You can take the rest of today off."

Charlotte stopped playing the piano. "Thank you, Mr. George," she said politely. Then she put her head on one side and smiled at Gideon. "Do you get the rest of the day off now, too?"

Hello? Was she about to ask if he'd like to go to the cinema with her? I held my breath.

But Gideon shook his head. "No, I'm going to elapse with Gwyneth."

Charlotte and I must have looked equally surprised.

"You are not," said Mr. George. "You've already fulfilled your quota for today."

"And you look exhausted," said Charlotte. "Which isn't surprising. You ought to use the time to catch up on some sleep."

For once I entirely agreed with Charlotte. If Gideon came with me, I wouldn't be able to collect the key or go in search of my grandfather.

"On her own, Gwyneth would be spending four totally pointless hours in the cellar," said Gideon. "If I go with her, she can learn something while she's there." He added, with a slight smile, "For instance, the difference between right and left. I'm sure she can get the hang of the minuet."

Oh, for God's sake! Not more dancing lessons!

"I have homework to do," I said in as unfriendly a tone as possible. "And my Shakespeare essay is due tomorrow."

"I can help you with that, too," said Gideon, looking at me. It was difficult to interpret his expression. To anyone who didn't know him, it might seem innocent, but I knew better.

Charlotte was still smiling, but without the pretty little dimples now.

Mr. George shrugged his shoulders. "Well, if you say so. Then Gwyneth won't be on her own, and there'll be nothing to be afraid of."

"I like being on my own," I said despairingly. "'Specially when I've been with people all day, like now." With totally stupid people.

"Oh, yes?" asked Charlotte sarcastically. "But then you're never really alone, because you have all your invisible friends, don't you?"

"Exactly," I said. "Gideon, you'd only be in the way."

Go to the cinema with Charlotte. Or found a book club or something, why don't you?

Well, that's what I thought. But did I really mean it? On one hand there was nothing I wanted more than to talk to my grandfather and ask what he'd found out about the Green Rider. On the other hand, vague memories of all that *oh* and *hmm* and *more!* stuff from yesterday were surfacing in my mind.

Oh, hell! I must pull myself together and think of all the things I'd found to hate about Gideon.

But he didn't give me time for that. He was already holding the door open for me and Mr. George. "Come on, Gwyneth. Off we go to 1953."

I was fairly sure that Charlotte's eyes would have been burning holes in my back if they could.

ON THE WAY down to the old alchemical laboratory, Mr. George blindfolded me again—not without apologizing first—and then, sighing, took my hand. Gideon had to carry my school bag.

"I know Mr. Giordano is not an easy man," said Mr. George when we had the climb down the spiral staircase behind us. "But maybe you could make a little effort for him."

I snorted. "He could make a bit more of an effort for *me*! Reiki master, creative jewelry designer, fashion designer . . . what on earth is he doing in the Lodge? I thought all the Guardians were top-flight scientists and politicians."

"You could call Mr. Giordano the odd one out among the Guardians," Mr. George admitted. "But he has a brilliant mind. As well as pursuing his . . . well, rather exotic professions, which incidentally have made him a multimillionaire, he is recognized as a good historian, and—"

"And five years ago at the latest, when he published an essay using previously unknown sources of material concerning a secret society which is based in London and has connections with the Freemasons and the legendary figure of Count Saint-Germain, the Guardians decided they must get to know him better as a matter of urgency," said Gideon from somewhere ahead of us. His voice echoed back from the stone walls.

Mr. George cleared his throat. "Er, yes, there's that, too. Careful, we're coming to a step."

"I get the idea," I said. "Giordano was made one of the Guardians so that he couldn't give the rest of them away. What kind of unknown sources were they?"

"Every member brings the Society something that makes it stronger," said Mr. George, without actually answering my question. "And Mr. Giordano's abilities are particularly varied."

"You bet," I agreed. "Who else do you know who can glue a rock to his own fingernail?"

I heard Mr. George cough as if choking back a laugh. For a while we went on side by side in silence. I couldn't hear Gideon at all, not even his footsteps, so I assumed he'd gone on ahead (my blindfold meant that we were crawling along at a snail's pace). Finally I plucked up the courage to ask, keeping my voice down, "Exactly why do I have to go to this soirée and then a ball, Mr. George?"

"Oh, hasn't anyone told you? Yesterday evening—or rather, it was last night—Gideon went to see the count to tell him about that last . . . adventure the two of you had. And he came back with a letter in which the count expressly says he wants you and Gideon to accompany him to a soirée given by Lady Brompton and a big ball a few days later. In addition you'll be paying him an afternoon call in the Temple. The whole idea is for the count to get to know you better."

I thought of my first meeting with the count and shuddered. "I can understand that he wants to know more about me. But why does he want me to mix with a lot of strangers? Is it some kind of test?"

"Well, it shows, yet again, that there is really no point in trying to keep you out of everything. To be honest, I was glad to hear of his letter. It shows that the count has far more confidence in you than many of our Guardian friends, those who think you just have a walk-on part in the game."

"And they also think I'm a traitor," I said, with Dr. White in mind.

"*Or* they think you're a traitor," said Mr. George casually. "Opinions differ. Well, here we are, my dear. You can take the blindfold off."

Gideon was already waiting for us. I tried, one last time, to get rid of him by saying I had a Shakespeare sonnet to learn by heart, and I could only do that by reciting it out aloud, but he just shrugged his shoulders and said he had his iPod with him, so he wouldn't be listening to me. Mr. George liberated the chronograph from the safe and warned us not to leave anything lying around in the past. "Not the smallest snippet of paper, do you hear, Gwyneth? You will bring the entire contents of your school bag back to this room. And the bag itself, of course. Understand?"

I nodded, took my bag back from Gideon, and clutched it firmly. Then I held my finger out to Mr. George. My little finger this time—my forefinger had been punctured enough already. "Suppose someone comes into the room while we're in it?"

"That won't happen," Gideon assured me. "It's the middle of the night there."

"So? Someone could get the idea of holding an inspiratorial meeting in the cellar."

"Conspiratorial," said Gideon. "Even so."

"Even so, what?"

"Don't worry," said Mr. George, putting my finger into the chronograph through the open flap. I bit my lip as the now familiar roller-coaster feeling took me over, and the needle went into my flesh. The room was bathed in ruby-red light, and then I landed in pitch-darkness.

"Hello?" I asked quietly. No answer, but a second later, Gideon landed beside me, and immediately switched on a flashlight.

"There, you see, it's not so uncomfortable here," he said as he went over to the door and pressed the switch. It was still only a naked electric lightbulb hanging from the ceiling, but the rest of the room had improved a lot since my last visit. My first glance was at the wall where Lucas had been going to make our secret hiding place. There were chairs stacked in front of it, but much more neatly than last time. There was no more old junk lying around. Compared with five years ago, the room was positively clean and tidy, and much emptier. Apart from the chairs against the wall, the only pieces of furniture were a table and a sofa covered with shabby green velvet.

"Yes, definitely more comfortable than on my last visit," I said. "I was scared a rat might come out and nibble me all the time then."

Gideon tried the handle of the door and rattled it once. It was obviously locked.

"Just once this door was left open," he said with a grin. "That was a really good evening. From here there's a secret passage down to underneath the Royal Courts of Justice. It goes on even deeper, into catacombs with bones and skulls . . . and not far from here, there's a wine cellar. At least, there is in 1953."

"We need a key." I looked surreptitiously at the wall again. Somewhere behind a loose brick, there *was* a key. I sighed. What a shame that it was no use to me now. But it was also kind of a good feeling to know something when, for once, Gideon had no idea of it. "Did you drink any of the wine?"

"What do you think?" Gideon took one of the chairs from the stack by the wall and put it down at the table. "Here you are, all yours. Have fun with the homework."

"Oh. Thanks." I sat down, took my things out of my bag, and pretended to be immersed in a book. Meanwhile Gideon stretched out on the sofa, took an iPod out of his jeans pocket, and put the earphones in his ears. After a couple of minutes, I risked glancing at him and saw that his eyes were closed. Had he gone to sleep? No wonder, really, when you stopped to think that he'd been time traveling again last night.

I lost myself for a while in looking at his long, straight nose, pale skin, soft lips, and those thick, curving eyelashes. Relaxed like that, he seemed much younger than usual, and suddenly I could imagine what he must have looked like as a little boy. Very cute, anyway. His chest was rising and falling regularly, and I wondered if I might venture to—no, too dangerous. And I mustn't look at that wall anymore, not if I wanted to keep the secret I shared with Lucas.

Since there was nothing else to do, and I could hardly spend four whole hours watching Gideon asleep (although the idea did have its good points), I finally devoted myself to my homework, first the mineral resources of the Caucasus, then irregular French verbs. The essay on Shakespeare's life and work only needed some kind of conclusion. I made a determined effort and summed it up in a single sentence: *Shakespeare spent the last five years of his life in Stratford-upon-Avon, where he died in 1616.* There, done it. Now all I had to do was learn a sonnet by heart. As they were all the same length, I picked one at random. *"Mine eye and heart are at a mortal war, how to divide the conquest of thy sight,"* I murmured.

"Do you mean me?" asked Gideon, sitting up and taking the earphones out.

Unfortunately I couldn't stop myself going red. "It's Shakespeare," I said.

Gideon smiled. *"Mine eye my heart thy picture's sight would bar, my heart mine eye the freedom of that right.* Or something like that."

"No, exactly like that," I said, slamming the book shut.

"You don't know it by heart yet," said Gideon.

"I'd have forgotten it again by tomorrow anyway. I'd better learn it first thing in the morning just before school. Then I have a fair chance of remembering it in Mr. Whitman's English class."

"Good, now we can practice the minuet." Gideon stood up. "There's plenty of room for us here, anyway."

"Oh, no! Please let's not!"

But Gideon was already bowing to me. "May I have the pleasure of this dance, Miss Shepherd?"

"There's nothing I'd like better, sir," I assured him, fanning myself with the book of Shakespeare sonnets, "but I am sorry to say that I've sprained my ankle. Perhaps you'd like to ask my cousin there. The lady in green." I pointed to the sofa. "She'd be happy to show you how well she can dance."

"But I want to dance with you—I found out how your cousin dances long ago."

"I meant my cousin Sofa, not my cousin Charlotte," I said. "I can assure you, you'll have more fun with Sofa than with Charlotte. Sofa may not be quite as pretty, but she's softer, she has much more charm, and she has a kinder disposition."

Gideon laughed. "As I said, I'm exclusively interested in dancing with you. Do let me have the honor!"

"Surely a gentleman like you will show consideration for my sprained ankle?"

"No, sorry." Gideon took the iPod out of his jeans pocket. "Wait a moment, the music's still too far away from you." He put the earphones in my ears and pulled me to my feet.

"Oh, good, Linkin Park," I said, while my pulse shot right up because Gideon was suddenly so close to me.

"What? Sorry, just a moment, and I'll have the right

track." His fingers moved over the display. "Right, Mozart—that will do." He handed me the iPod. "No, put it in your skirt pocket. You need both hands free."

"But you can't hear the music at all," I said as violins scraped away in my ears.

"I can hear enough, you don't have to shout like that. Okay, let's imagine this is for a set of eight dancers. There's another gentleman beside me on the left, two more on my right. Opposite us the same lineup, but with ladies. Curtsey, please."

I made him a curtsey and hesitantly put my hand in his. "But I'm stopping the moment you say *stupid girl* to me."

"Which I would never do," said Gideon, leading me straight past the sofa. "And we make polite conversation while dancing, that's important. May I ask how you developed your dislike of dancing? Most young ladies love it."

"Shh, I must concentrate." So far it was going really well. I was surprised at myself. The *tour de main* worked perfectly, once to the left, once to the right. "Can we do that bit again?"

"Raise your chin, that's it. And look at me. You must never take your eyes off me, never mind how good-looking my neighbor may be."

I had to grin. What was all this—fishing for compliments? Well, I wasn't going to play ball. Although I had to admit that Gideon danced really well. It wasn't a bit like dancing with Puffylips. The steps seemed to go smoothly all by themselves. I might actually end up getting some fun out of this minuet business.

Gideon noticed, too. "There, you see, you can do it after all! Right hand, right shoulder, left hand, left shoulder—very good."

He was right. I could do it! It really was child's play. I triumphantly twirled around with one of the invisible gentlemen, and then put my hand back in Gideon's. "There! So now who says I'm as graceful as a windmill?"

"Never mind what Giordano says, that would be an outrageous comparison," agreed Gideon. "You outclass any windmill as a dancer."

I chuckled. Then I jumped. "Oops—we're back to Linkin Park."

"Never mind." While "Papercut" pounded in my ears, Gideon led me unerringly through the last figure and finally bowed. I was almost sorry it was over.

I made a deep curtsey and took the earphones off. "Here. It was very nice of you to teach me how to do it."

"Pure self-interest," said Gideon. "After all, otherwise I'm the one who'd look foolish dancing with you. Forgotten that?"

"No." My good mood instantly passed off. Before I could prevent myself, I let my eyes wander to the wall with the chairs in front of it.

"Hey, we haven't finished," said Gideon. "That was very good, yes, but not perfect yet. What's the idea of giving me such a dark look all of a sudden?"

"Why do you think Count Saint-Germain is so keen for me to go to a soirée and a ball? After all, he could just tell me to be here in the Temple, and then I wouldn't risk making an idiot of myself in front of strangers. No one would have to wonder about me and maybe leave an account of my odd behavior for posterity."

Gideon looked down at me for a little while before answering. "The count likes to keep his cards close to his chest, but there's a brilliant plan behind every single one of his ideas. He has a definite suspicion about those men who attacked us in Hyde Park, and I think he wants to lure whoever was behind it out into the open by taking us both to large society events."

"Oh," I said. "You mean we're going to have men with swords after us again?"

"Not while we're in company," said Gideon. He perched on the arm of the sofa and crossed his arms over his chest. "All the same, I do think it's too dangerous—for you, anyway."

I leaned against the table. "Didn't you suspect that Lucy and Paul were mixed up with the attack in Hyde Park?"

"Yes and no," said Gideon. "A man like Count Saint-Germain makes quite a few enemies in the course of his life. There are several accounts of assassination attempts on him in the *Annals*. I only suspect that for their own ends Lucy and Paul may have joined forces with one of those enemies of his. Or several of them."

"Does the count think so too?"

Gideon shrugged his shoulders. "I hope so."

I thought about this for a while. "I'm in favor of breaking the rules again. Take one of those James Bond pistols with you," I suggested. "That would show those characters with their swords something! Where did you get it from, by the way? I'd feel better myself if I had a thing like that."

"A weapon can usually be turned against you, if you don't know how to use it," said Gideon.

I thought of my Japanese vegetable knife. Not a nice idea to think of it being turned against me.

"Is Charlotte good at fencing? And can she use a pistol?"

Another shrug of his shoulders. "She's had fencing lessons since she was twelve—of course she's good."

Of course. Charlotte was good at everything. Except being nice. "I'm sure the count would have liked her," I said. "I obviously wasn't his type."

Gideon laughed. "Well, you can still revise his idea of you. The main reason why he wants to know you better is to see whether the prophesies may be right in what they say about you after all."

"The magic of the raven and so on?" I felt uncomfortable. I always did when anyone talked about that. "Do the prophesies also say what it is?"

Gideon hesitated for a moment, and then said softly, "*The raven red, on ruby pinions winging its way between the worlds, hears dead men singing. It scarce knows its strength, the price it scarce knows, but its power will arise and the Circle will close.*" He cleared his throat. "You've come out in goose bumps."

"It sounds so eerie. Specially the bit about the dead men singing." I rubbed my arms. "Does it go on?"

"No, that's more or less all. You have to admit it doesn't sound much like you."

He was probably right there. "Is there something about you in the prophesies as well?"

"Of course," said Gideon. "There's a prophesy about each of the time travelers. I'm the lion with the diamond mane at the sight of which the sun . . ." For a moment, he suddenly seemed embarrassed. Then he went on, grinning, "Blah blah blah. Oh, and your great-great-grandmother, our stubborn friend Lady Tilney, is a fox. Very suitable. A jade fox hiding under a linden tree."

"Can anyone make any sense of these prophesies?"

"Oh, yes—they're teeming with symbols. It's just a question of how to interpret them." He looked at his watch. "We have some time left. I think we ought to go on with our dancing lessons."

"Will there be dancing at the soirée, too?"

"Probably not," said Gideon. "Only eating, drinking, talking—and making music. You're sure to be asked to play or sing something."

"Hm," I said. "I ought to have had piano lessons instead of going to those hip-hop classes with Lesley. I can sing all right, though. At Cynthia's party last year I won the karaoke contest hands down. With my own version of "Somewhere Over the Rainbow." Even though I was in costume as a bus stop, which didn't suit me."

"Er . . . yes. If anyone asks you to sing, you simply say you never have any voice when you have to sing in company."

"So I can say that, but I can't say I've sprained my ankle?"

"Here, put the earphones on. Repeat performance." He bowed to me.

"What do I do if someone else—I mean, not you—asks me to dance or sing or something?" I sank into my curtsey.

"Exactly the same as if I do," said Gideon, taking my hand. "But as far as that's concerned, everything was very formal in the eighteenth century. You didn't just ask a girl you didn't know to dance without being officially introduced to her."

"Unless she made some kind of obscene movement with her fan." The dance steps were beginning to come naturally. "Whenever I flicked my fan even an inch upstairs there, Giordano had a nervous breakdown, and Charlotte shook her head like a sad spaniel flapping its ears."

"She only wants to help you," said Gideon.

"Yes, and the earth is flat," I snorted, although I'm sure snorting wasn't allowed when you were dancing a minuet.

"Anyone might think you two didn't like each other much."

Oh, might they indeed?

"Apart from Aunt Glenda, Lady Arista, and our teachers, I don't think there's anyone who likes Charlotte."

"I don't believe that," said Gideon.

"Ah. Of course I was forgetting Giordano and you. Oops, now I've gone and rolled my eyes. I bet that's forbidden in the eighteenth century."

"Could you possibly be a little jealous of Charlotte?"

I had to laugh. "Take my word for it, if you knew her as well as I do, you wouldn't ask such a silly question."

"Oh, I know her quite well," said Gideon quietly, taking my hand again.

Yes, but only her chocolate-coated side, I wanted to say, but then I realized what that remark of his meant, and all at once, I really was terribly jealous of Charlotte. "How well *do* you know each other, then . . . exactly?" I removed my hand from Gideon's and gave it to his nonexistent neighbor in the set instead.

"I'd say as well as people know each other when they've spent a lot of time together." As he passed, he gave me a mocking smile. "And we neither of us had very much time for other . . . er, friendships."

"I see. You have to take what you can get." I couldn't bear it a second longer. "And what's Charlotte like at kissing?"

Gideon took my hand, which was at least six inches too high in the air. "You're making great progress in the art of conversation—but all the same, a gentleman doesn't talk about such things."

"I'd let that pass as an excuse if you *were* a gentleman."

"If I've ever given you reason to think I don't behave like a gentleman, then—"

"Oh, shut up! Whatever's going on with you and Charlotte, I'm not interested one little bit. But it's a bit much, you thinking it would be funny to go snogging me at the same time."

"Snogging? What a crude expression. I'd be grateful if

you'd tell me why you're in such a bad temper—and think of your elbows at the same time. They ought to be pointing down in this figure."

"It's not funny!" I spat. "I'd never have let you kiss me if I'd known that you and Charlotte were—" Ah, Mozart was over, we were back with Linkin Park. Good. They suited my mood much better.

"That I and Charlotte were what?"

"More than just good friends."

"Who says so?"

"You?"

"I didn't."

"Oh. Then you two have never . . . shall we say kissed?" I skipped the curtsey and glared at him instead.

"I didn't say that either." He bowed and reached for the iPod in my pocket. "Once again, you must practice what to do with your arms, but apart from that, it was great."

"I can't say the same for your conversation. It leaves a lot to be desired," I said. "Is there something between you and Charlotte or not?"

"I thought you weren't a bit interested in what was going on between me and Charlotte?"

I was still glaring at him. "Too right!"

"Then that's okay." Gideon handed me the iPod back. "Hallelujah" was coming over the earphones, the Bon Jovi version.

"That's the wrong track," I said.

"No, no." Gideon was grinning. "I thought you needed something soothing."

"You . . . you are such a . . ."

"Yes?"

"Such a shit."

He came a step closer, so that at a guess there was exactly half an inch of space left between us. "There, you see, that's the difference between you and Charlotte. She'd never say a thing like that."

I suddenly found breathing difficult. "Maybe because you don't give her any reason to."

"No, that's not it. I guess she just has better manners."

"Yes, and stronger nerves," I said. For some reason, I couldn't help staring at Gideon's mouth. "Just in case you were thinking of trying it again, if we find ourselves hanging around in a confessional somewhere twiddling our thumbs, I'm not letting you take me by surprise a second time!"

"You mean you wouldn't let me kiss you a second time?"

"Got it in one," I whispered, unable to move.

"That's a pity," said Gideon, and his mouth was so close to mine that I felt his breath on my lips. I realized I wasn't necessarily acting as if I meant it seriously. And I didn't. I thought it was much to my credit that I didn't throw my arms around Gideon's neck. But anyway I'd missed out on the moment for tearing myself free or pushing him away some time ago.

Obviously that was how Gideon saw it, too. His hand began stroking my hair, and then, at last, I felt the gentle touch of his lips.

"And every breath we drew was hallelujah," sang Bon Jovi in my ear. I'd always loved that song—it was one of those I could listen to fifteen times running—but now I supposed it would be connected with the memory of Gideon for ever and ever.

Hallelujah.

THE MONTROSE FAMILY TREE

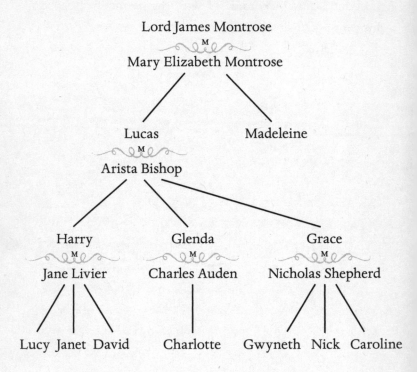

Lord James Montrose
M
Mary Elizabeth Montrose

Lucas   Madeleine
M
Arista Bishop

Harry   Glenda   Grace
M   M   M
Jane Livier   Charles Auden   Nicholas Shepherd

Lucy Janet David   Charlotte   Gwyneth Nick Caroline

HIC RHODOS
HIC SALTA

(Motto on the Montrose coat of arms.
Freely translated: *Show what you can really do.*)

SIX

THIS TIME we weren't disturbed either by traveling through time or a cheeky gargoyle demon. While "Hallelujah" was running, the kiss was gentle and careful, but then Gideon buried both hands in my hair and held me very close. It wasn't a gentle kiss anymore, and my reaction surprised me. I suddenly felt very soft and lightweight, and my arms went around Gideon's neck of their own accord. I had no idea how, but at some point in the next few minutes, still kissing without a break, we landed on the green sofa, and we went on kissing there until Gideon abruptly sat up and looked at his watch.

"Like I said, it really is a shame I'm not allowed to kiss you anymore," he remarked rather breathlessly. The pupils of his eyes looked huge, and his cheeks were definitely flushed.

I wondered what I looked like myself. As I'd temporarily mutated into some kind of human blancmange, there was no way I could get out of my half-lying position. And I realized, with horror, that I had no idea how much time had passed since Bon Jovi stopped singing "Hallelujah." Ten minutes? Half an hour? Anything was possible.

Gideon looked at me, and I thought I saw something like bewilderment in his eyes.

"We'd better collect our things," he said at last. "And you need to do something about your hair—it looks as if some idiot has been digging both hands into it and dragging you down on a sofa. Whoever's back there waiting for us will put two and two together—oh, my God, don't look at me like that."

"Like what?"

"As if you couldn't move."

"But I can't," I said, perfectly seriously. "I'm a blancmange. You've turned me into blancmange."

A brief smile brightened Gideon's face, and then he jumped up and began stowing my school things in my bag. "Come along, little blancmange, stand up. Do you have a brush or comb with you?"

"In there somewhere," I said vaguely.

Gideon held up Lesley's mother's spectacle case. "In this?"

"No!" I cried, and in my alarm my blancmange existence came to a sudden end. I jumped up, snatched the case containing the Japanese vegetable knife from Gideon's hand, and flung it back in my bag. If Gideon was surprised, he didn't show it. He put the chair back by the wall and looked at his watch again, while I took out my hairbrush.

"How much time do we have left?"

"Two minutes," said Gideon, picking up the iPod from the floor. How it had ended up there I had no idea. Or when.

I hastily brushed my hair.

Gideon was watching me with a serious expression on his face. "Gwyneth?"

"Hm?" I lowered the hairbrush and returned his gaze as calmly as I could. Oh, my God—he looked so incredibly good, and a part of me was trying to turn back into blanc-mange again.

"Do you . . . ?"

I waited. "What?"

"Oh, nothing."

The familiar dizzy feeling was spreading through me. "I think we're off," I said.

"Hold tight to your bag. Whatever happens, you mustn't let go of it. And come this way a bit, or you'll land on the table."

Even as I was moving toward him, everything blurred in front of my eyes. Only fractions of a second later, I made a soft landing on my feet, right in front of the wide-eyed Mr. Marley. The gargoyle was looking over his shoulder, grinning.

"At last," said Xemerius. "I've had to listen to Ginger here talking to himself for the last fifteen minutes."

"Are you all right, Miss Shepherd?" asked Mr. Marley, taking a step back.

"She's fine," said Gideon, who had landed behind me

and was now looking me up and down. When I smiled at him he quickly moved aside.

Mr. Marley cleared his throat. "I'm to tell you you're expected in the Dragon Hall, sir. The Inner Cir—Number Seven has arrived and wants to see you. If you'll allow me, I'll take Miss Shepherd to her car."

"Miss Shepherd doesn't have a car," said Xemerius. "She doesn't even have a driving license, dimwit."

"No need, I'll take her upstairs with me." Gideon picked up the black blindfold.

"Do I really have to wear that thing?"

"Yes, you do." Gideon tied the scarf together behind my head. As he did so, he caught a couple of my hairs in the knot, and it tweaked them, but I wasn't going to squeal, so I just bit my lip. "If you don't know where the chronograph is kept, then you can't give the secret away, and we won't find anyone lying in wait for us here when we land in this room some other time."

"But this cellar belongs to the Guardians, and the ways in and out are always guarded," I said.

"First, there are more passages in this vault than alleys running past the buildings in the Temple, and second, we can never rule out the possibility that someone in our own ranks might be interested in a surprise meeting."

"*Trust no one. Not even your own feelings,*" I murmured. They were all so suspicious here.

Gideon put a hand on my waist and propelled me forward. "Exactly."

I heard Mr. Marley say good night, and then the door

latched behind us. We walked along side by side in silence. There were a lot of things I'd have liked to say, but I didn't know where to begin.

"My instinct tells me you two have been at it again," remarked Xemerius. "My instinct and my sharp eyes."

"Nonsense," I said, and Xemerius burst into a cackle of laughter.

"You take my word for it, I've been on this earth since the eleventh century, and I know what a girl looks like when she's just been rolling in a stack of hay."

"Hay?" I repeated indignantly.

"Are you talking to me?" asked Gideon.

"Who else?" I said. "I was going to say hey, I'm ravenous—I could eat a horse. What's the time?"

"Nearly seven thirty." Gideon suddenly let go of me. A whole series of electronic beeps could be heard. Then my shoulder rammed into the wall.

"What's the idea?"

Xemerius cackled with laughter again. "That's what I call a real gentleman."

"Sorry. The wretched mobile doesn't get a signal down there, of course. Thirty-four calls in my absence, oh, great! That can only . . . oh, God, my mother!" Gideon sighed heavily. "She rang me eleven times."

I was feeling my way forward along the wall. "Look, either you take this stupid blindfold off or you'll have to guide me!"

"Okay." His hand was back again.

"I could say a thing or two about guys who blindfold

their girlfriends so they can check up on mobiles at their leisure," observed Xemerius.

I wasn't too keen on it either. "Has something bad happened?"

Another sigh. "I suppose so. We don't often call each other. Still no reception here."

"Watch out, there's a step," Xemerius warned me.

"Maybe someone's sick," I said. "Or you forgot something important. The other day my mum called goodness knows how many times to remind me to send my uncle Harry a birthday card. Ouch."

If Xemerius hadn't warned me, the knob at the end of the banisters would have caught me in the pit of the stomach. Gideon still didn't notice. I felt my way up the spiral staircase as well as I could for myself.

"No, that's not it. I never forget a birthday." He sounded harassed. "It must be something to do with Raphael."

"Your little brother?"

"He's always doing dangerous stuff—driving without a license, diving off cliffs, climbing without safety gear. No idea who he's trying to impress. Last year he had an accident paragliding and spent three weeks in hospital with a brain trauma. You'd think that would teach him a lesson, but no, he got Monsieur Po-Face Bertelin to give him a speedboat for his birthday. Of course that idiot goes along with everything Raphael wants." Once we were at the top of the stairs, Gideon quickened his pace, and I stumbled several times. "Ah, at last! Here we go." Obviously he was listening to his voice mail as we went along. Unfortunately I couldn't hear anything.

"Oh, shit!" I heard him mutter several times, that was all. He had let go of me again, and I was groping my way blindly forward.

"If you don't want to run into a wall, you'd better turn left now," Xemerius told me. "Ah—looks like it's suddenly occurred to him that you don't have built-in radar."

"Okay," murmured Gideon. His hands briefly touched my face and then the back of my head. "Gwyneth, I'm sorry." He did sound sorry about something, but I strongly suspected it wasn't me. "Can you find your way back from here by yourself?" He undid the scarf, and I blinked at the light. We were standing outside Madame Rossini's sewing room.

Gideon fleetingly stroked my cheek and gave me a wry smile. "You do know the way, right? Your car's waiting. See you tomorrow."

He had turned away before I could say anything.

"And off he goes," commented Xemerius. "Lacking in the finer feelings department, if you ask me."

"But what's happened?" I called after Gideon.

"My brother's run away from home," he called back, without turning or slowing down. "Give you three guesses where he's heading!" But he had gone around the next corner before I could make even one guess.

"Well, not Fiji, I bet," I murmured.

"If you ask me, you'd have done better not to roll about in any haystacks with him," said Xemerius. "Now he thinks you're easy pickings, so he won't go to any more trouble."

"Shut up, Xemerius. You're getting on my nerves with all this talk about haystacks. We kissed a bit, that's all."

"No reason to go beet red, darling."

I put my hands to my glowing cheeks, feeling cross with myself. "Come on, let's go. I'm hungry. At least I have a chance of getting some supper today. And maybe on our way we can catch a glimpse of these mysterious men from the Inner Circle."

"I wouldn't bother if I were you. I've been listening in on them all afternoon," said Xemerius.

"Oh, good! Tell me more."

"Boring, boring, *boring*. I thought they'd be drinking blood out of skulls and painting mysterious runes on their arms. No such luck. They just sat about in suits and ties, talking."

"What about?"

"Let's see if I can still remember." He cleared his throat. "Basically it was whether they could break their own golden rules to outwit Black Tourmaline and Sapphire. Great idea, said some of them. Nope, no way, said others. Then the first lot said, But we must, you cowards, or we'll never get anywhere with saving the world, and the second lot said no, terrible thing to do, also dangerous, what about the continuum and morality, and the first lot said, Yes, but never mind all that if it means saving the world. Then there was a lot of unctuous waffle—I think I slept through most of that. But then they all agreed that unfortunately

Diamond is inclined to act on his own initiative, while Ruby seems to be a little idiot, unsuitable for time-travel missions Operation Opal and Operation Jade on account of being too stupid. Are you with me so far?"

"Er . . ."

"Of course I stood up for you, but they weren't listening to me," said Xemerius. "They were saying all information had to be kept from you as far as possible. They thought your ignorance and naivete, the result of an inadequate education, already made you a security risk, and you were also indiscretion personified. Oh, and they're going to keep an eye on your friend Lesley too."

"Oh, shit."

"The good news is that they blame your inadequacies on your mother. Women are always to blame for everything, our friends the mystery mongers all agreed there. And then they started talking about evidence, dressmakers' bills, letters, sound human understanding, and after a good deal of talk, they agreed that Paul and Lucy had gone back to 1912 with the chronograph and that's where they're living now. Though in this case *now* isn't quite the right word for it." Xemerius scratched his head. "Never mind, that's where the two of them are, anyway, our friends are sure of that, and at the next opportunity your wonderful, strong hero is supposed to track them down, get some of their blood, and bring back the original chronograph while he's about it. Then off they started from the beginning again, blah blah blah, golden rules, unctuous waffle—"

"Interesting," I said.

"You think so? Well, if you do, that's because of my witty and amusing way of summing up all that boring twaddle."

I opened the door into the next corridor, and I was about to answer Xemerius when I heard a voice. "You're still just as arrogant as you used to be!"

That was my mum. And sure enough, when I turned the corner, there she was, standing in front of Falk de Villiers with both her fists clenched.

"And you are as pigheaded and obstructive as ever," Falk was saying. "You've done considerable damage to the cause with your attempts—for whatever reason you made them—to cover up the facts about Gwyneth's birth."

"The *cause*! Your precious cause was always more important to all of you than any human beings who got caught up in it!" snapped my mother.

I closed the door as quietly as possible behind me and slowly walked toward them.

Xemerius was working his way along the top of the wall, hand over hand. "Wow, she looks furious."

He was right. My mum's eyes were glittering, her cheeks were flushed, and her voice was unusually high. "We agreed that Gwyneth would be kept out of it. Wouldn't be put in any danger! And now you want her served up to the count on a platter. Although she's . . . she's completely helpless!"

"That's your own fault," said Falk de Villiers coldly.

Mum bit her lip. "As Grand Master of this Lodge, you're responsible!"

"If you'd shown your cards openly from the first, then Gwyneth wouldn't be unprepared now. For your information, you may be able to deceive Mr. George with your story of wanting to make sure your daughter had a carefree childhood, but you don't fool me. I am still extremely interested to know what that midwife will have to tell us."

"You haven't found her yet?" My mother's voice wasn't quite so shrill.

"It's only a matter of days, Grace. We have our agents everywhere." Now he noticed that I was there with them, and the cold, angry expression on his face disappeared.

"Why are you alone, Gwyneth?"

"Darling!" My mum rushed to me and gave me a hug. "I thought that before it all went on as late as last night, I'd come and pick you up."

"And take the opportunity of tearing me off a strip," added Falk, with a slight smile. "Why isn't Mr. Marley with you, Gwyneth?"

"I was told I could go the last of the way back alone," I said evasively. "What were you quarreling about?"

"Your mother thinks your expeditions into the eighteenth century will be too dangerous," said Falk.

Well, I couldn't blame her for that. And she didn't know a fraction of the dangers. No one had told her anything about the men who attacked us in Hyde Park. I for one would sooner have bitten my tongue off. She didn't know about Lady Tilney and the pistols either. As for Count Saint-Germain and the very sinister way he'd threatened me, so far I hadn't told anyone but Lesley about that. Oh, and my grandpa, of course.

I scrutinized Falk. "I'm getting the hang of all that stuff about fanning myself and dancing the minuet," I said casually. "It really isn't risky, Mum. Come to think of it, the only danger is I might break the fan over Charlotte's head."

"There you are, Grace," said Falk, his eyes twinkling at me.

"Who do you think you're kidding, Falk?" My mum gave him one last dark look, then took my arm and led me away. "Come along—the others will be waiting for us before they start supper."

"See you tomorrow, Gwyneth," Falk called after us. "And . . . er . . . see you sometime, Grace."

"See you," I muttered. Mum muttered something too, but I couldn't make out what it was.

"If you ask me, *haystacks* again," said Xemerius. "They don't fool me with their quarrels. I know people who fancy rolling in the hay when I see them."

I sighed. Mum sighed as well, and held me closer to her as we went the last of the way to the front door. I stiffened slightly, but then I put my head on her shoulder. "You don't have to quarrel with Falk over me. You're worrying too much, Mum."

"Easy for you to say so. . . . It's not a nice feeling, thinking you've done everything wrong. I can tell you're angry with me." She sighed again. "And you're right, really."

"But I love you all the same," I said.

Mum was fighting back tears. "And I love you more

than you can imagine." She murmured. We had reached the street outside the house, and she was looking around as if she was afraid of someone lying in wait for us in the dark. "I'd give anything for us to be a perfectly normal family living a perfectly ordinary life."

"What exactly is normal?" I said.

"Not us, anyway."

"It's all a question of attitude. So how was your day?" I asked with a touch of irony.

"Oh, the usual." Mum grinned faintly. "First a little argument with my mother, then a bigger argument with my sister, a bit of an argument with my boss at work, and finally another argument with my . . . former boyfriend, who just happens to be Grand Master of that amazingly secret Secret Lodge."

"Told you so," said Xemerius cheerfully. "Rolling in the hay!"

"There, you see, Mum. Perfectly normal."

Mum smiled, all the same. "And how was *your* day, darling?"

"Oh, nothing special worth mentioning. Some trouble with Mr. Squirrel at school, next some dancing and etiquette lessons with that obscure secret society that goes in for time travel, and then, just before I got around to strangling my dear cousin, a little excursion to the year 1953 to do my homework in peace and quiet, so as to avoid more trouble with Mr. Squirrel at school tomorrow."

"Doesn't sound too bad." Mum's heels were clicking on the sidewalk. She looked around again.

"I really don't think there's anyone following us," I re-assured her. "They're all too busy. The place is swarming with amazingly secret people."

"The Inner Circle is meeting—that doesn't often hap-pen. They last all met when Lucy and Paul stole the chro-nograph. Usually they're distributed all over the world."

"Mum. Don't you think it's about time to tell me what you know? It does no one any good to keep me in the dark."

"In every sense of the word," said Xemerius.

Mum stopped. "You're overestimating me! The little I do know wouldn't be any use to you. It would probably just confuse you even more. Or worse—it might actually put you in danger."

I shook my head. I wasn't giving up that easily. "Who or what is the Green Rider? And why don't Lucy and Paul want the Circle to close? Or *do* they want it to close, but only because they want to make use of the secret themselves?"

Mum rubbed her forehead. "Today's the first I heard of any Green Rider. And as for Lucy and Paul, I'm sure their motives weren't selfish. You've met Count Saint-Germain. He has ways and means of—" She stopped. "Oh, darling, believe me, nothing I could say would be any use to you."

"Please, Mum! It's bad enough with those men acting so mysterious and not trusting me, but you're my mother!"

"Yes," she said, and there were tears in her eyes again. "Yes, I am." But obviously that argument wasn't going to get me anywhere. "Come along, the taxi's been waiting half an hour. It's probably going to cost me half this month's salary."

I sighed, and followed her down the street. "We could go by Tube."

"No, you need something hot inside you as soon as possible. And Nick and Caroline miss you terribly. They'd hate to have supper without you yet again."

SURPRISINGLY, it was a peaceful, comfortable evening, because my grandmother and Aunt Glenda and Charlotte had gone to the opera.

"*Tosca*," said Great-aunt Maddy, sounding pleased, and she shook her blond curls. "Let's hope they come home feeling edified." She gave me a mischievous wink. "Good thing Violet had the tickets available."

I looked inquiringly around at everyone. It turned out that Great-aunt Maddy's friend (a nice old lady by the beautiful name of Mrs. Violet Purpleplum, who always knitted us scarves and socks for Christmas) had been going to the opera with her son and her future daughter-in-law, but now it turned out that the future daughter-in-law was going to be someone else's future daughter-in-law instead.

We all immediately relaxed, as usual when Lady Arista and Aunt Glenda were out of the house. It was a bit like being in elementary school when the teacher leaves the classroom. Even in the middle of supper, I had to jump up and show my brother and sister, Great-aunt Maddy, Mum, and Mr. Bernard how Puffylips and Charlotte had taught me to dance the minuet and flutter a fan, and Xemerius prompted me if I forgot anything. Looking back, I thought it was more comic than tragic myself, and I could see why the others were so amused. After a while, they were all dancing (except for Mr. Bernard, and even he was tapping the toe of his shoe in time to our rhythm), talking through their noses like Mr. Giordano, and telling each other, "Stupid thing! See how Charlotte does it!" and "Right! No, right is where your thumb is on the left!" and "I can see your teeth! That's unpatriotic!"

Nick demonstrated twenty-three ways of communicating without words by fanning himself with a napkin. "This one means *oops, your fly is open, sir*, and if you lower the fan a little and look at someone over the top of it, it means *wow, I'd like to marry you*. But if you do it the other way around, it means *ha ha, we are now at war with Spain*."

Nick showed a lot of acting talent, you had to give him that. Finally Caroline kicked her legs so high while she was dancing—it was more of a cancan than a minuet—that one of her shoes flew off and landed in what was left of the Bavarian cream we'd had for pudding.

That sobered us up a little, until Mr. Bernard fished the shoe out the dish, put it on Caroline's plate, and said with a perfectly straight face, "I'm glad there's plenty of that pudding left. Miss Charlotte and the ladies are sure to want a little something to eat when they get home from the opera."

My great-aunt beamed at him. "You're always so thoughtful, dear Mr. Bernard!"

"It is my duty to look after you all," said Mr. Bernard. "I promised your brother I would before his death."

I looked thoughtfully at the two of them. "I wonder if Grandpa ever told you anything about a Green Rider, Mr. Bernard? Or you, Aunt Maddy?"

Aunt Maddy shook her head. "Green Rider? What's that supposed to mean?"

"I've no idea," I said. "I know I have to find him, that's all."

"If I want to look for something, I usually go to your grandfather's library," said Mr. Bernard, and his owlish brown eyes looked very bright behind his glasses. "I have always found what I want there. If you need help, I know my way around the library very well, because I'm the one who dusts the books."

"That's a good idea, dear Mr. Bernard," said Great-aunt Maddy.

"Always at your service, ma'am." Mr. Bernard put more wood on the fire before wishing us good night.

Xemerius followed him. "I want to see if he takes his glasses off when he goes to sleep," he said. "And I'll tell you if he steals out of the house at night to play bass in a heavy-metal band."

My brother and sister were really supposed to go to bed early during the week, but today my mother let them stay up. After laughing till we were worn out, we settled down in front of the fire. Caroline cuddled up in Mum's arms, Nick nestled against me, and Great-aunt Maddy sat in Lady Arista's wing chair, blew a blond curl away from her face, and looked at us contentedly.

"Will you tell us about the old days, Aunt Maddy?" asked Caroline. "When you were a little girl, and you had to visit your horrible cousin Hazel in the country?"

"Oh, you've heard that so often already," said Aunt Maddy, putting her pink felt slippers on the footstool. But she didn't take much persuading. All her stories about her horrible cousin Hazel began "Hazel was about the most conceited girl you can imagine," and then we would say in chorus, "Just like Charlotte!" and Great-aunt Maddy would shake her head and say, "No, Hazel was much, much worse. She picked up cats by their tails and swung them around her head."

As I rested my chin on Nick's hair and listened to the story, in which Aunt Maddy, aged ten, avenged all the tortured cats in Gloucestershire by tipping Cousin Hazel into a pool of liquid manure, my thoughts went to Gideon. Where was he now? What was he doing? Who was with him? And was he maybe thinking of me, too—with that odd, warm feeling somewhere deep inside? Probably not.

I suppressed a deep sigh, with difficulty, as I thought of the moment when we parted outside Madame Rossini's sewing room. Gideon hadn't so much as looked at me again, even though only a few minutes earlier, we'd been kissing.

Again. Although I'd sworn over the phone to Lesley last night that it would never happen again. "Not until we've finally decided just what's going on between us."

Lesley had only laughed. "Oh, come on, who do you think you're kidding? It's obvious what's going on. You're head over heels in love with the guy!"

But how could I be in love with a boy I'd only known for a few days? A boy whose behavior was impossible most of the time? Although at those moments when it wasn't he was just so . . . so . . . so incredibly—

"Here I am!" crowed Xemerius, landing in sweeping style on the dining-room table next to the candle. Caroline, who was sitting on Mum's lap, gave a small start of surprise and stared his way.

"What's the matter, Caroline?" I asked quietly.

"Oh, nothing," she said. "I thought I saw a shadow, that's all."

"Really?" I looked at Xemerius in surprise.

He just shrugged one shoulder and grinned. "It's nearly full moon. Sensitive people can sometimes see us then, usually just out of the corners of their eyes. Then if they look more closely, we're not there at all." Now he was dangling from the chandelier again. "That old lady with the golden curls sees and senses more than she's letting on. When I put a claw on her shoulder, just to find out what would happen, she reached up to the place . . . not that that surprises me, in your family."

I looked lovingly at Caroline. A sensitive child—not that she'd inherited Great-aunt Maddy's talent for seeing visions.

"Now comes my favorite bit," said Caroline, her eyes shining, and Great-aunt Maddy threw herself into the story of sadistic Hazel with her best Sunday dress on, standing up to her neck in the liquid manure, screeching, "Just you wait, Madeleine, I'll pay you back for this!"

"And so she did, too," said Great-aunt Maddy. "More than once."

"But we'll listen to that story another time," said Mum firmly. "You children must go to bed. You have school in the morning."

We all sighed, Great-aunt Maddy loudest of all.

FRIDAY WAS PIZZA DAY, and no one skipped school lunch. Pizza was about the only edible dish the school ever served. I knew that Lesley would die for that pizza, so I didn't let her stay in the classroom with me. I had a date with James there.

"Go and have lunch," I said. "I'd hate for you to miss pizza on my account."

"But then there'll be no one here to act as lookout for you. And I want to hear more about yesterday, with you and Gideon and the green sofa—"

"Look, with the best will in the world, I can't tell you any more than I already did," I said.

"Then tell me again. It's so romantic!"

"Go eat that pizza!"

"You absolutely must get his mobile number," said Lesley. "I mean, it's a golden rule: never kiss a boy if you don't have his phone number."

"Delicious cheese and pepperoni . . . ," I said.

"But—"

"Xemerius is here with me," I said, pointing to the

windowsill where he was sitting, chewing the end of his pointy tail and looking bored.

Lesley caved in. "Okay. But make sure you get something to eat today. All that waving Mrs. Counter's pointer about does no one any good! And if anyone sees what you're up to, you'll be carted off to the loony bin in short order, remember that."

"Oh, go away," I said, pushing her out of the doorway just as James was coming through it.

James was glad we'd be on our own this time. "That freckled girl gets on my nerves, always butting in! She treats me like thin air."

"That's because so far as she's concerned you *are* . . . oh, forget it!"

"Well, so how can I help you today?"

"I thought maybe you could tell me how to say hello at a soirée in the eighteenth century."

"*Hello?*"

"Yes. Hello. Hi. Good evening. You must know what people used to say when they met. And what they did. Shaking hands, kissing hands, a bow, a curtsey, Your Highness, Your Serene Highness . . . it's all so complicated, and there's so much I could do wrong."

James had a self-satisfied expression on his face. "Not if you do as I tell you. The first thing you should know is how to curtsey to a gentleman of the same social rank as your own."

"Oh, wonderful," said Xemerius. "The only problem is, how will Gwyneth know what his social rank is?"

James stared at him. "What's that? Shoo, kitty, shoo! Go away!"

Xemerius snorted disbelievingly. "What did you say?"

"Oh, James, take a closer look," I said. "This is my friend Xemerius, the gargoyle demon. Xemerius, this is James, another friend of mine."

James shook a handkerchief out of his sleeve, and the scent of lilies of the valley wafted through the air. "Whatever it is, I want it to go away. It reminds me that I'm in the middle of a terrible nightmare, a feverish dream in which I have to teach a pert minx how to behave."

I sighed. "James, when are you going to face the facts? Over two hundred years ago, you may have had a feverish dream, but since then you've been . . . well, you and Xemerius are both . . . you're—"

"Dead," said Xemerius. "Strictly speaking." He put his head on one side. "It's true, you know. Why won't you face it, like she said?"

James flicked his handkerchief. "I don't want to hear this. Cats can't talk."

"Do I look like a cat, you stupid ghost?" cried Xemerius.

"You do, rather," said James, without looking. "Except for the ears, maybe. And the horns. And the wings. And the funny tail. Oh, how I hate these fevered fantasies!"

Xemerius planted himself in front of James. His tail was lashing furiously. "I am not a fantasy. I'm a demon," he said, and in his annoyance, he spat out a torrent of water on the floor. "A *powerful* demon. Conjured up by magicians and architects in the eleventh century, as you reckon time, to protect the tower of a church that isn't standing any-more these days. When my sandstone body was destroyed, hundreds of years ago, this was all that was left of me—a shadow of my former self, so to speak, condemned to wander this earth until the world falls apart. Which could take another few million years, I should think."

"Tralala, I'm not listening," said James.

"You're pathetic," said Xemerius. "Unlike you, I have no choice—I'm bound to this earth by a magician's curse. But you could give up your pitiful ghostly existence and go wherever human beings do go when they're dead."

"I'm not dead, you stupid kitty cat!" cried James. "I'm only sick in bed with horrible feverish hallucinations. And if we don't change the subject this minute, I'm leaving!"

"Okay," I said, trying to use the board eraser to mop up the puddle Xemerius had made. "Let's go on. Curtsey-ing to a gentleman of the same social rank . . ."

Xemerius shook his head and flew away over our heads to the door. "I'll stand guard for you. Think how embar-rassing it'd be if anyone found you here curtseying."

The lunch break wasn't long enough to learn all the tricks James wanted to teach me, but in the end, I could curtsey in three different ways and hold out my hand to be kissed. (A good thing that custom has died out, if you ask me.) When the other students came back, James bowed to me and left, while I whispered a quick word of thanks.

"So?" asked Lesley.

"James thinks Xemerius is a funny kind of cat, part of his fevered fantasies," I told her. "I can only hope that what he's taught me isn't also distorted by the fever. If not, then now I know what to do if I'm introduced to the Duke of Devonshire."

"Oh, good," said Lesley. "So what *do* you do?"

"Sink into a deep curtsey and stay there for a long time," I said. "Almost as long as before the king, and for longer than if I was curtseying to a marquis or a count. It's quite simple, really. And I always have to hold out my hand to be kissed like a good girl and keep on smiling."

"Well, fancy that! I'd never have expected James to come in useful." Lesley looked around appreciatively. "You'll wow them in the eighteenth century."

"Let's hope so," I said. But nothing could cloud my good mood for the rest of the classes. Charlotte and stupid Puffylips would be amazed to find out that I even knew the difference between a Serene Highness and an Illustrious Highness, although they'd done their level best to make it sound as complicated as possible.

"And by the way, I've worked out a theory about the magic of the raven," said Lesley after school, on the way from the classroom to our lockers. "It's so simple that no one's thought of it yet. Let's meet tomorrow morning at your house, and I'll bring everything I've found out. So long as my mum hasn't decided it's house-cleaning day again and handed out rubber gloves to everyone—"

"Gwenny?" Cynthia Dale, coming up behind us, slapped me on the back. "Do you remember Regina Curtis who was in the same class as my sister until last year? She's in hospital with anorexia now. Is that where you want to end up as well?"

"No," I said, baffled.

"Okay, then eat this! *At once!*" Cynthia threw me a caramel. I caught it and obediently unwrapped it. But as I was about to put it in my mouth, Cynthia grabbed my arm. "Stop! Are you really going to eat it? So you're not on a starvation diet?"

"No," I said again.

"Then Charlotte was lying. She said you kept skipping lunch because you want to be as thin as her. Give me my caramel back. You're not anorexic after all." Cynthia put the caramel in her own mouth. "Here, your invitation to my birthday party. It's going to be fancy dress again. And this year the theme is "Greensleeves." You can bring your boyfriend with you."

"Er—"

"It's a funny thing, but Charlotte said the same. I don't mind which of you brings that guy, I just want him to be at my party."

"She's crazy," Lesley whispered to me.

"I heard that," said Cynthia. "You can bring Max, Lesley."

"Cyn, Max and I haven't been together for the last six months."

"Oh, bother," said Cynthia. "Sounds like too few boys this time. Either you bring some with you or I'll have to uninvite a few girls again. Aishani, for instance, although she probably won't come anyway, because her parents don't let her go to mixed parties . . . oh, my God, who's *that*? Please, someone pinch me!"

"That" was a tall boy with fair hair cut short. He was standing outside the principal's office with Mr. Whitman. And he seemed to me curiously familiar.

"Ouch!" screeched Cynthia, because Lesley had taken her at her word and pinched her.

Mr. Whitman and the boy turned around. When those green eyes under thick, dark eyelashes glanced at me, I knew at once who the strange boy was. Good heavens! Maybe Lesley ought to pinch me too.

"Ah, just the right moment," said Mr. Whitman. "Raphael, these three girls are from your class. Cynthia Dale, Lesley Hay, and Gwyneth Shepherd. Meet Raphael Bertelin, girls. He'll be joining your class on Monday."

"Hi," Lesley and I murmured, and Cynthia said, "Is this for real?"

Raphael grinned at us, hands casually in his pockets. He really did look very like Gideon, although he was a bit younger. His lips were fuller, and his skin was bronzed as if he was just back from a month in the Caribbean. I supposed the lucky people there in the south of France all looked bronzed.

"Why are you changing school in the middle of the school year?" asked Lesley. "Did you do something to get yourself thrown out of your old one?"

Raphael's grin grew broader. "Depends how you look

at it," he said. "I'm really here because I was fed up to the teeth with school. But for some reason or other—"

"Raphael has moved here from France," Mr. Whitman interrupted him. "Come along, Raphael, Mr. Gilles is waiting."

"See you Monday," said Raphael, and I had the feeling he was speaking exclusively to Lesley.

Cynthia waited until Mr. Whitman and Raphael were in the principal's office, and then she raised both arms in the air and cried, "Thank you, God, thank you for answering my prayer!"

Lesley dug her elbow into my ribs. "You look as if a bus had just run over your foot."

"Wait till I tell you who that is," I whispered. "Then you'll look the same."

Every period of time is a sphinx that throws itself into the abyss as soon as its riddle has been solved.

HEINRICH HEINE

SEVEN

WHAT WITH MEETING Gideon's little brother and my hasty conversation with Lesley afterward (she asked, "Are you sure?" ten times; I said, "Absolutely sure" ten times; and then we both said, "Crazy!" and "I don't believe it!" and "Did you see his eyes?" about a hundred times), well, what with all that, I arrived at the waiting limousine several minutes after Charlotte today. Mr. Marley had been sent to pick us up again, and he seemed more nervous than ever. Xemerius was squatting on the car roof swishing his tail back and forth. Charlotte was already in the back of the limousine. She looked annoyed with me. "Where the hell have you been all this time?" she snapped. "One doesn't keep a man like Giordano waiting. I don't think you realize what a great honor it is to be taught by him."

Mr. Marley, looking embarrassed, helped me into the car and closed the door.

"Anything wrong?" I had a nasty feeling that I'd

missed out on something important, and Charlotte's expression confirmed that idea.

When the car began to move, Xemerius slipped through the roof into the interior and flopped down on the seat opposite me. Like last time, Mr. Marley was sitting in front beside the driver.

"It would be nice if you could take more trouble today," said Charlotte. "All this is terribly embarrassing for me, you know. After all, you're my cousin."

I laughed out loud. "Oh, come on, Charlotte! You don't have to pretend with me! You just *love* to see me making a fool of myself!"

"That's not true!" Charlotte shook her head. "Typical of you to think like that! You're so childish, you see yourself at the center of everything. The rest of us just want to help you so that you won't spoil everything because you aren't fit for your task. Although maybe that possibility won't come up again. I can imagine them calling the whole thing off. . . ."

"What makes you say so?"

Charlotte looked at me for a while in silence. Then she said, almost gleefully, "You'll find out soon enough, I expect."

"Has something happened?" I asked, but I was asking Xemerius, not Charlotte. I wasn't stupid. "Did Mr. Marley say something before I got here?"

"Only cryptic stuff," said Xemerius, as Charlotte compressed her lips and looked out of the window. "There was obviously some kind of incident this morning when

whatsisname, your boyfriend, sparkly jewel thingy . . ."
He scratched his eyebrows with the tip of his tail.

"Don't make me worm it all out of you!"

Charlotte, who understandably thought I was talking
to her, said, "If you hadn't been late, then you'd know."

"*Diamond*, that's it," said Xemerius. "Well, he went
traveling in time and someone—how can I put this? Seems
like someone hit him over the head."

My stomach muscles contracted painfully. "What?"

"Don't upset yourself," said Xemerius. "He'll live. Or
so I gathered from what Ginger there was stammering.
Oh, good heavens, you're white as a sheet! Not going to
throw up, are you? Pull yourself together!"

"I can't," I whispered. I really did feel terrible.

"You can't what?" snapped Charlotte. "The first thing
gene carriers learn is to put their own wishes last and do
their best for the cause. While you are just the opposite."

In my mind's eye, I saw Gideon lying on the ground
covered with blood. I was finding it difficult to breathe.

"Other people would do anything to be taught by Giordano, and you act as if we were setting out to torture you."

"Oh, do shut up for once, Charlotte," I said.

Charlotte turned back to the window. I began
trembling.

Xemerius put one claw comfortingly on my knee.
"Listen, I'll find your boyfriend and report back, okay? But
please don't cry, or I'll get upset and spew water all over
this showy leather upholstery, and your cousin will think
you've wet yourself!"

With a jerk, he disappeared through the roof of the car and flew away. It was a dreadful hour and a half before he finally came back. An hour and a half in which I imagined the most terrible things, feeling more dead than alive. It made matters no better that meanwhile we had arrived at the Temple, where the implacable Giordano was waiting for me. But I was in no fit state to take in what he was saying about colonial policy in the eighteenth century or to imitate Charlotte's dance steps either. Suppose Gideon had been attacked by swordsmen again, and this time he hadn't been able to defend himself? When I wasn't seeing him lying on the ground covered with blood, I imagined him hooked up to thousands of tubes in intensive care, looking whiter than the sheets on his bed. Why wasn't there anyone here to tell me how he was?

Then, at last, Xemerius came flying straight through the wall and into the Old Refectory.

"Well?" I asked, ignoring Giordano and Charlotte. They were in the middle of teaching me how to clap when you were applauding something in the eighteenth century. Not the way I did it, of course.

"You're playing *pat-a-cake, pat-a-cake, baker's man*, you stupid creature," Giordano was saying. "That's the way toddlers clap in the sandbox when they're pleased—oh, what's she looking at *now*? I am going right out of my mind."

"Nothing to worry about, haystack girl," said Xemerius, grinning cheerfully. "Something came down *boing* on your friend's head, put him out of action for an hour or so, but his skull must be hard as diamond itself—he didn't even get concussion. And the wound on his forehead makes him look kind of . . . er . . . oh, no, don't go all pale again. I told you he's all right."

I took a deep breath. I felt dizzy with relief.

"That's better," said Xemerius. "No need to hyperventilate. Lover boy still has all his nice white teeth. And he's cursing under his breath nonstop, which I guess is a good sign."

Thank God. Thank God. Thank God.

In fact the person about to hyperventilate was Giordano. Go ahead, I thought, why don't you? Suddenly his screeching didn't bother me anymore. Far from it—it was very amusing to watch his complexion turning from dark pink to purple in between those crisscross lines of beard.

Mr. George arrived just in time to prevent the furious Puffylips from slapping my face.

"It was even worse today, if that's possible." Giordano sank down on a delicate little chair and mopped the sweat from his face with a handkerchief as purple as his present skin color. "She just stared ahead with glazed eyes all the time—if I didn't know better, I'd have thought she was on drugs!"

"Giordano, please!" said Mr. George. "We have none of us had a particularly good day today—"

"How is . . . *he* doing?" asked Charlotte quietly, with a sideways glance at me.

"As you might expect in the circumstances," replied Mr. George gravely.

Once again Charlotte cast me a brief, searching glance.

I stared darkly back. Did it give her some kind of sick satisfaction to know something I didn't know, although she thought it would be of burning interest to me?

"Oh, nonsense," said Xemerius. "He's doing fine, trust me, darling! He just ate an enormous veal schnitzel with French fries and green vegetables. Does that sound like *as you might expect in the circumstances*?"

Giordano was getting cross because no one was listening to him. "I just hope I won't be held to blame!" he said shrilly, pushing his little chair aside. "I have worked with unacknowledged talents, I have worked with the truly great men of this world, but never, never in my life has anything like *this* come my way."

"My dear Giordano, you know how much we esteem you here. And no one would have been more suitable to teach Gwyneth the . . ." Here Mr. George fell silent, because Giordano had pushed his lower lip forward in a sulky pout, throwing his head with its cement hairdo right back.

"Just don't say I didn't warn you," he snapped. "That's all I ask."

"Very well," said Mr. George, sighing. "I . . . yes, well, I'll pass the message on. Coming, Gwyneth?"

I'd already taken off the hooped skirt and hung it up over the piano stool. "See you sometime," I said to Giordano.

He was still pouting. "I am afraid there will be no avoiding that."

ON THE WAY down to the old alchemical laboratory, which I knew almost by heart now, even blindfolded,

Mr. George told me what had happened in the morning. He was a little surprised that Mr. Marley hadn't passed the news on to me, and I didn't go to the trouble of explaining.

They had sent Gideon back to the past by chronograph (Mr. George wasn't telling me what year), to carry out a little errand (Mr. George didn't say just what that was either), and two hours later, they'd found him unconscious in a corridor not far from the chronograph room. With a lacerated wound on his forehead, obviously made by something hard and heavy. Gideon couldn't remember anything about it, but the attacker must have been lying in wait for him.

"But who . . . ?"

"We don't know. It's worrying, particularly in the present situation. We had him thoroughly examined, and there was no sign of any puncture on him to suggest that his blood had been taken—"

"Wouldn't the blood from his forehead have been enough?" I asked, shuddering slightly.

"Possibly," agreed Mr. George. "But if someone had . . . well, wanted to make sure, that's not how he'd have gone about getting Gideon's blood. There are countless explanations. No one knew Gideon was going to be there that evening, so it's unlikely that someone was lying in wait for him on purpose. It's much more likely to have been a chance meeting. In certain years, these cellars were swarming with subversive, lowlife characters—smugglers, criminals, creatures of the underworld in every sense. My own belief is that it was an unfortunate coincidence. . . ." He cleared his throat. "In any case, Gideon seems to have survived the adventure pretty well—at least, Dr. White found no serious injuries. So the two of you will be able to set off on Sunday at midday as planned, to attend that soirée." He laughed a little. "Funny idea: a soirée in the middle of the day on Sunday."

Yes, ha ha, hilarious. "Where's Gideon now?" I asked impatiently. "In hospital?"

"No, he's resting—at least, I hope so. He only went to hospital for a scan, and as it found nothing, thank God, he discharged himself. The fact is, he had an unexpected visit from his brother yesterday evening."

"I know," I said. "Mr. Whitman registered Raphael at my school today."

I heard Mr. George sigh heavily. "The boy ran away from home after getting into some kind of trouble along with his friends. Falk has this crazy idea of keeping Raphael in England. In these turbulent times, we all have better things to do—Gideon in particular—than bother about difficult boys, but Falk could never refuse Selina anything, and it seems this is Raphael's only chance of finishing high school with some kind of certificate, away from the friends who have such a bad influence on him."

"Selina . . . is that Gideon and Raphael's mother?"

"Yes," said Mr. George. "They both inherited those striking green eyes from her. Here we are. You can take the blindfold off now."

This time we were alone in the chronograph room.

"Charlotte said that in the circumstances you'd be

calling off our planned visit to the eighteenth century," I suggested hopefully. "Or postponing it? Just to give Gideon time to recover, and maybe I could practice a bit more—"

Mr. George shook his head. "No, we won't be doing that. The timing of your visits was very important to the count. Gideon and you will go to the soirée the day after tomorrow—that's definite. Any particular year you'd like to elapse to today?"

"No," I said, taking care to sound indifferent. "I don't suppose it makes any difference if I'm shut up in a cellar, does it?"

Mr. George was carefully taking the chronograph out of its velvet wrapping. "No, it doesn't. We usually send Gideon to the year 1953, a nice quiet year. We just have to take care he doesn't meet himself." He smiled. "I imagine it would feel rather eerie to be shut up somewhere with your double." He patted his round little paunch and looked thoughtful. "How about 1956? Another quiet year."

"Sounds perfect," I said.

Mr. George handed me the flashlight and took his ring off. "Just in case . . . but don't worry, there won't be anyone around in the small hours, not at two thirty A.M."

"Two thirty A.M.?" I repeated, horrified. How was I going to find my grandfather in the middle of the night? No one was going to believe I'd lost my way down in the cellars at two thirty A.M. There might not be anyone at all in the building. Then our plan would fall through! "Oh, Mr. George, please don't send me into those eerie catacombs in the middle of the night all by myself!"

"Gwyneth, it makes no difference when you're in a locked room deep underground."

"But I . . . I get scared at night! Please, don't send me off all alone in the dark." I was so desperate that tears came to my eyes of their own accord; I didn't have to help them along.

"Very well," said Mr. George, his little eyes looking at me indulgently. "I was forgetting that you . . . well, let's just pick another time of day. How about three in the afternoon?"

"That's better," I said. "Thank you, Mr. George."

"There's nothing to thank me for." Mr. George looked up from the chronograph for a moment and smiled at me. "We really do ask a lot of you—I think in your place I'd feel rather uneasy alone in a cellar myself. Particularly as you sometimes see things that other people don't. . . ."

"Yes, thanks for reminding me," I said. Xemerius wasn't with us. He'd probably have been very cross at being described as a "thing." "What about all those tombs full of bones and skulls just around the corner?"

"Oh, dear," said Mr. George. "I didn't mean to add to your worries."

"I'm not worried," I said. "I'm not afraid of the dead. In my experience, they can't hurt you—unlike the living." I saw Mr. George raise his eyebrows and added quickly, "Though of course I think they're dreadfully uncanny, and I certainly wouldn't like to be sitting around here at night next to a lot of catacombs." I gave him my hand, clutching my school bag with the other one. "Try the fourth finger this time, please. That one hasn't been punctured yet."

MY HEART was pounding like crazy as I took the key out of its hiding place behind the bricks and unfolded the note that Lucas had left there with it. The password for the day seemed to me unusually long, and I didn't even try to memorize it; I took a ballpoint out of my bag and wrote it on the palm of my hand. Lucas had also drawn me a plan of the cellar vaults. According to his diagram, I had to turn right once I was outside the door and then turn left three times running until I came to the big staircase where the first guards would be stationed. The door opened easily when I turned the key in the lock. I thought for a moment and then decided not to lock it again, just in case I was in a hurry on the way back. There was a musty smell down here, and the walls clearly showed how old these vaults were. The ceiling was low and the passages very narrow. Every few yards, another corridor branched off or a door was let into the wall. Without my flashlight and Lucas's plan, I'd probably have been lost, even though it felt oddly familiar down here. As I turned left in the last corridor before the staircase, I heard voices. I took a deep breath.

Now I had to convince the guards that there was a really good reason for letting me through. Unlike the guards in the eighteenth century, this couple didn't look at all dangerous. They were sitting at the foot of the stairs playing cards. I marched firmly up to them. When they saw me, one of them dropped his cards; the other jumped up and looked frantically around for his sword, which was propped against the wall.

"Good afternoon," I said bravely. "Don't let me disturb you."

"What . . . who . . . how?" stammered the first guard. The second guard had picked up his sword and was staring at me undecidedly.

"Isn't a sword rather an exotic weapon for the twentieth century?" I asked, baffled. "What are you going to do if someone comes this way with a hand grenade? Or a machine gun?"

"People don't come this way at all much," said the guard with the sword. He grinned awkwardly. "It's more a kind of a traditional weapon that . . ." He shook his head, as if calling himself to order, then pulled himself together and stood up very straight. "Password?"

I glanced at the palm of my hand. "*Nam quod in iuventus non discitur, in matura aetate nescitur.*"

"That's right," said the guard still sitting on the stairs. "But where do you come from, may I ask?"

"The Royal Courts of Justice," I said. "There's this useful shortcut through to here from them. I can show you sometime if you like. But now I have a very important appointment with Lucas Montrose."

"Mr. Montrose? I don't know if he's in the building today," said the guard with the sword.

The other one said, "We'll take you up, Miss . . . ? You'll have to tell us your name first. For the records."

I told them the first name to come into my mind. Maybe I was a little too quick about it.

"Violet Purpleplum?" repeated the guard with the sword incredulously, while the other guard stared at my legs. I guessed the skirt length of our school uniform wasn't fashionable in 1956. Never mind, he'd have to put up with it.

"Yes," I said, in a slightly aggressive tone of voice, because I was annoyed with myself. "No need to grin like that. Not everyone can be called Smith or Jones. Can we get on with this?"

The two men had a brief argument over which one was going to escort me up, then the guard with the sword said his friend could go, and made himself comfortable at the foot of the stairs again. On the way, the other guard asked if I had ever been here before. I said yes, several times, and wasn't the Dragon Hall beautiful? Half my family were members of the Guardians, I added, and then the guard thought he suddenly remembered seeing me at the last garden party here in the Temple.

"Weren't you the girl pouring lemonade? Along with Lady Gainsley."

"Yes, that's right," I said, and then we launched into cheerful gossip about the party, the roses, and a bunch of people I didn't know from Adam. Not that I let that stop me commenting at length on Mrs. Lamotte's hat and the fact that Mr. Mason, of all people, was having a relationship with an office girl—who'd have thought it?

As we passed the first windows, I looked curiously out—it all seemed very familiar. But it was kind of odd to know that outside these venerable walls the city would look quite different from in my own time. I felt as if I wanted to rush out at once and see it before I could believe it.

Up on the first floor, the guard knocked at an office door. I read my grandfather's name on a plate outside the door and was overcome by a wave of pride. I'd actually made it to here!

"A Miss Purpleplum for Mr. Montrose," said the guard, opening the door just a crack.

"Thank you for bringing me up," I said as I walked past him and into the office. "See you at the next garden party, then."

"I'll look forward to that," he said, but I had already shut the door in his face. I turned triumphantly around. "There, now what do you say?"

"Miss . . . er . . . *Purpleplum?*" The man at the desk stared at me, wide-eyed. He was clearly not my grandfather. I stared back in alarm. He was very young, not much more than a boy, really, and he had a round, smooth face with a pair of bright, friendly little eyes which struck me as more than familiar.

"*Mr. George?*" I asked incredulously.

"Have we met?" Young Mr. George had risen to his feet.

"Yes, of course. At . . . at the last garden party," I stammered, while a jumble of ideas went around in my head. "I was the girl pouring the . . . but where's my grand . . .

where's Lucas? Didn't he tell you we had an appointment today?"

"I'm his assistant, but I haven't been here very long," said Mr. George, shyly. "No, he didn't say anything about an appointment, but he ought to be back any time now. Would you like to sit down and wait for him, Miss—er . . ."

"Purpleplum!"

"Of course. Can I get them to bring you a coffee?" He came around the desk and pulled out a chair for me. I was very glad of it; my legs felt quite wobbly.

"No, thank you, no coffee," I said.

He looked at me undecidedly. I stared silently back.

"Are you . . . are you in the Girl Guides?"

"What?"

"I mean . . . because of the uniform."

"No." I couldn't help it, I just had to keep staring at Mr. George. It was unmistakably him! He was still very much the same when he was fifty-five years older, except for having no hair left, wearing glasses, and being as broad as he was tall.

Young Mr. George, on the contrary, had plenty of hair, neatly parted and kept in place with some kind of hair cream, and he was positively slender. Obviously he didn't like being stared at, because he went red, sat down at the desk again, and leafed through some papers. I wondered what he would say if I took his signet ring out of my pocket and showed it to him.

We sat in silence like that for at least fifteen minutes

before the office door opened and my grandfather came in. When he saw me, his eyes almost popped out of his head for a split second, before he had control over himself again and said, "Well, look who's here—my dear little cousin!"

I jumped up. Since our last meeting, Lucas Montrose had definitely grown older. He was wearing an elegant suit and a bow tie, and he had a mustache that didn't really suit him. The mustache tickled when he kissed me on both cheeks.

"How good to see you, Hazel! How long are you going to be in town? Have your dear parents come with you?"

"N-no," I stammered. Was I going to have to pretend I was horrible Hazel? "They're at home, with the cats. . . ."

"By the way, this is my new assistant, Thomas George. Thomas, this is Hazel Montrose from Gloucestershire. I told you she was probably going to visit me sometime."

"I thought her name was Purpleplum," said Mr. George.

"Yes," I said. "So it is. Part of my name. Hazel Violet Montrose Purpleplum, but who can possibly remember all that rigmarole?"

Lucas looked at me, frowning. Then, turning to Mr. George, he said, "I'm going for a little walk with Hazel. All right? If anyone wants me, say I'm in a meeting with a client."

"Yes, Mr. Montrose, sir," said Mr. George, trying to keep an indifferent expression on his face.

"See you later," I told him.

Lucas took my arm and led me out of the room. We both kept strained grins on our faces, and it wasn't until we had closed the heavy front door of the building behind us and were out in the sunny road that we spoke again.

"I don't want to be horrible Hazel," I said reproachfully, looking around. The Temple didn't seem to have changed much in fifty-five years, if you ignored the cars. "Do I look like someone who picks up cats by their tails and swings them in the air?"

"Purpleplum!" said Lucas, just as reproachfully. "I suppose you couldn't think of anything even more striking?" Then he took me by the shoulders and examined my face. "Let's take a look at you, granddaughter! Why, you look just the same as you did eight years ago."

"Yes, but for me that was only the day before yesterday."

"Amazing," said Lucas. "And all these years I thought I might just have been dreaming the whole thing."

"I elapsed to 1953 yesterday," I said, "but I wasn't on my own."

"How long do we have today?"

"I arrived at three o'clock your time, so I'll be traveling back at six thirty."

"Then at least we have a little time to talk. Come along. There's a café where we can get a cup of tea around the corner." Lucas took my arm, and we walked toward the Strand. "You won't believe it, but I'm a father now!" he said as we walked on. "The baby was born three months ago. I must say it's a nice feeling. And I think Arista was a good choice. Claudine Seymour has rather lost her figure, and they say she drinks. Even in the morning." We went down a small alley and then out of the arched gateway into the street. I stood there staring. Traffic was roaring up and down the Strand as usual, but all the cars were vintage models. Even the noisy red double-decker buses looked like museum pieces, and most of the people on the sidewalk wore hats—men, women, even children! There was a film poster on the wall of the building over the road, advertising *High Society*, starring wonderfully beautiful Grace Kelly and incredibly ugly Frank Sinatra. I looked left and right with my mouth open and could hardly take a step. It all looked like something out of a nostalgia picture postcard in the retro style, only much more colorful.

Lucas took me to a pretty corner café and ordered tea and scones. "You were hungry last time," he remembered. "They make good sandwiches here, too."

"No, thanks," I said. "Grandpa, about Mr. George! In the year 2011, he acts as if he'd never seen me before!"

Lucas shrugged his shoulders. "Don't worry about the boy. It's going to be another fifty-five years before he meets you again. He'll probably have simply forgotten you by then."

"Yes, maybe," I said, looking around, irritated, at all the smokers here. Right beside us a fat man was sitting at a kidney-shaped table with an ashtray the size of a skull on it, smoking a cigar. Hadn't they heard of lung cancer yet in 1956? "Have you found out anything about the Green Rider since we last met?"

"No, but I can tell you something much more important. Now I know why Paul and Lucy will steal the chronograph." Lucas looked briefly around and moved his chair a little closer to mine. "Since your first visit, Lucy and Paul have been here several times to elapse, and nothing special happened. We drank tea together, I tested them on their French verbs, and we spent four boring hours. They couldn't leave the building, that was the rule, and that sneak Kenneth de Villiers made sure we kept it. I did once smuggle Lucy and Paul out so that they could see a film and look around for a while, but the stupid thing was that we were caught at it. Oh, why pretend? *Kenneth* caught us at it. There was a terrible row. I was disciplined, and for the next six months, a guard was always posted outside the Dragon Hall when Paul and Lucy were with us. That went on until I'd reached the rank of Adept Third Degree. Oh, thank you very much." That was to the waitress, who looked just like Doris Day in *The Man Who Knew Too Much*. Her tinted blond hair was short, and she wore a pretty, floaty dress with a full skirt. She put our order down in front of us with a beaming smile, and I wouldn't have been a bit surprised if she'd burst out singing "Que Sera, Sera."

Lucas waited until she was out of earshot and then went on. "Of course, at first I wanted to find out what kind of reason they could possibly have for going off with the chronograph, but I was on the wrong track. Their only problem was that they were madly in love with each other. Obviously no one looked kindly on that connection in their own time, so they kept it secret. According to them, only a few people did know about it, apparently including me and your mother, Grace."

"Then they escaped into the past because they couldn't be together? Like Romeo and Juliet! Wow, how romantic!"

"No," said Lucas. "No, that wasn't the reason." He stirred his tea, while I looked greedily at the little basket of warm scones lying under a cloth napkin, smelling very tempting.

"I was the reason," Lucas went on.

"What, *you*?"

"Well, not directly. But it was my fault. One day, you see, I got the crackbrained idea of sending Lucy and Paul a little farther back into the past."

"With the chronograph? But how . . ."

"I told you it was a crackbrained idea. But there we were, shut up for four hours a day in that wretched Dragon Hall, along with the chronograph. So it's hardly surprising if such crazy thoughts occurred to me. I looked at old maps, I studied the count's secret writings and the *Annals* thoroughly, and then I borrowed costumes from the stock, and finally we read Paul and Lucy's blood into the chronograph here. Then I sent them back on a two-hour trial journey to the year 1590. It worked without a hitch. When the two hours were up, they traveled back to me in 1948, and no one had noticed that they'd ever been gone. And half an hour later, they traveled back again to their own year, 1992. It went perfectly smoothly."

I put a scone heavily laden with clotted cream into my mouth. I could think better if I was munching. A whole lot of questions came into my mind, and I tackled the first of them. "But 1590—there weren't any Guardians at that time, were there?"

"Exactly," said Lucas. "Even the building didn't yet exist. And that was our good luck. Or bad luck, depending how you look at it." He sipped more tea. He still hadn't eaten a thing, and I was beginning to wonder how he was ever going to put on those extra pounds that I remembered. "Looking at the old maps, I'd found out that the building with the Dragon Hall would go up on a site which, from the late sixteenth to the end of the seventeenth century, was a small square with a fountain in the middle of it."

"I don't quite understand."

"Hang on a minute. This discovery was our ticket to ride. Lucy and Paul could travel from the Dragon Hall to that square further back in the past, and then they only had to find their way back to it in good time to travel automatically back to the Dragon Hall. Are you still with me?"

"But suppose they landed in the square in broad daylight? Wouldn't they have been arrested and burnt for witchcraft?"

"It was a quiet little place; they usually passed entirely unnoticed. And if anyone did see them, they probably just rubbed their eyes in surprise and thought they hadn't been attending for a split second. Of course it was still very dangerous, but we thought it was a positively brilliant idea. We congratulated ourselves on thinking it up and tricking everyone, and Lucy and Paul had a great time. So did I, even if I was always on tenterhooks in the Dragon Hall waiting for them to come back. Imagine if someone had come in just then—"

"It was very brave," I said.

"Yes," admitted Lucas, looking a little guilty. "You only do that kind of thing when you're young. I certainly wouldn't do it today. But I thought if it really turned dangerous, then my wise old self from the future would intervene, do you see?"

"What wise old self from the future?"

"Well, me!" Lucas cried, and immediately lowered his voice again. "I mean, I thought that in 1992 I'd still remember what Lucy and Paul and I had been up to in 1948, and then, if it had gone wrong, I could have warned them to ignore my reckless younger self . . . or so I thought."

"Okay," I said slowly, helping myself to another scone. Good food for the brain. "But you didn't?"

Lucas shook his head. "Evidently not, fool that I was. And so we got more and more reckless. When Lucy was studying *Hamlet* at school, I sent them off to the year 1602. Over three days in succession, they saw the premiere of the play by the Lord Chamberlain's Men at the Globe Theatre."

"In Southwark?"

Lucas nodded. "Yes, it was quite tricky. They had to cross London Bridge to get to the south bank of the Thames, try to see as much of the play as possible in one go, and be back before they were due to travel forward in time. It worked well for the first two days, but on the third day, there was an accident on London Bridge, and Lucy and

Paul were witnesses to a crime. They didn't make it to the north bank in time, so they landed in Southwark in the year 1948 still half in the river, while I was going out of my mind with worry." He obviously still remembered that vividly, because he went pale around the nostrils. "They reached the Temple just for a moment, dripping wet in their seventeenth-century costumes, before traveling on again to 1992. I didn't hear what had happened until their next visit."

My head was spinning with all these different dates. "What kind of a crime did they witness?"

Lucas moved his chair a little closer still. Behind his glasses, his eyes were dark and serious. "That's the point! Lucy and Paul saw Count Saint-Germain murder someone."

"The count?"

"Lucy and Paul had met the count only twice before, but they were sure it was him. After their initiation journey, they'd been introduced to him in the year 1784. The count himself decided on that date; he didn't want to meet the time travelers who would be born after him until near the end of his own life. I wouldn't be surprised if it was the same with you." He cleared his throat. "Will be the same with you. Whatever way around it is. Anyway, the Guardians traveled with Lucy and Paul and the chronograph specially to north Germany, where the count spent the last years of his life. I was with them myself. Will be with them. As Grand Master of the Lodge, would you believe it?"

I frowned. "Could we maybe . . . ?"

"I'm trying to think of too many things all at once, right? It's still more than I can grasp, knowing that these things are still going to happen although they took place long ago. Where were we?"

"How could the count commit a murder in 1602 . . . oh, I see! He did it on one of his own journeys back in time!"

"Yes, exactly. And when he was a very much younger man. It was an amazing coincidence that Lucy and Paul happened to be in just the same place at just the same time. If you can talk about coincidences at all in this connection. The count himself writes, in one of his many books, *Those who believe in coincidence have not understood the forces of destiny.*"

"Who did he murder? And why?"

Lucas looked around the café again. "That, my dear granddaughter, is something that we ourselves didn't know at first. It was weeks before we found out. His victim was none other than Lancelot de Villiers. Amber. The first time traveler in the Circle."

"He murdered his own ancestor? But why?"

"Lancelot de Villiers was a Flemish baron who moved to England with his whole family in 1602. The chronicles, and the writings of Count Saint-Germain that he left for the Guardians, say that Lancelot died in 1607, which threw us off the track for a while. But the fact is—I'll spare you the details of our detective work—the baron's throat was cut as he sat in his own coach in the year 1602. . . ."

"I don't understand," I murmured.

"I haven't been able to fit all the pieces of the jigsaw together myself yet," said Lucas, taking a pack of cigarettes out of his pocket and lighting one. "In addition, there's the fact that I never saw Lucy and Paul again after 24 September 1949. I suspect that they went back to a time before my own, taking the chronograph with them, or they'd have visited me by now. Oh, *damn* . . . don't look that way!"

"What's the matter? And how long have you been smoking?"

"Here comes Kenneth de Villiers with his battle-ax of a sister." Lucas tried to get into cover behind the menu.

"Just say we don't want to be disturbed," I whispered.

"I can't—he's my boss. In the Lodge and in everyday life. He owns those legal chambers. . . . If we're in luck, they won't see us."

We weren't in luck. A tall man in his mid-forties and a lady wearing a turquoise hat were making purposefully for our table. They sat down, unasked, on the two free chairs.

"Both of us playing hookey this afternoon, eh, Lucas?" said Kenneth de Villiers affably, slapping Lucas on the shoulder. "Not that I wouldn't have turned *two* blind eyes after you brought the Parker case to such an excellent conclusion yesterday. My congratulations again. I heard that you had a visitor from the country." His amber eyes were subjecting me to close scrutiny. I tried to look back as naturally as possible. It was weird the way the de Villiers men, with their pronounced cheekbones and straight, aristocratic noses, looked so like each other through the years. Kenneth was another impressive specimen, if not quite as good-looking as, say, Falk de Villiers in my own time.

"Hazel Montrose, my cousin," Lucas introduced me. "Hazel, meet Mr. and Miss de Villiers."

"We're brother and sister," said Miss de Villiers, giggling. "Oh, good, you have some cigarettes—I really must cadge one."

"I'm afraid we were just leaving," said Lucas as he gallantly gave her a cigarette and lit it for her. "I have to look through some files."

"But not today, my dear fellow, not today!" His boss's eyes had a friendly twinkle in them.

"It's so boring with only Kenneth," said Miss de Villiers, puffing the smoke from her cigarette out through her nostrils. "One can't talk to him about anything but politics. Kenneth, please order more tea for us all. Where do you come from, my dear?"

"Gloucestershire," I said, coughing slightly.

Lucas sighed, resigned. "My uncle, Hazel's father, has a large farm there with a lot of animals."

"Oh, how I love the country life," said Miss de Villiers enthusiastically. "And I do so love animals."

"Me too," I said. "Particularly cats."

0700h: Novice Cantrell, reported missing during the nocturnal Ariadne test, reaches the way out seven hours late, unsteady on his feet and smelling of alcohol, suggesting that although he failed the test, he found the lost wine cellar. For once, I allow him in on yesterday's password. Otherwise, no unusual incidents.

Report: J. Smith, Novice, morning shift

1312h: We see a rat. I am in favor of running it through with my sword, but Leroy feeds it the rest of his sandwich and christens it Audrey.

1515h: Miss Violet Purpleplum reaches the way out after taking a path unknown to us, a shortcut from the Royal Courts of Justice. She is word-perfect in the password of the day. At her request, Leroy escorts her up to the offices.

1524h: Audrey comes back. Otherwise, no unusual incidents.

Report: P. Ward. Novice, afternoon shift

1800h to 0000h: no unusual incidents

Report: N. Cantrell, Novice, evening shift

0000h to 0600: no unusual incidents.

Report: K. Elbereth, M. Ward, Novices

From *The Annals of the Guardians*
"Records of the Cerberus Watch"
24–25 July 1956

"Nam quod in iuventus non discitur, in matura aetate nescitur."

EIGHT

THE GUARD at the foot of the stairs was fast asleep with his head against the banister.

"Poor Cantrell," whispered Lucas as we stole past the sleeping man. "I'm afraid he'll never make the grade to Adept if he goes on drinking like a fish. . . . Still, all the better for us. Come on, quick!"

I was already breathless. We'd had to run the whole way back from the café. Kenneth de Villiers and his sister had kept us there forever, talking for what seemed like hours about country life in general; country life in Gloucestershire in particular (here I'd managed to steer the conversation around to some anecdotes about my cousin Madeleine and a sheep called Clarissa); about the Parker case (all I understood about that was that my grandfather had won it); about that cute little boy Charles, the heir to the throne (hello?); and about all the Grace Kelly films and the star's marriage to the Prince of Monaco. Now and then, I coughed and tried to interest them in the health risks of smoking, but I got nowhere. When we were finally able to leave the café, it was so late that I didn't even have time to go to the toilet, although I had pints of tea in my bladder.

"Another three minutes," gasped Lucas. "And there was so much else I wanted to say to you. If my wretched boss hadn't turned up—"

"I didn't know you *worked* for the de Villiers family," I said. "After all, you're the future Lord Montrose, you'll be a member of the Upper House of Parliament."

"Yes," replied Lucas gloomily, "but until I inherit from my father, I still have to earn a living for my family. And I was offered this job . . . never mind that, listen! Before Saint-Germain died, he censored everything he left to the Guardians: his secret writings, the letters, the chronicles, the entire lot. All the Guardians know is what Saint-Germain saw fit to tell them, and all the information that we do have obviously aims to get later generations putting all their efforts into closing the Circle. But the Guardians don't know the whole secret."

"Then you do?" I cried.

"Shh! No, I don't know it either."

We turned the final corner, and I flung open the door of the old alchemical laboratory. My stuff was lying on the table just where I'd left it.

"But I'm convinced that Lucy and Paul *do* know the secret. The last time we met, they were on the point of finding the missing documents." He looked at his watch. "Damn."

"Go on!" I begged him, as I snatched up my school bag and the flashlight. At the last moment I remembered to give him back the key. The familiar flip-flop sensation was already taking me over. "Oh, and please shave that mustache off, Grandpa!"

"The count had enemies who are mentioned only briefly in the Chronicles," gasped Lucas, speaking as fast as he could. "In particular, there was an old secret society with close ties to the Church that had its knife into him. It was called the Florentine Alliance, and in 1745, the year when the Lodge was founded here in London, the Alliance got its hands on some documents that Count Saint-Germain had inherited— Don't you think the mustache suits me, then?"

The room was beginning to spin around.

"I love you, Grandpa!" I called.

"Some documents showing, among other things, that reading the blood of all twelve time travelers into the chronograph isn't the whole story! The secret will be revealed only when—" I heard Lucas say, before I was swept off my feet.

A fraction of a second later, I was blinking at bright light. And I was close up to a white shirt front. Half an inch to the left, and I'd have landed right on Mr. George's feet.

I let out a small cry of alarm and took a few steps back.

"We must remember to give you a piece of chalk next time, to mark the spot where you land," said Mr. George, shaking his head, and he took the flashlight from my hand.

He hadn't been waiting for my return on his own. Falk de Villiers stood beside him; Dr. White sat on a chair at the table; the little ghost boy, Robert, was peering at me from behind his father's legs; and Gideon, with a large white plaster on his forehead, was leaning against the wall by the door.

At the sight of him, I had to take a deep breath.

He was in his usual attitude—arms crossed over his chest—but his face was almost as pale as his plaster, and the shadows under his eyes made the irises look unnaturally green. I felt an overpowering desire to run to him, fling my arms around him, and kiss his forehead better, the way I always used to with Nick when he hurt himself.

"Everything all right, Gwyneth?" asked Falk de Villiers.

"Yes," I said, without taking my eyes off Gideon. Oh, God, I'd missed him. Only now did I realize how much! Had that kiss on the green sofa been only a day ago? Not that you could describe it as *one* kiss.

Gideon looked back at me impassively, almost indifferently, as if he was just seeing me for the first time. Not a trace of yesterday was left in his eyes.

"I'll take Gwyneth upstairs so that she can go home," said Mr. George calmly, putting his hand on my back and propelling me gently past Falk to the door. And right past Gideon.

"Have you . . . are you all right again?" I asked.

Gideon didn't reply. He just looked at me. But there was something very wrong with the way he did it. As if I wasn't a person at all, only an object. Something ordinary and unimportant, something like a . . . a chair. Maybe he did have concussion after all, and now he didn't know who I was? I suddenly felt very cold.

"Gideon ought to be in bed, but he has to elapse for a few hours if we don't want to risk an uncontrolled journey through time," Dr. White brusquely explained. "But it's ridiculous to let him go alone—"

"Only to spend two hours in a peaceful cellar in 1953, Jake," Falk interrupted him. "On a sofa. He'll survive."

"How right you are," said Gideon, and his look became if anything even darker. Suddenly I felt terrible.

Mr. George was opening the door. "Come along, Gwyneth."

"Just a moment, Mr. George." Gideon was holding my arm. "There's one thing I'd like to know. What year did you send Gwyneth to?"

"Just now, you mean? Nineteen fifty-six. July 1956," said Mr. George. "Why?"

"Well—because she smells of cigarette smoke," said Gideon, and his grip on my arm tightened until it hurt. I almost dropped my school bag.

Automatically, I sniffed the sleeve of my blazer. He was right. Hours in that smoky café had left obvious clues behind. How on earth was I going to explain that?

All eyes in the room were on me now, and I realized that I needed to think up a good excuse in a hurry.

"Okay—I admit it," I said, looking at the floor. "I did smoke, just a little. But only three cigarettes. Honestly!"

Mr. George shook his head. "Gwyneth, surely I'd made it perfectly clear to you. You can't take—"

"I'm sorry," I said, interrupting him. "But it's so boring in that dark cellar, and a cigarette helps me not to get scared." I was trying my best to look embarrassed. "I collected the stubs carefully and brought them all back. You don't have to worry someone will find a pack of Marlboros and be surprised."

Falk laughed.

"It seems that our little princess here isn't quite such a good girl as she makes out," said Dr. White, and I breathed a sigh of relief. "Don't look so shocked, Thomas. I smoked my first cigarette at the age of thirteen."

"So did I. My first and also my last." Falk de Villiers was leaning over the chronograph again. "Smoking really isn't a good idea, Gwyneth. I'm sure your mother would be rather shocked if she knew."

Even little Robert nodded hard and looked at me reproachfully.

"It does your looks no good, either," added Dr. White. "You get bad skin and ugly teeth from smoking."

Gideon said nothing. But he still hadn't relaxed his firm grip on my arm. I forced myself to look him in the eye as naturally as possible, trying to summon up an apologetic smile. He looked back at me with his eyes narrowed, shaking his head very slightly. Then he slowly let go of me. I swallowed hard, because I suddenly had a lump in my throat.

Why was Gideon acting like this? Nice to me one moment, kind and affectionate, next moment chilly and unapproachable? It was more than anyone could bear. Well, I couldn't for one. What had happened down here, between him and me, had felt real. And right. And now all he could find to do was expose me to the entire team at the first chance he got? What was his idea?

"Come along," Mr. George told me again.

"I'll see you the day after tomorrow, Gwyneth," said Falk de Villiers. "Your big day."

"Don't forget to blindfold her," said Dr. White, and I heard Gideon laugh briefly as if Dr. White had made a bad joke. Then the heavy door closed behind me and Mr. George, and we were out in the corridor.

"You'd think he didn't like smokers," I said quietly, though I felt like bursting into floods of tears.

"Let me put the blindfold on, please," said Mr. George, and I stood still until he had tied the scarf into a knot behind my head. Then he took my school bag from me and carefully helped me forward. "Gwyneth . . . you really must be more careful."

"A couple of cigarettes won't kill me stone dead this minute, Mr. George."

"That's not what I meant."

"What did you mean, then?"

"I meant you should be careful about showing your feelings."

"What? What feelings?"

I heard Mr. George sighing. "My dear child, even a blind man could see that you . . . you really should take care where your feelings for Gideon are concerned."

"But I—" I stopped. Obviously Mr. George saw more than I'd given him credit for.

"Relationships between two time travelers have never turned out well," he said. "Nor, come to that, have any relationships at all between the de Villiers and Montrose families. In times like these, we have to keep reminding ourselves that, fundamentally, no one is to be trusted." Maybe I was only imagining it, but I thought his hand on my back was trembling. "Unfortunately it's an incontrovertible fact that sound common sense flies out of the window as soon as love comes in through the door. And sound common sense is what you need most of all at this point. Careful, there's a step coming."

We made our way up from the chronograph room in silence, and then Mr. George took off the blindfold. He looked at me very seriously. "You can do it, Gwyneth. I firmly believe in you and your abilities."

His round face was covered with little beads of perspiration again. I saw nothing but concern for me in his bright eyes—it was the same with my mother when she looked at me. A huge wave of affection swept over me.

"Here's your signet ring," I said. "How old are you, Mr. George? If you don't mind me asking."

"Seventy-six," said Mr. George. "It's no secret."

I stared at him. Although I'd never thought of it before, I'd have guessed he was a good ten years younger. "Then in 1956 you were . . . ?"

"Twenty-one. That was the year when I began work as a legal clerk in the chambers here and became a member of the Lodge."

"Do you know Violet Purpleplum, Mr. George? She's a friend of my great-aunt's."

Mr. George raised one eyebrow. "No, I don't think I do. Come along, I'll take you to your car. I'm sure your mother will be anxious to see you."

"Yes, I think so, too. Mr. George . . . ?"

But Mr. George had already turned to move away. I had no option but to follow him. "You'll be collected from home tomorrow," he said. "Madame Rossini needs you for a fitting, and after that Giordano will try teaching you a few things. And after that, you'll have to elapse."

"Sounds like a wonderful day," I said wearily.

"BUT THAT . . . that's not *magic!*" I whispered, shocked.

Lesley sighed. "Not in the sense of hocus-pocus magical rituals, maybe, but it's a magical ability. The magic of the raven."

"More of an eccentricity, if you ask me," I said. "Something that makes people laugh at me—and anyway no one believes I can do it."

"Gwenny, it's not eccentric to have extrasensory perception. It's a gift. You can see ghosts and talk to them."

"And demons," Xemerius pointed out.

"In mythology, the raven stands for the link between human beings and the world of the gods. Ravens carry messages between the living and the dead." Lesley turned her file my way, so that I could read what she had found on the Internet about ravens. "You have to admit your abilities suit that very well."

"Your hair too," said Xemerius. "Black as a raven's wings."

I was biting my lower lip. "But in the prophesies it sounds so—oh, I don't know, so important and powerful and all that. As if the magic of the raven was some kind of secret weapon."

"It could be that as well," said Lesley. "You have to stop thinking it's only a kind of strange eccentricity allowing you to see ghosts."

"And demons," Xemerius repeated.

"I'd love to know exactly what those prophesies say," said Lesley. "It would be so interesting to have the full text."

"Charlotte can certainly rattle them all off by heart," I said. "I think she learnt them when she was being taught the mysteries. And everyone talks about them in rhyme. The Guardians. Even my mum. And *Gideon*."

I quickly turned away so that Lesley wouldn't see my eyes suddenly filling with tears, but it was too late.

"Oh, sweetie, don't start crying again!" She handed me a tissue. "You're making too much of it."

"No, I'm not. Remember how you cried for days on end over Max?" I said, sniffing.

"Of course," said Lesley. "It was only six months ago."

"Well, now I can imagine how you felt at the time. *And* I suddenly understand why you wished you were dead."

"How stupid could I get! You sat with me the whole time telling me Max wasn't worth another thought, not after the way he'd behaved. And you told me to brush my teeth—"

"Yes, and we were listening to Abba's 'The Winner Takes It All' played in an endless loop."

"I can play that song for you," offered Lesley, "if it'd make you feel any better."

"It wouldn't. But you can hand me the Japanese vegetable knife. Then I can commit hara-kiri." I let myself drop on my bed, and closed my eyes.

"Girls always have to be so dramatic!" said Xemerius. "The boy's in a bad temper, looks grouchy because someone hit him on the head, and you think it's the end of the world."

"It's because he doesn't *love* me," I said despairingly.

"You can't know that," said Lesley. "With Max, unfortunately, I did know, because half an hour after he dumped me, he was seen snogging in the cinema with that Anna. You can't accuse Gideon of doing a thing like that. He's rather . . . changeable, that's all."

"But why? You should have seen the way he looked at me! Kind of *repelled*. As if I was a . . . a woodlouse! I can't bear it."

"A moment ago, you said you were a chair." Lesley shook her head. "Come on, pull yourself together. Mr. George is right: love comes in at the window and common sense flies out. Listen, we're on the point of making a tremendous breakthrough!"

Earlier that morning, when she had just arrived and we were sitting comfortably on my bed together, Mr. Bernard had knocked at my bedroom door—something he never usually did—and put a tea tray down on my desk.

"A little refreshment for you young ladies," he had said.

I'd looked at him in astonishment. I couldn't remember ever having seen him up on this floor of the house before.

"Since you were asking about it recently, I took the liberty of searching in the library," Mr. Bernard had gone on, studying us gravely with his owlish eyes above the rim of his glasses. "And as I expected, I found what I wanted."

"What is it?" I'd asked.

Mr. Bernard had lifted the napkin on the tray to reveal a book lying there. *"The Green Rider,"* he had said. "If I remember correctly, this is what you were looking for."

Lesley had jumped to her feet and picked up the book. "Oh, but I've already looked at this in the public library," she said. "It's nothing special."

Mr. Bernard had smiled indulgently. "The reason you say that, I think, is that the copy you found in the public library was never the property of Lord Montrose. However, this one may interest you." Then he left the room, with a little bow, and Lesley and I had fallen on the book at once. A piece of paper on which someone had written masses of numbers in tiny handwriting had fluttered to the floor. Lesley's cheeks had turned red with excitement.

"Oh, my God, it's a code!" she had exclaimed. "How absolutely *wonderful*! I always wanted to find something like this. Now all we have to do is find out what it means."

"Right," said Xemerius, who was dangling from my

curtain rail. "I've heard that before. I think it fits the category of famous last words. . . ."

But it hadn't taken Lesley five minutes to crack the code and work out that the figures related to separate letters in the text. "The first number is always the page, the second is the line, the third is the word, the fourth is the letter, get it? Fourteen, twenty-two, six, three—that's page fourteen, line twenty-two, word six, and the third letter in that word." She shook her head. "What a cheap trick! People use this code in every other kids' book, as far as I remember. Never mind, that means the first letter is an *f.*"

Impressed, Xemerius had nodded. "Listen to your friend."

"Don't forget, this is a matter of life and death," said Lesley. "You think I want to lose my best friend just because she couldn't think straight after a bit of snogging?"

"My own opinion exactly!" That was Xemerius.

"This is important. You must stop crying and find out what Lucy and Paul discovered instead," Lesley went on forcefully. "If you get sent to elapse to 1956 again today— and you'll only have to ask Mr. George to fix that—you must insist on a private talk with your grandfather! What a crackpot idea to go out to a café! And this time you must write down all he tells you, every last little detail, understand?" She sighed. "Are you sure he said *Florentine Alliance*? I couldn't find anything useful online about that. We just have to get a look at those secret writings left to the

Guardians by Count Saint-Germain. If only Xemerius could move objects, he could search the archives—he'd simply have to go through the wall and read everything."

"That's right, so I'm useless. Go ahead and rub it in, why don't you?" said Xemerius, offended. "It's only taken me seven centuries to get used to not even being able to turn the pages of a book."

There was a knock at my door, and Caroline looked into the room. "Lunch is ready! Gwenny, you and Charlotte are being collected in an hour's time."

I groaned. "Charlotte as well?"

"Yes, that's what Aunt Glenda said. They're imposing on poor Charlotte, she said, making her coach people with no talent at all. Or something like that."

"I'm not hungry," I said.

"We'll be right down," said Lesley, digging me in the ribs. "Come along, Gwenny. You can wallow in self-pity later. Right now you need something to eat!"

I sat up and blew my nose. "My nerves aren't strong enough to listen to Aunt Glenda's nasty remarks. And we only just got started on the code!"

"I'll keep working on it, don't worry. Meanwhile, you're going to need strong nerves in the immediate future." Lesley pulled me to my feet. "Charlotte and your aunt will be good practice for when the going gets tough. If you survive lunch, you can get through that soirée, no problem."

"And if not, you can always commit hara-kiri," said Xemerius.

* * *

MADAME ROSSINI clasped me to her ample bosom when I arrived. "My leetle swan-necked beauty, 'ere you are at last. I 'ave missed you."

"I've missed you, too," I said, and I meant it. The mere presence of Madame Rossini, with her overflowing kindness and her wonderful French accent (*leetle swan-necked beauty*! If only Gideon could hear that!), was invigorating and reassuring at the same time. She was balm to my wounded self-esteem.

"You will be *enchantée* when you see what I 'ave made for you. Monsieur Giordano, 'e almost wept when 'e saw your clothes, zey are so beautiful."

"I believe you," I said. Giordano would have been weeping because he couldn't wear the clothes himself. Still, he'd been reasonably friendly today, not least because I did rather well with the dancing this time—and thanks to being prompted by Xemerius, I'd been able to say which great lords of the time supported the Tories and which the Whigs. (Xemerius had simply looked over Charlotte's shoulder from behind and read her list.) Also thanks to Xemerius, I was word-perfect in my own cover story— Penelope Mary Gray, born 1765—including all the first names of my dead parents. I was still not much good with a fan, but Charlotte had made the constructive suggestion that I didn't need to carry one at all.

At the end of the lesson, Giordano had handed me another list full of words that I mustn't under any circumstances use. "Learn those by heart for tomorrow," he had said in his nasal voice. "Remember, there are no buses in the eighteenth century, no news anchormen, no Hoovers, nothing is super, wicked, or cool, they knew nothing about splitting the atom, colllagen skin creams, or holes in the ozone layer."

Who'd have thought it? I tried to imagine why on earth, when I was at an eighteenth-century soirée, I'd want to come out with a sentence about anchormen, holes in the ozone layer, and collagen skin creams. However, I politely said, "Okay," which had Giordano screeching, "Nooo! Not okay. There was no *okay* in the eighteenth century, you stupid girl."

Madame Rossini laced the corset behind my back. Once again I was surprised to find how comfortable it was. You automatically stood up straight wearing something like that. She strapped a padded wire framework around my hips (the eighteenth century must have been a very relaxing time for women with big bums and broad hips), and then put a dark red dress over my head. She did up a long row of little hooks and buttons behind me, while I stroked the heavy, embroidered silk, admiring it. Wow, it was so amazing!

Madame Rossini walked slowly around me, and a satisfied smile spread over her face. "Entrancing. *Magnifique*."

"Is this the ball dress?" I asked.

"No, it is ze gown for ze soirée." Madame Rossini pinned tiny, perfectly formed silk roses in place around the deep décolletage. As her mouth was full of pins, she spoke indistinctly through her teeth. "Zere, you can wear your 'air unpowdered, and ze dark color will look fantastic with ze red. Just as I thought!" She winked at me mischievously. "You will attract attention, my swan-necked beauty, *n'est-ce pas*—although zat is not ze idea, but what can I do?" She wrung her hands, but unlike Giordano when he was wringing his, dumpy little Madame Rossini looked cute. "You *are* a leetle beauty, zere is no denying it, putting you in neutral colors would not 'elp. Zere we are, little swan neck, and now for ze ball dress."

The ball dress was pale blue with cream embroidery and frills, and it fitted as perfectly as the red dress. It had, if possible, an even more spectacularly plunging neckline than the red dress, and the skirt swung around me for what looked like yards. Madame Rossini weighed up my hair, which was in a braid today, in both hands, looking worried. "I am not sure 'ow we should do ze 'air. A wig is not comfortable, not with all that 'air of your own 'idden underneath. But your 'air is so dark, with powder it will probably be a 'ideous gray. *Quelle catastrophe!*" She frowned. "Never mind. With powder you would be à la mode—but dear 'eaven, what a 'orrible mode!"

For the first time that day, I couldn't help smiling. *'Ideous! 'Orrible!* Oh, how right she was. It wasn't just the fashionable hair powder, Gideon was *'ideous* and *'orrible* as well, so far as I was concerned, and from now on, I was going to look at him that way, so there!

Madame Rossini didn't seem to realize how good she was for my peace of mind. She was still getting indignant about the eighteenth century. "Boys, girls, 'aving to powder their 'air to look like their *grandmères*—'orrible. Now try on zese shoes. You must dance in zem, remember, but we still 'ave time to get zem altered."

Like the corset, the shoes, embroidered red for the red dress, pale blue with golden buckles for the ball dress, were surprisingly comfortable, although they looked as if they came out of a museum. "Those are the most beautiful shoes I've ever worn in my life," I said appreciatively.

"I should 'ope so," said Madame Rossini, beaming all over her face. "Zere, my little angel, you are ready. Mind you 'ave a good night's rest tonight. You will 'ave an exciting day tomorrow." As I slipped back into my jeans and favorite dark blue pullover, she draped the dresses over her headless tailor's dummies. Then she looked at the clock on the wall and frowned in annoyance. "Oh, zat unreliable boy! 'E was to be 'ere fifteen minutes ago!"

My pulse rate instantly shot up. "Gideon?"

Madame Rossini nodded. "'E do not take zis seriously, 'e think it does not matter 'ow 'is breeches fit. But ze fit of ze breeches is very, very important."

'Ideous! 'Orrible! I tested my new mantra.

Someone knocked on the door. Only a slight sound, but all my good intentions vanished into thin air.

Suddenly I couldn't wait to see Gideon again. And at the same time, I was scared to death of meeting him. I wouldn't survive those dark glances of his a second time.

"Ah," said Madame Rossini. "'Ere 'e is. Come in!"

My whole body stiffened, but it wasn't Gideon coming through the doorway, it was red-haired Mr. Marley. Nervous and awkward as usual, he stammered, "I'm to take the Ruby . . . er, Miss Gwyneth down to elapse."

"Okay," I said. "We'll be finished with this in a moment." Behind Mr. Marley, Xemerius was grinning at me. I'd sent him away before the fittings began.

"I just flew through a real live home secretary," he said cheerfully. "It was cool!"

"And where is ze boy?" asked Madame Rossini crossly. "'E was coming for a fitting!"

Mr. Marley cleared his throat. "I saw the Diam—Mr. de Villiers just now with the other Rub—with Miss Charlotte. He was with his brother."

"*Tiens!* I couldn't care less about zat," said Madame Rossini, annoyed.

I could, though, I thought. In my mind I was texting Lesley. Just one word: *hara-kiri*.

"If 'e does not come 'ere at once, I am complaining of 'im to ze Grand Master," said Madame Rossini. "Where's my telephone?"

"I'm sorry," murmured Mr. Marley. Looking embarrassed, he was turning the black scarf this way and that in his hands. "May I . . . ?"

"Go ahead," I said, sighing, and I let him blindfold me.

"I'm afraid that young hopeful is telling the truth," said Xemerius. "Your sparkly-stone friend is flirting with your cousin for all he's worth. So's his pretty brother. What do boys see in redheads? I think they're all going off to the cinema. I didn't want to tell you myself in case you started crying again."

I shook my head.

Xemerius looked up at the ceiling. "I could keep an eye on them for you. Would you like that?"

I nodded vigorously.

All the way down to the cellar Mr. Marley persistently kept silent, and I was deep in my own gloomy thoughts. Not until we'd arrived in the chronograph room and Mr. Marley took off the blindfold did I ask, "Where are you going to send me today?"

"I . . . we're waiting for Number Nine, I mean Mr. Whitman," said Mr. Marley, looking at the floor instead of meeting my eyes. "Of course I don't have permission to set the chronograph myself. Please sit down."

But as soon as I had sat down on a chair, the door opened again and Mr. Whitman came in. With Gideon right behind him.

My heart missed a beat.

"Hello, Gwyneth," said Mr. Whitman, with his most charming squirrel smile. "Good to see you." He pushed back the tapestry that hid the safe. "Right, so now we'll send you off to elapse."

I scarcely heard what he was saying. Gideon still looked very pale, but much better than yesterday evening. The thick white plaster was gone, and I could see the wound going up to his hairline. It was about four inches long and was now held together by lots of narrow strips of plaster. I waited for him to say something, but he just looked at me.

Xemerius came leaping through the wall and landed right beside Gideon. I gasped with alarm.

"Oops. Here he is already," said Xemerius. "I wanted to warn you, sweetheart, but I couldn't decide which of them to follow. Obviously Charlotte's taken over babysitting duties for Gideon's little brother this afternoon. They've gone off to eat ices, and then they're going to the cinema. Looks to me like cinemas are the haystacks of the modern era."

"Everything all right, Gwyneth?" asked Gideon, raising one eyebrow. "You look nervous. Would you like a cigarette to calm your nerves? What was your favorite brand, did you say? Marlboros?"

I could only stare at him speechlessly.

"Leave her alone," said Xemerius. "Can't you see she's unhappy in love, bonehead? All because of you! What are you doing here, anyway?"

Mr. Whitman had taken the chronograph out of the safe and put it on the table. "Then let's see where to send you today . . ."

"Madame Rossini is expecting you for a fitting, sir," said Mr. Marley, turning to Gideon.

"Damn," said Gideon, put off his stroke. He looked at his watch. "I totally forgot it. Was she very cross?"

"She did seem rather annoyed," said Mr. Marley. At that moment the door opened again, and Mr. George came in. He was out of breath, and as always when he'd been making an effort, his bald patch was covered with tiny beads of sweat. "What's going on here?"

Mr. Whitman frowned. "Thomas? Gideon said you were still deep in conversation with Falk and the home secretary."

"So I was. Until I had a call from Madame Rossini and heard that Gwyneth had already been fetched to go and elapse," said Mr. George. This was the first time I'd seen him really angry.

"But—Gideon said you'd asked us to—" said Mr. Whitman, clearly confused.

"I hadn't! Gideon, what's going on?" All the kindliness had vanished from Mr. George's little eyes.

Gideon had crossed his arms over his chest. "I thought you might be glad if we relieved you of that task," he said smoothly.

Mr. George mopped the beads of sweat off with his handkerchief. "How very thoughtful of you," he said, with a distinct sarcastic undertone. "But there was no need for that. You'd better go straight up to Madame Rossini."

"I'd be happy to go with Gwyneth," said Gideon. "After yesterday's events, it might be better for her not to be on her own."

"Nonsense," said Mr. George. "There's no reason to suppose there's any danger for her, as long as she doesn't travel too far back."

"Quite true," said Mr. Whitman.

"Like for instance to the year 1956?" asked Gideon slowly, looking Mr. George straight in the eyes. "I was leafing through the *Annals* this morning, and I must say the year 1956 certainly sounds peaceful enough. The reports of the men on guard say *no unusual incidents* more often than anything else. A report like that is music to our ears, wouldn't you say?"

By now my heart was in my mouth. The way Gideon was acting, he must have found out what I'd really been doing yesterday. But how on earth *could* he know? After all, I'd only smelt of cigarette smoke, which might be suspicious but couldn't possibly have told him what had really happened back in 1956.

Mr. George returned his glance without batting an eyelash. At the most, he looked slightly irritated. "That wasn't a request, Gideon. Madame Rossini is waiting. Marley, you can go too."

"Yes, Mr. George, sir," muttered Mr. Marley. He almost saluted.

When the door had latched shut behind Marley, Mr. George, eyes flashing, looked at Gideon. Mr. Whitman, too, was looking at him in surprise.

"What are you waiting for?" asked Mr. George coolly.

"Why did you let Gwyneth land in the afternoon, in broad daylight? Isn't that against the rules?" asked Gideon.

"Uh-oh," said Xemerius.

"Gideon, it is not your—" Mr. Whitman began.

"It makes no difference what time of day or night she landed," Mr. George interrupted him. "She traveled to a locked room in the cellars."

"I was scared," I said quickly, and perhaps my voice was a little too shrill. "I didn't want to be alone in that cellar in the middle of the night, right beside the catacombs—"

Gideon turned his gaze briefly to me, raising one eyebrow again. "Ah, yes, you're such a timid, shrinking little thing. I'd quite forgotten." He laughed softly. "Nineteen fifty-six—that was the year when you became a member of the Lodge, wasn't it, Mr. George? What a strange coincidence."

Mr. George frowned.

"I don't see what you're getting at, Gideon," said Mr. Whitman. "But I would suggest you go up to Madame Rossini now. Mr. George and I will look after Gwyneth."

Gideon looked at me again. "Let *me* make the following suggestion: I get the fitting over with, and then you can simply send me on to join Gwyneth, never mind where or when. Then even if it's night, she won't have to be scared of anything."

"Except you," said Xemerius.

"You've already fulfilled your quota for today," pointed out Mr. Whitman. "However, if Gwyneth is afraid . . ." He looked at me sympathetically.

I couldn't bear him a grudge for that. I supposed that I really did look kind of terrified. My heart was still in my mouth, and I was totally unable to say anything.

"Well, I don't mind if we do it that way," said Mr. Whitman, shrugging. "Any objections, Thomas?"

Mr. George slowly shook his head, although he looked as if he wanted to do the opposite.

A smile of satisfaction spread over Gideon's face, and he finally moved from his rigid position beside the door. "See you later, then," he told me triumphantly. It sounded like a threat.

When the door closed behind him, Mr. Whitman

sighed. "He's been acting very strangely since he got that knock on the head, don't you think, Thomas?"

"Definitely very strangely," said Mr. George.

"Maybe we should talk to him, mention the tone to be taken with senior members of the Lodge," said Mr. Whitman. "For his age, he is extremely . . . ah, well. He's under great pressure. We have to take that into consideration." He looked at me encouragingly. "Well, are you ready, Gwyneth?"

I stood up. "Yes," I said. I was lying through my teeth.

The raven red, on ruby pinions winging
its way between the worlds, hears dead men singing.
It scarce knows its strength, the price it scarce knows,
but its power will arise and the Circle will close.

The lion—as proud as the diamond bright,
Though the spell may be clouding that radiant light—
In the death of the sun what's amiss will then mend,
While the raven, in dying, discloses the end.

From the Secret Writings of
Count Saint-Germain

NINE

I HADN'T ASKED what year they'd sent me to, because it made no difference anyway. In fact, the place looked the same as on my last visit. The green sofa still stood in the middle of the room, and I cast it an angry glance, as if everything was all that sofa's fault. Chairs were stacked up against the wall where Lucas had made his hiding place for the key, the same as last time, and I struggled with myself. Should I clear out the hiding place? If Gideon suspected its existence—and he definitely did—then searching the room was the first thing he'd think of, right? I could put the contents of the hidey-hole behind the loose brick out in the corridors somewhere, and come back into the room before Gideon arrived.

I began frantically pushing the chairs aside, but then I changed my mind. First, I couldn't hide the key outside the room, because I'd have to lock the door again, and second, even if Gideon did find the hiding place, how was he going to prove that it was meant for me? I'd simply make myself look silly.

Carefully, I put the chairs back where they had been before, wiping away any telltale traces I'd left in the dust. Then I made sure the door really was locked and sat down on the green sofa.

I was feeling rather like I did four years ago over that frog incident, when Lesley and I had to wait in Mr. Gilles the principal's room until he had time to tell us off. We hadn't really done anything wrong. It was Cynthia who had run over the frog on her bike. She didn't seem to have any guilty conscience about it—"It was only a silly old frog"—so Lesley and I got angry and decided to avenge the frog. We were going to bury it in the park, but first, since it was dead already, we thought it might shake Cynthia up and make her a little more sensitive to frogs in future if she saw it again in her soup. No one could have guessed that the sight would send her into a fit of hysterical screaming. . . . Mr. Gilles, anyway, had treated us like a couple of serious offenders, and unfortunately he had never forgotten the incident. If he met us somewhere in the corridors, even today, he always said, "Aha, the evil-minded frog girls," and then we felt terrible all over again.

I closed my eyes for a moment. There was no reason for Gideon to treat me like that. I hadn't done anything bad. They all kept saying I wasn't to be trusted, they blind-folded me, no one would answer my questions—so it was only natural for me to try finding out what was really going on here for myself, wasn't it?

Where was Gideon, anyway? The electric bulb hanging from the ceiling was fizzing; the light flickered for a moment. It was very cold down here. Maybe they'd sent me to one of those cold postwar winters that Aunt Maddy was always talking about. Great. Winters when the water pipes froze and dead animals lay about the streets frozen stiff. I tested my breath to see if it would form little white clouds in the air in front of me. But it didn't.

The light flickered again. I was getting scared. Suppose I suddenly found myself sitting here in the dark? This time no one had thought of giving me a flashlight—in fact you couldn't say I'd been treated with any consideration at all. I felt sure the rats would come out of their holes in the dark. Maybe they were hungry . . . and where there were rats, cockroaches wouldn't be far behind. Then there was the ghost of the one-armed Knight Templar, the one Xemerius had mentioned. He might feel like taking a little trip down here.

Fzzzzz.

That was the lightbulb.

I was gradually coming to the conclusion that Gideon's presence would at least be better than rats and ghosts. But he didn't arrive. Instead the lightbulb flickered in its death throes.

When I was scared in the dark as a child, I always used to sing, and I automatically did that now. First very quietly, then louder and louder. After all, there was no one here to listen in on me.

Singing helped. I didn't feel so scared, or so cold. After

the first few minutes the lightbulb even stopped flickering. It started again when I began on Adele songs, and it didn't seem to like Katy Perry, either. However, when I tried old Abba songs, it rewarded me with a steady, regular beam of light. A pity I couldn't remember more of them, particularly the words. But the lightbulb was ready to accept *lalala, one chance in a lifetime, lalalala.*

I sang for hours, or that's what it felt like. After "The Winner Takes It All," Lesley's ultimate unrequited-love song, I started again with "I Wonder." I danced around the room at the same time so as not to get too cold. After the third encore of "Mamma Mia," I felt sure that Gideon wasn't going to turn up.

Damn. I could have stolen out of the cellar and gone upstairs after all. I tried "Head over Heels," and when I got to "Wasting My Time," he was suddenly standing there beside the sofa.

I closed my mouth and looked at him accusingly. "Why are you so late?"

"I imagine it seemed a long time to you." His glance was still as cold and peculiar as a little while ago. He went over to the door and rattled the handle. "At least you had enough sense not to leave this room. You couldn't know when I might come after you."

"Ha, ha," I said. "Is that meant to be a joke?"

Gideon leaned back against the door. "Gwyneth, you needn't bother to act all innocent with me."

I could hardly bear that chilly expression. The green

eyes that I usually liked so much had gone the color of pea soup—the nasty sort we had in the school dining room, of course.

"Why are you being so . . . so horrible to me?" I asked. The lightbulb flickered again. It was probably missing my Abba songs. "You don't by any chance have a lightbulb with you, I suppose?"

"It was the cigarette smoke that gave you away." Gideon was playing with the flashlight he held in one hand. "So then I did a little research, and I put two and two together."

I swallowed. "What's so terrible about smoking a cigarette?"

"You didn't. And you can't tell lies half as well as you think. Where's the key?"

"What key?"

"The key that Mr. George gave you so that you could visit him and your grandfather in 1956." He took a step toward me. "If you're clever, you've hidden it somewhere in here, if not, then it's still on you." He went right up to the sofa, picked up the cushions, and threw them on the floor one by one. "Well, it's not here, anyway."

I stared at him, horrified. "Mr. George didn't give me any key! Really he didn't. And as for the cigarette smoke, that's totally—"

"It wasn't just cigarette smoke. You'd been somewhere near a cigar as well," he said calmly. He looked around the room, and his eyes lingered on the chairs stacked in front of the wall.

I was beginning to feel very cold again, and even the lightbulb seemed to be trembling worse than ever in sympathy. "I . . . ," I began uncertainly.

"Yes?" Now Gideon sounded positively friendly. "You smoked a cigar as well, did you? In addition to the three Marlboros? Is that what you were going to tell me?"

I said nothing.

Gideon bent down to shine the flashlight under the sofa. "Did Mr. George write the password on a piece of paper for you, or did you learn it by heart? And how did you get past the Cerberus Watch on the way back? They never mentioned it in the records."

"What on earth do you think you're talking about?" I said. I meant to sound outraged, but I'm afraid it came over more intimidated.

"Violet Purpleplum—what a very remarkable name, don't you agree? Ever heard it before?" Gideon had straightened up again and was looking at me. No, greengage jelly wasn't the right comparison for his eyes. They were a positively toxic green.

Slowly, I shook my head.

"That's funny," he commented. "And she's a friend of your family, too. When I happened to mention the name to Charlotte, by chance, she told me kind Mrs. Purpleplum always knitted scratchy scarves for you all."

Oh, damn Charlotte! Couldn't she ever keep her mouth shut? "No, that's wrong," I said all the same. "She knits the scratchy ones specially for Charlotte. The rest of us get nice soft scarves."

Gideon leaned against the sofa and crossed his arms. He shone the beam of the flashlight at the ceiling, where the bulb was still flickering nervously. "For the last time, where's the key, Gwyneth?"

"Mr. George didn't give me any key. I swear it," I said, with a desperate attempt at damage limitation. "He doesn't have anything to do with it."

"Oh, no? I told you before, I don't think you're a good liar." He shone the flashlight over the chairs. "If I were you I'd have tucked the key away behind a cushion somewhere."

Okay, so let him search the cushions. At least that would give him something to do until we traveled back. It couldn't be much longer now.

"On the other hand"—Gideon swung the beam around to shine it right on my face—"On the other hand, that might be a labor of Sisyphus."

I stepped aside and said, angrily, "Stop it!"

"And we shouldn't always draw conclusions from what we'd do ourselves," Gideon went on. His eyes looked darker and darker in the flickering light, and suddenly I felt afraid of him. "Maybe you simply put the key in your jeans pocket. Give it here." He put out his hand.

"I don't *have* a key, damn it!"

Gideon came slowly toward me. "Again, if I were you, I'd hand it over of my own accord. But like I said, we shouldn't draw conclusions about other people from ourselves."

At that moment the lightbulb finally fizzled out and expired.

Gideon was right in front of me, the beam of the flash-light shining somewhere on the wall. Apart from that beam, which acted as a spotlight, it was pitch-dark. "Well?"

"Don't you dare come any closer." I took a couple of steps back, until I came up against the wall. The day before yesterday he couldn't have been too close for my liking. But now I felt as if I were confronting a stranger. Suddenly I lost my temper. "What's the matter with you?" I spat. "I haven't done anything to you! I don't see how you can kiss me one day and then hate me the next. *Why?*" My tears were coming so fast that I couldn't keep them from streaming down my cheeks. A good thing he couldn't see that in the dark.

"Maybe because I don't like being told lies." In spite of my warning, Gideon was advancing on me, and this time, I couldn't retreat any further. "Particularly by girls who throw themselves at me one day and get me knocked over the head the next."

"What on earth are you talking about?"

"I *saw* you, Gwyneth."

"What? Saw me where?"

"When I traveled back in time yesterday morning. I had a small errand to run, but I'd gone only a couple of yards when you were suddenly standing there in front of me—like a mirage. You looked at me and smiled as if you were pleased to see me. Then you turned and disappeared around the next corner."

"When is this supposed to have been?" I was so con-fused that I stopped crying for a few seconds.

Gideon ignored my question. "When I went around the same corner a moment later, I was hit over the head, so I'm afraid I was in no position to have a conversation with you to clear things up."

"You think . . . you think *I* knocked you out?" The tears were flowing again.

"No," said Gideon. "I don't think that. You weren't holding anything when I saw you, and I doubt whether you could have hit so hard. No, you just lured me around the corner because someone was waiting for me there."

Impossible. Totally, absolutely impossible.

"I'd never do a thing like that," I finally managed to say reasonably clearly. "Never!"

"Yes, I was a little shocked myself," said Gideon in an offhand tone. "When I was thinking we were . . . friends. But when you came back from elapsing yesterday evening smelling of cigarette smoke, it occurred to me that you might have been lying to me all along. Now, give me that key!"

I wiped the tears off my cheeks. Unfortunately more kept coming. I only just managed to suppress a sob, hating myself even more for crying. "If that's true, then why did you tell everyone you hadn't seen who hit you?"

"Because it's true. I didn't see who it was."

"But you didn't say anything about me, either. Why not?"

"Because I didn't want Mr. George to . . . you're not *crying*, are you?" The beam of the flashlight shone on my face again, dazzling me so that I had to close my eyes. I probably looked like a chipmunk, all stripy. Why had I bothered to put on mascara?

"Gwyneth." Gideon switched off the flashlight.

Now what? A body search in the dark?

"Go away," I said, sobbing. "I do *not* have any key on me, I swear I don't. And whoever you saw, it can't have been me. I would never, *never* let anyone hurt you."

Although I couldn't see a thing, I sensed that Gideon was standing right in front of me. His body warmth was like a radiant heater in the darkness. When his hand touched my cheek, I flinched. He quickly withdrew it again.

"I'm sorry," I heard him whisper. "Gwen, I . . ." Suddenly he sounded helpless, but I was far too upset to feel any kind of satisfaction.

I don't know how much time passed as we simply stood there. I was still shedding floods of tears. Whatever he was doing, I couldn't see it.

After a while, he switched the flashlight on again, cleared his throat, and shone the beam on his watch. "Another three minutes before we travel back," he said in a matter-of-fact tone. "You'd better come away from that corner, or you'll be landing on the chest in the chronograph room." He went back to the sofa and picked up the cushions he had thrown on the floor. "You know, of all the Guardians, Mr. George has always struck me as one of the most loyal. Someone to be trusted whatever happened."

"But Mr. George really didn't have anything at all to do with it," I said, hesitantly moving away from my corner. "It wasn't like that at all." I mopped the tears off my face with the back of my hand. I'd better tell him the truth so that at least he couldn't suspect poor Mr. George of disloyalty. "When I was sent to elapse alone for the first time, I met my grandfather here by chance." Okay, maybe not the *whole* truth. "He was looking for the wine cel—well, never mind that. It was a peculiar meeting, especially once we'd realized who we were. He left the key and the password in hiding in this room for my next visit, so that we could talk again. And that's why yesterday, I mean in 1956, I borrowed the name of Violet Purpleplum when I came back here. To meet my grandfather! He's been dead for a few years now, and I miss him dreadfully. Wouldn't you have done the same if you could? Talking to him again was so . . ." I fell silent once more.

Gideon said nothing. I stared at his outline and waited.

"How about Mr. George, then? He was already your grandfather's assistant at the time," he said at last.

"I did see him, but not for long, and my grandfather told him I was his cousin Hazel. He must have forgotten that ages and ages ago—to him it was an unimportant meeting a good fifty-five years in the past." I put my hand on my midriff. "I think . . ."

"So do I," said Gideon. He reached out his hand, but then obviously thought better of it. "Any moment now," he said, lamely. "Come another step or so this way."

The room began going around and around, then I was blinking at a bright light, swaying slightly on my feet, and Mr. Whitman said, "Ah, there you two are."

Gideon put his flashlight on the table and cast me a

brief glance. Maybe I was imagining it, but this time I thought there was something like sympathy in his eyes. I surreptitiously wiped my face once more, but all the same, Mr. Whitman could see I'd been crying. There was no one else here. Xemerius had probably felt bored and gone away.

"What's the matter, Gwyneth?" asked Mr. Whitman, in the kindly tone he used to suggest that he was a teacher to be trusted. "Is something wrong?" If I hadn't known better, I might have been tempted to indulge in more tears and pour out my heart to him. ("Horrible, horrible Gideon has been so, soooo nasty to me!") But I knew him too well. He'd sounded just the same last week when he asked us who had drawn the caricature of Mrs. Counter on the board. "I'd certainly say that the artist has talent," he had said, with a smile of amusement. So Cynthia (of course!) told him Maggie had done it, and Mr. Whitman had stopped smiling and entered a bad mark against Maggie's name in the class register. "I meant it about the talent, by the way," he had added. "Your talent for getting yourself into trouble, Maggie, is truly remarkable."

"Well?" he said now, with the same sympathetic and trustworthy smile. But I definitely wasn't falling for that one.

"A rat," I muttered. "You said there weren't any . . . and then the lightbulb gave out, and you hadn't given me a flashlight, and there I was all alone in the dark with that horrible rat." I very nearly added "I'm going to tell my mum," but I managed to stop myself just in time.

Mr. Whitman looked a little distressed. "I'm sorry," he

said. "We'll remember that next time." Then he went back to his usual instructive teacher's tone. "You'll be taken home now, and I recommend you go to bed early. Tomorrow is going to be a strenuous day for you."

"I'll take her to the car," said Gideon, picking up the black scarf that they always used to blindfold me. "Where's Mr. George?"

"In a meeting," said Mr. Whitman, frowning. "Gideon, I think you should consider your conversational tone. We let a good deal pass, because we know you're not having an easy time at present, but you ought to show a little more respect for the members of the Inner Circle."

Gideon's face gave nothing away, but he said politely, "You're right, Mr. Whitman. I'm sorry." Then he held his hand out to me. "Coming?"

I almost took it, too. A pure reflex action. And it gave me a pang to think I couldn't do it without losing face. I was on the point of bursting into tears again.

"Good night," I said to Mr. Whitman, staring at the floor as hard as I could.

Gideon opened the door.

"See you tomorrow," said Mr. Whitman. "And remember, both of you, plenty of sleep is the best preparation."

The door closed behind us.

"All alone in a dark cellar with a horrible rat, were you?" said Gideon, grinning at me.

I could hardly make any sense of it. Nothing but cold looks from him for the last two days—and in fact for the last couple of hours, glances that almost made me freeze as stiff as a board, like those poor animals in the postwar winters. And now this? A joke, as if everything was the same as before? Maybe he was a sadist and couldn't smile unless he'd been horrible to me first?

"Aren't you going to blindfold me?" I wasn't in any mood for more of his silly jokes, and I wanted him to know it.

Gideon shrugged. "I imagine you know the way by now. We can forget about the blindfold. Come on." Another friendly grin.

This was my first sight of the cellar corridors in our own time. They were neatly plastered, with lights let into the walls, some of them with movement detectors. The way up again was well lit.

"Not very impressive, is it?" said Gideon. "All the corridors leading out of the cellars have special doors and alarm systems fitted, and these days it's as safe as the Bank of England down here. But none of these security devices were fitted until the 1970s. Before that, you could go through half of London below the ground starting from here."

"I'm not interested," I said sullenly.

"What would you like to talk about, then?"

"Nothing." How could he act as if nothing at all had happened? His silly grin and all this small talk made me truly furious. I walked faster, and although I kept my lips firmly compressed, I couldn't keep the words from tumbling out of me. "I can't do it, Gideon! I can't make out the way you kiss me one moment and then act as if you loathed me like poison the next!"

Gideon said, after a brief pause, "I'd much rather be

kissing you the whole time than loathing you, but you don't exactly make it easy for me."

"I haven't done anything to you," I said.

He stopped. "Oh, come off it, Gwyneth! You don't seriously believe I'm swallowing that story about your grandfather? As if he just happened by chance to be in the room where you were elapsing! It's as unlikely as Lucy and Paul just happening to be at Lady Tilney's. Or those men attacking us in Hyde Park by chance."

"Oh, of course, I fixed all that in person, because I'd always wanted to stick a sword through someone. Not forgetting that I wanted to see what a man looks like with half his face shot away!" I snapped.

"What you may do in the future, and why—"

"Oh, be quiet!" I cried, angrily. "I'm sick and tired of all this! Ever since last Monday, I've felt like I was living in a nightmare that's never going to end. When I think I've woken up, I find I'm still dreaming. There are millions of questions that no one will answer going around in my head, and everyone expects me to do my best for something I don't understand one little bit!" I was walking on again, almost running, but Gideon easily kept up with me. There was no one on the stairs to ask us for the password. Why bother, if all the ways in and out were as secure as Fort Knox? I went up the stairs two steps at a time. "No one asked me if I wanted to be involved in this at all. I have to be pestered by crazy dancing masters and have my dear cousin show me all the things she can do but I'll never be able to learn, and you . . . you . . ."

Gideon shook his head. "Hey, can't you put yourself in my position for a change?" He was losing his own temper now. "It's the same for me! How would you act if you knew for certain that sooner or later, I was going to make sure someone attacked you and hit you over the head with a heavy instrument? In the circumstances, I don't suppose you'd still think I was lovable and innocent, would you?"

"I don't anyway!" I said firmly. "You know something? By now I could well imagine bringing that heavy instrument down on your head myself."

"Well, there we are!" said Gideon, grinning again.

I just snorted angrily. We were passing Madame Rossini's sewing room. Light fell out into the corridor from under the door; she was probably still at work on our costumes.

Gideon cleared his throat. "Like I said, I'm sorry. Can we talk to each other normally again?"

Normally! That was a joke.

"So what are you planning to do this evening?" he asked in his best casually friendly tone.

"Oh, practice dancing the minuet, of course, and just before I go to sleep, I'll think up sentences that don't contain words like *Hoover, jogging,* and *heart transplant,*" I replied caustically. "How about you?"

Gideon looked at his watch. "I'm going to meet Charlotte and my little brother and then . . . well, we'll see what we do. After all, it's Saturday evening."

Of course. They could do anything they liked. I'd had it up to here.

"Thank you for escorting me upstairs," I said in as

chilly a tone as I could muster. "I can find my way to the car by myself."

"As it happens, I'm going the same way," said Gideon. "And you can stop running. I'm supposed to avoid too much exertion. On Dr. White's instructions."

Even though I was so cross with him, my conscience did prick me, just for a moment. I took a surreptitious look at him. "Well, if someone hits you on the head with something around the next corner, don't go saying I lured you that way."

Gideon smiled. "No, you wouldn't do a thing like that *yet*."

I wouldn't do a thing like that ever was the thought that shot through my head. However badly he'd treated me. I would never allow anyone to hurt him.

The arched gateway ahead of us was lit briefly by the flash from a camera. Although it was dark, there were still a number of tourists out and about in the Temple. The black limousine I already knew was standing in its usual parking slot. When he saw us coming, the driver got out and opened the door for me. Gideon waited until I was in the car and then bent down to me. "Gwyneth?"

"Yes?" It was too dark for me to see his face properly.

"I wish you'd trust me more." That sounded so serious and honest that, for a moment, it deprived me of speech.

Then I said, "I wish I could." Only when Gideon had closed the door and the car was moving off did it occur to me that I'd have done better to say, "I wish you'd do the same with me."

* * *

MADAME ROSSINI'S eyes shone with enthusiasm. She took my hand and led me over to the full-length mirror on the wall so that I could see the result of her efforts. At first glance, I hardly knew myself. That was mostly because my hair, usually straight, had been curled into countless ringlets and pinned up into a towering pile on top of my head, like the way my cousin Janet had her hair done for her wedding. Single strands corkscrewed down to my bare shoulders. The dark red of the dress made my skin even paler than usual, but not as if I were sick; I looked radiant. Madame Rossini had discreetly powdered my nose and forehead, and rubbed a little rouge into my cheeks. Thanks to her skill with makeup, I had no shadows left under my eyes, even though I'd been up so late last night.

"Like Snow White in ze fairytale," said Madame Rossini, dabbing her eyes with a scrap of fabric. "Red as blood, white as snow, black as ebony. Zey will be cross with me if you look like ze dog's breakfast. Show me your fingernails— *oui, très bien*, clean and short. Now, shake your 'ead. No, shake it 'arder. Zis 'airstyle must last all evening."

"Feels a bit like wearing a hat."

"You will get used to it," said Madame Rossini, as she fixed the pile of hair with yet more spray. As well as about eleven pounds of ordinary hairpins holding it in place, there were some just for show, decorated with the same little roses as the neckline of the dress. They were cute! "There. Ready, my leetle swan-necked beauty! Shall I take photos again zis time?"

"Oh, yes please!" I looked around for my bag with the mobile in it. "Lesley would murder me if I didn't put this on record!"

"I'd like to take some of you both," said Madame Rossini, after she'd snapped me from all sides about ten times. "You and zat badly be'aved boy, just to show 'ow perfectly and also discreetly ze costumes match! I 'ave refused to argue about ze need for colored stockings again. Enough is enough!"

"The stockings I'm wearing aren't at all bad," I said.

"Zat is because zey may look like stockings of ze time, but elastane makes zem far more comfortable," said Madame Rossini. "In ze old days, a garter like zat probably cut your thigh in 'alf. Of course I 'ope no one will look under your skirt, but if zey do, zey cannot complain, *n'est-ce pas?*" She clapped her hands. "*Bien,* now I will call zem upstairs and say you are ready."

While she was phoning, I stood in front of the mirror again. I was feeling excited. I'd tried to put Gideon firmly out of my mind since this morning, and I'd been fairly successful, but only at the price of thinking about Count Saint-Germain all the time. My fears of meeting the count again were now mixed with excitement as I looked forward to the soirée, a feeling that I couldn't really explain to myself.

Mum had said Lesley could sleep over with us last night, so somehow it had turned into a nice evening. Analyzing what had happened in detail with Lesley and Xemerius had done me good. Maybe they were saying it only to cheer me up, but neither Lesley nor Xemerius thought there was any reason for me to jump off a bridge into the Thames because of unrequited love. They both said that considering the circumstances, Gideon's reasons for behaving the way he did had been justified, and Lesley said that in the interests of sexual equality, boys should be allowed their own bad moods, and she felt sure that deep down inside, he was a really nice guy.

"You don't know him!" I had shaken my head. "You're only saying that because you know I want to hear it!"

"Yes, and because I also want it to be true!" she had said. "If he turns out an absolute bastard in the end, I'll go and see him and beat him up in person! That's a promise!"

Xemerius had been late coming home, because I'd asked him to shadow Charlotte, Raphael, and Gideon first. Unlike him, Lesley and I didn't think it was at all boring to hear what Raphael was like.

"If you ask me, that lad is a little too good-looking," said Xemerius critically. "And doesn't he just know it!"

"Well, he's in good hands with Charlotte," said Lesley, satisfied. "So far our Ice Princess has managed to take the joys of life out of everyone."

We'd perched on my big window seat while Xemerius sat on the table, curled his tail neatly around him, and began on his report.

First Charlotte and Raphael had gone out for an ice, then to the cinema, and finally they'd met up with Gideon in an Italian restaurant. Lesley and I had wanted to know every tiny detail, from the title of the film to the pizza toppings, plus every word they had said. According to Xemerius, Charlotte and Raphael had insisted on talking at cross-purposes the whole time. While Raphael wanted to know the differences between French and English girls and how far English girls would go, Charlotte had droned on forever about the winners of the Nobel Prize for Literature over the last ten years, with the result that Raphael had been visibly bored and occupied himself with ostentatiously looking at other girls. And at the cinema, much to the surprise of Xemerius, Raphael didn't even try making a grab at Charlotte. Far from it. After about ten minutes, he fell fast asleep and stayed asleep. Lesley said that was the best thing she'd heard in a long time, and I entirely agreed. Then, of course, we wanted to know whether Gideon, Charlotte, and Raphael had been talking about me in the Italian restaurant, and Xemerius—slightly reluctantly—had regaled us with the following conversation. I did a kind of simultaneous translation of it for Lesley.

Charlotte: *Giordano is terribly afraid Gwyneth will get everything wrong tomorrow that she can get wrong.*

Gideon: *Pass the olive oil, please.*

Charlotte: *Politics and history are a closed book to Gwyneth. She can't even remember names—they go in at one ear and straight out of the other. She can't help it, her brain doesn't have the capacity. It's stuffed with the names of boy bands and long, long cast lists of actors in soppy romantic films.*

Raphael: *Gwyneth is your time-traveling cousin, right? I saw her yesterday in school. Isn't she the one with long dark hair and blue eyes?*

Charlotte: *Yes, and that birthmark on her temple, the one that looks like a little banana.*

Gideon: *Like a little crescent moon.*

Raphael: *What's that friend of hers called? The blonde with freckles? Lily?*

Charlotte: *Lesley Hay. Rather brighter than Gwyneth, but she's a wonderful example of the way people get to look like their dogs. Hers is a shaggy golden retriever crossbreed called Bertie.*

Raphael: *That's cute!*

Charlotte: *You like dogs?*

Raphael: *Especially golden retriever crossbreeds with freckles.*

Charlotte: *I see. Well, you can try your luck. You won't find it particularly difficult. Lesley gets through even more boys than Gwyneth.*

Gideon: *Really? How many . . . er, boyfriends has Gwyneth had?*

Charlotte: *Oh, my God! This is kind of embarrassing. I don't want to speak ill of her, it's just that she's not very discriminating. Particularly when she's had a drink. She's done the rounds of almost all the boys in our class and the class above us. . . . I guess I lost track at some point. I'd rather not repeat what they call her.*

Raphael: *The school mattress?*

Gideon: *Pass the salt, please.*

When Xemerius had reached this point in his story, I'd jumped up at once to go down to Charlotte's room and strangle her, but Lesley wouldn't let me. She reminded me that revenge is a dish best eaten cold, and she wouldn't agree when I said my motive wasn't revenge, it was pure murderous bloodlust. She added that if Gideon and Raphael were even a quarter as bright as they were good-looking, they wouldn't believe a word Charlotte said anyway.

"I think Lesley really does look a bit like a golden retriever," Xemerius had said, and when I looked at him reproachfully he was quick to add, "I like dogs, you know I do! Such clever animals."

And Lesley really was clever. She had solved the mystery of the *Green Rider* book, although the result of all her efforts was rather disappointing. All she had come up with was another number code with two letters and funny little marks in it.

Five one zero three zero four one dot seven eight n comma zero zero zero eight four nine dot nine one w.

It was nearly midnight when we stealthily made our way right through the house and into the library. At least, Lesley and I stealthily made our way right through the house. Xemerius had flown on ahead.

We must have spent an hour searching the shelves for more clues. The fifty-first book in the third row . . . the fifty-first row, thirtieth book, page four, line seven, word eight . . . but wherever we tried beginning to count, nothing made sense. In the end we were just taking books out at random and shaking them, hoping for more notes to drop to the floor. But Lesley was confident, all the same. She'd written the code down on a piece of paper, and she kept taking it out of her jeans pocket and looking at it. "It must mean something," she murmured to herself. "And I'm going to find out what."

After that we finally went to bed. My alarm clock had roused me from my dreamless sleep in the morning—and from then on, I'd thought of almost nothing but the soirée.

"'Ere comes Mr. George to collect you," said Madame Rossini, bringing me back to the present. She handed me a little bag—the reticule, that would be—and I wondered whether to smuggle the vegetable knife into it at the last moment after all. I'd turned down Lesley's advice to tape it to my thigh. With my luck, I'd probably have hurt no one but myself, and how I was going to get the tape off my leg under the huge skirt in an emergency was a mystery to me anyway. When Mr. George came into the room, Madame Rossini was draping a large, lavishly embroidered shawl around my shoulders. She kissed me on both cheeks. "Good luck, my leetle swan-necked beauty," she said. "Mind you bring 'er back to me safe and sound, Monsieur George."

Mr. George gave a rather forced smile. He didn't seem quite as friendly as usual. "I'm afraid that's out of my hands, Madame Rossini. Come along, Gwyneth. There are a few people who want to meet you."

It was already early afternoon when we went another floor up to the Dragon Hall. Getting dressed and having my hair done had taken over two hours. Mr. George was unusually silent, and I concentrated on not tripping over the hem of my dress on the stairs. I remembered our last visit to the eighteenth century and thought how difficult it was going to be to escape from any men armed with swords in all these bulky clothes.

"Mr. George, could you tell me about the Florentine Alliance, please?" I asked on a sudden impulse.

Mr. George stopped. "The Florentine Alliance? Who mentioned that to you?"

"No one, really," I said, sighing. "But now and then, I catch people saying something about it. I was only asking because . . . well, I'm scared. It was those Alliance guys who attacked us in Hyde Park, wasn't it?"

Mr. George looked at me gravely. "Maybe, yes. In fact probably. But there's nothing for you to be afraid of. I don't think the two of you need fear an attack today. Together with the count and Rakoczy, we've taken all imaginable precautions."

I opened my mouth to say something, but Mr. George got in first. "Oh, very well, or you won't give me any peace: we do indeed have to assume that in the year 1782 there's a traitor among the Guardians, maybe the same man who leaked information in previous years that led to the attempts on Count Saint-Germain's life in Paris, Dover, Amsterdam, and Germany." He passed his hand over his bald patch. "But that man is never mentioned by name in the *Annals*. Although the count successfully crushed the Florentine Alliance, the traitor among the Guardians was never unmasked. Your visits to the year 1782 are intended to put that right."

"Gideon thinks Lucy and Paul may have had something to do with it."

"There are indeed indications that such an idea isn't too wide of the mark." Mr. George pointed to the door of the Dragon Hall. "But there's no time for us to go into more detail now. Whatever happens, keep close to Gideon, and if you do happen to get separated, hide somewhere you can wait safely until you travel back."

I nodded. Suddenly my mouth felt very dry.

Mr. George opened the door and let me go first. I could hardly get past him in my hooped skirt. The room was full of people staring at me, and I felt so embarrassed that the blood shot into my face. Apart from Dr. White, Falk de Villiers, Mr. Whitman, Mr. Marley, Gideon, and the unspeakable Giordano, there were five other men in dark suits, with serious expressions, all standing under the huge dragon on the ceiling. I wished Xemerius was here to tell me which of them was the home secretary and which was the Nobel Prize winner, but Xemerius had been sent off on another mission. (By Lesley, not me, but more about that later.)

"Gentlemen, may I introduce Gwyneth Shepherd to you?" announced Falk de Villiers solemnly. It was probably a rhetorical question. "She is our Ruby. The last time traveler in the Circle of Twelve."

"This evening traveling under the name of Penelope Gray, ward of the fourth Viscount Batten," added Mr. George, and Giordano murmured, "Probably to go down in history, after this evening, as the *Lady Without a Fan*."

I glanced quickly at Gideon, whose dark red embroidered coat really did go very well with my dress. To my great relief, he wasn't wearing a wig, because all tensed up as I was, I'd probably have burst into hysterical laughter at the sight of it. But there was nothing ridiculous about him. He looked simply perfect. His brown hair was tied back in a braid behind his head; one lock fell over his forehead as if by mistake, cleverly covering up his injury. As so often, I couldn't really interpret the expression on his face.

I had to shake hands with the unknown gentlemen one by one. Each told me his name (which went in at one ear and straight out of the other; Charlotte was right about my brain capacity), and I murmured something like "How do you do?" or "Good evening, sir," to each of them. All in all, they seemed a very serious bunch. Only one of them smiled. The others just looked as if they were about to have a leg amputated. The one who was smiling must have been the home secretary. Politicians do more smiling than other people, it's part of the job.

Giordano looked me up and down, and I was expecting some kind of comment, but instead he just sighed very heavily. Falk de Villiers wasn't smiling, either, although at least he said, "That dress really suits you beautifully, Gwyneth. The real Penelope Gray would have been glad to look as good as that. Madame Rossini has done wonderful work!"

"That's true—I've seen a portrait of the real Penelope Gray. No wonder she never married and she spent her life out in the wilds of Derbyshire," Mr. Marley blurted out. Next moment he went bright red and stared at the floor in embarrassment.

Mr. Whitman quoted Shakespeare—at least, I strongly suspected it was Shakespeare. Mr. Whitman was crazy about the man. Something like *Oh then, what graces in my love do dwell, that she can make a heaven into hell?* "No need to blush, Gwyneth," he added.

I gave him a cross look. Silly Mr. Squirrel! If I'd gone red before, it was certainly nothing to do with him. Apart from which I didn't understand the quotation—you could take it equally well as a compliment or the opposite.

Unexpectedly, Gideon came to my aid. "*The conceited man overestimates his own deserts,*" he told Mr. Whitman in a friendly tone. "Aristotle."

Mr. Whitman's smile turned a little tight-lipped.

"Mr. Whitman only meant to say how terrific you look," Gideon told me, and the blood promptly shot into my cheeks again.

Gideon acted as if he didn't notice. But when I glanced at him again a few seconds later, he was smiling to himself in a satisfied way. Mr. Whitman, on the other hand, looked as if he was having difficulty suppressing another quote from Shakespeare.

Dr. White looked at his watch. Little Robert was hiding behind his legs, gazing at me wide-eyed. His father looked at his watch. "It's about time we started off. The priest has a christening at four o'clock."

The *priest*?

"You're not traveling back to the past from the cellars here today," explained Mr. George. "You leave from a church in North Audley Street instead. That will save you time getting to Lord Brompton's house."

"And it will also minimize the danger of an attack on

the way there or back," said one of the strangers I'd met, earning himself a glance of annoyance from Falk de Villiers.

"The chronograph is ready," said Falk, pointing to a silver-handled chest standing on the table. "There are two limousines waiting outside. Well, gentlemen . . ."

"Good luck," said the man I thought was the home secretary. Giordano heaved another heavy sigh.

Dr. White, carrying a doctor's bag (what for?), held the door open. Mr. Marley and Mr. Whitman took one handle of the chronograph chest each and carried it out as solemnly as if it were the Lost Ark.

Gideon was beside me in a moment and gave me his arm. "Come on, young Penelope, let's introduce you to the cream of London society," he said. "Ready?"

No. I wasn't ready in the least. And Penelope was a horrible name. But I had no choice. I tried to seem as relaxed as possible as I looked up at Gideon. "Ready when you are."

I vow to be honorable and courteous,
show compassion and decency,
right wrongs,
help the weak,
and preserve the secrets
contained in the Golden Rules,
from this day to the day of my death.

FROM THE OATH OF THE ADEPTS,
CHRONICLES OF THE GUARDIANS,
VOL. 1: *THE KEEPERS OF THE SECRET*

TEN

WHAT I WAS MOST afraid of was seeing Count Saint-Germain again. The last time we met, I'd heard his voice in my mind, and his hand had squeezed my throat although he'd been standing more than a dozen feet away from me. *I don't know exactly what part you are playing, girl, or whether you are of any importance. But I will not have my rules broken.*

I could take it for granted that I'd broken some of his rules since then—although it had to be admitted that I didn't know what they were, which made me feel rather defiant. If no one could be bothered to explain any of these rules to me, or the reasons for them, they couldn't really be surprised if I didn't keep them.

But I was also afraid of all kinds of other things. I was secretly convinced that Giordano and Charlotte were right: I was going to make a total mess of pretending to be Penelope Gray, and everyone would realize that there was something wrong about me. For a moment, I couldn't even remember the name of the place she came from in Derbyshire. Something beginning with *B*. Or *P*. Or *D*. Or . . .

"Have you learnt the guest list by heart?" Mr. Whitman, next to me, wasn't exactly helping to calm me down. Why on earth would I learn the guest list by heart? I shook my head. Mr. Whitman responded with a slight sigh.

"I don't know it by heart either," said Gideon. He was sitting opposite me in the limousine. "It spoils the fun if you always know in advance who you'll be meeting."

I'd have loved to know if he felt as edgy as I did. Were the palms of his hands sweating, was his heart beating as fast as mine? Or had he traveled back to the eighteenth century so often that it was nothing special to him now?

"You're going to make your lip bleed, biting it like that," he said.

"I'm feeling . . . kind of nervous."

"I can see that. Would it help if I held your hand?"

I shook my head vigorously.

No, it would only make things worse, you idiot! Quite apart from the fact that I'm at a total loss to understand the way you're treating me now anyway! Not to mention our relationship in general. What's more, Mr. Whitman is looking at us like some kind of know-it-all squirrel!

I almost groaned aloud. Would I feel any better if I told him any of what I was thinking? I thought about doing just that for a moment, but I didn't.

At last we arrived outside the church. When Gideon helped me out of the car (in a dress like mine you needed a helping hand, if not two of them, for that maneuver), I noticed that this time he wasn't wearing a sword. How reckless of him!

Passersby looked at us curiously. In the porch, Mr. Whitman held the church door open for us. "Hurry up, please," he said. "We don't want to attract attention." No, sure, there was nothing likely to attract attention in two black limousines parking in North Audley Street in broad daylight so that men in suits could carry the Lost Ark out of the trunk of one of the cars, over the sidewalk, and into the church. Although from a distance the chest carrying it could have been a small coffin. . . . The thought gave me goose bumps.

"I hope at least you remembered the pistol," I whispered to Gideon.

"You have a funny idea of what goes on at a soirée," he said, in a normal tone of voice, arranging the scarf around my shoulders. "Did anyone check what's in your bag? We don't want your mobile ringing in the middle of a musical performance."

I couldn't keep from laughing at that idea, because just then my ringtone was a croaking frog. "There won't be anyone there who could call me except you," I pointed out.

"And I don't even know your number. Please may I take a look inside your bag?"

"It's called a reticule," I said, shrugging and handing him the little bag.

"Smelling salts, handkerchief, perfume, powder . . . excellent," said Gideon. "All just as it should be. Come along." He gave me the reticule back, took my hand, and led me through the church porch. Mr. Whitman bolted the door again behind us. Gideon forgot to let go of my hand once we were inside the church, which was just as well, because otherwise I'd have panicked at the last moment and run away.

In front of the altar, and under the skeptical gaze of the priest (in all his vestments, ready to conduct a church service), Falk de Villiers and Mr. Marley were taking the chronograph out of the Lost Ar—I mean its chest. Dr. White, striding around to measure the space, said, "Eleven steps to the left from the fourth column and then you can't miss it."

"I don't know whether I can guarantee that the church will be completely empty at six thirty," the priest said nervously. "The organist likes to stay a little longer, and there are some members of the congregation who stop to talk to me at the door on their way out, and I can't very well—"

"Don't worry," said Falk de Villiers. The chronograph was now standing on the altar. The afternoon sunlight coming through the stained-glass church windows made the jewels set in it look enormous. "We'll be here, helping you to get rid of your flock." He looked at us. "Are you two ready?"

Gideon finally let go of my hand. "I'll go first," he said. The priest's jaw dropped when he saw Gideon simply disappear in a whirling eddy of bright, clear light.

"Gwyneth." As Falk took my hand and inserted my

finger into the chronograph, he smiled encouragingly at me. "We'll meet again in exactly four hours' time."

"Let's hope you're right," I muttered, and then the needle was going into my flesh, the room filled with red light, and I closed my eyes.

When I opened them again, I staggered slightly, and someone was holding my shoulder to steady me. "It's all okay," Gideon whispered in my ear.

You couldn't see much. Only a single candle lit up the chancel, while the rest of the church lay in eerie darkness.

"Soyez les bienvenus," said a hoarse voice out of that darkness, and although I'd been expecting it, I jumped. A man's figure emerged from the shadow of a column, and in the candlelight I recognized the pale face of the count's friend Rakoczy. He reminded me of a vampire, just as he had at our first meeting; there was no brightness in his black eyes, and in the dim light, they looked like uncanny black holes again.

"Monsieur Rakoczy," said Gideon in French, bowing politely. "I am glad to see you. You've already met my companion."

"Of course. Mademoiselle Gray, for this evening. My pleasure." Rakoczy sketched a bow.

"Ah, très . . . ," I murmured, and then I gave it up. After all, you never knew what you might say by mistake in a foreign language, particularly when you were likely to get stuck speaking it.

"My men and I are escorting you to Lord Brompton's house," said Rakoczy.

There wasn't anything to be seen of these men of his, but the scary part was that I could hear them, breathing and moving in the darkness as we followed Rakoczy down the nave of the church and over to the door. I couldn't see anyone out in the street, either, although I looked around several times. It was cool, with a light drizzle of rain falling, and if there were any streetlights at all at this period, they'd all gone wrong this evening. It was so dark that I couldn't even see Gideon's face beside me properly, and all the shadows seemed to be coming alive, breathing, clinking slightly. My hand clutched Gideon's. I only hoped he wouldn't let go of me now!

"These are my men," whispered Rakoczy. "Good, battle-hardened Kurucs, every one. I am sure we'll be escorting you on the way back as well."

How reassuring.

It wasn't far to Lord Brompton's house, and the closer we came, the more the dismal gloom lifted. When we reached the fine house in Wigmore Street, it was brightly lit and looked really inviting, almost cozy. Rakoczy's men stayed behind in the shadows while he took us into the house, where we found Lord Brompton himself waiting in the big entrance hall. A grand staircase with curving banisters led up to the first floor. Lord Brompton was just as fat as I remembered him, and in the light of all the candles, his face shone greasily.

The hall was empty except for his lordship and four footmen lined up neatly beside a door, waiting for further instructions. The party we were going to was nowhere to be seen, but I could hear the muted sound of babbling voices, and a few bars of a tune played on a tinkling keyboard.

As Rakoczy bowed and withdrew, I realized why Lord Brompton was receiving us here before anyone else could talk to us. He said how glad he was to see us, and how much he had enjoyed our last meeting, but added that—er, well, it would be better not to mention that meeting in front of his wife.

"Just in case of any misunderstanding," he said. He kept winking as if he had something in his eye, and he kissed my hand at least three times. "The count tells me that you are from one of the most distinguished families in England, Miss Gray, and I do hope you will forgive my impertinence at our amusing conversation about the twenty-first century, and my *ridiculous* notion that you were an actress." He was still winking for all he was worth.

"I'm sure that was partly our own fault, said Gideon smoothly. "The count was doing his best to put you on the wrong track. And since we are on our own now, don't you think the count is a remarkable old gentleman? My foster sister and I are used to his jokes, but those who know him less well must often find him rather strange." He took my shawl off my shoulders, and handed it to one of the footmen. "Well, however that may be, we have heard that your salon contains an excellent pianoforte and has wonderful acoustics. We were delighted to receive Lady Brompton's kind invitation."

Lord Brompton spent a few more seconds staring at

my plunging neckline before he said, "And we are equally delighted to see you here. Come along. All the other guests are here." He offered me his arm. "Miss Gray?"

"My lord." I glanced at Gideon, and he smiled encouragingly as he followed us to the salon, which was on the other side of a handsome double door at the far end of the entrance hall.

I'd thought that a salon would be something like a living room, but the room we now entered could almost have rivaled our ballroom at home in Bourdon Place. A fire blazed in a large hearth on one of the longer walls, and a pianoforte stood in front of the heavily curtained windows. My eyes moved over delicate little tables with curving legs ending in feet like animal paws, sofas with colorful patterned upholstery, and chairs with gilded arms. The whole room was lit by hundreds of candles hanging and standing everywhere, lending it such a magical glitter that for a moment I was speechless with delight. Unfortunately the candles also lit up a great many strangers, and my admiration of the scene (remembering Giordano's stern warnings, I kept my lips firmly closed so as not to let my mouth drop open by mistake) was mingled with fear again. Was this supposed to be an intimate little evening party? If so, what would the ball be like?

I didn't get around to taking a closer look, because Gideon was firmly leading me on into the crowd. Many pairs of eyes examined us curiously, and a moment later, a small, plump woman who turned out to be Lady Brompton came hurrying toward us.

She wore a light brown dress trimmed with velvet, and her hair was hidden under a voluminous wig, which, considering all the candles here, must be a high-risk fire hazard. Our hostess had a nice smile—she welcomed us warmly. I automatically sank into a low curtsey, while Gideon took this opportunity of leaving me alone, or rather of letting Lord Brompton lead him farther into the throng. Before I could decide whether to feel cross about that, Lady Brompton was deep in conversation with me. Luckily I remembered the name of the place where I lived—where Penelope Gray lived, that is—just in time. Encouraged by Lady Brompton's enthusiastic nods, I assured her that it was a very quiet, peaceful spot, but short of the delightful entertainments that looked like positively overwhelming me here in London society.

"You won't think *that* anymore if Genoveva Fairfax gets a chance to run through her entire repertory on the pianoforte again today." A lady in primrose yellow came over to us. "In fact I am sure that you'll be longing for the simple pleasures of country life again."

"Oh, hush!" said Lady Brompton, but she giggled. "How unkind of you, Georgiana!" When she smiled at me in that conspiratorial way, she suddenly seemed quite young. How had she come to marry that fat old man?

"Unkind, maybe, but true!" The lady in yellow (such an unflattering color, even by candlelight) told me, lowering her voice, that at the last soirée where Miss Fairfax performed, her husband had fallen asleep and started snoring loudly.

"That can't happen today," Lady Brompton assured me. "After all, we have the extraordinary, mysterious Count Saint-Germain among our guests. He is going to delight us later by playing his violin, while Lavinia can hardly wait to sing to the accompaniment of our dear Mr. Merchant."

"Well, you'll have to make sure Mr. Merchant gets plenty to drink first," said the lady in yellow, giving me a broad smile and showing her teeth without a moment's hesitation. I automatically smiled just as broadly. There, I'd known it! Giordano was nothing but a stupid know-it-all!

Both ladies were acting much more naturally than I'd expected.

"Such a difficult balancing act!" sighed Lady Brompton, and her wig trembled slightly. "Too little wine, and Mr. Merchant won't perform on the pianoforte at all; too much, and he breaks into song himself—improper sailors' ditties. My dear, do you know Count Saint-Germain?" she asked me.

That brought me down to earth at once, and I instinctively looked around. "I was introduced to him a few days ago," I said, gritting my teeth to keep them from chattering. "My foster brother . . . er, knows him." I caught sight of Gideon standing near the fire in the hearth, talking to a slender young woman in the most beautiful green dress. They looked as if they'd known each other for a long time. She was laughing so much that you could see her teeth. They were lovely teeth, too, not rotten stumps with gaps in them, which was what Giordano had tried to persuade me all teeth looked like at this period.

"Isn't the count incredible? I could listen to him for hours on end when he tells his tales," said the lady in yellow, after informing me that she was Lady Brompton's cousin. "I particularly enjoy the stories he tells of France!"

"Yes, those *spicy* stories," said Lady Brompton. "Not for the innocent ears of a debutante, of course."

Searching the room with my eyes for the count, I found him sitting in a corner, talking to two other men. From a distance, he looked elegant and ageless, and as if he had sensed that I was looking at him, he turned his dark eyes on me.

The count was dressed like all the other men in the salon—he wore a wig, a frock coat, rather ridiculous knee breeches, and funny buckled shoes. But unlike the others, he didn't look to me as if he came straight out of some costume drama on film, and for the first time, I realized fully what I'd landed myself in here.

His lips curled into a smile, and I bowed my head courteously, while I felt I had goose bumps all over. I had difficulty suppressing an instinctive urge to raise my hand to my throat. I didn't want to go putting ideas into his head.

"Your foster brother is a very good-looking young man, my dear," said Lady Brompton. "Contrary to the rumors we have heard."

I took my eyes off Count Saint-Germain and looked at Gideon again. "Yes, you're right. He really is very . . .

good-looking." The lady in green seemed to think so, too. She was just straightening his cravat with a flirtatious smile. Giordano would probably have murdered me for such behavior. "Who is the lady who's fl—who's talking to him?"

"Lavinia Rutland, the loveliest widow in London."

"But there's no need to feel sorry for her," the primrose-yellow lady added. "She found consolation long ago in the arms of the Duke of Lancashire, much to the duchess's displeasure, and at the same time she's developed a taste for rising young politicians. Is your brother interested in politics?"

"I don't think they're talking politics at this precise moment," said Lady Brompton. "Lavinia looks as if she'd just been given a present to unpack." Once again, she looked Gideon up and down. "Well, rumor said he had a sickly constitution and a stout, clumsy figure. How delightful to find that rumor was wrong!" Suddenly a horrified expression crossed her face. "Oh, but you have nothing to drink!"

Lady Brompton's cousin looked around, saw a young man standing near us, and nudged him in the ribs. "Mr. Merchant? Make yourself useful, please, and bring us two glasses of Lady Brompton's special punch. And a glass for yourself, too. We want to hear you perform today."

"And this is the enchanting Miss Penelope Gray, Viscount Batten's ward," said Lady Brompton. "I'd introduce you more thoroughly, Merchant, but she has no dowry to speak of, and you are a fortune-hunter—so I can't indulge my passion for matchmaking with you two."

Mr. Merchant, who was a head shorter than me—like many of the men in this room, in fact—didn't look particularly insulted, but made a gallant bow and said, staring hard at my décolletage, "That doesn't blind me to the charms of such a delightful young lady."

"I'm . . . I'm glad for your sake," I said uncertainly, and Lady Brompton and her cousin burst out laughing.

"Oh, no—Lord Brompton and Miss Fairfax are advancing on the pianoforte!" said Mr. Merchant, rolling his eyes. "I fear the worst!"

"Quick, our glasses of punch!" ordered Lady Brompton. "No one can endure this fully sober!"

I sipped the punch hesitantly at first, but it tasted wonderful. It had a strong flavor of fruit, a touch of cinnamon, and there was something else in it, too. It made me feel nice and warm inside. For a moment, I was perfectly relaxed, and I began enjoying the sight of this beautifully candlelit room full of well-dressed people. Then Mr. Merchant made a grab for my décolletage from behind, and I almost spilled the punch.

"One of those dear, pretty little roses slipped out of place," he claimed, with an insinuating grin. I stared at him, baffled. Giordano hadn't prepared me for a situation like this, so I didn't know the proper etiquette for dealing with Rococo gropers. I looked at Gideon for help, but he was so deep in conversation with the young widow that he didn't even notice. If we'd been in my own century, I'd have told Mr. Merchant to keep his dirty paws to himself or I'd hit back, whether or not any little roses had really slipped. But in the circumstances, I felt that his reaction was rather—discourteous. So I smiled at him and said, "Oh, thank you, how kind. I never noticed."

Mr. Merchant bowed. "Always glad to be of service, ma'am." The barefaced cheek of it! But in times when women had no vote, I suppose it wasn't surprising if they didn't get any other kind of respect either.

The talking and laughter gradually died away as Miss Fairfax, a thin-nosed lady wearing a reed-green dress, went over to the pianoforte, arranged her skirts, and placed her hands on the keys. In fact, she didn't play badly. It was her singing that was rather disturbing. It was incredibly . . . well, high-pitched. A tiny bit higher, and you'd have thought she was a dog whistle.

"A refreshing punch, isn't it?" said Mr. Merchant, topping up my glass. To my surprise (and rather to my relief), he was now unashamedly groping Lady Brompton's bosom, on the pretext that she had a stray hair lying there. Lady Brompton didn't seem bothered; she only called him a naughty rogue and tapped his fingers smartly with her fan. (So that's what fans were really for!) Then she and her cousin took me over to a sofa upholstered in a flowery blue pattern close to the windows and sat me down between them.

"You'll be safe from sticky fingers here," said Lady Brompton, patting my knee in a motherly way. "Only your ears will still be in danger."

"Drink up!" her cousin advised me. "You're going to need it. Miss Fairfax has only just begun."

The sofa felt unusually hard, and the back curved so much that I couldn't possibly lean against it unless I wanted to sink right into its depths with all my skirts. Obviously you weren't meant to lounge around on sofas in the eighteenth century.

"I don't know—I'm not used to alcohol," I said doubtfully. My only experience with alcohol dated to exactly two years ago. It had been at a pajama party at Cynthia's house. A perfectly harmless party. No boys, but plenty of chips and *High School Musical* DVDs. And a large salad bowl full of vanilla ice cream, orange juice, and vodka. . . . The sneaky thing about the vodka was that all the vanilla ice cream kept you from tasting it, and the stuff obviously had different effects on different people. After three glasses, Cynthia flung the windows open and announced, "Zac Efron, I love you!" to the whole of Chelsea, while Lesley was crouched head down over the lavatory bowl throwing up, Maggie had made Sarah a declaration of love ("you're sho, sho beautiful, marry me!"), and Sarah was shedding floods of tears without knowing why. It hit me worst of all. I had jumped on Cynthia's bed and was bawling out "Breaking Free" in an endless loop. When Cynthia's father came into the room, I'd held Cynthia's hairbrush up to him like a microphone and called out, "Sing along, baldie! Get those hips swinging!" Although next day I couldn't even begin to explain why to myself.

After that rather embarrassing episode, Lesley and I had decided to give the demon drink a wide berth in future (we gave Cynthia's father a wide berth as well for a couple of months), and we had stuck to that resolution. Although it was sometimes odd to be the only sober person when everyone else was tipsy. Like now, for instance.

From the opposite side of the room, I sensed Count Saint-Germain's eyes resting on me again, and the back of my neck tingled uncomfortably.

"They say he knows the art of reading thoughts," whispered Lady Brompton beside me, and I decided to lift the alcohol ban for now. Only for this one evening. To help me forget how scared I was of Count Saint-Germain. And everything else.

Lady Brompton's special punch took effect surprisingly fast, and not just on me. After the second glass, everyone already thought Miss Fairfax's singing was distinctly less terrible. After the third glass, we began jiggling our feet in time, and I decided I'd never been to such a good party before. Really, people here were much more free and easy than I'd expected. Even more free and easy than in the twenty-first century, now I came to think of it. And the lighting was terrific. Why hadn't I ever noticed before that hundreds of candles made people's faces look as if they were covered with gold leaf? Even the count's face as he stood at the far end of the room, smiling at me from time to time.

My fourth glass finally silenced the warning inner voice telling me, "Stay alert! Trust no one!" Only the fact that Gideon seemed to have eyes only for the woman in the green dress still bothered me.

"Our ears have now had sufficient training," decided Lady Brompton at last. She rose to her feet, clapping, and went over to the pianoforte. "My dear, *dear* Miss Fairfax. Once again, that was absolutely exquisite," she said, kissing Miss Fairfax on both cheeks and firmly guiding her into the nearest chair. "But now I will ask you all to give a warm welcome to Mr. Merchant and Lady Lavinia—no, no protests, either of you, we know that you've been rehearsing in secret."

Beside me, Lady Brompton's cousin screeched like a teenie boy-band fan when the bosom groper sat down at the keyboard and played an arpeggio with great verve. The lovely Lady Lavinia gave Gideon a radiant smile and came forward with her green skirts rustling. I could see now that she wasn't quite as young as I'd thought. But her singing was great! She sang like Anna Netrebko when we heard her at the Royal Opera House in Covent Garden two years ago. Well, maybe her singing wasn't quite as great as Anna Netrebko's, but it was a pleasure to listen to her, all the same. If you liked ornate Italian operatic arias. Which normally I didn't, to be honest, but thanks to the punch, I did today. And obviously, Italian operatic arias went down tremendously well in the eighteenth century. The people in the room were really enjoying themselves now. Only the poor dog-whist . . . I mean Miss Fairfax was looking cross.

"Can I steal you away for a moment?" Gideon had come up behind the sofa and was smiling down at me. Of course, now the green lady was otherwise occupied, he'd remembered me again. "The count would be glad to enjoy a little of your company."

Oh. That was something else. I took a deep breath, picked up my glass, and tipped the contents right down my throat. When I stood up, I felt a pleasant dizzy sensation in my head. Gideon took the empty glass out of my hand and put it down on one of those tables with the cute little paws.

"Was there by any chance anything alcoholic in that?" he whispered.

"No, only punch," I whispered back. Oops, the floor was kind of uneven here. "I don't drink alcohol on principle, understand? One of my iron principles. You can have fun even without alcohol."

Gideon raised one eyebrow and offered me his arm. "I'm glad you're having a good time."

"The feeling's mutual," I assured him. Wow, these eighteenth-century floors really did wobble. Funny that I hadn't noticed it earlier. "I mean, she may be a little old for you, but don't let that bother you. Or the consolation the Duke of Wherever offers her. This really is a great party. People here are a lot nicer than I expected. So happy to make contact . . . physical contact." I looked at the piano-playing groper and the second-rate Netrebko. "And they obviously like to sing. Very nice. Makes you feel like jumping up at once to join in."

"Don't you dare," whispered Gideon, leading me over to the sofa where the count was sitting. When he saw us coming, he rose with the flexible ease of a much younger man, curving his lips into an expectant smile.

Okay, I thought, lifting my chin. Let's act as if I didn't know that Google says you're not a real count at all. Let's act as if you really had an aristocratic title and weren't a con man of unknown origin. Let's act as if you didn't half strangle me last time we met. And let's act as if I were stone-cold sober.

I let go of Gideon, picked up my heavy red silk skirts, spread them out, and sank into a deep curtsey. Only when the count reached out his hand with its many rings, all set with jewels, did I come up from it.

"My dear child," he said, and there was a glint of amusement in his dark brown eyes as he patted my hand, "I do admire your elegance. Others can't even speak their own names after four glasses of Lady Brompton's special punch."

Oh, so he'd been counting. I lowered my eyes guiltily. In fact it had been five glasses, but they'd been worth it, they really had! I couldn't be sorry I'd shaken off that oppressive, vague feeling of anxiety. And I didn't miss my inferiority complex, either. I liked my tipsy self. Even if I did feel rather unsteady on my legs.

"*Merci pour le compliment,*" I murmured.

"Delightful!" said the count.

"I'm sorry. I ought to have been watching more closely," said Gideon.

The count laughed softly. "My dear boy, you were otherwise occupied. And after all, today we are first and foremost intent on amusement, are we not? Particularly as

Lord Alastair, to whom I was extremely anxious to introduce this charming young lady, is not yet here. However, I have been brought word that he is on his way."

"Alone?" asked Gideon.

The count smiled. "That makes no difference."

The downmarket Anna Netrebko and the bosom groper ended the aria with a rousing final chord, and the count let go of my hand so that he could clap. "Isn't she wonderful? A really fine talent, and so beautiful, too."

"Yes," I said quietly, clapping as well and taking care not to play pat-a-cake. "It's quite something to make the chandeliers ring like that." The clapping upset my sensitive sense of balance, and I staggered slightly.

Gideon caught me. "I can't make it out," he said angrily, his lips close to my ear. "We haven't been here two hours, and you're totally drunk! What on earth were you thinking of?"

"You said *totally*. I'm going to tell on you to Giordano," I giggled. In all the noise, no one else could hear us. "Anyway, it's too late. No point in locking the stable door after the horse has gone." A hiccup interrupted me—*hic.* "Sorry." I looked around me. "But everyone else is much more drunk than me, so leave out the moral indignation, okay? I have everything under control. You can let go of me again. I stand here as steady as a rock among the breakers."

"I'm *warning* you," whispered Gideon, but he did let go of me.

For safety's sake, I braced my legs a little farther apart. Well, no one could see that, not underneath my huge skirt.

The count, amused, had been watching us. His expression gave away nothing but a certain grandfatherly
pride. I glanced at him surreptitiously and was rewarded
by a smile that warmed my heart. Why had I been so
scared of him? It was only with difficulty that I could remember what Lucas had told me—how this same man
had cut his own ancestor's throat. . . .

Lady Brompton had quickly come up to the pianoforte again to thank Mr. Merchant and Lady Lavinia for
their performance. Then—before Miss Fairfax could get
to her feet again—she asked for a warm round of applause
for today's guest of honor, the famous, much-traveled
Count Saint-Germain, a man surrounded by mystery. "He
has promised me to play something on his violin today,"
she said, and Lord Brompton came hurrying up with a
violin case as fast as his potbelly allowed. The audience,
spaced out on punch, roared their enthusiasm. This really
was a *super-cool* party.

The count smiled as he took the violin out of its case
and began tuning it. "I would never dream of disappointing you, Lady Brompton," he said in a soft voice. "But my
old fingers are not as agile as they used to be when I played
duets with the notorious Giacomo Casanova at the French
court . . . and my gout troubles me a little these days."

A collective whispering and sighing ran through the
room.

"So this evening I would like to hand the violin over
to my young friend here," the count went on.

Gideon looked slightly shocked and shook his head.

But when the count raised his eyebrows and said, *"Please!"* he bowed, took the instrument and the bow, and went over to the pianoforte.

The count took my hand. "And we two will sit on the sofa and enjoy the music, shall we? No need for you to tremble! Sit down, my child. You don't know it, but since yesterday afternoon we have been the best of friends, you and I. We had a really, really intimate conversation, and we were able to settle all our differences."

What?

"Yesterday afternoon?" I repeated.

"From my point of view," said the count. "From yours, that meeting is still in the future." He laughed. "I like it to be complicated, you see!"

I stared at him, baffled. But at that moment Gideon began to play, and I entirely forgot what I had been going to ask the count. Oh, my God! Maybe it was the punch—but wow! That violin was really sexy! Even the way Gideon raised it and tucked it under his chin! He didn't have to do more than that to carry me away with him. His long lashes cast shadows on his cheeks, and a lock of hair fell over his face as he began passing the bow over the strings. The first notes filling the room almost took my breath away, they made such tender, melting music, and suddenly I was close to tears. Until now, violins had been way down on my list of favorite instruments, and I really liked them only for accompanying certain moments in films. But this was just incredibly wonderful—well, all of it was: the bittersweet melody and the boy enticing it out of the instrument. All the people in the room listened with bated breath, and Gideon played on, immersed in the music as if there were no one else there.

I didn't notice that I was crying until the count touched my cheek and caught a tear gently with his finger. Then I jumped in alarm.

He was smiling down at me, and I saw a warm glow in his dark brown eyes. "Nothing to be ashamed of," he said quietly. "If it were otherwise, I'd have been very disappointed."

I was surprised to find myself smiling back at him—really! How could I? This was the man who had strangled me!

"What's that tune?" I asked.

The count shrugged his shoulders. "I don't know. I assume it has yet to be composed."

A storm of applause broke out in the room when Gideon came to the end of the piece. He bowed, smiling, and successfully declined to play an encore, although he was less successful in eluding the embrace of the lovely Lady Lavinia. She clung to his arm, and he had no alternative but to bring her over to our sofa.

"Wasn't that marvelous?" cried Lady Lavinia. "But when I saw those hands, I knew at once that they could work miracles."

"I bet," I muttered. I would have liked to get up from the sofa, if only so that Lady Lavinia couldn't look down at me like that, but it was beyond me. The punch had had an unfortunate effect on my muscles.

"It's a wonderful instrument, sir," said Gideon to the count, giving him back the violin.

"A Stradivarius. Made for me by the master himself," replied the count in a tone of reverie. "I would like you to have it, my boy. This evening is probably the right moment for me to pass it solemnly on to you."

Gideon went a little red. With delight, I assumed. "That . . . oh, I can't . . ." He looked into the count's dark eyes, but then lowered his own and added, "You do me great honor, sir."

"The honor is all mine," replied the count gravely.

"My word," I murmured to myself. The two of them seemed to have formed a mutual admiration society.

"And are you as musical as your foster brother, Miss Gray?" asked Lady Lavinia.

No, probably not. But I bet I'm as musical as you, I thought. "I like to sing, that's all," I said.

Gideon shot me a warning glance.

"You like to sing!" cried Lady Lavinia. "As indeed so do I, and our dear Miss Fairfax."

"I'm afraid I can't reach such high notes as Miss Fairfax," I said firmly. Well, I wasn't a bat, was I? "And my lungs don't have the capacity of yours. But I do like singing, all the same."

"I think we've had enough music for this evening," said Gideon.

Lady Lavinia looked hurt.

"Of course we would be delighted if *you* would honor us again," Gideon was quick to add, giving me a dark look.

I was so happily drunk that, for once, I couldn't have cared less.

"You . . . you played wonderfully," I said. "It made me cry! It really did."

He grinned as if I'd told a joke and put the Stradivarius away in its case.

Lord Brompton came up, out of breath, bringing us two glasses of punch, and assured Gideon that he was absolutely delighted by his guest's virtuoso performance. It was a shame, he added, that poor Alastair had missed what was undoubtedly the high point of the soirée.

"Do you think Alastair may yet find his way here this evening?" asked the count, with a touch of annoyance.

"I'm sure of it," said Lord Brompton, handing me one of the glasses. I took a greedy gulp. Was this stuff good! I just had to sniff it, and I was on a high. Ready to snatch up a hairbrush, jump on a bed, and sing "Breaking Free" with or without Zac Efron!

"My lord, you really must persuade Miss Gray to offer us something from her repertory," said Lady Lavinia. "She so likes to sing!"

There was an odd undertone in her voice that made me prick up my ears. In a way, she reminded me of Charlotte. She might not look like her, but there was another Charlotte somewhere deep inside that bright green dress, I felt sure of it. The kind of person who always wanted you to notice how absolutely wonderful and unique she herself was by comparison with you and your mediocre talents.

"Very well," I said, trying to get up from the sofa again.

This time it worked. I could even keep on my feet. "Then I'll sing."

"What?" said Gideon, shaking his head. "On no account will she sing—I'm afraid that the punch—"

"Miss Gray, it would be a great pleasure for us all if you would sing to us," said Lord Brompton, winking at me so hard that his fifteen double chins wobbled like crazy. "And if we owe it to the punch, so much the better! Come up to the front with me and let me announce you."

Gideon firmly held my arm. "This is not a good idea," he said. "Lord Brompton, please—my foster sister has never before performed in public."

"There's a first time for everything," said Lord Brompton, guiding me on. "We're all friends together here. Don't spoil sport for us!"

"Exactly. Don't be such a spoilsport," I said, shaking off Gideon's hand. "Do you happen to have a hairbrush with you? I sing better holding a hairbrush."

Gideon looked rather despairing. "Definitely not," he said, following me and Lord Brompton over to the piano.

I heard the count laughing quietly behind us.

"Gwen," whispered Gideon, "do please stop this nonsense."

"Penelope," I corrected him, draining the rest of my punch in one draft and handing him the empty glass. "Do you think they'd like 'Over the Rainbow'? Or," I added, with a giggle, 'Hallelujah'?"

Gideon groaned. "You really can't do this. Come back with me now!"

"No, 'Hallelujah' is too modern, isn't it? Let's see . . ." In my mind I went over my entire playlist, while Lord Brompton announced me in pompous terms. Mr. Merchant, the groper, came over to join us at the pianoforte. "Does the lady need a competent accompanist on the instrument?" he asked.

"No, the lady needs . . . needs something entirely different," said Gideon, sitting down on the piano stool himself. "Please, Gwen . . ."

"*Pen*, if you must," I said. "I know what to sing! 'Don't Cry for Me, Argentina.' I know all the words, and musicals are timeless, don't you agree? But maybe they don't know about Argentina. . . ."

"You're not really going to make a fool of yourself in front of all these people, are you?"

It was a nice try at scaring me, but useless in the circumstances. "Listen," I said in a confidential whisper. "I couldn't care less about these people. First, they've been dead for two hundred years and, second, they're also as good as dead drunk anyway—except for you, of course."

Groaning, Gideon leaned his forehead on the palm of his hand, hitting a whole series of notes on the pianoforte keyboard in the process.

"Do you happen to know . . . yes, 'Memory'?" I asked Mr. Merchant. "From *Cats*?"

"Oh—no, I'm sorry," said Mr. Merchant.

"Never mind, then I'll just sing it a capella," I said confidently, turning to my audience. "This song is called 'Memory,' and it's about . . . about a cat who's unhappy in love, but basically it fits us humans as well. In the widest sense."

Gideon had raised his head again and was looking at me incredulously. "Please," he tried again.

"We just won't tell anyone about it," I said. "Okay? This will be our secret."

"And now comes the great moment!" cried Lord Brompton. "The wonderful, unique, and beautiful Miss Gray will sing for us! Her first performance in public!"

I ought to have felt alarmed, because all the talk died down, and all eyes were on me, but I didn't. That punch was just divine! I absolutely must get the recipe.

What was it I'd said I was going to sing?

Gideon struck a couple of notes on the keyboard, and I recognized the opening bars. "Memory." Yes, right, that was it. I smiled gratefully at Gideon. How kind of him to prompt me and join in. I took a deep breath. The first note of this song was particularly important. If you got it wrong, you might just as well give up right away. The word *midnight* had to come out clear as glass and yet ring all around the room.

I was pleased, because I sounded just like Barbra Streisand singing it. *"Not a sound from the pavement, has the moon lost her memory? She is smiling alone."*

Guess what? Gideon could obviously play the piano, too. And not badly either. Oh, God, if I hadn't been head over heels in love with him already, I'd have fallen in love with him now. He didn't even have to look at the keys, he was just looking at me. And he seemed slightly surprised, like someone who has just made an unexpected discovery. Maybe that the moon was a *she*?

"All alone in the moonlight I can dream of the old days," I sang, just for him. This salon had great acoustics; it was almost as if I were singing into a mike. Or else it was because no one was making a sound. *"Let the memory live again."* This was much more fun than playing SingStar. It was really, really great. And even if the whole thing was just a lovely dream and Cynthia's father was about to march into the room and kick up an almighty row, this moment was worth it.

No one would ever believe me.

Time ain't nothin' but time.
It's a verse with no rhyme.
Man, it all comes down to you.

Bon Jovi, "Next 100 Years"

ELEVEN

THE ONLY STUPID THING was that it's such a short song. I was tempted to make up another verse of my own, but that might have just spoiled the general good impression, so I didn't. Instead, a little regretfully, I sang my favorite lines—*"If you touch me, you'll understand what happiness is. Look, a new day has begun"*—and thought, yet again, that the song couldn't have been specially written for *Cats*. Maybe it was the punch—in fact it was certainly the punch—but the guests at this soirée seemed to like our performance just as much as the earlier Italian operatic arias. At least, they applauded enthusiastically, and while Lady Brompton hurried forward, I bent down to Gideon and said, meaning it, "Thank you! That was really nice of you! And you play so well!"

He leaned his head on his hand again, as if he couldn't believe what he had just done.

Lady Brompton hugged me, and Mr. Merchant kissed

me exuberantly on both cheeks, called me his "golden-voiced charmer," and demanded an encore.

I was in such a good mood that I would have launched right into one, but at this point Gideon came back to life, stood up, and grabbed my wrist. "I'm sure Andrew Lloyd Webber would be delighted to know that you already appreciate his music here, but my sister has to rest. Until last week, she was suffering from a nasty throat infection, and now, on medical advice, she has to spare her voice—or she might lose it forever."

"Oh, for heaven's sake!" cried Lady Brompton. "Why didn't you say so before? The poor girl!"

I was happily humming "I Feel Pretty," out of *West Side Story*.

"There certainly is something special about your punch," said Gideon. "I think it tempts us to throw caution to the winds."

"To be sure it does!" said Lady Brompton, beaming all over her face. Lowering her voice, she went on, "You've just revealed the secret of my success as a society hostess. All London envies us our famous parties. People scramble for invitations. But it took me years to perfect the recipe, and I don't intend to give it away until I'm on my deathbed."

"What a pity," I said. "But you're right. Your soirée is so much more fun than I expected! I was told it would be a boring, stiffly correct—"

"Her governess is rather conservative," Gideon interrupted me. "And it can indeed be said that social life in Derbyshire is a little behind the times."

Lady Brompton giggled. "Dear me, yes, I'm sure it is. Oh, here's Lord Alastair at last!" She looked at the doorway, where Lord Brompton was welcoming a new arrival. His guest was probably middle-aged (difficult to be sure because of his snow-white wig), and he wore a frock coat so heavily embroidered with little stones and glittery thread that from a distance it seemed to sparkle. The glittery effect was enhanced by the contrast with his companion, a man dressed entirely in black who stood beside him. He was wrapped in a black cloak, he had pitch-black hair and an olive complexion, and even from some way off, I could see that his eyes, just like Rakoczy's, resembled huge dark holes. He was like some foreign body in this colorful company flashing its jewels around.

"I was just thinking," Lady Brompton told me, "that Alastair wasn't going to give us the honor of his company today. Which wouldn't have been entirely disastrous, if you ask me. His presence doesn't usually contribute much to a relaxed, cheerful atmosphere. I'll try to persuade him to take a glass of punch and then show him where they're playing cards in the next room. . . ."

"And we will try to cheer him with a little singing," said Mr. Merchant, sitting down at the piano again. "Would you do me the honor, Lady Lavinia? Something from *Così Fan Tutte*?"

Gideon placed my hand on his arm and led me a little way aside. "How much have you drunk, for heaven's sake?"

"A couple of glasses," I admitted. "I'm sure the secret ingredient isn't alcohol. Absinthe, maybe? Like in that sad film *Moulin Rouge* with Nicole Kidman." I sighed. "*The greatest thing you'll ever learn is just to love and be loved in return.* I bet you can play that, too."

"Let's get one thing clear: I *hate* musicals," said Gideon. "Do you think you can hold out for a few minutes longer? Lord Alastair has finally arrived, and once we've been introduced to him, we can go."

"So soon?" I said. "What a shame!"

Gideon looked at me, shaking his head. "You've obviously lost all sense of time. I'd hold your head under cold water if I could."

Count Saint-Germain came up to us. "That was a . . . a very remarkable performance," he said, looking at Gideon with raised eyebrows.

"I'm sorry," said Gideon, sighing. He glanced at the two newcomers. "Lord Alastair looks a little fatter than he used to."

The count laughed. "Don't cherish any false hopes! My enemy is still in brilliant form. Rakoczy saw him fence at Galliano's this afternoon—none of the young dandies could compete with him. Follow me. I can't wait to see his face."

"He's being so *nice* today," I whispered to Gideon as we followed in the count's wake. "You know, he terrified me last time, but today I feel almost as if he was my grandfather or something. I almost like him. And it was so kind of him to give you the Stradivarius. I'm sure it would be worth a fortune if you auctioned it on eBay. Oops, the floors are still so wobbly here."

Gideon put a hand on my waist. "I swear I'm going to murder you when we're through with this," he muttered.

"Am I babbling?"

"Not quite yet," he said. "But I expect that will be next."

"Didn't I tell you he might turn up at any moment?" Lord Brompton placed one hand on the shoulder of the man in the glittery clothes and the other on the count's. "I've been told that you know each other already. Lord Alastair, you never told me that you were personally acquainted with the famous Count Saint-Germain."

"It's not something one cares to boast of," said Lord Alastair arrogantly, and the black-clad man with the olive complexion standing a little way behind him added, in a grating voice, "Very true!" His black eyes were almost burning holes in the count's face, leaving no one in any doubt of his profound hatred for him. For a moment, I wondered if he had a sword hidden under that black cloak and might draw it at any time. Why he wore a thick, gloomy cloak like that at all was a mystery to me. First, it was hot enough in here, and second, it seemed odd and discourteous in these festive surroundings.

Lord Brompton looked around him, beaming cheerfully, as if he hadn't caught on to the hostile atmosphere at all.

The count stepped forward. "Lord Alastair, how delightful! Although our acquaintanceship lies some years in the past, I have never forgotten you."

I was standing behind Count Saint-Germain, so I couldn't see his face, but he sounded as if he was smiling.

His voice was friendly and cheerful. "I, too, still remember our conversation about slavery and morality, and how surprising I thought it that you were so well able to keep the two apart—just like your father," he said.

"The count never forgets anything," said Lord Brompton effusively. "His brain is phenomenal! During these last few days in his company I've learnt more than in all my life before. Did you know, for instance, that the count is able to make artificial jewels?"

"Yes, I was aware of that." Lord Alastair's expression became, if possible, even colder, and his companion was breathing heavily like someone about to run amok.

"Science is not necessarily among Lord Alastair's hobbies, if I remember correctly," said the count. "Oh, how remiss of me!" He stepped to one side, allowing Lord Alastair a full view of Gideon and me. "I wished to introduce these two delightful young people to you. To be honest, that was my sole reason for being here today. A man of my age avoids society and goes to bed early."

At the sight of Gideon, Lord Alastair's eyes widened incredulously.

Lord Brompton squeezed his massive bulk between Gideon and me. "Lord Alastair, may I introduce Viscount Batten's son? And the Viscount's ward, the enchanting Miss Gray?"

My curtsey fell a little short of the deference prescribed by etiquette. There were two reasons for that: (a) I was afraid of losing my balance, and (b) Lord Alastair seemed so arrogant that I quite forgot I was playing the part of

Viscount Batten's penniless ward. I mean, I was the grand-daughter of Lord Lucas Montrose, wasn't I? I was descended from a long line of famous ancestors, and what's more, your origins didn't make any difference in my own time, when everyone was equal, right?

At any other time, Lord Alastair's glance would have frozen the blood in my veins, but the punch was good anti-freeze, so I returned it as haughtily as I could. He didn't give me his attention for long anyway. Instead, he returned his gaze to Gideon, while Lord Brompton went on chattering happily.

No one took the trouble to introduce Lord Alastair's black-clad companion, and no one seemed to notice when he stared at me over Lord Alastair's shoulder and growled, "You! Demon with the sapphire eyes! You will soon be on your way to hell!"

I beg your pardon? That was really going too far! In search of help, I looked at Gideon, whose rather tense smile was only for show. But he didn't say anything until Lord Brompton said he was going to fetch his wife—and a couple of glasses of punch.

"Please don't trouble, Lord Brompton," said Gideon. "We have to leave soon anyway. My sister is still a little weak after her long illness and not used to staying up late." He put his arm around my waist again and took my forearm with his other hand. "As you see, she is slightly unsteady on her legs."

How right he was! The floor was swaying very unpleasantly beneath my feet. Gratefully, I leaned on Gideon.

"Oh, I'll be back in a moment!! cried Lord Brompton. "I'm sure my wife will be able to persuade you to stay."

Count Saint-Germain watched him go with a smile. "Such a good-hearted soul! Fond as he is of harmony, he could never bear it if we were to quarrel."

Lord Alastair was still inspecting Gideon with undisguised hostility. "If my memory serves me rightly, when we met before, this young man was traveling under the name of Marquis Weldon. And now he is the son of a viscount. I expect, Saint-Germain, that like you, your young friend is inclined to indulge in empty boasting. How very regrettable!"

"It's what one calls a diplomatic pseudonym," said the count, still smiling. "Nothing that you would understand. Be that as it may, I heard that you greatly enjoyed that little fencing match when you met eleven years ago."

"I enjoy *any* fencing match," said Lord Alastair. He acted as if he didn't hear his companion, who was whispering, "Smite the enemies of God with the swords of the angels and archangels!" Lord Alastair went on, unmoved, "And I have learnt a few tricks since then. Whereas your young friend seems to have aged by only a few days in those eleven years—and as I was recently able to convince myself, he has had no time to improve his technique."

"Convince *yourself*?" said Gideon, with a derisive smile. "For that you'd have had to be *there* yourself. But you sent your men, and my technique was perfectly adequate to dealing with them. Yet more proof that if you want something done, it is better to do it yourself."

"Can you mean . . . ?" Lord Alastair's eyes narrowed. "Ah, you are speaking of the incident in Hyde Park last Monday. True—I ought to have given it my own attention. In any case, it was just an idea on the spur of the moment. But without the help of black magic . . . and a *girl*, you would hardly have survived."

"I'm glad to hear you speak so frankly," said the count. "For since your men's attempt on the lives of my young friends here, I have been rather . . . well, annoyed. I thought it was I on whom your aggression was turned. I am sure you understand that I will not tolerate such a thing."

"You'll do as you think you ought to do, and I'll do as I must do," said Lord Alastair, and his companion growled, "Death! Death to the demons!" in such a weird way that I couldn't rule out the idea that he might have a laser sword hidden under that cloak. He was clearly a nutcase. I didn't think I ought to ignore his peculiar behavior any longer.

"We haven't been introduced, I know, and I admit to having my own problems with correct manners at this period," I said, looking him straight in the face. "But if you ask me, all this talk of demons and death is definitely out of order."

"Speak not to me, demon!" said Darth Vader harshly. "I am invisible to your sapphire eyes! And your ears cannot hear me."

"Chance would be a fine thing," I said, and suddenly I wanted to go home. Or at least back to that sofa, however uncomfortable it was. The whole room was swaying around me like a ship at sea.

Gideon, the count, and Lord Alastair seemed to have lost the thread of their own conversation for now. They forgot to go on flinging cryptic accusations at each other, and stared at me with baffled expressions on their faces.

"The swords of my descendants will pierce your flesh, the Florentine Alliance will avenge what was done to my family, and will wipe that which is displeasing to God off the face of the earth," said Darth Vader, addressing no one in particular.

"Who are you talking to?" whispered Gideon.

"Him over there," I said, clutching Gideon a little more tightly and pointing to Darth Vader. "Someone ought to tell him that his cloak is sh . . . isn't exactly the latest fashion. And that I am not a demon, if he doesn't mind, and I don't want to be pierced by the swords of his descendants and wiped off the face of the earth. *Ow!*"

Gideon's hand had closed hard on my forearm.

"What does this farce mean, Count?" inquired Lord Alastair, adjusting a showy brooch in his cravat.

The count took no notice of him. Under their heavy lids, his eyes were resting on me. "This is interesting," he said softly. "She can obviously see straight into your black soul, my dear Alastair."

"I'm afraid she's drunk so much wine that she's imagining things," said Gideon, hissing into my ear, "Shut up, for goodness' sake!"

My stomach contracted painfully with shock, because all at once I realized that the others couldn't see or hear Darth Vader, and the reason why they couldn't was that he was a ghost! If I hadn't been so drunk, this obvious idea would have occurred to me sooner. How stupid could you get? Neither his clothes nor his hairstyle was right for the eighteenth century, and by the time he launched into his emotional ramblings, if not earlier, I ought to have realized who I had before me, or rather what.

Lord Alastair threw back his head and said, "We both know, Count, whose soul belongs to the Devil, and with God's help, I will ensure that these . . . these *creatures* are never born at all!"

"Pierced by the swords of the Holy Florentine Alliance," Darth Vader unctuously concluded.

The count laughed. "You still don't understand the laws of time, Alastair. The mere fact that these two are here in front of you proves that your plan will not succeed. So maybe you shouldn't rely on God's help in this business too much. Or on my continued forbearance." Suddenly there was an icy chill in his eyes and his voice, and I saw Lord Alastair flinch. For a split second all the arrogance was gone from his face, and his expression was one of naked fear.

"By changing the rules of the game, you have forfeited your life," said the count in exactly the same voice as he had used to frighten me out of my wits at our last meeting. Suddenly I was convinced all over again that he was capable of cutting an enemy's throat with his own hands.

"Your threat means nothing to me," whispered Lord Alastair, but his face gave him the lie. Pale as death, he put a hand to his Adam's apple.

"Oh, my dears, surely you're not really leaving us already?" Lady Brompton came hurrying up, skirts rustling, looking happily around at us.

Count Saint-Germain's features relaxed again, and there was nothing but goodwill in them. "Ah, here is our charming hostess. I must say you do your reputation credit, my lady. It's a long time since I passed such an entertaining evening."

Lord Alastair rubbed his throat. The color was slowly coming back into his cheeks.

"*Satanas! Satanas!*" cried Darth Vader angrily. "We will crush you, we will tear out your lying tongue with our own hands. . . ."

"My young friends here are as sorry as I am that we really have to leave now," the count continued with a smile. "But you will soon be seeing them again at Lord and Lady Pympoole-Bothame's ball."

"A party is only as interesting as its guests," said Lady Brompton. "So I would be very happy to welcome you here again soon. And your delightful young friends. It has been a great pleasure for us all."

"The pleasure was entirely ours," said Gideon, cautiously letting go of me as if he wasn't sure whether I could stand on my own. Although the room was still swaying like a ship, and my thoughts seemed to be suffering a bad bout of seasickness too, when we said good-bye, I managed to pull myself together and do credit to my training by Giordano and, above all, James. I wasn't even going to spare a glance for Lord Alastair and the ghost, who was still uttering savage threats. But I bobbed a curtsey to Lord and Lady Brompton, thanking them for the delightful evening, and I didn't bat an eyelash when Lord Brompton left the trail of a moist kiss on my hand.

I sank in a very deep curtsey before the count, but I dared not look him in the face again. When he said quietly, "We shall see each other yesterday afternoon, then," I just nodded and waited with downcast eyes until Gideon was beside me again, taking my arm. This time I let him lead me out of the salon.

"FOR GOD'S SAKE, Gwyneth, that wasn't a party with your school friends! How could you?" Gideon was impatiently putting my shawl around my shoulders. He looked as if he'd like to shake me.

"I'm sorry," I said for the umpteenth time.

"Lord Alastair is accompanied only by a page and his coachman," whispered Rakoczy, materializing behind Gideon like some kind of jack-in-the-box. "The road and the church are safe. All the entrances to the church are guarded."

"Come on, then," said Gideon, taking my hand.

"I could carry the young lady," Rakoczy suggested. "She seems rather unsteady on her feet."

"A charming idea, but no thank you," said Gideon. "She can manage that short distance on her own, can't you?"

I nodded firmly.

It was raining harder now. After the Bromptons' brightly lit salon, the way back to the church through the dark was even eerier than when we had set out. Once again the shadows seemed to be alive, once again I suspected that there could be a figure ready to pounce on us in every nook and cranny. ". . . *will wipe that which is displeasing to God off the face of the earth*," the shadows seemed to whisper.

Gideon didn't seem to like the look of the road either. He walked so fast that I had trouble in keeping up with him, and he didn't say a single word. Unfortunately the rain did nothing to clear my head, nor did it stop the ground swaying. So I was extremely relieved when we arrived at the church and Gideon made me sit down on one of the pews in front of the altar. While he exchanged a few words with Rakoczy, I closed my eyes and cursed my stupidity. Granted, that punch had also had positive side effects, but all things considered, I'd have done better to stick to the no-alcohol pact that Lesley and I had made. It's always easy to be wise after the event.

There was only a single candle burning on the altar, as there had been when we arrived, and apart from that small, flickering light, the church lay in darkness. When Rakoczy left—"All the doors and windows will be guarded by my men until you travel back"—I was overcome by fear. I looked up at Gideon, who had come back to my pew.

"It's just as scary in here as outside. Why doesn't he stay with us?"

"Out of politeness. He doesn't want to listen to me shouting at you. But don't worry, we're on our own. Rakoczy's men have searched every last corner."

"How much longer before we travel back?"

"Not long now, Gwyneth. I suppose you realize that you did almost precisely the opposite of what you ought to have done? As usual, come to think of it."

"You shouldn't have left me alone—I bet that was also almost precisely the opposite of what *you* ought to have done!"

"Don't go blaming me! First you get drunk, then you sing songs from modern musicals, and finally you behave like a lunatic in front of Lord Alastair, of all people! What was all that stuff about swords and demons?"

"I didn't begin it. It was that black, uncanny gho—" But here I bit my lip. I couldn't simply tell him about the ghosts I saw. He thought I was peculiar enough as it was.

Gideon totally misunderstood my sudden silence. "Oh, no! Please don't throw up! Or if you must, do it somewhere well away from me." He looked at me with slight revulsion. "Good heavens, Gwyneth, I can see that there's something tempting in the idea of getting drunk at a party, but not *that* party!"

"I don't feel like throwing up." Not yet, at least. "And I never drink at parties—whatever Charlotte's told you."

"She hasn't told me anything," said Gideon.

I had to laugh. "No, sure. *And* she never claimed that Lesley and I have been out with all the boys in our class and almost all the boys in the class above, did she?"

"Why would she say a thing like that?"

Let's think . . . maybe because she's a sly, mean, red-haired witch? I tried to scratch my head, but my fingers couldn't get through the pile of ringlets. So I pulled out a hairpin and scratched with that instead. "Oh, I'm sorry, really! You can say what you like about Charlotte, but I'm sure she would never even have *sniffed* that punch."

"You're right," said Gideon, and suddenly he smiled. "Although then those people would have never have heard Andrew Lloyd Webber two hundred years ahead of time, and that would have been a real pity."

"Right . . . although tomorrow I'll probably want to sink into the ground with shame." I buried my face in my hands. "In fact, come to think of it, that's how I feel right now."

"Good," said Gideon. "It means the effect of the alcohol is wearing off. One question, by the way: what did you want a hairbrush for?"

"I wanted it as a substitute for a mike," I murmured through my fingers. "Oh, my God! I'm so horrible."

"But you have a pretty voice," said Gideon. "Even I liked it, and I told you I hate musicals."

"Then how come you can play songs from them so well?" I put my hands in my lap and looked at him. "You were amazing! Is there *anything* you can't do?" Good heavens, I heard myself sounding like a groupie.

"No. Go ahead, you're welcome to think me some kind of god!" He was grinning now. "It's rather sweet of you! Come on, we'll be traveling back soon now. We'd better get into position."

I got to my feet, trying to stand up as straight as possible.

"Over here," Gideon told me. "Don't look so remorseful. Basically the evening was a success. It went according to plan, if not exactly *as* planned. Hey, keep standing." He put both hands on my waist and pulled me close, until my back was against his chest. "You can lean on me if you like." He paused and then said, "Sorry I was so nasty to you just now."

"All forgotten." That wasn't strictly true, but it was the first time I'd heard Gideon apologize for his behavior, and maybe it was the alcohol, or the fact that its effects were wearing off, but I was very touched.

We stood there for a while in silence, still looking ahead in the flickering candlelight. Like the light, the shadows between the columns seemed to be moving, casting dark patterns on the floor and the church roof. "That man Alastair," I said. "Why does he hate the count so much? Is it something personal?"

Gideon began playing with one of the ringlets falling on my shoulder. "Depends how you look at it. The organization that so pompously calls itself the Florentine Alliance has really been a kind of family firm for centuries. On his travels through time in the sixteenth century, the count happened by chance to meet the Conte di Madrone's family in Florence. So . . . well, let's say they entirely mistook his abilities. The Conte di Madrone's religious views rejected the mere idea of time travel. In addition, there seems to have been some kind of trouble involving his daughter—anyway, the Conte was sure he was confronting a demon, and he felt that God had given him a mission to rid the world of what he thought was spawned by hell." Suddenly Gideon's voice was very close to my ear, and before he went on, his lips touched my neck. "When the Conte di Madrone died, his son inherited that mission, and his own son after him, and so on. Lord Alastair is the last in a line of fanatically obsessed demon-hunters, if that's the way to put it."

"I see," I said, which was not entirely true. But it did seem to explain a bit of what I'd recently seen and heard. "Er . . . at this moment, are you *kissing* me?"

"No, only almost," murmured Gideon, with his lips just above my skin. "I mean, no way do I want to exploit the fact that you're drunk and may be mistaking me for some kind of god right now. But it doesn't come easy. . . ."

I closed my eyes and leaned my head against his shoulder, and he held me closer.

"Like I said, you really don't make things easy for me. You always give me the wrong sort of ideas in churches. . . ."

"There's something you don't know about me," I said, with my eyes closed. "Sometimes I see . . . I can . . . well, sometimes I can see and hear people who've been dead a long time. And I can hear what they say. Like just now. I think the man I saw with Lord Alastair could have been that Italian Conte di Madrone."

Gideon said nothing. He was probably wondering how he could most tactfully recommend me to see a good psychiatrist.

I sighed. I ought to have kept it to myself. Now, in addition to everything else, he must think me crazy.

"Here we go, Gwyneth," he said, pushing me a little further off and turning me around so that I could look at him. It was too dark to see the expression on his face, but I could tell that he wasn't smiling. "It would be a good thing if you could stay standing right here for the few seconds after I've gone. Ready?"

I shook my head. "Not really."

"I'm letting go of you now," he said, and at the same moment, he disappeared. I was alone in the church with all those dark shadows. But only a few seconds later, I registered the dizzy feeling inside me, and the shadows began going around in circles.

"There she is," said Mr. George's voice. I blinked. The church was brightly lit, and after the golden glow of candles in Lady Brompton's salon, the halogen lighting was quite hard on the eyesight.

"Everything's all right," said Gideon, after scrutinizing me quickly. "You can close your medical bag, Dr. White."

Dr. White growled something I couldn't make out. In fact there were all kinds of instruments on the altar that you'd be more likely to see on a trolley in an operating room.

"Good heavens, Dr. White, are those surgical clamps?" Gideon laughed. "Now we know what you think of an eighteenth-century soirée!"

"I like to be ready for all eventualities," said Dr. White, putting the instruments back in his bag.

"We're anxious to hear your report," said Falk de Villiers.

"I want to get some of this stuff off first." Gideon was undoing his cravat.

"Did it all . . . work out?" asked Mr. George, glancing nervously at me.

"Yes," said Gideon, throwing the cravat aside. "Everything went according to plan. Lord Alastair arrived a little later than expected, but in plenty of time to see us." He grinned at me. "And Gwyneth played her part to perfection. Viscount Batten's real ward couldn't have done it better."

I couldn't help blushing.

"It will be a pleasure for me to tell Giordano that," said Mr. George, with a note of pride in his voice. He offered me his arm. "Not that I expected anything else."

"No, of course not," I murmured.

I WOKE TO HEAR Caroline whispering, "Gwenny, stop singing! It's so embarrassing! You have to go to school."

I abruptly sat up and stared at her. "Was I *singing*?"

"What?"

"You told me to stop singing."

"I told you to wake up!"

"Then I wasn't singing?"

"You were asleep," said Caroline, shaking her head. "Hurry up, you're already late. And Mum says you're not on any account to use her shower gel."

Under the shower I tried to suppress my memories of yesterday as far as possible. But I wasn't very successful, so I wasted several minutes pressing my forehead to the door of the shower cubicle, muttering to myself, "It was all just a dream!" My headache did nothing to make me feel better.

When I finally came down to the dining room, luckily breakfast was all but over. Xemerius was hanging head down from the chandelier. "Sobered up again, have you, little tippler?"

Lady Arista looked me up and down. "Did you make up only one eye on purpose?"

"Er, no." I was about to turn and go back to my room, but my mother said, "Breakfast first! You can put your mascara on later."

"Breakfast is the most important meal of the day," Aunt Glenda informed us.

"Nonsense!" said Aunt Maddy. She was sitting in the armchair beside the hearth in her dressing gown, with her knees drawn up like a little girl. "You can always leave out breakfast and save the calories to invest in a little glass of wine in the evening. Or two or three little glasses of wine."

"A liking for the bottle seems to run in your family," remarked Xemerius.

"We can see that from her figure," whispered Aunt Glenda.

"I may be a little plump, Glenda, but I am not hard of hearing," said Aunt Maddy.

"You ought to have stayed in bed," said Lady Arista. "Breakfast is more relaxed for all concerned if you have your beauty sleep."

"I'm afraid I didn't get the chance," said Aunt Maddy.

"She had another of her visions last night," Caroline explained to me.

"Yes, I did," said Aunt Maddy, "and it was horrible. So *sad*. It really upset me. There was this beautiful polished ruby heart sparkling in the sun. . . . It was lying on a rocky ledge above a precipice."

I wasn't sure that I wanted to know what happened next.

My mum smiled at me. "Eat something, darling. At least a little fruit. And don't listen to her."

"And then along came this lion." Aunt Maddy sighed. "With a lovely golden coat."

"Uh-oh!" said Xemerius. "And sparkling green eyes, I bet."

"You have felt pen on your face," I told Nick.

"Shh," he replied. "This is where it gets exciting."

"And when the lion saw the heart lying there, he gave it a push with his paw, and it fell down and down into the ravine below," said Aunt Maddy, dramatically putting her hand to her bosom. "When it hit the bottom, it smashed into hundreds of tiny pieces, and when I looked more closely, I saw that they were all drops of blood."

I swallowed. Suddenly I felt queasy.

"Oops," said Xemerius.

"Then what happened?" asked Charlotte.

"Nothing," said Aunt Maddy. "That was all—and quite nasty enough, too."

"Oh," said Nick, disappointed. "It started so well."

Aunt Maddy's eyes flashed at him angrily. "Young man, I'm not writing film scripts."

"Thank God," murmured Aunt Glenda. Then she turned to me, opened her mouth, and shut it again.

Charlotte spoke up instead. "Gideon says you did all right at the soirée. I must say I'm very relieved. I think *everyone* will be very relieved."

I ignored her and looked reproachfully up at the chandelier.

"I was going to tell you yesterday evening that your pushy cousin had supper at Gideon's place. But you were—how can I put it? You were a little indisposed," said Xemerius.

I snorted.

"Well, I can't help it if your sparkly diamond friend invites her to stay and eat, can I?" Xemerius took off and flew across the table to Aunt Maddy's empty place, where he sat upright on her chair and curled his lizard tail neatly around his feet. "I mean, I'd have done the same in his place. For one thing, she spent all day babysitting his little brother, and then she tidied up his apartment and ironed his shirts."

"*What?*"

"I said, I can't help it. Anyway, he was so grateful that he decided he had to show her how fast he could conjure up a spaghetti dish for three. . . . Wow, he was in a really good mood. Like he'd scored points or something. Now close your mouth. They're all looking at you."

They were, too.

"I'm going to finish doing my other eye," I said.

"Maybe a touch of rouge on your cheeks, too?" said Charlotte. "Just a friendly hint."

"I HATE HER!" I said. "I hate her. I hate her!"

"Oh, come on! Just because she ironed his stupid shirts?" Lesley looked at me, shaking her head. "I mean, that is plain *silly*!"

"He *cooked* for her!" I wailed. "She spent all day in his apartment!"

"Yes, but he was snogging with you in that church," said Lesley, sighing.

"He wasn't."

"Well, no, but he'd have liked to."

"He kissed Charlotte!"

"Only a good-bye kiss. On her cheek!" Xemerius shouted right into my ear. "If I have to tell you that once again, I'm going to explode. I'm off. All this girly stuff is more than I can take." He flapped his wings a few times, flew up to the school roof, and made himself comfortable there.

"I don't want to hear another word about it," said Lesley. "Right now it's much more important for you to remember everything you heard yesterday. And I mean things that really count. Matters of life and death!"

"I've told you everything I know," I assured her, rubbing my forehead. My headache had gone, thanks to three aspirins, but it left a dull sensation behind my temples.

"Hm." Lesley was poring over her notes. "Why didn't

you ask Gideon how he'd met up with this Lord Alastair eleven years ago and what fencing match they were talking about?"

"There's a whole lot more I didn't ask him, believe you me!"

Lesley sighed again. "I'll make you a list. Then you can ask a casual question now and then, when there's a good strategic moment and your hormones let you." She put her notepad away and looked at the school entrance. "Come on, we must go up or we'll be late. And I don't want to miss it when Raphael Bertelin walks into our classroom for the first time. Poor boy—he probably feels the school uniform is like a convict's outfit."

We made a brief detour past James's niche. In all the pushing and shoving of morning school, no one noticed if I spoke to him, particularly when Lesley acted as if I might be talking to her.

James raised his perfumed handkerchief to his nose and looked around cautiously. "Ah, I see you didn't bring that badly behaved cat today."

"Guess what, James, I was at Lady Brompton's soirée last night," I said. "And I curtseyed just the way you taught me."

"Lady Brompton, hm," said James. "She does not necessarily have the reputation of moving in the highest circles. They say her parties can be very free and easy."

"If that's what they say, they're right. I hoped that was normal in eighteenth-century polite society."

"Thank God, no!" James pursed his lips, looking offended.

"Well, anyway, I think I've been invited to a ball given by your parents, Lord and Lady Pympoole-Bothame."

"I find that hard to imagine," said James. "My mother sets great store by the impeccable social standing of her guests."

"Well, thank you very much," I said, turning to go. "What a snob you are!"

"I didn't mean it as an insult," James called after me. "And what's a snob?"

Raphael was already leaning in the doorway when we reached our classroom. He looked so gloomy that we stopped dead.

"Hi. I'm Lesley Hay, and this is my friend Gwyneth Shepherd," said Lesley. "We met on Friday outside the principal's office, remember?"

A faint grin lit up his face. "Well, I'm glad you recognize me, anyway. I had problems with that when I saw myself in the mirror just now."

"Yup," said Lesley. "You look like a steward on a cruise ship. Never mind. You'll get used to it."

Raphael's grin widened.

"You just have to take care the school tie doesn't dip into your soup," I said. "Happens to me all the time."

Lesley nodded.

"And by the way, school lunches usually taste frightful. Apart from that, it's not so bad here. I'm sure you'll soon feel at home."

"Never been in the south of France, have you?" asked Raphael, with a touch of bitterness.

"No," said Lesley.

"I can tell. I'll never feel at home in a country where it rains for twenty-four hours on end."

"We Brits don't really like it when people talk about our weather like that," said Lesley. "Oh, look, here comes Mrs. Counter. You're in luck—she's a Francophile, and if you mix a few French words into your essays by mistake, she'll love you."

"*Tu es mignonne*," said Raphael.

"I know," said Lesley, "but I'm not a Francophile."

"He fancies you," I said, putting my books down on our table.

"Maybe," said Lesley, "but I'm afraid he's not my type."

I couldn't help laughing. "No, of course not!"

"Oh, come on, Gwenny. It's bad enough for one of us to lose her mind. I know his sort. They just give you trouble. Anyway, he's only interested because Charlotte told him I was a pushover."

"And because you look like your dog, Bertie," I said.

"Yes, exactly, because of that, too." Lesley laughed. "Anyway, he'll forget all about me the moment Cynthia throws herself at him. Look, she's been to the hairdresser specially to have highlights done."

But Lesley was wrong. Raphael obviously wasn't interested in talking to Cynthia. When we were sitting on the bench under the chestnut tree at break and Lesley was studying the note with the Green Rider code on it yet again, Raphael came strolling over, sat down beside us uninvited, and said, "Oh, cool. Geocaching."

"What?" Lesley looked at him with annoyance.

Raphael pointed to the note. "Don't you know about geocaching? It's a kind of modern treasure hunt using GPS navigational devices. Those numbers look like geographical coordinates."

"No, they're only . . . oh! Do they really?"

"Let me see." Raphael took the note from her. "Yes, assuming a few of the zeros are superscript zeros so they mean *degree*, and the strokes are minutes and seconds."

A shrill sound came over the yard to us. Cynthia was standing on the steps, gesticulating wildly as she talked to Charlotte, and that made Charlotte look our way with a nasty expression.

"Oh, my God," Lesley was all excited. "Then it means *51 degrees, 30 minutes, 41.78 seconds north*, and *0 degrees, 08 minutes, 49.91 seconds west*?"

Raphael nodded.

"So it's the description of a place?" I asked.

"That's right," said Raphael. "Rather a small place, measuring about four and a half square yards. So what do you find there? A cache?"

"If only we knew," said Lesley. "We don't even know where the place is."

Raphael shrugged his shoulders. "Well, that's easy to find out."

"How? Do we need one of these GPS things? How do they work? I've no idea about them at all," said Lesley excitedly.

"I do, though. I could help you," said Raphael. "*Mignonne.*"

I glanced at the steps again. Sarah had now joined Cynthia and Charlotte, and all three were looking daggers at us. Lesley didn't notice.

"Okay. But it'll have to be this afternoon," she said. "We have no time to lose."

"Same here," said Raphael. "Let's just meet in the park at four. I'll have shaken Charlotte off somehow by then."

"Better not expect it to be easy." I looked at him sympathetically.

Raphael grinned. "I think you underestimate me, little time-travel girl."

The illimitable, silent, never-resting thing called Time, rolling, rushing on, swift, silent, like an all-embracing ocean-tide, on which we and all the Universe swim like exhalations, like apparitions which are, and then are not: this is forever very literally a miracle; a thing to strike us dumb—for we have no word to speak about it.

Thomas Carlyle

TWELVE

"I COULD JUST HAVE worn last week's dress," I said, as Madame Rossini put a little girl's dream of a dress over my head. It was lavishly embroidered with cream and wine-red flowers. "The blue flowered dress, I mean. It's hanging in the wardrobe at home—you only had to say."

"Shh, my leetle swan-necked beauty," said Madame Rossini. "What do you think zey pay me for 'ere? For you to wear ze same dress twice?" She concentrated on doing up the little buttons at the back. "I am only sorry you 'ave ruined ze 'airstyle. In ze Rococo age, a work of art like that 'ad to last for days. Ze ladies slept sitting up on purpose."

"Well, I could hardly have gone to school with it piled up like that," I said. I'd probably have got stuck in the door of the bus. "Is Giordano helping Gideon to get dressed?"

Madame Rossini clicked her tongue. "Huh! Zat boy say 'e does not need 'elp. Meaning 'e will wear dull colors again and take no care with 'is cravat. But I 'ave given 'im up! Now, what can we do with your 'air? I will get ze curling wand, and zen we will simply put a ribbon in it, *et bien!*"

While Madame Rossini worked on my hair with the curling wand, I had a text message from Lesley. "Will wait another two minutes. If *le petit français* isn't here then, he can forget about *mignonne.*"

I texted back. "Your date isn't for another fifteen minutes. At least give him ten!"

But I didn't get an answer back, because Madame Rossini took the mobile away from me to take the now-obligatory souvenir photos. The pink suited me better than I'd expected (it wasn't my color at all in real life), but my hair looked as if I'd spent the night with my fingers plugged into an electric socket. The pink ribbon threaded through it looked like a vain attempt to tame my exploding curls. When Gideon arrived to collect me, he burst out laughing.

"You can stop zat! We might just as well laugh at *you!*" Madame Rossini snapped at him. "Ha! What do you zink you look like?"

Oh, wow, what *did* he look like? There ought to be a law against looking so good—even in silly dark knee-breeches and an embroidered bottle-green coat that made his eyes shine.

"You 'ave no idea of fashion, young man! Or you would 'ave put on ze emerald brooch zat go with zat outfit. And zat sword—you are supposed to be a gentleman, not a soldier!"

"I'm sure you're right," said Gideon, still laughing.

"But at least my hair doesn't look like those wire-wool pads I use to scour my pans."

I did my best to look haughty. "The wire-wool pads *you* use to scour your pans? Aren't you mixing yourself up with Charlotte?"

"What?"

"I thought she was cleaning up your apartment these days."

Gideon looked a little embarrassed. "That's . . . that's not quite correct," he muttered.

"Huh! In your place I'd feel bad about it too," I said. "Give me the hat, please, Madame Rossini." The hat, a monstrous creation crowned with pale pink feathers, would at least look better than that hair. Or so I thought. A glance in the mirror showed that I'd made an unfortunate mistake.

Gideon was still laughing.

"Can we get moving now?" I asked crossly.

"Take care of my leetle swan-necked beauty, do you 'ear me?"

"Don't I always, Madame Rossini?"

"You must be joking," I said, out in the corridor. I pointed to the black scarf he was holding. "No blindfold today?"

"No, we can do without that. For reasons we both know," Gideon replied. "And because of the hat."

"Do you still think I'm about to lure you around a corner and hit you over the head with something?" I straightened my hat. "And by the way, I've been thinking about that again, and it's my belief that there's a perfectly simple explanation for the whole thing."

"Which is?" Gideon raised his eyebrows.

"You imagined it all after the event. While you were lying unconscious, you were dreaming about me, and so you decided later that it was all my fault."

"Yes, that possibility has occurred to me, too," he said, to my surprise. Then he took my hand and made me walk on. "But, no, I know what I saw."

"So why didn't you tell anyone that—apparently—I had lured you into a trap?"

"I didn't want them to think even worse of you than they do already." He grinned. "Well . . . do you have a headache?"

"I didn't really drink all that much," I said.

Gideon laughed. "No, sure. Basically you were stone cold sober."

I shook his hand off. "Could we please talk about something else?"

"Oh, come on! Surely I'm allowed to wind you up a bit! You were so sweet yesterday evening. Mr. George really thought you were totally exhausted when you went to sleep in the limousine."

"For two minutes at the most," I said, feeling embarrassed. I'd probably dribbled or done something else terrible.

"I hope you went straight to bed."

"Hm," I said. All I remembered, vaguely, was Mum taking all four hundred thousand hairpins out of my hair, and how I fell asleep as soon as my head hit the pillow. But

I wasn't going to tell him that. After all, he'd gone off to have a good time with Charlotte, Raphael, and the spaghetti.

Gideon stopped so suddenly that I collided with him and promptly forgot to breathe.

He turned to face me. "Listen," he murmured. "I didn't want to say this yesterday, because I thought you were too drunk, but now that you're sober again and as prickly as ever . . ." His fingers carefully stroked my forehead, and I was about to hyperventilate. Instead of going on, he kissed me. I had closed my eyes before his lips touched mine. The kiss was more intoxicating than yesterday evening's punch. It left me weak at the knees, and with a thousand butterflies in my stomach.

When Gideon let go of me again, he seemed to have forgotten what he wanted to say. He propped one arm on the wall beside my head and looked at me seriously. "We can't go on like this."

I tried to get my breath under control.

"Gwen . . ."

There were footsteps in the corridor behind us. Gideon quickly withdrew his arm and turned around. A moment later Mr. George was standing in front of us. "So there you are. We've been waiting for you. Why isn't Gwyneth blindfolded?"

"I quite forgot. You do it, please," said Gideon, giving Mr. George the black scarf. "I'll . . . I'll go on ahead."

Mr. George sighed as Gideon walked off. Then he looked at me and sighed again. "I thought I'd warned you,

Gwyneth," he said as he tied the cloth in front of my eyes. "You ought to be careful where your emotions are concerned."

"Hm," I said, touching my treacherously burning cheeks. "Then you shouldn't let me spend so much time with him. . . ."

Typical Guardians' logic again! If they'd wanted me not to fall in love with Gideon, they should have made sure he was an unattractive idiot with a silly quiff of hair, grubby fingernails, and a speech impediment. And they could have left out the violin stuff.

Mr. George led me through the darkness. "Maybe it's just too long ago that I was sixteen years old. But I do remember how easily one is impressed at your age."

"Mr. George, have you told anyone that I can see ghosts?"

"No," said Mr. George. "That's to say, I did try, but no one would listen to me. You see, the Guardians are scientists and mystics, but they won't meddle with parapsychology. Careful, there's a step here."

"Lesley—she's my best friend, but you probably know that—well, Lesley thinks that my . . . my ability is the magic of the raven."

Mr. George said nothing for a while. Then he replied, "Yes. I think so, too."

"And how exactly is the magic of the raven supposed to help me?"

"My dear child, if only I could tell you. I wish you'd rely more on sound human reason, but . . ."

"But I'm a hopeless case, you were going to say?" I couldn't help laughing. "You're probably right."

Gideon was waiting for us in the chronograph room, with Falk de Villiers, who paid me a rather absentminded compliment on my dress as he set the little cogwheels of the chronograph moving.

"Right, Gwyneth, today your conversation with Count Saint-Germain takes place. It's afternoon, the day before the soirée."

"I know," I said, with a surreptitious glance at Gideon.

"It's not a particularly arduous task," said Falk. "Gideon will take you up to the count's rooms and collect you again."

That had to mean I was to be left alone with the count. I began to feel anxious at once.

"Don't worry. You were getting on so well yesterday, remember?" Gideon put his finger into the chronograph and smiled at me. "Ready?"

"Ready when you are," I said softly, while the room filled with white light and Gideon disappeared before my eyes.

I stepped forward and gave Falk my hand.

"Today's password is *qui nescit dissimulare nescit regnare*," said Falk, as he pressed the needle into my finger. The ruby lit up, and everything went around in a swirl of red.

When I landed, I had forgotten the password again.

"Everything's all right," said Gideon's voice right beside me.

"Why is it so dark here? The count's expecting us. He might have been kind enough to light us a candle."

"Yes, but he doesn't know exactly where we land," said Gideon.

"Why not?"

I couldn't see him, but I felt that he was shrugging his shoulders. "He's never asked, and I have a vague feeling he wouldn't be very happy to think of us using his beloved alchemical laboratory as a runway for taking off and landing. Go carefully—this place is full of fragile objects."

We groped our way to the door. Out in the corridor, Gideon lit a torch and took it out of its holder. It cast eerie, moving shadows on the wall, and I instinctively moved a step closer to Gideon. "What was that wretched password again? Just in case anyone hits you on the head."

"*Qui nescit dissimulare nescit regnare.*"

"Why Nessie swims Loch Ness in the rain?"

He laughed and put the torch back in its holder.

"What are you doing?"

"I only wanted to . . . I mean, just now, when Mr. George interrupted us, there was something very important I wanted to say to you."

"Is it about what I told you in the church yesterday? I mean, I can understand that you may think me crazy because I see these beings, but a psychiatrist wouldn't make any difference."

Gideon frowned. "Just keep quiet for a moment, would you? I have to pluck up all my courage to make you a declaration of love. . . . I've had absolutely no practice in this kind of thing."

"What?"

"Gwyneth," he said, perfectly seriously, "I've fallen in love with you."

My stomach muscles contracted as if I'd had a shock. But it was joy. *"Really?"*

"Yes, *really!*" In the light of the torch I saw Gideon smile. "I do realize we've known each other for less than a week, and at first I thought you were rather . . . childish, and I probably behaved badly to you. But you're terribly complicated, I never know what you'll do next, and in some ways you really are terrifyingly . . . er . . . naive. Sometimes I just want to shake you."

"Okay, I can see you were right about having no practice in making declarations of love," I agreed.

"But then you're so amusing, and clever, and amazingly sweet," Gideon went on, as if he hadn't heard me. "And the worst of it is, you only have to be in the same room and I need to touch you and kiss you. . . ."

"Yes, that's really too bad," I whispered, and my heart turned over as Gideon took the hatpin out of my hair, tossed the feathered monstrosity into the air to fall on the floor, drew me close, and kissed me. About three minutes later, I was leaning against the wall, totally breathless, making an effort to stay upright.

"Hey, Gwyneth, try breathing in and out in the normal way," said Gideon, amused.

I gave him a little push. "Stop that! I can't believe how conceited you are!"

"Sorry. It's just such a . . . a heady feeling to think you'd forget to breathe on my account." He took the torch out of the holder again. "Come on. I'm sure the count is waiting for us."

Only when we turned into the next corridor did I remember my hat, but I didn't feel like going back for it.

"It's funny, but I was just thinking I wouldn't mind a repeat of that boring evening when we elapsed to 1953," said Gideon. "Just you and me and Cousin Sofa."

Our footsteps echoed through the long corridors, and I gradually emerged from my rose-tinted sense of walking on air, reminding myself where we were. Or rather, *when* we were. "If I took the torch, you could draw your sword, just to be on the safe side," I suggested. "You never know. What year was it when you got hit on the head?" (This was one of the many questions that Lesley had written down for me to drop into the conversation when the state of my hormones allowed it.)

"I've just noticed that I made you a declaration of love, but you didn't make me one," said Gideon.

"Didn't I?"

"Not in words, at least, and I'm not sure if anything else counts. Shh!"

I had squealed, because right ahead of us a fat, dark brown rat was crossing our path at its leisure, looking not in the least afraid of us. Its eyes glowed red in the torchlight. "Have we been immunized against the plague?" I asked, and as we walked on, I clutched Gideon's hand more tightly.

THE ROOM on the first floor chosen by Count Saint-Germain as his office in the Temple was small and looked decidedly unassuming for the Grand Master of the Guardians' Lodge, even if he didn't spend much time in London. One wall was entirely covered by shelves of leather-bound books reaching to the ceiling, and in front of those stood a desk with two armchairs upholstered in the same fabric used for the curtains. There was no other furniture. Outside, the September sun was shining, and there was no fire in the hearth. Even without one, the room was warm enough. The window looked out on the small inner courtyard with the fountain that was still there in our own time. Both the window seat and the desk were covered with papers, quill pens, candles for melting sealing wax, and books, some of them stacked dangerously high. If the piles toppled, they would knock over the inkwells standing so confidently amidst the confusion. It was a comfortable little room, and there wasn't a soul in it, yet when I entered it, for some reason the fine hairs on the back of my neck stood up.

A morose secretary in a white Mozart-style wig had brought me here, and with the words "I am sure the count won't keep you waiting long," he had closed the door behind me. I hadn't liked being separated from Gideon, but after handing me over to the grumpy secretary, he had gone off through the nearest door looking cheerful and like someone who knew his way around here very well.

I went over to the window and looked out into the quiet inner courtyard. It all seemed very peaceful, but I couldn't shake off the uncomfortable feeling that I wasn't alone. Maybe, I thought, someone was watching me through the wall behind the books. Or the mirror over the mantelpiece was a window on the other side, like police detectives have in their interrogation rooms.

For a while, I just stood there feeling uncomfortable, but then I thought if I just stood around looking unnaturally awkward, the secret observer might notice that I felt I was being watched. So I took the top book off one of the piles on the wide window seat and opened it. Marcellus, *De Medicamentis*. Aha. Marcellus—whoever he had been— had obviously discovered some unusual medical treatments, and they'd been collected in this little book. I found a nice passage telling you how to cure liver disease. All you had to do was catch a green lizard, remove its liver, tie the liver to a red cloth or a naturally black rag (what did he mean, naturally black?), and hang the rag or the cloth on the right-hand side of the sick person. Then if you let the lizard run away, saying *ecce dimitto te vivam* and some other Latin words like that, the invalid would be cured. The only question, I thought, was whether the lizard *could* run away once you'd removed its liver. I closed the book again. This Marcellus must have lost his marbles. The book next to it on top of the pile was bound in dark brown leather, and very fat and heavy, so I let it lie where it was as I leafed through it. Gold lettering on the cover told me that it was *Of All Manner of Demons, and How They May Render Assistance to Both the Magician and the Common Man*. Although I wasn't a magician, or a "common man" either, I felt curious, and opened it somewhere in the middle. The picture of an ugly dog looked at me out of the page, with a caption underneath saying that this was Jestan, a demon of the

Hindu Kush, who brought disease, death, and war. I disliked Jestan at sight, so I went on leafing through the book. A strange distorted face with horny growths on its skull (rather like one of the Klingons in the Star Trek films), stared at me from the next page, and as I was staring back, repelled, the Klingon closed its eyes, rose off the paper like smoke from a chimney, and swiftly solidified into a complete figure entirely clad in red. The figure towered up and glared down at me with glowing eyes. "Who dares to summon the great and mighty Berith?" it called.

Naturally I felt a little queasy, but experience had taught me that while ghosts might look dangerous and utter nasty threats, as a rule, they couldn't touch and move anything, not even a breath of air. And I very much hoped that this Berith was nothing but a ghost, a copy of the real demon trapped between the covers of this book, and the real demon, as it was also to be hoped, wasn't around anymore.

So I said politely, but unimpressed, "No one summoned you."

"Berith, demon of lies, Grand Duke of Hell," Berith introduced himself in a ringing voice. "Otherwise known as Bolfri."

"Yes, that's what it says here," I agreed, looking at the book again. "You also improve the voices of singers." A nice gift, that one. However, once you'd summoned him with an invocation (which looked tricky, since it was obviously written in ancient Babylonian), if you wanted him to improve your voice, you had to make him assorted sacrifices, including aborted monstrosities, preferably still alive. And that was nothing compared with what you had to do to get him to turn other metals into gold, which he could also do. As a result, the Sichemites—whoever they were—had worshipped Berith. Until Jacob and his sons came along and "put all the men of Sichem to death by the sword, torturing them most horribly." So far, so good.

"Berith commands twenty-six legions," he announced grandly.

But he hadn't done anything to me so far, and I felt even braver. "I think people who talk about themselves in the third person are peculiar," I said, and turned the page. Just as I'd hoped, Berith disappeared back into the book like smoke blown away by the wind. I breathed a sigh of relief.

"An interesting choice of reading matter," said a quiet voice behind me. I spun around. Count Saint-Germain, unnoticed, had entered the room. He was leaning on a stick with an elaborately carved handle, his tall, lean figure was as impressive as ever, and his dark eyes were bright and watchful.

"Yes, very interesting," I murmured rather uncertainly. But then I pulled myself together, shut the book, and sank into a deep curtsey. When I emerged from my huge skirts again, the count was smiling.

"I'm glad you have come," he said, taking my hand and raising it to his lips. I could hardly feel their touch. "It seems to me advisable for us to get to know each other better, for our first meeting was a little . . . unfortunate, was it not?"

I said nothing. At our first meeting I'd concentrated mainly on singing all the verses of the national anthem in my head, the count had made some offensive remarks about the low IQ of women in general and me in particular, and finally he had half strangled me and threatened me in a distinctly unconventional way. He was dead right: the whole thing had been more than a little unfortunate.

"How cold your hand is," he said. "Come along, sit down. I am an old man. I can't spend a long time standing." He smiled, let go of my hand, and sat down in the chair behind the desk. Against the background of all those bookshelves, he once again looked like his own portrait, an ageless man with distinguished features, lively eyes, and a white wig, surrounded by an unmistakable aura of mystery and danger. I had no option but to sit down on the other chair.

"Are you interested in magic?" he asked, pointing to the stack of books.

I shook my head. "Not at all until last Monday, to be honest."

"Yes, the situation is rather strange, don't you agree? All these years, your mother has kept you thinking of yourself as an ordinary girl. And from now on, you have to remember that you play an important part in the history of one of the greatest secrets of mankind. Can you imagine why she did it?"

"Because she loves me." I meant it to sound like a question, but it came out as a firm statement.

The count laughed. "Yes, that's the way women think! *Love!* The fair sex really does overwork that word. Love is the answer—I am always moved to hear that reply. Or amused, depending on circumstances. What women will never understand is that they and men have entirely different notions of love."

I didn't reply.

The count tilted his head slightly to one side. "Without a woman's wholehearted commitment to love, it would be far more difficult for her to subordinate herself to a man in every respect."

I tried to keep my expression neutral. "In fact, that's kind of changed in my own time." (And thank goodness, I thought.) "In the twenty-first century, men and women have equal rights. No one has to feel worth less than anyone else."

The count laughed again, this time at some length, as if I'd told a really funny joke. "Yes," he said at last. "Yes, I've been told that before. But believe me, whatever rights women may be granted, it makes no difference to human nature."

What could I say to that? Nothing would probably be best. As the count had just acknowledged, it's hard to change human nature. That might easily apply to his own nature, as well.

He went on looking at me for some time, his mouth curving in amusement. Then he said, suddenly, "But magic . . . according to the prophesies, you ought to know something about that. *Ruby red, with G major, the magic of the raven, brings the Circle of Twelve home into safe haven.*"

"Yes, I've heard that several times before," I said. "But no one has been able to tell me what the magic of the raven really is."

"*The raven red, on ruby pinions winging its way between the worlds, hears dead men singing. It scarce knows its strength, the price it scarce knows, but its power will arise and the Circle will close.*"

I shrugged my shoulders. No one could make head or tail of these cryptic lines of verse.

"It's only a prophesy of dubious origin," said the count. "It isn't necessarily accurate." He leaned back and went on scrutinizing me intently. "Tell me something about your parents and your home."

"My parents?" I was rather surprised. "There isn't really much to tell. My father died of leukemia when I was seven. Before he fell sick, he was a lecturer at Durham University. We lived in Durham until he died. Then my mum moved back to my grandparents' house in London, with my little brother and sister and me. We live there with my aunt and my cousin and our great-aunt Maddy. My mother works as a hospital administrator."

"And she has red hair, like all the Montrose girls, doesn't she? Like your brother and sister, am I right?"

"Yes, they all have red hair except me." Why was he harping on that? "My father had dark hair."

"All the other women in the Circle of Twelve are red-haired. Did you know that? Until not so long ago, hair of that color was enough to get you burnt as a witch in many countries. At all times, and in all cultures, people have found magic both fascinating and threatening. That is also why I have studied it in such depth. Once you know about something, there is no reason to fear it." He leaned forward and placed his fingertips together. "In particular, I take a burning interest in the magic of Far Eastern cultures. On my travels in India and China, I was fortunate enough to meet many teachers who were prepared to pass on their knowledge. I was initiated into the mysteries of the Akasha Chronicle and learnt much that would be beyond the intellectual capacity of most Western cultures. Knowledge that would drive the Inquisition, even today, to take violent action. There is nothing the Church fears more than the discovery by human beings that God is not sitting far away in heaven, determining our fate, but is within us." He looked at me hard and then smiled. "It is always refreshing to discuss such blasphemous notions with you children of the twenty-first century, who do not bat an eyelash at the thought of heresy."

Well, I don't expect we would, even if we knew exactly what it was.

"The Asiatic masters are far ahead of us on the path of spiritual development," said the count. "It is from them that I learned many small . . . abilities such as the one I demonstrated to you last time we met. My teacher was a monk, a member of a secret order in the distant Himalayas. He and his monastic brothers communicate without using their vocal cords, and they can defeat their enemies without lifting a finger, so strong is the power and imagination of their minds."

"That must be useful," I said cautiously. I didn't want him thinking he'd like to show me all over again. "I think you were trying out that ability on Lord Alastair at yesterday evening's soirée."

"Ah, the soirée." He smiled again. "From my point of view, it won't take place until tomorrow. How delightful to know that we shall really be meeting Lord Alastair there. Does he appreciate my little performance?"

"He seemed impressed, anyway," I replied. "But not really intimidated. He said he was going to see to it that Gideon and I were never born at all. And he called us *these creatures*."

"Yes, he has an unfortunate tendency to make uncivil remarks," said the count. "Although in that he can't compete with his ancestor, the Conte di Madrone. I should have killed the conte when I had the chance. However, I was young at the time, and regrettably naive. . . . Well, that's not a mistake I'll make a second time. Even if I cannot lay him low with my own hands, Lord Alastair's days are numbered, however many men he gathers around him for protection, and however expert his swordplay. If I were a young man, I would challenge him myself. But now my descendant can take over that role. Gideon's skill at fencing is considerable."

At the mention of Gideon's name, I felt warm all over, as usual. I thought of what he had said a little while ago, and felt even warmer.

Instinctively, I looked at the door. "Where has Gideon gone?"

"Oh, for a little outing, I expect," said the count casually. "He has enough time to pay a call on a charming young woman of my acquaintance. She lives quite close, and if he takes the coach, he can be with her in a few minutes."

What?

"Does he do that often?"

The count smiled again, a warm, friendly smile, but there was something else lurking in it. Something that I couldn't interpret. "He hasn't known her very long. It was only recently that I introduced them. She is a clever and very attractive young widow, and I am of the opinion that it does a young man no harm to spend a little time in the company of . . . well, let's call her an experienced woman."

I was unable to say a word to that, but obviously I wasn't expected to.

"Lavinia Rutland is one of those delightful women who enjoy passing on the benefit of their experience to the opposite sex," said the count.

You bet she did. I'd thought so myself. Upset, I stared at my hands, which had clenched into fists entirely of their own accord. Lavinia Rutland, the lady in the green dress. So that's why they'd seemed so much at ease with each other yesterday evening.

"I have an impression that you do not quite like the idea," said the count in a soft voice.

He was dead right. I didn't like it one little bit. It took me a great effort to look the count in the eye again.

He was still smiling that warm, kindly smile. "My dear, it is important to learn early that no woman can claim rights of any kind over a man. Women who do so end up unloved and lonely. The cleverer a woman is, the sooner she will come to terms with the nature of men."

What stupid twaddle!

"Ah, but of course you are still *very* young, are you not? Much younger, it seems to me, than other girls of your own age. You have probably just fallen in love for the first time."

"No," I muttered.

Yes, though. Yes! Or at least it felt like the first time. It was so special. So necessary to me. So painful. So sweet.

The count laughed quietly. "It's nothing to be ashamed of. I would be disappointed if it were otherwise."

He had said the same thing at the soirée, when I burst into tears at the sound of Gideon's violin playing.

"Fundamentally, it is very simple: a woman in love would not hesitate to die for the object of her affections," said the count. "Would you give your life for Gideon?"

Well, I'd rather not. "I've never thought about it," I said, confused.

The count sighed. "Regrettably—and thanks to the dubious motives of your mother in protecting you—you and Gideon have not yet spent very much time together, but I am already impressed to see how well he has played his part. Love positively shines out of your eyes. Love and jealousy!"

Played what part?

"Nothing is easier to calculate than the reactions of a woman in love. No one is more easily controlled than a woman whose actions are determined by her feelings for a man," the count went on. "I explained that to Gideon the very first time we met. Of course I am a little sorry that he wasted so much energy on your cousin—what is her name again? Charlotte?"

Now I was staring at him. For some reason, I thought about Aunt Maddy's vision of the ruby heart lying on a rocky ledge above a precipice. I'd have liked to put my hands over my ears to shut out the sound of his gentle voice.

"In that respect, at least, he is more sophisticated than I was at his age," said the count. "And it must be admitted that nature has equipped him with many advantages! The body of a young Adonis! Such a handsome face, such charm, so many gifts! He hardly has to do anything to attract girls. *The lion roars loud in F sharp, his mane is diamond bright, multiplicatio is his, his star the sun gives light.*"

The truth hit me like a punch in the solar plexus. Everything Gideon had done, his touch, his gestures, his kisses, his loving words, they were all intended only to manipulate me. So that I'd fall in love with him, like Charlotte before me. So that we could be controlled more easily.

And the count was so right. Gideon hadn't needed to do much. My stupid heart had gone straight to him of its own accord and fallen at his feet.

In my mind's eye, I saw the lion go over to the ruby heart at the top of that precipice and sweep it aside with one blow of his paw. It fell in slow motion, hit the bottom of the ravine far below, and broke into a thousand tiny drops of blood.

"And have you heard him play the violin? If not, then I'll make sure that you do—there's nothing better than music for conquering a woman's heart." Lost in reverie, the count looked up at the ceiling. "That was another of Casanova's tricks. Music and poetry."

I was going to die. I felt absolutely sure of it. Where my heart had been just now, an icy cold was spreading. It seeped into my stomach, my legs, feet, arms and hands, and last of all, into my head. Like a trailer for a film, the events of the last few days ran through my mind, to the theme tune of "The Winner Takes It All." From the first kiss in that confessional to his declaration of love just now in the cellar. All of it manipulation on the grand scale—and except for a few interruptions, when he'd probably been his real self, all perfectly carried out. And that damn violin had been the finishing touch.

Although I tried to remember it later, I had no clear idea of the rest of my conversation with the count, because once the chill took me over, nothing mattered anymore. The good thing was that he did most of the talking on his own. In his soft, pleasant voice, he told me about his childhood in Tuscany, the shame of his illegitimate birth, his difficulties in tracking down his real father, and how even in his youth he had studied the mysteries of the chronograph and the old prophesies. I really did try to listen, if only because I knew that I'd be expected to repeat every word he said to Lesley. But it was no good. My thoughts were just circling around my own stupidity. And I badly wanted to be alone so that I could cry my eyes out.

"Sir?" The grumpy secretary had knocked and opened the door. "The archbishop's delegation is here."

"Ah, good," said the count, rising. He winked at me. "Politics in these times are still greatly influenced by the Church."

I scrambled up too and made him a curtsey.

"I have so enjoyed talking to you," said the count. "And now I look forward eagerly to our next meeting."

I murmured some kind of agreement.

"Please give Gideon my regards and say I am sorry not to have seen him myself today." The count took his stick and went to the door. "And if I may give you a piece of advice: a clever woman succeeds in concealing her jealousy. Otherwise we men always feel so sure of ourselves. . . ."

I heard that faint, soft laugh one last time, and then I was alone at last. But not for long, because a few minutes later, the morose secretary came in and said, "Follow me, please."

I had sunk into my chair again, and I was waiting for the tears, with my eyes closed, but they wouldn't come. Maybe it was better that way. In silence, I followed the secretary downstairs, and then we stood around for a while, also in silence (I kept thinking I was going to fall over and die), until the man looked at the clock on the wall. Frowning, he said, "He's late."

At that moment, the door opened and Gideon came in. My heart forgot that it was already broken and lying smashed at the bottom of a rocky ravine, and it beat quickly a couple of times. Wild anxiety took over from the chill in my body. Considering the disordered state of his clothes, his tousled, sweaty hair, his flushed cheeks, and the almost feverish gleam in his green eyes, I might possibly have put it all down to Lady Lavinia, but there was also a long tear in his sleeve, and the lace at his neck and cuffs was drenched in blood.

"You're injured, sir!" cried the morose secretary in alarm, taking the words out of my mouth. (Okay, except for the *sir*.) "I'll get someone to call a doctor."

"No, don't do that," said Gideon, looking so self-confident that I could have hit him. "It's not my blood. Or not all of it, anyway. Come on, Gwen. We must hurry. I was slightly held up."

He took my hand and led me on. The secretary followed us down to the next flight of stairs, stammering a couple of times, "But what happened, sir? Shouldn't we tell the count . . . ?" Gideon said only that there was no time and he'd visit the count again as soon as possible to tell him what had happened.

"We'll go on our own from here," he said as we reached the foot of the stairs, where the two guards were standing with their swords drawn. "Give the count my regards! *Qui nescit dissimulare nescit regnare.*"

The two Guardians let us pass, and the secretary bowed a good-bye. Gideon took a torch out of its holder and made me go on. "Come along, we have another two minutes at the most!" He seemed to be in high spirits, if untidy. "Have you worked out yet what the password means?"

"No," I said, surprised at myself to find that my heart, having grown back, refused to fall into the ravine again. It was acting as if everything was all right, and the hope that after all my heart might not be wrong was almost too much for me. "But I did find out something else. Whose blood is that on your sword?"

"*He who does not know how to dissimulate does not know how to rule,*" said Gideon, holding up the torch to show us the way around the next corner. "Louis XI."

"Very suitable, I'm sure," I said.

"To be honest, I haven't the faintest idea of the name of the man who got his blood all over these clothes. Madame Rossini is going to throw a fit." Gideon opened the laboratory door, and put the torch in a holder on the wall. By its flickering light, I saw a large table covered with strange apparatus, glass bottles, little flasks, and beakers filled with liquids and powders in many different colors. The walls were in shadow, but I could see that they were almost entirely covered by diagrams and writing, and just above the torch, a roughly sketched death's-head with pentagrams instead of eyes was grinning at us.

"Come over here," said Gideon, leading me around to the other side of the table. Then he let go of my hand at last. But only to put both his own hands on my waist and draw me close to him. "How did your conversation with the count go?"

"It was very . . . enlightening," I said. The phantom heart in my breast was fluttering like a small bird, and I swallowed the lump in my throat. "The count explained how you . . . you and he share the same weird opinion that a woman is easier to control if she's in love. It must have been really annoying to put in all that strenuous work on Charlotte and then have to begin again at the beginning with me, wasn't it?"

"What on earth are you talking about?" Gideon looked at me, frowning.

"You did it really well, all the same," I went on. "The count thinks so, too, by the way. Of course you didn't have a particularly difficult time with me. . . . My God, I'm so ashamed when I think how easy I made it for you." I couldn't look at him anymore.

"Gwyneth—" He interrupted himself. "Look, we'll be traveling back any minute. Maybe we should continue this conversation later. In peace and quiet. I haven't the faintest idea what you're getting at. . . ."

"I only want to know whether it's true," I said. Of course it was true, but as everyone knows, hope dies hard. I was getting the familiar feeling that we were about to travel forward in time again. "Whether you really planned to make me fall in love with you—the same as you did with Charlotte before me."

Gideon let go of me. "This isn't the moment," he said. "Gwyneth. We'll talk about it when we get back. I promise you."

"No! Now." The knots tying up my throat broke apart, and my tears began to flow. "Just say yes or no—that'll do. Did you plan it all?"

Gideon was rubbing his forehead. "Gwen—"

"Yes or no?" I sobbed.

"Yes," said Gideon, "but—oh, please stop crying."

And for the second time that day, my heart—only this time its second edition, the phantom heart that had grown out of sheer hope—fell over the precipice and smashed into thousands of tiny little pieces at the bottom of the ravine. "Okay, that's really all I wanted to know. Thanks for being so honest."

"Gwen. I want to explain. . . ." Gideon disappeared into thin air in front of me. For a few seconds, as the chill came back into my body, I stared at the flickering torchlight and the death's-head, tried to suppress my tears, and then everything blurred before my eyes.

It took me a few seconds to get used to the light in the chronograph room of my own time, but I heard the alarm in Dr. White's voice and the sound of ripping fabric.

"It's nothing," said Gideon. "Only a tiny cut. It hardly bled at all. I don't even need a plaster for it, Dr. White, and you can put those clamps away again! Nothing happened."

"Hello, haystack girl!" said Xemerius. "You'll never guess what we've found out! Oh, no! You haven't been crying again, have you?"

Mr. George took hold of me with both hands and swung me once around my own axis. "She's not injured!" he said, with relief in his voice.

Not injured, no, except for my heart.

"Let's get out of here," said Xemerius. "Bonehead's brother and your friend Lesley have something very interesting to tell you! Guess what? They've tracked down the place described by the coordinates in the Green Rider code. You'll never believe it!"

"Gwyneth?" Gideon was looking at me as if he was afraid I might throw myself under the first bus to come along, all because of him.

"I'm fine," I said, without looking him in the eye. "Mr. George, could you please take me upstairs? I have to go home. It's urgent."

"Of course." Mr. George nodded.

Gideon made a movement, but Dr. White was holding him. "Oh, keep still, for heaven's sake!" He had torn the sleeves of Gideon's jacket and the shirt he was wearing under it right off. The bare arm was encrusted with blood, and I saw a small cut up almost by Gideon's shoulder. The little ghost boy Robert was staring at all the blood in horror.

"Who did this? It will have to be disinfected and stitched," said Dr. White gloomily.

"Certainly not," said Gideon. He was pale, and there was nothing left of the high spirits he'd shown back in the eighteenth century. "We can see about that later. I have to talk to Gwyneth first."

"There's really no need," I said. "I know all I want to know. And now I have to go home."

"I should just about think so!" said Xemerius.

"Tomorrow is another day," Mr. George told Gideon, as he picked up the black scarf. "And Gwyneth looks tired. She has to go to school tomorrow morning."

"Exactly!" said Xemerius. "And tonight she's going on

a treasure hunt. Or a hunt for whatever those coordinates lead us to."

Mr. George blindfolded me. The last thing I saw was Gideon's eyes, looking unnaturally green in his pale face.

"Good night, everyone," I said, and then Mr. George led me out of the room. No one had answered me anyway, except for little Robert.

"Okay, I'll put you out of your suspense," said Xemerius. "Lesley and Raphael had a lot of fun this afternoon—unlike you, I guess from the look of you. Well, anyway, the two of them managed to locate the place described in the coordinates precisely. You can have three guesses where it is."

"Here in London?" I asked.

"Bingo!" cried Xemerius.

"What did you say?" Mr. George asked me.

"Nothing," I said. "Excuse me, Mr. George."

Mr. George sighed. "I hope your conversation with Count Saint-Germain went well."

"Oh, yes," I said bitterly. "It was very instructive in all sorts of ways."

"Hello! I'm still here, you know," said Xemerius, and I felt his damp aura as he clung to my back like a monkey, with his arms around my neck. "And I have really, really interesting news. Listen to this: the hiding place we're looking for is here in London. And even better, it's in Mayfair. To be precise, in Bourdon Place. And to be even more precise, at number 81 Bourdon Place. Now what do you say?"

In my own home? The coordinates described a place in

our own house? For heaven's sake, what would my grandfather have hidden there? Maybe another book? One with drawings that would finally help us to get somewhere?

"So far the doggy girl and the frog-eater have done a good job," said Xemerius. "Admittedly, I had no idea of that coordinates stuff myself. But now I can be really useful. Because only the unique, the wonderful, the brilliantly clever Xemerius can stick his head through walls and see what's hidden behind them. We're both going on a treasure hunt tonight."

"Would you like to talk about it?" asked Mr. George.

I shook my head. "No, it can wait until tomorrow," I said, and I was speaking to both Mr. George and Xemerius.

Tonight I was going to lie awake in mourning for my broken heart. I wanted to wallow in self-pity and high-flown metaphors. And maybe I'd listen to Bon Jovi and "Hallelujah" while I wallowed. After all, everyone needs her own soundtrack for a tragic case like this.

EPILOGUE

London,
29 September 1782

HE LANDED with his back to the wall, placed his hand on the hilt of his sword, and looked around him. There was no one about in the yard of the inn, just as Lord Alastair had promised. Washing lines stretched across it from wall to wall, and the white sheets hanging on them moved slightly in the wind.

Paul looked up at the windows that reflected the afternoon sun. A cat lay on one windowsill, giving him a mocking glance, one paw dangling casually over the edge of the sill. The cat reminded him of Lucy.

He took his hand off the sword hilt and shook out the lace cuffs around his wrists. These Rococo clothes all looked the same to him, stupid knee breeches, weird, impractically long tailcoats, embroidery and lace everywhere. Frightful. He had intended to wear the wig and costume left over from his visits to the year 1745, but Lucy and Lady Tilney had insisted on having a completely new outfit made for him. They said everyone would notice if he went about in 1782 wearing clothes dating back to 1745, and when he said, who cared, he was only going to a remote yard for a short time to meet Lord Alastair and exchange the papers, they refused to see his point. He slipped his hand between his coat and his shirt, where the folded copies lay in a brown envelope.

"Excellent. You are punctual."

The cool voice made him spin around. Lord Alastair stepped out of the shadow of the arched entrance to the yard, as elegantly dressed as ever, even if his clothes were very colorful, and their embroidery and the jewels he wore sparkled in the sunlight. He looked exotic against the plain background of the sheets. Even the hilt of his sword seemed to be made of pure gold and was set with gemstones. They gave the weapon the appearance of being harmless, almost ridiculous.

Paul glanced quickly through the arch, where green turf ran beside the road and down to the Thames. He could hear horses snorting, so he assumed that Lord Alastair had come in a coach.

"Are you alone?" asked his lordship. His tone of voice was extremely arrogant, although he also sounded like a man with a chronically stuffy nose. He came closer. "What a pity! I would have liked to see your pretty red-haired companion again. She had such . . . such an unusual way of expressing her opinion."

"She was only disappointed that you didn't make use of the advantage our last information gave you. And she's suspicious about what you intend to do with it."

"Your information was incomplete."

"It was complete enough! The Florentine Alliance hadn't thought its plans through properly! In forty years, five attempts on the count's life have failed, and you were personally responsible for two of them. Last time—and that was eleven years ago—you seem to have been so certain of yourself!"

"Have no fear! The next attempt won't fail!" said Lord Alastair. "Until now, my ancestors and I have always made the mistake of fighting the so-called count as if he were an ordinary human being. We have tried to unmask him, spread defamatory rumors about him, destroy his reputation. We have also tried to help lost souls like you back to the straight and narrow path, before we realized that you were all lost long ago—because you inherited his demonic blood."

Paul frowned with annoyance. He had never been able to make head or tail of the unctuous remarks uttered by his lordship and the other men of the Florentine Alliance.

"We have tried to destroy him, like any ordinary man, with poison, the sword, bullets," Lord Alastair went on. "How ludicrous!" He gave a hoarse laugh. "But whatever we did, he always seemed to be one step ahead of us. Wherever we went, he was always there first. He seemed invincible. He has influential friends and protectors everywhere, and like him, they are experts in black magic. The members of his Lodge are among the most powerful men of our time. It has taken me decades to understand that a demon cannot be defeated by human methods. But now I know better."

"Glad to hear it," said Paul, casting a quick glance to one side. Two more men, clad in black and carrying drawn swords, had appeared in the arched entrance. Damn it— Lucy had been right! Alastair had no intention of keeping his word. "Do you have the letters?"

"Of course," said Lord Alastair, taking a thick bundle of papers tied together with a red cord out of his coat pocket. "These days—and not least thanks to you and your excellent information—I have succeeded in getting a good friend of mine to infiltrate the ranks of the Guardians. He is now providing me with important news every day. Did you know that the count is back in town at this moment? Ah, but of course you did!" He weighed up the bundle in his hand, and then tossed it to Paul.

Paul caught it neatly with one hand. "Thank you. I'm sure you've had copies of them made."

"There was no need," said his lordship, with his usual arrogance. "And what about you? Have you brought me what I asked for?"

Paul stowed the bundle of letters away under his coat and held up the brown envelope. "Five pages of the family tree of the de Villiers family, beginning in the sixteenth century with Lancelot de Villiers, the first time traveler, and ending with Gideon de Villiers, born in the twentieth century."

"And the female line?" asked Lord Alastair, and now he almost sounded excited.

"It's all in there as well. Beginning with Elaine Burghley and ending with the name of Gwyneth Shepherd." Speaking her name gave Paul a pang. He cast a quick glance at the two men. They had stopped under the arch, hands on the hilts of their swords, as if they were waiting for something. Gritting his teeth, he admitted to himself that he could guess what it was.

"Good. Then give it to me."

Paul hesitated. "You haven't kept to our agreement," he said, trying to gain time. He pointed to the two men. "You were going to come alone."

Lord Alastair followed his gaze with indifference. "A gentleman of my social rank is never alone. My servants accompany me everywhere." He took another step forward. "Now, give me the papers! I'll see to the rest of it myself."

"And suppose I change my mind?"

"It doesn't matter to me whether I take those papers from your hands when you're dead or alive," said his lordship, and his hand went to the ornate hilt of his sword. "In other words, it makes no difference whether I kill you before or after I have them."

Paul put his hand on his own sword. "You swore an oath."

"Huh!" cried Lord Alastair, drawing his sword. "A man doesn't outwit the Devil by means of morality! So give me those papers!"

Paul took two steps back and drew his own sword.

"Didn't you say it was no use trying to defeat us with ordinary weapons?" he asked, raising one eyebrow as derisively as possible.

"We'll see about that," said his lordship. *"En garde,* demon!"

Paul would rather have gone on talking, but Lord Alastair seemed to have been just waiting for his opportunity. He lunged, obviously fiercely determined to kill Paul. That ferocity and his brilliance as a swordsman were not an ideal combination.

Paul realized as much when, two minutes later, he had his back to the wall. He had parried the attack as well as he could, had ducked down under the sheets, and tried to drive Lord Alastair into a corner himself. It didn't work.

The cat from the windowsill, spitting, jumped down and ran away through the arched entrance. All was still behind the windows. Damn it, why hadn't he listened to Lucy when she begged him to set the chronograph to a shorter window of time? Then he might have been able to hold out long enough to disappear into thin air before his lordship's eyes.

Alastair's weapon flashed in the sun. His next stroke was so hard and forceful that it almost knocked Paul's sword out of his hand.

"Wait!" he cried, gasping even more than he really had to. "You win! I'll give you the papers."

Lord Alastair lowered his sword. "Very sensible of you."

Appearing to breathe with difficulty, Paul pushed himself off from the wall and tossed the brown envelope to

Lord Alastair. At the same time he rushed after it himself, but Lord Alastair seemed to have been prepared for that. He let the envelope drop to the ground, and easily parried Paul's attack.

"I can see through any demon's cunning tricks!" he cried, laughing. "And now let's take a look at the color of your blood!" He feinted neatly, and Paul felt Lord Alastair's blade slit open the sleeve of his coat and, under it, his skin. Warm blood ran down his arm. It didn't hurt too badly, so he assumed it was only a slight scratch, but the malicious grin on his adversary's face, and the fact that Alastair hardly seemed to be at all out of breath, while he himself was gasping for air, didn't strike him as a promising state of affairs.

"What are you waiting for?" Lord Alastair called over his shoulder to the two servants. "We mustn't give him time, or do you want to see him vanish into thin air before your eyes, like the last of them you fought?"

The black-clad men reacted at once. As they ran past the sheets and toward him, Paul knew he had lost. At least, the thought went through his head, Lucy was safe. If she had come with him, she would have died as well.

"Speak your last words," said Lord Alastair, and Paul thought of dropping his sword, falling on his knees, and starting to pray. Maybe his devout lordship would wait a little while on the grounds of piety before murdering him. Or maybe he would be dead even before his knees touched the ground.

At that moment, he caught sight of a movement on

the other side of the sheets and one of Lord Alastair's men collapsed without a sound before he could finish turning toward it. After a split second of alarm, the other lunged with his sword at the newcomer, a young man in a green coat who now emerged from behind the sheets and casually parried the stroke with his own sword.

"Gideon de Villiers!" Paul exclaimed as he plucked up new courage and tried to defend himself against Lord Alastair's swordplay. "I'd never have expected to be so glad to see you, boy."

"I felt curious, that was all," said Gideon. "I saw the coach with Lord Alastair's crest on the panels standing out there in the street, and I thought I'd see what was going on in this deserted backyard—"

"My lord, this is the demon who killed Jenkins in Hyde Park!" Lord Alastair's man gasped.

"Do what you're paid to do," Lord Alastair spat at him, seeming to redouble his own strength. Paul felt it himself for the second time, on the same arm but a little higher up. This time the pain went right through him.

"My lord . . ." The servant seemed to be in difficulty.

"You deal with this one!" Lord Alastair cried angrily. "I'll see to the other!"

Relieved, Paul gasped for air as his lordship moved away. He cast a brief glance at his arm—it was bleeding, but he could still hold his sword.

"We've met before!" Lord Alastair was standing opposite Gideon, his sword blade dark with Paul's blood.

"Quite correct," replied Gideon, and Paul admired—if

rather reluctantly—the calm assurance of his manner. Had the boy no fear at all? "Eleven years ago, shortly after your failed attempt on Count Saint-Germain's life, we met at Galliano's fencing school."

"Marquis Weldon, wasn't it?" said his lordship scornfully. "I remember. You brought me a message from the devil himself."

"I brought you a warning, which, unfortunately, you ignored." There was a dangerous glint in Gideon's green eyes.

"Demon riffraff! I knew it as soon as I set eyes on you. And you parried neatly, but you may recollect that I won our little fencing match."

"I remember it very well," replied Gideon, shaking the lace cuffs at his wrists as if they were bothering him. "As if it were only last week. Which from my point of view, in fact, it was. *En garde!*"

Metal clashed against metal, but Paul couldn't see who had the upper hand, for the remaining servant had gathered his wits together and was making for him with his drawn sword.

The man fought less elegantly than his master, but very fiercely, and Paul felt the strength in his injured arm quickly failing him, in spite of that short breathing space.

When would he finally travel back? It couldn't be much longer now! He gritted his teeth and feinted. For several minutes, no one spoke—there was only the clashing of blades and hard breathing to be heard—and then, out of the corner of his eye, Paul saw Lord Alastair's valuable sword fly through the air. It landed on the paving of the yard with a dull clang.

Thank God!

The servant took a couple of steps back. "My lord?"

"That was a sly trick, *demon!*" said his lordship angrily. "Against all the rules! I was winning!"

"Seems to me you're a bad loser," said Gideon. He was bleeding from a wound to his arm.

Lord Alastair's eyes were burning with rage. "Kill me if you dare!"

"Not today," said Gideon, putting his sword back into his belt.

Paul noticed the slight movement of Lord Alastair's head and saw the servant tense his muscles. Quick as lightning, Paul threw himself between them and parried the stroke before the point of the servant's sword could drive in between Gideon's ribs. At the same moment, Gideon had drawn his own sword again. He ran the man through the chest with it. Blood spurted from the wound, flowing profusely, and Paul had to turn away.

Lord Alastair had used the moment to pick up his sword and spit the brown envelope lying on the paving on the point of it. Without another word, he turned and ran away through the arched entrance of the yard.

"Coward!" shouted Paul angrily. Then he turned to Gideon. "Are you hurt, boy?"

"No, it's only a scratch," said Gideon. "But you don't

look so good. Your arm . . . all that blood . . ." He pressed his lips together and picked up his sword. "What were those papers you gave Lord Alastair?"

"Family trees," said Paul unhappily. "The ancestral lines of the male and female time travelers."

Gideon nodded. "I knew you two were the traitors, but I didn't expect you to be quite so stupid! He's going to try killing all the count's descendants! And now he knows the names in the female line. If he gets his way, we'll never be born."

"You ought to have killed him when you had the chance," said Paul bitterly. "He took us for a ride. Listen, I don't have much time left. I'll be traveling back any moment now, but it's important for you to listen to me."

"Not likely!" Those green eyes flashed angrily at him. "If I'd known I was going to find you here today, I'd have brought a test tube with me."

"It was a mistake to get in touch with the Alliance," said Paul quickly. "Lucy was against it from the first. But I thought that if we could help them to render the count harmless . . ." He put his hand to his stomach. As he did so, his fingers met the package of letters that he had stowed away under his coat. "Damn! Here, take this, boy!"

Hesitantly, Gideon took the package. "Stop calling me boy. I'm taller than you."

"These are part of the prophesies that the count has always kept from the Guardians. It's important for you to read them before you get the idea of running straight off to your friend the count to tell tales of us. Shit, Lucy will murder me if she hears about this!"

"How do I know they're not fakes?"

"Just read them! Then you'll know why we stole the chronograph. And why we have to keep the count from closing the Circle of Blood." He was gasping for air. "Gideon, you have to look after Gwyneth," he said quickly. "And you must protect her from the count."

"I'd protect Gwyneth from anyone!" There was an arrogant look in Gideon's eyes. "But I don't know what that has to do with you."

"It has a great deal to do with me, boy!" Paul had to exercise self-control not to come to blows with the lad. God, if only he had the faintest idea!

Gideon folded his arms. "Alastair's men almost killed Gwyneth and me in Hyde Park the other day, all because of your treachery! So you can hardly expect me to swallow this sudden concern for her welfare!"

"You have no notion—" Paul interrupted himself. He was running out of time. "Never mind. Listen." He thought of what Lucy had said and tried to put all his sense of urgency into his voice. "A simple question, a simple answer: do you love Gwyneth?"

Gideon never took his eyes off him. But something flickered in his gaze, Paul clearly saw that. Was it uncertainty? Wonderful—the boy could use a sword, but he seemed to be something of a beginner in emotional matters.

"Gideon, I have to know the answer!" His voice was sharp.

Some of the anger left the boy's face. "Yes" was all he said.

Paul felt his own fury evaporate. Lucy had known it. How could he ever have doubted her? "Then read those papers," he said quickly. "That's the only way you can understand the part that Gwyneth is really playing and how much there is at stake for her."

Gideon stared at him. "What do you mean?"

Paul leaned forward. "Gwyneth is going to die if you don't prevent it. You're the only one who can. And the only one she trusts, it seems."

He tightened his grip on Gideon's arm as he felt the dizzy sensation threaten to overwhelm him. What he wouldn't have given for one or two minutes' delay!

"Promise me, Gideon!" he said desperately.

But he couldn't hear Gideon's answer. Everything around him blurred. He was torn off his feet and flung through time and space.

THE CAST OF
MAIN CHARACTERS

IN THE PRESENT

IN THE MONTROSE FAMILY:

Gwyneth Shepherd, in Year Ten at school, discovers one day
    that she can travel in time

Grace Shepherd, Gwyneth's mother

Nick and Caroline Shepherd, Gwyneth's younger brother and
    sister

Charlotte Montrose, Gwyneth's cousin

Glenda Montrose, Charlotte's mother, Grace's elder sister

Lady Arista Montrose, grandmother of Gwyneth and
    Charlotte, mother of Grace and Glenda

Madeleine (Maddy) Montrose, Gwyneth's great-aunt, sister of
    the late Lord Montrose

Mr. Bernard, butler in the Montrose household

Xemerius, ghost of a demon in the form of a stone gargoyle

AT ST. LENNOX HIGH SCHOOL:

Lesley Hay, Gwyneth's best friend

James Augustus Peregrine Pympoole-Bothame, the school ghost

THE CAST OF MAIN CHARACTERS

Cynthia Dale, in Gwyneth's class
Gordon Gelderman, in Gwyneth's class

AT THE HEADQUARTERS OF THE GUARDIANS
IN THE TEMPLE:
Gideon de Villiers, like Gwyneth, can travel in time
Raphael de Villiers, Gideon's younger brother
Falk de Villiers, Gideon's uncle twice removed, Grand Master
 of the Lodge of Count Saint-Germain, to which the
 Guardians belong
Thomas George, member of the Inner Circle of the Lodge
Mr. William Whitman, member of the Inner Circle of the
 Lodge, teacher of English and history at St. Lennox
Dr. Jacob White, medical doctor and member of the Inner
 Circle of the Lodge
Mrs. Jenkins, secretary
Madame Rossini, dress designer and wardrobe mistress

IN THE PAST

Count Saint-Germain, time traveler and founder of the
 Guardians
Miro Rakoczy, his close friend, also known as the Black
 Leopard
Lord Brompton, acquaintance and patron of the count's
Lady Brompton, his lively wife
Margaret Tilney, time traveler, Gwyneth's great-great-
 grandmother, Lady Arista's grandmother
Paul de Villiers, time traveler, younger brother of Falk de
 Villiers

THE CAST OF MAIN CHARACTERS

Lucy Montrose, time traveler, niece of Grace, daughter of Grace and Glenda's elder brother, Harry

Lucas Montrose, later Lord Lucas Montrose, Lucy's grandfather, Glenda and Grace's father, Grand Master of the Lodge until his death

Mr. Merchant, Lady Lavinia Rutland, guests at Lady Brompton's soirée

Lord Alastair, English peer descended from Italian forefathers, head of the Florentine Alliance in the eighteenth century

ACKNOWLEDGMENTS

"When you change, everything around you changes.
That's magic!"

While I was writing this book, an amazing number of wonderful things happened, and I met more delightful people than I can count. Let me just say how extremely grateful I am for all the magical events that brought me together with them. And no—I don't believe in coincidences.

My thanks to all the readers—your approval and your enthusiasm were incredibly helpful in motivating me.

Thanks to Daniela Kern, Eva Schöffmann-Davidoff, Thomas Frotz—you are the very best!

Thanks to all those who have been so patient with me this year—I've been really lucky with you.

For reasons of time, I will thank only four people by name: my wonderful agent Petra Hermanns, my excellent editor Christiane Düring, my dear friend Eva, and my tireless little mama.

Thanks for everything, Mama, including the way you read these books with the enthusiasm of a fourteen-year-old. Eva, without your moral support, there would have been many days when I didn't write a word. Petra, I am sure you were sent to me by heaven! Christiane, I don't know how you do it, but in the end I always think the ideas were all my own, although the best of them were yours! Thank you both, too, for those wonderful days in London.

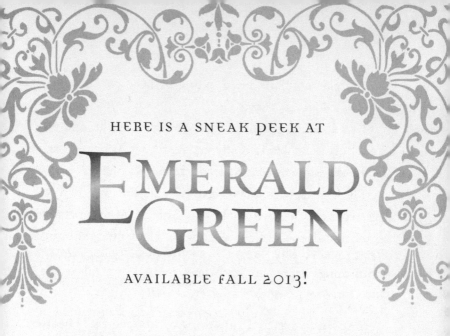

HERE IS A SNEAK PEEK AT

EMERALD GREEN

AVAILABLE FALL 2013!

THE END OF THE SWORD was pointing straight at my heart, and my murderer's eyes were like black holes threatening to swallow up everything that came too close to them. I knew I couldn't get away. With difficulty, I stumbled a few steps back.

The man followed me. "I will wipe that which is displeasing to God off the face of the earth!" he boomed. "The ground will soak up your blood!"

I had at least two smart retorts to these sinister words on the tip of my tongue. (Soak up my blood? Oh, come off it, this was a tiled floor.) But I was in such a panic that I couldn't get a word out. The man didn't look as if he'd appreciate my little joke at this moment anyway. In fact he didn't look as if he had a sense of humor at all.

I took another step back, and came up against a wall. The killer laughed out loud. Okay, so maybe he did have a sense of humor, but it wasn't much like mine.

"Die, demon!" he cried, plunging his sword into my breast without any more ado.

I woke up, screaming. I was wet with sweat, and my heart hurt as if a blade really had pierced it. What a horrible dream! But was that really surprising?

My experiences of yesterday (and the day before) weren't exactly likely to make me nestle down comfortably in bed and sleep the sleep of the just. Unwanted thoughts were writhing around in my mind like flesh-eating plants gone crazy. *Gideon was only pretending*, I thought. *He doesn't really love me.*

"He hardly has to do anything to attract girls," I heard Count Saint-Germain saying in his soft, deep voice, again and again. And, "Nothing is easier to calculate than the reactions of a woman in love."

Oh yeah? So how does a woman in love react when she finds out that someone's been lying to her and manipulating her? She spends hours on the phone to her best friend, that's how, then she sits about in the dark, unable to get to sleep, asking herself why the hell she ever fell for the guy in the first place, crying her eyes out at the same time because she wants him so much . . . right, so it doesn't take a genius to calculate that.

The lighted numbers on the alarm clock beside my bed said 3:10, so I must have nodded off after all. I'd even slept for more than two hours. And someone—my mum?—must have come in to cover me up, because all I could remember was huddling on the bed with my arms around my knees, listening to my heart beating much too fast.

Odd that a broken heart can beat at all, come to think of it.

"It feels like it's made of red splinters with sharp edges, and they're slicing me up from inside so that I'll bleed to death," I'd said, trying to describe the state of my heart to Lesley (okay, so it sounds at least as corny as the stuff the character in my dream was saying, but sometimes the truth *is* corny). And Lesley had said sympathetically, "I know just how you feel. When Max dumped me I thought at first I'd die of grief. Grief and multiple organ failure. Because there's a grain of truth in all those things they say about love: it goes to your kidneys, it punches you in the stomach, it breaks your heart and . . . er . . . it scurries over your liver like a louse. But first, that will all pass off; second, it's not as hopeless as it looks to you; and third, your heart isn't made of glass."

"Stone, not glass," I corrected her, sobbing. "My heart is a gemstone, and Gideon's broken it into thousands of pieces, just like in Aunt Maddy's vision."

"Sounds kind of cool—but no! Hearts are really made of very different stuff, you take my word for it." Lesley cleared her throat, and her tone of voice got positively solemn, as if she were revealing the greatest secret in the history of the world. "Hearts are made of something much tougher, it's unbreakable, you can reshape it any time you like. Hearts are made to a secret formula."

More throat-clearing to heighten the suspense. I instinctively held my breath. "They're made of stuff like *marzipan!*" Lesley announced.

"Marzipan?" For a moment I stopped sobbing and smiled instead.

"That's right, marzipan," Lesley repeated in deadly earnest. "The best sort, with lots of real ground almonds in it."

I almost giggled. But then I remembered that I was the unhappiest girl in the world. I sniffed, and said, "If that's so, then Gideon has *bitten off* a piece of my heart! And he's nibbled away the chocolate coating around it too! You ought to have seen the way he looked when . . ."

But before I could start crying all over again, Lesley sighed audibly.

"Gwenny, I hate to say so, but all this miserable weeping and wailing does no one any good. You have to stop it!"

"I'm not doing it on purpose," I told her. "It just keeps on breaking out of me. One moment I'm still the happiest girl in the world, and then he tells me he . . ."

"Okay, so Gideon behaved like a bastard," Lesley interrupted me. "Although it's hard to understand why. I mean, *hello*? Why on earth would girls in love be easier to manipulate? I'd have thought it was just the opposite. Girls in love are like ticking time bombs. You never know what they'll do next. Gideon and his male chauvinist friend the count have made a big mistake."